LT Harris
Harris, E. Lynn
Mama dearest /

34028074222531
CC $31.95   ocn429750202
10/22/09

D0284382

WITHDRAWN

MAMA DEAREST

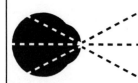

This Large Print Book carries the
Seal of Approval of N.A.V.H.

MAMA DEAREST

E. LYNN HARRIS

THORNDIKE PRESS

A part of Gale, Cengage Learning

Detroit • New York • San Francisco • New Haven, Conn • Waterville, Maine • London

Copyright © 2009 by E. Lynn Harris.
Thorndike Press, a part of Gale, Cengage Learning.

ALL RIGHTS RESERVED
This book is a work of fiction. Names, characters, places, and incidents either are products of the author's imagination or are used fictitiously. Any resemblance to actual events or locales or persons, living or dead, is entirely coincidental.
Thorndike Press® Large Print African-American.
The text of this Large Print edition is unabridged.
Other aspects of the book may vary from the original edition.
Set in 16 pt. Plantin.
Printed on permanent paper.

LIBRARY OF CONGRESS CATALOGING-IN-PUBLICATION DATA

Harris, E. Lynn.
   Mama dearest / by E. Lynn Harris.
      p. cm. — (Thorndike Press large print African-American)
   ISBN-13: 978-1-4104-2088-6 (alk. paper)
   ISBN-10: 1-4104-2088-4 (alk. paper)
   1. African American women singers—Fiction. 2. African American actresses—Fiction. 3. Mothers and daughters—Fiction. 4. Large type books. I. Title.
   PS3558.A64438M36 2009b
   813'.54—dc22   2009032508

Published in 2009 by arrangement with Pocket Books, a division of Simon & Schuster, Inc.

Printed in the United States of America
1 2 3 4 5 6 7 13 12 11 10 09

Dedicated to Four Great Mamas
My own lovely mother, Etta W. Harris
My loving aunt, Jessie L. Phillips
And two wonderful ladies who give
me motherly love and friendship
Laura Gilmore and Jean Nail

and to Frank McCourt,
a friend who will be missed

■ ■ ■ ■

PART ONE

■ ■ ■ ■

PROLOGUE

I had that dream again last night. It's been tormenting me for a long time. It plays in my mind as clearly as a movie on the silver screen, with me in my most glamorous role ever. I'm the star of this imaginary filmstrip, taking center stage, with all my dreams coming true for the world to see.

But this beautiful dream always turns tragic. It turns ugly in a million different ways, as if Satan is writing the script and has so many ideas for horrible endings that he's making me watch every one of them while I sleep.

But oh, the beginning is so sweet.

As always, I'm wearing a glittery silver gown that makes me look like a statue of pure diamonds. My hair is laid and I'm dripping in bling, with too many icy karats to count, sparkling in my earrings, necklace and eye-popping ring.

I look so hot, the TV cameras can't help

but keep returning to show off my glam to the world by focusing on me in my aisle seat just a few feet from the gleaming stage. I see myself on the giant screens, framed by rows of Hollywood's who's who, all decked out in tuxedos and sparkling gowns. Beside me, my date's face is a brown oval blur, but I know he's handsome and sporting that tux like a Sean John model. His mouth and eyes come into focus; he's smiling at me lovingly, like I'm the most beautiful woman in the world. And in my dream, I am and the world knows it.

Then Denzel Washington steps up to the microphone carrying a single white envelope. His world-famous face beams with a huge smile. He keeps looking at me like he knows a juicy secret. Sometimes he gives me a wink. Other times all I get is a mischievous grin.

In his best movie-star voice, Denzel looks at the teleprompter and says: "The nominees for best actress in a motion picture are Meryl Streep for *The Token*, Angela Bassett for *The Beyonce Knowles Story*, Beyonce Knowles for *The Sasha Fierce Story*, Jennifer Lewis for *Mamadem* and Yancey Harrington Braxton for *Her Mother's Daughter*. And the Oscar goes to —"

Denzel pauses as he opens the envelope.

He smiles, looks at me and announces: "Yancey Harrington Braxton."

My head spins. I'm smiling so hard that my cheeks ache. Tears of joy sting my eyes. I feel like my body is floating up on a cloud. Until I press my lips to the warm cheek of my date, who's smiling and joining the thunderous applause.

I'm so floaty with happiness that I don't feel my silver stilettos touch the plush red carpet as I walk toward the stage. The black steps are a blur through tears that stream down my face. This is the moment that I've been dreaming about all my life. I've rehearsed my acceptance speech over and over.

But with this tingly jolt of excitement shooting through me, would I remember to thank all the people in my life who had made this magic moment happen? I grip my sparkly purse containing the note that will help me remember to thank all those who have supported me, those who have loved me. The crowd is clapping and screaming at a fever pitch and I have never felt so important and loved in my entire life.

Finally, I make it up to the stage. Denzel kisses my cheek and hands me my gold statue. Then in a magical wave, his long arm directs me to the podium and my loyal subjects. The lights are so bright and hot. I'm nervous, but I'm ready. From my purse, I retrieve that paper that I wrote on when I won my first pageant.

"First I would like to thank God, even though I don't know Him." I smile at the audience with a great deal of bravado. My voice sounds smooth and strong, despite the fact that every muscle in my body is shaking with excitement. "I would like to thank the Academy, even though I can't understand why it has taken you so long. I would like to thank my producers and directors, even though you made it perfectly clear that I got this role because Halle Berry and Vanessa Williams turned you down."

I pause for dramatic effect. I'm loving the captivated expressions on all the important Hollywood people's faces as I deliver an acceptance speech that's way more bodacious than anything they've ever heard.

"I would like to thank my agent, even though he wouldn't return my phone calls until I withheld a commission payment." The crowd is laughing and cheering me on at the same time.

"You tell it, Yancey!" they shout. "Go on, girl, with your bad self!"

But then the back door of the auditorium opens with a blaze of light. Out walk several people from my past. They're smiling, so I assume they're here to congratulate me. There's my first boyfriend, my first vocal and dance teacher and Nicole Springer, an actress and former friend until I showed my ass. Here comes John Basil Henderson, the dangerously handsome man I almost married; he's carrying a bouquet of red roses. Also coming toward me is a beautiful young girl whom I don't recognize. She looks so excited and happy to see me as she skips past all my friends.

"Yancey!" a familiar voice calls. I look offstage. It's my mother. She's wearing the same silver dress that I have on, the same jewels and — even though I'm certain it's a wig — her hair is styled exactly like mine.

The sight of her makes me feel like this fantastic bubble of excitement and accomplishment and recognition of my talent by the world is suddenly about to pop. Her sharp, disapproving glare could pierce a hole through me and the silver screen where this dream is coming true. And I literally hear a popping sound as she speaks:

"Yancey, Yancey." She says my name like I am in trouble; her voice shoots through the cheer and excitement in a way that makes me feel like I've been smacked in the face. "So you think you're big time now, huh?

13

You still got that birthmark?"

She's walking toward me as if I'm still a kid and she has a switch in her hand, ready to whup my behind for doing something bad. She is coming toward me dressed like a black June Cleaver, carrying an iron with a massively fake smile. And even though I'm standing on the stage with the adoring smiles and applause of Denzel and an auditorium full with superstars, I cower and tremble. Suddenly my voice sounds meek:

"No, Mother, I wouldn't be here without you."

"You got that right," she snaps with a disgusted twist of her mouth. "So, when you gonna thank me?"

I point to the bottom of my list. "I'm getting to that. See? Look here. Here's your name."

My mother smirks with a crooked grin, then shouts:

"You still ain't shit, bitch!"

Then, as always, the curtains fall on this dream-turned-nightmare.

I wake up. My body trembles under a cold sweat. My eyes burn with hot tears. And I fear my real dreams will always be out of my grasp.

CHAPTER 1

As I savor the first sip of my second glass of wine, my eyes move to the television and I say to myself, "Yancey, that's the bitch who got your life."

Here I am in a third-rate hotel (it used to be a Days Inn) down the street from the Jackie Gleason Theater near South Beach in Miami. I'm in the second week of my role as Deena Jones in a bus-and-truck company of *Dreamgirls.* The producers aren't extravagant when it comes to lodging, and I can't wait until this tour is over and I can get my beautiful ass back to New York City where I belong.

I'm sitting here watching the DVD of the 2007 Grammys, and there is Beyonce singing and gliding across the stage with Tina Turner. That should've been me singing with Tina or on the stage alone, but things haven't turned out the way I'd planned. And I don't have much time before

15

it will be too late.

My name is Yancey Harrington Braxton, and I'm a singer and actress. I've been close to stardom and even had a big pop hit at the beginning of the decade, but just as I got near Beyonce and Tina status, something happened that slammed the door in my face.

I'm thirty-six in actress years, which really means I'm a sneeze away from turning forty. At times that scares me, but thank God I still have my looks, especially a body that could compete with a twenty-year-old on the beach and in the bedroom.

I had come to Miami with a plan to make a second comeback but I'm running out of ideas. Maybe I need a stalker; then people would feel sorry for me. I could do the drug thing and go into rehab. It looks like it might work for Miss Whitney and Lord knows it ain't hurting that crazy singer from England, Amy Winehouse. I'm much too vain to put on a few pounds and then become a spokesperson for one of the weight-loss companies like Queen Latifah. But there has to be something legal that I can do to push myself back onto the national scene one last time. This is a time when it seems everybody and their mama has a reality show. Surely there is still room

16

for a legitimate star of my caliber. Yeah, that's the ticket — I need my own reality show.

I took this job even though I hate working with a bunch of no-talent people who've never set foot on a Broadway stage unless they were pushing a broom across it, but I'd run into some tough times with my finances. Besides, I've played the role of Deena Jones since I was in my twenties and could do it in my sleep. Gone are the days when I can demand first-class transportation, suites and car service. Let's not forget my name over the title on the theater marquee. Most producers and directors aren't savvy enough to recognize talent and class in one package.

Thank God I still own a really nice town house on the Upper East Side. I'd always planned to use it as my nest egg but now when I need to sell it, the real estate market has gone to hell in a handbasket. A lot of people were interested in purchasing it, but with the banks tight with money, even so-called rich white folks are having a hard time getting a loan. My real estate agent told me that my best hope for getting my asking price is if some rich Russian falls in love with it and pays cash. I told her that she needs to get her ass on a plane to Russia quick, fast and in a hurry.

If I sell the house, I'll get myself a smaller place and there will still be enough money left over to get new headshots and some new outfits and go sit my ass in some spa where rich men hang out. I just can't take another night in a seedy hotel when somebody with as little talent as Beyonce has all the things I'm supposed to have, including a rich, powerful husband. It should be me who's the toast of the red carpet, with my own clothing line and preparing for yet another world tour.

As I watched Tina and Beyonce complete their performances and take their bows I thought, "I can sing better than both of them." I'd give them a run for their money on the dancing as well. When did it all go wrong for me and why? I was born to be a star.

I'm a statuesque five feet eight inches, 125 pounds with a twenty-two-inch waist. A beige princess with a diamond-shaped face, golden brown eyes and auburn-tinted hair that falls just below my shoulders. My arms are long and slender, almost perfect . . . almost. I am still as beautiful as any actress, black or white, working today. I just need to remind Hollywood of that so I can move from the D-list back to the A-list.

As I tried to figure out what I could do to get some positive press, I thought back to almost ten years before when I was on Broadway starring in yet another *Dreamgirls* revival. I guess I should be thankful that Jennifer Hudson and Beyonce made the movie musical. Still, I'm pissed that I couldn't even get a role as an extra in the glitzy film. Maybe the first step for me should be to get another agent and by this I mean a good one. And I don't mean somebody calling himself an agent/producer like the current fool who represents me, Zeus Miller. First of all what kind of name is that? But for now he's the best that I can do.

I finished my glass of wine and looked around the tacky room for the rest of the bottle. Another glass would ensure me of at least a sound sleep and I wouldn't spend the night worrying about how I was going to keep the bank from foreclosing on my home before I could sell it and hopefully make a nice profit or at least break even.

Just as I got up, there was a knock at my door. I figured it was housekeeping finally bringing the extra towels I'd asked for three hours ago. If I was staying in a Four Seasons or the Ritz Carlton South Beach, I would have had those towels before I hung up the phone. I miss those days more than I can say. You get what you pay for.

I pulled together my robe and opened the door.

"You got a corkscrew I can borrow for a few?" It was Violet Smith, one of the understudies for the musical and my next-door neighbor. Violet is an okay-looking young girl when she has makeup on. She'd made it to the top ten on *American Star* a couple seasons back and landed a small part in the *Dreamgirls* movie, something she never fails to tell people when she meets them. Now with shows like *American Idol* and *So-You-Think-You-Can-Do-This-or-Do-That,* any clown can have a little time in the sun. Gets on my damn nerves. When I first entered the business you had to have talent before you appeared on stage or television, let alone being cast in a movie. I have sold millions of CDs, had a number-one hit and appeared on Broadway countless times. Damn, I was even nominated for a Tony Award. I should have won and would have if Patti Lupone had taken her old ass somewhere and sat down.

Violet stood there impatiently. "Yeah, but I'm not lending it out," I said. "Bring your bottle of wine to my room and I'll open it for you." Maybe Violet will have the decency to offer me a glass and I can save my corner for later on tonight in case I wake up.

Violet gave me an are-you-serious look. "Girl, quit playing," she said, "I promise to bring it right back. I got a real nice man I met at the after-hour's club off Lincoln in my room waiting on me. I know we normally hang out and talk but I can't tonight, hon. I got some catching up to do. Some of the cast is watching the semifinals of *American Star* in Dalton's room. Why don't you go down there? I think they got some drinks."

I ignored her suggestion that I join a bunch of sexually confused chorus boys watching a bunch of no-talent teenagers and walked over to the desk and picked up the corkscrew I'd stolen from the hotel we'd stayed at in Tampa. It was one of the few times we'd stayed in a hotel that had a wine list and twenty-four-hour room service. Still, it wasn't a five-star hotel, but more like a two and a half.

When I turned around, Violet had let herself into my room and was sitting in the chair making herself at home. I made a mental note to make sure to let Violet know I didn't like people invading my space without my permission. I don't have roommates on the road, no matter how much money it saves.

"Did you hear who was in the audience tonight?"

"Who, Michelle Obama?" I asked, being cute.

"No, honey, but I hope that she and the president will come to this show. That would really put us on the map. It was Nicole Springer. She was one of the Deena Jones that played in the show when it was on Broadway back in the day. Do you know her?"

"No" I lied. Of course I knew Nicole Springer, and if there was one person I despised more than Beyonce it was Nicole "Miss Perfect" Springer. I'd understudied her on Broadway and plotted her demise by spiking her coffee. I don't think she ever found out or suspected me because I was a better actress than she was. I have to admit that the reason I dislike her so is that everything came so easily to her. Talented, beautiful and nice to almost everyone, and to me that took just too much work.

"That's funny, she said she knew you. Dalton and I were going to bring her to your dressing room but we were so busy talking. Dalton used to take voice lessons from her in Atlanta and was a member of her theater group. She was the one who talked him into auditioning for this show,"

Violet said.

I was not going to engage her in this Nicole banter so I just handed her the corkscrew. "Now don't make me have to knock on your door to get this back."

"Thanks," she said popping up from the chair, "and don't worry, you won't have to. As soon as my company leaves I will bring it back. If you don't answer I'll leave it by your door."

"Don't do that because if it comes up missing, I'm still coming back to you. Understand?" What did it say about my depressed life that I was clutching a corkscrew the way a diabetic relies on insulin.

"I hear you. Thanks, Yancey. You're the best."

I shut the door and thought, I once was the best and very soon I'll be the best again. These bitches better get out of my way!

I was sitting at my dressing-room table removing my makeup when I heard a knock at the door.

"Come in," I shouted.

Dalton McGurdy, the understudy for C. C. White, stuck his head in and asked if he could talk to me for a moment.

I like Dalton more than most of the chorus boys but now I was a little apprehensive since he knew Nicole. He was talented and a bit unusual. I assumed he was gay but he was also in charge of the weekly Bible studies the cast held that I never attended. I didn't see how a gay boy could conduct biweekly Bible study. But this was the theater, where conventional rules didn't apply.

"Sure, Dalton, come on in."

Dalton was light brown and on the thin side. He had an unshaven face and had recently cut his dreads, which made him look boyish and not old enough to play the main character, Effie's brother, and my love interest in the first half of the show. Thank God we didn't have any kissing scenes.

"I only need to see you for a few moments. Here's a CD of some of the songs I've written. It's classic R & B kinda like Stephanie Mills and Angela Winbush used to sing. I think you have the perfect voice for the songs."

"Okay, lay it on my dresser and I'll listen to them when I get a chance."

Why did all of these kids think they could write music or choreograph dances just because they were in a show?

"Take your time because I just found out I might have a gig in New York after this show closes and we'll have plenty of time to talk about it."

"I thought you were going back to Atlanta."

"No, hon, I'm from Athens, Georgia, you know, the University of Georgia, go bulldogs."

"What?"

"Don't mind me, I was just making a little joke, or should I say making a little cheer."

"Whatever, Dalton."

"Danni — I told you my good friends call me Danni."

"Okay, Danni," I said, wondering when we had suddenly become good friends.

"See you at the next show or maybe back at the hotel."

"Okay, whatever. Hey, I heard you were really tight with Nicole Springer."

"You mean Nicole Springer-Stovall? Oh, I just love her. She is the greatest. Ms. Stovall said she knew you back in the day."

"What did she say about me?"

"Oh, that you were really talented, beautiful and a real go-getter."

"Really?"

"Yeah, I think she respects you a lot. She encouraged me with my songwriting."

"Then why didn't you give her the songs? I remember an okay voice," I said.

"Nicole is done with that side of the business. She told me she just loves teaching and being a wife and mother."

"Oh, I forgot what they say. Those who can't, teach," I said with a wicked grin.

"Well, let me get out of here," Dalton said with slight disappointment in his voice. If he wanted to really work with me he was going to have to get over his infatuation with Nicole Springer.

"Whatever, Dalton."

Dalton left my dressing room and it was back to my mirror time.

Sometimes I don't like what I see in the mirror and this evening before I left for the theater was no different. I decided to do something about it. In the cramped dressing room I looked into the tiny mirror on the wall that was chipped in two places and gave myself a much needed pep talk.

I spoke swiftly and with great conviction. "Yancey Harrington Braxton, stop feeling sorry for yourself. You a bad bitch! It's time to show the world what you're really made of. What you're capable of. It starts tonight when you open the stage door. You're as good as Vanessa L. Williams, Angela Bassett and Gabrielle Union. No! Not as good as, better than all those pretend divas. A setback

26

is a setup for a comeback, bitch. Now let's get to work."

CHAPTER 2

All Ava Middlebrooks wanted was for those loud-ass broads to quiet down so she could watch *American Star* in peace. Ava didn't know who she hated more — ghetto-girl whores or white trailer-trash bitches. Sadly, this prison was filled with both.

Her favorite singer, a teenaged girl from a little town in Ohio, was up there on the stage right now. Ava stared at the screen, mesmerized by how the satin-smooth notes of "Summertime" could ride such a big voice in such a little body.

"Yawl betta change the channel to *Dancing with the Stars*," Sheronda Jenkins shouted as her hulking figure blocked the TV in the beige-walled rec room of the women's prison.

"Get out the way!" Ava yelled, standing up. "You watched your show last week. It's our turn. So move!"

Sheronda stomped toward Ava, coming at

28

her like a bull in orange cotton. The fluorescent light glowed on the shiny skin between Sheronda's fresh cornrows. She squinted and spat: "That's yo ass, old bitch."

Unfazed, Ava crossed her arms and sat down on the couch between her girls, Lyrical and Cheryl. She craned to look around Sheronda to focus back on that girl with the magic voice on TV. That child represented everything that these prison broads didn't. Success. Talent. Reaching for your dreams. Living life to the fullest.

And that was exactly what Ava planned to be doing twenty-four hours from now, in the comfort of her own home in the free world. Her whole body tingled with the thrill of resuming her prominent place in society. She would go to the salon and stay there until she'd achieved perfection with her hair, nails, toes and skin. She would dine on gourmet meals. She would sink into the buttery leather seat of a luxury sedan. And her daughter had better have a big dinner party to welcome Ava home if she knew what was good for her.

"You hear me?" Sheronda shouted, standing at Ava's feet.

Ava looked up with a bored expression.

"I'm out of this hellhole tomorrow," Ava snapped, with a haughty tilt of her chin.

"And I'm not about to jeopardize my freedom by stooping to your ghetto ways."

"How is your ass getting out anyhow? Didn't your crazy ass shoot somebody? I thought they gave you fifteen to life."

"I know important people," Ava snapped.

"I bet you do but let's see how they treat you now that you're a convicted felon. I don't think the country club types take too kindly to people like us."

Ava stared up at Sheronda with disgust and pity. She and her ghetto girl crew were no different from the white trailer trash chicks who hung together. Black or white, they all came from the lower rungs of society, and because they didn't know any better, were destined to languish there forever.

But not Ava. She was about to rise back up to where she belonged. She simply shook her head and told Sheronda, "You *need* to get yourself some anger-management classes. Now move!"

Sheronda glared down at Ava with hate in her eyes. Her wide chest rose and fell with her heavy breathing. Those dark blue tattoos up and down her caramel-colored forearms rippled like a creeping rash as Sheronda clenched and unclenched her fists, over and over.

"Girl, move!" a woman on the couch behind them shouted. "We tryin' to watch!"

"Will you please move!" a white woman yelled.

"That ho always tryin' to start somethin'," another woman said. "You betta put your wide behind in a chair and watch the show."

"I ain't gon' watch that white shit!" Sheronda snapped. "I want *American Star.* That's *our* show."

"Yeah, turn it!" yelled another woman.

Ava rolled her eyes. "Turn around and look. A black girl is stealin' the show. Don't be so prejudiced. The judges love her. Just look at the judges' faces."

Sheronda pointed a finger at the dozen women sitting around the TV. "Last time I looked in the judge's face, I ended up in this joint —"

"Sit down and shut up!" Cheryl snapped, standing to face Sheronda. Cheryl was cool people. She was tiny, and her milk-white skin and spiky peroxide-yellow hair contrasted with Sheronda's. But she stared down the bigger woman without an ounce of fear.

"What you gon' do?" Sheronda threatened, hunching lower to glare at Cheryl nose to nose.

Good. Now Ava could see that girl sing

31

on TV. The beauty of her voice raised goose bumps on Ava's flesh. And when she sang the lyrics "your daddy's rich," Ava's eyes burned with tears. She had sung "Summertime" in her cabaret show once. Ava was thinking that soon she'd be rich again too.

Ava loved that powerful look in the singer's eyes. Like she owned the world. Soon as she stepped out of this place, Ava would look at everyone and everything just like that. The singer was nearing the end of the song, and Ava leaned forward to hear every beautiful note.

"Can't none a' y'all bitches watch!" Sheronda shouted. She stood in front of the TV, blocking the screen, reaching backward to wrap her arms around it. "How ya like me now?"

Two dozen women rushed up like a swarm of bees, yanking Sheronda's arms.

Ava remained seated, hoping they would extract Sheronda in time to hear the end of the girl's song and get the judges' responses.

Four guards stood around them.

"Sit down or all of you will return to your cells," the guard shouted. "Now!"

The women obeyed. And when they dispersed, a TV commercial was playing.

"Damn!" Ava snapped. "We missed it."

Beside her, Lyrical whispered, "Sit tight,

I'll take care of this bitch."

Sheronda shot a hate look at Ava as she crossed her arms, sitting with her group of bull-dykish broads who were probably lesbians. Ava suspected that all these women had some girl-on-girl tendencies. But she wasn't about to stoop to muff diving, no matter how hot and bothered her body had gotten in here.

No, she would let a man take care of all that, starting tomorrow. Whoever he was had better get ready to make up for all the lonely nights she'd had to take care of it herself here in prison. She'd almost lost her mind from the burning hunger —

A flash of yellow and brown caught her eye.

Cupcakes.

They were arranged on a tray made of newspapers carried by Lyrical, who carefully walked toward Ava. The other women surrounded them. Even Sheronda, but her big ass probably just wanted a cupcake.

"We'll miss your ass," Lyrical said, smiling as she offered the treats to Ava. "I made up a little rap I want to do for you after we eat. I call it 'The Classy Mama Anthem' and it ain't got no curse words in it."

Ava's heart softened. She could feel her face forming into an expression of shock.

Everyone and everything around her was so hard. Yet this was such a gentle and sweet gesture. Even her own rap song, though Mama wasn't a moniker Ava answered to.

"We got the cupcakes out of the vending machine," Cheryl said with a shrug. "The best we could do, you know?"

Ava smiled, refusing to let the threat of tears show up in her eyes. She couldn't get *that* soft. There was a tough world awaiting her and Ava knew it wasn't for sissies. Her own mother had taught her that.

"Take one," Cheryl said. "You first."

Ava took a yellow cupcake with white frosting drizzled across the top.

"Mmmmm," she said, loving the sweet taste and the attention. Yes, the sweetness.

Tomorrow, after she got out of here, she would be living the sweet life.

CHAPTER 3

Two days later, it's closing night in Miami and some wannabe socialite is throwing the cast a party at Crowbar, one of the hottest clubs on South Beach. I'm walking into the club like I'm appearing at an Oscars after party.

My hair is down and bone straight and I'm wearing this cute, short black-and-white dress I purchased at BC/BG on Lincoln Road. It's a strapless number and the top is white lace, pleated across the chest, and the bottom half is black satin. I have on a pair of black patent leather Christian Lacroix pumps and am carrying a small black beaded bag. No matter what LaNita Duncan thinks, I'm the star of this show.

LaNita is playing the role of Effie White (which some folks are foolish enough to consider the lead), and let's just say no fat suit required. The producers discovered her in some backwoods church in Tennessee and all of a sudden she thinks she's an actress. I spot her in the corner with a bunch of the boys from the cast clinking champagne glasses in the air, and so I head in the opposite direction to the bar.

A cute Cuban bartender smiles. "What can I get for you, pretty lady?"

"Let me get a mojito," I said, placing my purse on the bar.

I recognize a couple more castmates heading to the dance floor and sometimes I nod and other times I act like I don't see them. The producers are the only reason I've graced this little affair. They asked everybody to come because this socialite is thinking about investing some money, which might allow us a few more cities.

When we leave Miami we have two days in Tallahassee and then Raleigh before the tour is supposed to end. I really don't care if more cities are added because I'm ready to get back to New York. I also want to make sure that the producers remember my face in the place when my bonus comes up. Sometimes when you do things to piss producers off it takes them a little longer to deliver your check. This is another problem with doing a bus-and-truck production. If that happened during a New York production I would be on the phone with the union rep so fast heads would spin, and I would have my money.

The bartender sets my drink down. "Here you go; would you like some appetizers from the buffet table?"

"No thanks," I said. For a moment I wondered what it would be like if my mother, Ava, was here for the party. Due to a little time being served upstate, Ava isn't here tonight. But if she was, she would be shouting at the top of her lungs, "Who organized this chicken wing affair and where can a bitch get a drink to quench her thirst?" I smile to myself and remember how I miss Ava, even though she is the last of the original bitches from hell. She taught me everything I know on how to be a bitch-diva without really trying. And despite her numerous faults, Ava is my mother.

On most nights of this second-rate tour I'm ambivalent, at best, about being in this cast, but on nights like this I hate being forced to take this job. A hatred so deep I'm scared that if somebody says the wrong thing to me, the slapping will begin without hesitation. Then I'll have to worry about lawsuits and jail. One woman locked up in the family is enough.

I've been to hundreds of opening- and closing-night parties and I can tell by just looking around the club that this one will elude my memory before morning breaks.

I order myself another drink and look away from the bar for the producers. I want them to know I'm here so that I can get my ass back to the hotel, change and do some real clubbing. As my eyes wander around the bar I see the person I've avoided for most of the tour coming toward me, smiling.

Her name is Marshawn Dallas and she plays the role of Michelle, the new girl in the fictional group the Dreams. I hear she's the daughter of a wealthy interracial couple from outside of Boston and has attended Carnegie Mellon in Pittsburgh. I knew she was trouble when I walked into the auditions and I saw her whispering and laughing in my direction. It was such a middle-school move.

She walks up to me and smiles as if we are college girlfriends. Her light brown eyes dissect me, settling momentarily on my breasts. I know they are one of my best features but is this bitch a lesbo?

"Yancey, I was hoping you'd be here. We haven't had a chance to talk since we started rehearsals," Marshawn said, sitting on the stool next to me. She ordered a glass of red wine and then turned to face me.

"Hello, Marshawn," I said reluctantly.

"You know I was hoping to get to know you better."

"Why?"

"You're Yancey Braxton, that's why I googled you before we had the first meeting. I mean you've done everything — recording, stage. I know you didn't do much television and movies but I'm sure that's because you turned Hollywood down. Am I right?"

I study Marshawn to see if I can figure out what she is up to. She radiates spoiled bitch from the red bottom of her expensive shoes to the top of her sewn-in weave. Marshawn is in her early twenties, tall and lean, with a dancer's legs and Angela Bassett-like defined arms. But from what I've heard just a passable voice.

"You're a smart girl," I said, sipping my drink.

"So what happened?"

I spotted a good-looking light-skinned brother and I felt his eyes on me. "What?" I asked, looking back at Marshawn.

"What happened to your career?" she repeated. I'd played this game with this girl before so I anticipated her next move. "I know I'm doing this second-rate production because I'm young, beautiful and at the start of my career. But you should be further along, shouldn't you?"

Was I about to give out my first slap of the night? What was this Flavor of Love reject with the bleached teeth and too tight LBD (little black dress) trying to do? She can't fool me. She's bitch by birth, I'm one by choice, which means I work at it. It doesn't take me long to see through the bullshit. I've done it so many times before. I guess Google didn't inform her that I can flick the bitch switch in a split second.

I showed her what a truly phony smile looked like and said, "Sweetheart, I know you mean well, but my career is none of your concern. Why don't you try doing some exercises to increase the size of those avocado pits I think you might call breasts. Enjoy your night, honey." I grabbed my bag and stood.

Two hours later I wobbled in a pair of three-and-a-half-inch, open-toed, slingback Manolo Blahnik pumps, with my arms extended over my head, trying to hail a taxi. Music from the South Beach Club about four doors down from the Crowbar rang out behind me each time the door was opened and closed by clubgoers.

After leaving the casting party, I went back to the hotel, changed clothes and shoes and gave my luck another chance. I know I had drunk too much but it helps me forget my problems for a minute. No money, no man and if I'm honest with myself — no real career. Since I couldn't get a taxi right away I figured one more club wouldn't hurt. I picked one with a bright white façade that looked popular. Once inside, I could feel just about every man's eyes checking out the full package.

I walked up to a glass-cased bar. There was a rainbow of blinking lights within it that pulsed with the beat of the music. I sneaked a peek at myself in the mirror behind the bar, and my hair was almost perfect, even for a home perm. I have to do it myself these days. A sista don't have two or three hundred dollars to be handing out for a wash and blow dry.

My eyes lingered over the countless bottles of liquor that were stacked at the bar when a lean, chiseled bartender, sporting a Mohawk haircut, and a black, ribbed T-shirt that clung to him like a second skin, approached. "What will you have, sweetheart?"

I wanted to say, "I'll have the most expensive drink your tattooed hand can pour in a glass." But all I had in my purse was enough money to get me back to the hotel.

"Umm . . . ," I said, tapping my beautifully manicured fingertip to my chin as I stalled for time. No way should I have to buy my own drink.

After a couple of seconds, I felt a presence to my left. "What are you drinking, beautiful?" I didn't even turn to see what the man looked like. It doesn't matter; he'd uttered the magic words.

I flashed my Broadway smile, and said, "Cognac. Louis the Fourteenth." And that's the way the entire night flowed. Men stepped up, bought drinks and shot their best game, as though they were auditioning for a high-paying job. But I turned them away like they had lied on their resumes. I guess I still have something left. At least my beauty hasn't deserted me.

When I left the cast party for my quick change of clothes, my intentions were to find a tall, handsome man with one pocket full of paper, the other full of dick. A brotha who could leave my legs trembling after he climbed off me, but wouldn't hesitate to drop five hundred dollars on a nice dinner before he got up the nerve to ask me for some. But since that was nowhere in sight, I decided to accept the drinks men (and women if they had the courage) bought, and make the most of it. Tomorrow is a travel day and we aren't leaving until late in the day.

After what seemed like the fifth fat, short guy had tried to get me to go home with him, I asked a tall sista with a disturbing orange and purple ensemble, dancing by herself, what time it was.

"It's almost two," she said, her hand cupped to her mouth, screaming in my ear over the music.

It's later than I thought, and any self-respecting woman knows, if you linger in a club until daybreak, men will think you're just waiting for invitations to go home.

So I left the club a little past tipsy, but not yet pissy, trying to get a damn cab to stop. They raced past me like it was NASCAR, and I wondered did a sista have to yank down the front of her dress and flash the twins to get a lift.

Suddenly a car quickly stopped in front of me in the cab lane. It was a two-seater sports car with a pointy nose and huge wheels. Its color was a dark, dark blue, like a midnight sky, the streetlights reflecting off it like stars.

As casually as I could, I tilted my head a little, not wanting to seem like some busted-down ghetto girl, because I was intrigued by who could be inside. Maybe it was somebody from the Miami Heat or Miami

Dolphins. But the windows were tinted.

As if the driver was reading my mind, the dark window smoothly powered down.

With a little effort now, I could see inside, and what I saw was the profile of an incredibly gorgeous man. He had the complexion of lightly toasted bread. His hair was cut down to a shadow and lined razor sharp all around. I could only see him from the side, but his profile was nothing short of majestic.

The car sat there idling, the exhaust emitting a deep, throaty purr, as smoke spiraled from the two pipes into the night air.

I stalled as best I could, letting a couple of cabs pass. I wanted the man inside to turn so I could see if he was as handsome from the front, or if he had ears too big or gold teeth, but he just sat still like a statue, as if he was waiting for something. I was dying to be noticed but there was no way I was going to show it.

A cab pulled up behind him and the cabbie waved for me to get in. No, I thought, I'm not budging. This was the cab stand. If this fool wasn't trying to show off his new boy toy, the cab could've picked me up.

Another taxi pulled behind the first, then another, then they started honking their horns. But the man didn't seem to notice or care. He acted like he was deaf.

I saw my opening. "Uh, I think that honking is meant for you, guy," I yelled over the noise. Still nothing. So I took two steps to the car and lowered myself to the window. "Are you gonna move or —" He turned to look at me, and oh, yes, he was fine as a new mohair sweater. I stumbled over my words a moment, regained composure and finished my sentence. "You gonna move or what?" I asked, this time a little sweeter, a lot sexier.

He turned toward me. "Depends," he said, his voice a smooth baritone, like the baseline in a quiet storm slow jam. "If you'd rather ride in a taxi or an Aston Martin."

I wasn't sure he was saying what I thought he was saying, so as cool as possible, I said, "Depends. Is this your Aston Martin?"

He cracked a smile. A deep dimple appeared in his left cheek, and his straight, white teeth seemed to brighten the car's entire dim cabin.

My, my, he was phine!

With a gesture of his hand he said coolly, "Get in."

Just like that? Oh no, I had to set him straight. "What?" I said, wondering just who he thought I was. "I'm not just any female on the street a man barks an order to —"

"Get in," he said again, more forceful this time.

I looked at the fine man behind the wheel, and I don't know why, because I've never done anything like this, but there I was pulling on the door handle and lowering myself into his magnificent ride.

Cut to an hour later. I'm standing not six inches from the floor-to-ceiling windows of S. Marcus Pinkston's 54th floor, three-bedroom apartment at the Four Seasons in the Brickell area. The windows wrap all the way around the corner unit, and on one side you can see the sparkling lights of the downtown Miami skyline. On the other side, I'm staring down at the Miami harbor, stretched out, peaceful and placid, dotted with sailboats.

I'm barefoot on Brazilian wood floors, a glass of champagne with a splash of pomengrate juice in my hand. I'm with a man I don't even know. I guess I trust him. I know it's crazy. I trusted him enough to get in his car, and when he suggested he take me to his home instead of my hotel, I trusted him enough to agree. I guess he trusted me too, not knowing if I could be some Glenn Close *Fatal Attraction*–type stalker, for all he knows. Maybe he could be that stalker that

I needed.

Don't ask me why. Maybe it's all the drinks I'd consumed or his unquestionable good looks, or the fact that I'm tired of counting dimes and quarters to make ends meet, denying myself all the finer things I've been accustomed to. He seems to have the means and is prepared to let me experience all those things for just one night.

And if I lay it on him right, maybe he'll be my ticket back into the glamorous life that I deserve. Not to mention, he's so fine, I have no doubt he'll satisfy the craving for love that's been making my body ache for far too long.

I take a tiny sip of my drink. It splashes over my palate like sweet nectar. I'm in the house of a man I don't know, yet I feel totally comfortable. He had an aura about him that soothed me from the moment I jumped into his car.

"Tell me your name again, beautiful," he says, extending a hand and leading me to a low black leather couch.

I place my hand in his and follow, saying, "Yancey Harrington Braxton." His hand is soft as a velvet glove. "You must have rich blood by the feel of your hand. I bet you haven't worked a day in your life."

His voice is deep and seductive as he says,

"I use my brains, sweetheart, not my hands. I save them for other things."

The look in his eyes tells me it's not for praying. I decide to probe. "So how old are you?"

"Thirty-something," he says quickly.

"So what do you do? I mean, to be able to afford all this?" I asked as I waved the champagne flute like it was a conductor's baton.

"I used to manage a hedge fund and dabble in the futures market. It's the family business. Do you consider that working?"

"Yeah, I guess," I teased and turned up my charm. Judging from his place, I need to be on his team. "So you got me in your car. Do you always get what you want?"

S. Marcus smiled, showing those dimples again. He leaned in playfully. "Most of the time, because I know what I want. And I know how to ask."

You better believe he does. Don't blow this, Yancey, I tell myself. This could be your golden ticket back. "What does the S stand for? Steven?"

"Do I look like a Steven to you?"

"You could definitely be a Steven."

He gives a wink and says with a sip, "I can't reveal that until after our fifth date."

"Who said there would be a fifth date?" I

ask with a laugh. Deep down, I'm loving the idea that he sees me as more than a one-night stand. And once he gets a taste of my sweet stuff, he'll want to keep me in his life for a long time, to shower me with all this luxury.

My sassy response makes his eyes glow with intrigue, as if he's never been challenged.

"Oh, there *will* be a fifth date," he says confidently, looking at me like I'd be crazy not to stick around to share in his high life. "But if there isn't, then you'll never know who S. Marcus Pinkston is. Or what you'd missed out on."

I shook my head, not knowing whether to admire the hell out of this guy or be taken aback by his gall. "So sure of yourself, aren't you?"

"And you love it. So what is it that you do, Yancey Braxton?"

I hated that he knew my name and still had to ask, but I'd grown used to that. It hurts less than it did at first. "I'm an actress and I dabble in New York real estate."

"Are you making any money in either one?"

"I do all right," I lied.

"I bet you do. Listen," he said, rising, "I'm going to get more comfortable. Make yourself at home and try not to miss me too much." He then disappeared behind mahogany-paneled walls.

I'm still standing at the windows looking at the water when suddenly music pipes through the apartment. It is a seductive male voice I don't recognize at first and then realize it's neo-soul singer Anthony Hamilton. It has been a long time since I've been in a posh setting like this and I miss it terribly. I want to tell S. Marcus that I too once had it all, but who wants to explain how it all fell apart?

Just as I was feeling sorry for myself, the softest kiss brushes over on the curve of my neck. A hot wave of lust ripples through me. It feels so good, I don't move. Because it makes me realize just how much I've missed a man touching me like that.

My body hungers for him just as much as my entire being aches to return to the life of luxury. And right now I feel like I'll do anything to satisfy both cravings.

He put his heavy hand low on my hip. And I swear I could feel lightning shoot from his palm and his fingertips through my body. It didn't help that he was touching me way too close to a place that needed love more than anything else. I took in a deep, sharp breath — almost a gasp — as that lightning crackled through every inch of me and sparked a fire between my legs. It was a wonder that I could feel so wet and so on fire at the same time. All I wanted was for this gorgeous man to do whatever he says he does with his hands. I needed him to touch me there, then hammer into the heat until it exploded and cooled down, at the same time intoxicating him with an over-whelming need for Yancey in his life.

"Turn around," he whispers. "I want to see you."

I do as I'm told with the obedience of a child. It's not my style. But my body wants him so badly, I guess I can do it one night of my life. I turn, and he stands before me wearing nothing but a milk-white bath towel cinched around his waist.

I gasp, admiring his perfect anatomy. His body looks better than any guy on the cover of a fitness magazine. The sight of this magnificent piece of manhood makes my body burn even hotter. I cross my arms to hide my nipples, poking two hard points through my dress. But I can't take my eyes off this luscious vision of male perfection.

Being in the theater, I've seen my share of perfect bodies, from gay chorus boys to toned leading men. But this one is all mine. It is muscled, strong and hairless and can give Michelangelo's *David* a run for his money.

Then I saw something that let me know he was no Goody Two–shoes, that he could probably throw down like I needed him to. He had a circular Chinese tat around his waist that looks like a permanent belt. There was another tat with a red heart with the words *Mom* and *R.I.P.* I usually don't like tats but on Marcus they look marvelous. Maybe he was a straight-laced, pinstripe-suited financial wizard by day, but this man definitely had a freakier side that I was about to meet by night.

Marcus moves closer to me, his lips almost touching mine. His breath smells of mint mouthwash.

The sensation of a gorgeous man's lips this close to mine makes that blaze between my legs burn even hotter with need. I press my thighs together to massage the throbbing wetness that has created a creamy puddle in my panties; the friction sends a shiver through me that feels so good, I'm dizzy.

To steady myself, I rest my hand on his bicep, which is as hard as stone. If his dick is even half as hard as his arm, I am in for a sweet treat tonight. For a moment I think this is some type of dream and I must will myself never to wake up.

He moves even closer. He's pressing his lips softly to mine, as though he knows he doesn't have to ask permission. This isn't my first time at the fair. I feel his broad chest brushing against my naked shoulders, the head of his stiff dick pressing through the fabric of my short dress.

A soft moan escapes my lips. All I want is to feel that ramming up into me for as long as I can take it.

He steps back.

"You know I want you," he said.

"You said you always get what you want, right?" I asked playfully, wishing he would get on with the program. Men were always talking about the urgency of a hard dick. Well, if they ever felt the overwhelming urgency of a hot, hungry pussy, they'd understand that we need it just as much as they do.

"Yes," he said. "Because I know what I want, and —"

"You know how to ask," I finished for him, laughing. I look deep into his eyes. He seems like he'd be an attentive, unselfish lover. That's just what I need, what I've been needing for a long time. "You got protection?" I ask softly.

"Yes," he said, holding up a gold wrapper

he seemed to pull from thin air.

"Oh, I see we have a regular Boy Scout here," I smiled, relieved.

"Always prepared."

"The zipper's in the back," I said, turning around and lifting my hair up slightly over my shoulders.

S. Marcus unzipped my dress, and followed the path of the zipper with his tongue from the small of my back to the center of my ass. He might as well have been dragging a giant matchstick down my spine, because that man's tongue set off an inferno inside me. Every inch that he licked made my pussy ignite with a pulsating sensation that was like little flames licking at my moist flesh from the inside out.

Alicia Keyes's voice is playing in the background, but I need her ass to shut up so this man can hear how he is making my pussy sing.

He reaches up, pulls the dress down past my breasts, waist and finally my knees. I'm standing in nothing but sheer pink panties, staring at the sky, my palms pressed against the glass. The beautiful view and the even better sensations make me feel like I'm on top of the world. And I'm going to use this situation to stay here.

"Very pretty," he says, removing my panties with one swoop, obviously no stranger to the game. I love that this body looks so hard, but his touch and his kisses are so soft.

He continues kissing my cheeks, sucking them, sending bolts of electricity through my entire body. I close my eyes, seeing flashes of yellow and white — that lightning from his touch. On his knees, he spins me around, my ass slapping against the glass. I look down at him as he kisses my inner thighs, sinks his long, middle finger deep into his mouth, then aims it between my legs. I watch, panting with excitement.

"Aaahhh," I cry out as his fingertip slips across my clit. He slowly slides his finger inside me. And I toss my head back with the shock of intense pleasure. Because now those lightning bolts are shooting up through my insides as he moves his finger in and out, letting his thumb dance on my clit.

I am so hot, so aroused, that my whole body begins to tremor. I have never come this fast. Ever.

His eyes sparkle as I open mine long enough to look into his face. "Yeah, baby, come for me like that."

His thumb is rubbing so fast, round and round, back and forth, over my slippery berry, and his finger, stroking in and out —

"Ooh," he says, "you need it bad, and I got it for you."

A tingly sensation explodes between my legs, sending shivers through every inch of me. I'm crying out, gasping, shocked at the speed and intensity of this pleasure in this beautiful place with this gorgeous man.

Heaven. That word flashes in my head. Because I'm getting a little taste of heaven right at this moment. And I need him to keep looking at me like that, and keep making me feel like this, for a long time.

"I'm here to make you feel good," he whispers seductively. "You ain't seen nothin' yet." Ooh, I loved that he could switch from proper to slightly roughneck in the span of a whisper. That made me pulsate around his finger even harder as my clit danced under his expert touch.

When my moans let him know I've reached the limit, he stands. The towel falls.

And I gasp.

Because he has one of the most beautiful dicks I've ever seen. It's jutting out from a soft nest of black hair, curving slightly up. Can this man get more perfect?

"All that for me?" I ask, looking at him with hunger in my eyes.

"Is it enough, baby girl?"

"It looks like more than enough," I say,

wondering why all men need dick approval and how long it had been since a man called me baby girl. My body is so ready for him, I know this is one night I will never forget.

Lust burns in his eyes as he asks, "So what are you going to do with it?"

I don't say a word. Instead I grab it in my hand like a cob of corn I'm about to shuck. He moans as I feel it throb in my fist.

"You ready for it?" he asks with a teasing tone.

"I want it, now," I almost order. I love the power I feel right now, with him looking at me like I'm the most beautiful and desirable woman in the world.

But I don't like the way worry tightens his face when he catches a glimpse of my scar.

"What's that?" Marcus asks as he gently touches my shoulder blade. I usually covered it up with makeup, but tonight I hadn't. I just hope that my eyes didn't give me away.

"It's a birthmark," I said confidently, in a way that said I didn't want to talk about it or let it interfere with the pleasure at hand.

Marcus studied it for a few seconds. He sounded skeptical when he said, "That's an unusual-looking birthmark."

I looked up at him with my most seductive look, to quiet the questions in his head.

"Everything about me is different. Now let's get back to business, sir."

He spun me back around, gently pushing me against the glass, pressing my breasts and the side of my face into it. The corner of my mouth can barely rise as I smile, thrilled with anticipation. But the glass against my cheek — and a sudden pang of fear — remind me just how fragile my situation is. I feel so high with the world at my feet, but if I push too hard, I could literally plunge into tragedy.

Here I am dreaming that casual sex is going to open the door for me to stay in this man's luxurious life, yet as I look out at Biscayne Bay, for all I know, I might just be his catch of the day.

Behind me, the sound of him tearing open the condom wrapper underscores that thought. Was he just going to consume me and toss me out just like he'd flush that condom when we're done? Me and it, gone forever from here?

I feel so conflicted. My body is screaming for him. My mind is crying out for his life-style. Am I dreaming?

He grabs my ass, runs his fingertips over the slippery swollen flesh between my legs, and —

"Ooooh," I moan, closing my eyes. I know

no better feeling in the world than that first stroke of a big, hard dick sliding up into my hungry body. I squeeze around him.

"Yeah, girl," he groans. "I feel you."

He's so gentle; his stroke is careful and caring. He pushes deep, a little deeper, and then so deep it feels like he's tickling my stomach from the inside out.

Our bodies are now connected. But are our minds? I need to make sure he wants those five dates with me and much more.

He pauses, as if he, too, is stopping to savor just how good it feels. He takes a long, deep breath as I feel his dick pulsating and getting bigger.

That makes me gasp and press my palms to the glass. If it feels this good being still, I'm about to lose my mind when he —

Thrusts. With his hands gripping my waist, he pulls his hips back, then thrusts again. In, out. In, out. Faster, harder, making magic friction with this perfect fit.

If I thought his hands were sending lightning bolts through my body, his dick is doing the same, with a thousand times more intensity. It's like I can feel little waves of electricity dance up through every cell in my body. Goose bumps ripple across my skin. I cry out with the most intense pleasure I've ever felt.

For a second, I think about all the times I've gotten off with my vibrator. That does the job, but this is the real thing. A real dick, pounding relentlessly with the fierce force of a man, taking me to a place I could never describe because nobody has invented the words to explain how good this feels.

And another explosion is sparking between my legs. My whole body trembles; my pussy pulsates around his huge, rock-hard dick. I pull my cheek off the window for fear that his hammering might shatter the glass — and this fantasy experience. At the same time, I grip the glass so hard that my fingernails make scratching noises.

"I feel you, baby," he groans with delight. "Come for me again. Come for *me!*"

"Oh I am," I moan.

"Yeah, tell me how much you love it," S. Marcus whispers.

I arch my back, which lets him thrust even deeper. He responds with faster, harder strokes.

"Oh, yeah," I cry. "Yeah . . ."

"Come on, girl. Make it come for me!" he demands. I think this man doesn't know who he is messing with. I still have the flexibility of a sixteen-year-old gymnast and the sexual skills of a porn star.

I back my ass into him hard, grinding in a

circular motion. I look back. He's staring down at my gyrating hips and ass with absolute ecstasy in his eyes. So I go fast, then slow, over and over, until a glazed look in his eyes lets me know I've hypnotized him into submission to give me everything I want.

"Damn, baby girl, you'll make me come too quick like that," he groans, pounding even deeper.

And that sends me into another orgasmic explosion all over that long love stick of his.

His voice is raw and deep with passion as he shouts, "Oh baby girl, I'm comin' with you."

I feel his dick pulsate inside me as his body shudders behind me. At the same time, I shiver with pleasure and glimpse back at his face — lovestruck, luststruck, sprung — whatever you want to call it.

I'm calling it *This man is hooked on some Yancey. And he'll want more. And more. For as long as I want.*

Realizing that my work is done, my legs go weak, and I slide down the length of the window to the floor.

A few hours later, I wake up in soft, apple-green Egyptian cotton sheets, sunlight slicing thinly through long vertical bedroom blinds. S. Marcus is standing bare-chested at the foot of the bed, holding a silver tray with a single rose, bacon, eggs, sliced fruit and a glass of cranberry juice on it.

"After last night, I thought you might be hungry, so I got some breakfast for you."

I ran my hands through my hair, trying to compose myself. "You cooked for me?"

"Well, not really," he said, setting the tray across my lap and giving me a gentle kiss on my forehead. "My chef, Danni, made this. And then I gave her the day off. I hope you don't have plans. I want to spend the day with you."

I smile wider than I want and say, "I wish I could, but I leave today." I don't know what makes me happier, the breakfast or the fact that my dream boy has his own personal chef.

"Where are you going?"

"Tallahassee, then North Carolina. Raleigh-Durham, to be exact."

"For what?"

"I told you I'm an actress. I'm in a show and we open there tomorrow. I wish I could stay in Miami. I really do."

"Then I will come to Raleigh-Durham in a couple of days to see you."

"That would be nice," I said.

"How long is this tour thing?"

"Right now I don't know. The producers are talking about adding some cities, but quite honestly I'd just as soon go back to my home in New York."

S. Marcus sits down beside me and takes my hand tenderly. "Does it pay you a lot of money?"

"I do okay," I say with a sip of juice.

"How long have you been acting?"

Not willing to give up my age until I find out how old S. Marcus is, I say, "Not long. I'm looking for a big break."

"Have you ever thought about doing a reality show?" S. Marcus asks.

"Yeah, I have. Why do you ask?" Could this man be more perfect?

"I think a show about the life of a not-so-well-known actress might be interesting. They could follow you on the road with cameras. I have some investors trying to break into television and this might be the way in. They invested in some young singer a couple of years ago, but when she made it big, her daddy and stepmom cut them out."

"How do you know I'm not famous? I had a hit record a few years ago," I said proudly.

"So did that chick Sparkle. But now the only gig she's got is testifying in the R. Kelly trial." He paused, cupping my chin in his large hand. "I think we could make this happen."

"Really?" I said, thinking that if this man is as good in business as he is in bed, I might be on the verge of that comeback. But before I can say another word, he leans in and starts kissing me all over again.

Maybe my luck is changing.

CHAPTER 4

Ava Parker Middlebrooks stood before her daughter Yancey's Upper East Side town-house door, holding the gold key in her hand. She said a little prayer before attempting to slip the key into the lock. She hoped it would fit, hoped her daughter had not changed the locks in the seven years that Ava had been away.

Ava was given a fifteen-year sentence for attempted murder, but had been released yesterday morning on the condition that she stay in New York during the first two years of her probation. Ava practically had to beg Yancey to write a letter stating that her mother could stay with her. The clothes she had been dragged to prison in had been given back to her — a violet St. John's pant-suit. She was sure only the shoes, a pair of open-toed pumps, would now fit, she'd gained so much weight. The pantsuit sat on the prison's discharge counter, crudely folded, waiting for her to pick it up. Not that she wanted it, considering how terribly out of style it was now. Who said a St. John's purchase would never get old? She was also given back her two-tone Philippe Patek watch, a gold ring, a necklace and the small amount of cash she had on her, which totaled over four hundred dollars. This was a long way from the days of villas and yachts in Europe, where Ava had spent many of her adult years.

Standing in the drab gray release room, after counting all the money she had in the world, Ava realized that she didn't have enough to fly back to New York City. At least not first class, and there was no way in hell she was flying anything but.

"Is it all there, Ava?" asked a burly older corrections officer with broad shoulders and salt-and-pepper, close-cropped hair. He had been working there all seven years that Ava had been incarcerated, but this was the first time she had given him a second look. He was actually quite handsome. He appeared to be five years or so younger than Ava, so he was really the right age. But she figured even if he received a bonus or overtime, he only made fifty grand tops. For Ava to even consider him, he'd have to add at least two more zeros to the end of that figure. Besides, wealthy men would be lining up once they heard that Ava was free and single again. She still saw herself as a traffic-stopping beauty with big doe-brown eyes and long, thick lashes. The country girl called Miss Brickhouse by boys in her hometown when she strolled down the street in Jackson, Tennessee. The girl who had become a woman and lived her life large with few regrets and fewer attachments. Ava had dined with Moroccan royalty, partied with rich Frenchmen, married a count and been pursued by wealthy men all over the world. But her fall from grace was a long, hard fall because of how high she had climbed so fast.

"Yes," Ava smiled, batting her eyes at the muscular man. "Everything is here."

After five hours of freedom, Ava found herself in seemingly the most disgusting place on earth — a small-town Greyhound bus station, wearing her outdated, too-tight fashions at that.

She had landed there after countless failed attempts at reaching her daughter to have her wire money for clothes, a first-class plane ticket, and some extra cash to get her nails, hair and eyebrows done. Ava couldn't even think about stepping on a plane looking the way she did. What if she were seated next to an eligible, aging man on her flight to New York City? A man with, let's say, millions in the bank. A generous man with a failing heart, who knew he had only a limited time left on this earth, but wanted to marry a beautiful, incredibly fabulous, middle-aged woman and leave her his fortune.

After standing around next to pay phones for hours, waiting for Yancey to call her back, Ava finally accepted the fact that she would have to use the bus ticket provided by the state to get back to New York.

Why hadn't Yancey returned her calls? Ava wondered. The two had called a truce over their mother-daughter battles while Ava was in jail. Yancey had accepted her collect calls during the seven years Ava was away and had even visited her mother at least twice a year. Maybe Yancey didn't know that Ava was being released early.

With ticket in hand and the bus in sight, Ava made one final attempt to get in touch with Yancey. When she couldn't, Ava lowered her head and sadly boarded the bus as if its destination was not New York, but back to the prison she was released from.

The ride was a horrible nine-hour affair, filled with the noise of a screaming infant, a quarreling couple and a group of immigrants arguing in a language that Ava didn't understand.

Ava huddled in a window seat, staring out at the darkened, star-filled sky as the countless miles sped past her. This was the lowest she had ever felt. Lower than when she was convicted and sent to jail. At least there she was considered a diva among her fellow inmates, passing out makeup tips and sharing stories of life among the rich and famous. At that moment on that speeding dark bus, with the portable bathroom only three seats down from her, smelling so bad it made her stomach do somersaults, Ava vowed she would never sink this low again.

When Ava reached the Port Authority on 42nd Street in New York, she quickly hailed a cab and was taken to more familiar, appropriate surroundings — Yancey's fancy East Side town house.

And that is where Ava stands now, staring down at the key in her hand. She exhales, points the key in the direction of the lock and then pushes it into the tiny slit. The tumblers flip and Ava looks toward the sky and smiles as she pushes open the door.

"Yancey, sweetheart," Ava calls into the vast space that was Yancey's town house. "Your darling mother is home. Free at last." There is no response.

Closing the door behind her, Ava steps

down the three stairs that lead into the sunken living room. She turns in a circle looking around at the apartment she helped her daughter purchase. Yancey had done nothing with the place in seven years. Ava thought the child would've at least updated the furniture, had the place repainted, something.

"Yancey, darling," Ava calls again, walking toward the kitchen. Still not receiving a response, she opens the refrigerator door, pulls out a quart of skim milk and twists off the top. She brings the plastic container to her nose and, as expected, it is spoiled. Ava doesn't notice any fresh flowers in the house, which Yancey always loves to keep. This makes her suspect that her daughter hasn't been home for some time.

Ava examines the stamped date on the plastic bottle and notices that the milk expired almost two months ago.

Suddenly, the phone rings, startling Ava. She walks quickly across the thick Persian living room rug to answer it.

"Hello."

"Hello," a somewhat high-pitched, girlish voice says. "Is this Ms. Yancey Braxton?"

Ava thought for a moment, figuring that maybe this call could give her information as to where her daughter is. "Yes. This is

Ms. Braxton. How may I help you?"

"This is Sharon Dale, Mrs. Weeks your real estate agent's assistant."

"Oh, yes, hello, Sharon."

"I have a very wealthy couple from Russia who are extremely interested in your apartment. They saw it online and Mrs. Weeks thinks they're ready to make an offer. I have even more good news. If they like it, and I know they will, it will be a cash sale."

"Really?" Ava said, wondering why Yancey would want to sell this prime property. Yancey had purchased this exclusive 2,700-square-foot town house with Ava's help. At least that's what she led Yancey to believe, but the money actually came from a life insurance policy her own mother had left Yancey. Essie Dean had left everything to Yancey to spite Ava, whom she never forgave for getting pregnant in high school and leaving Jackson, Tennessee, soon after to pursue a career on Broadway. But Yancey never knew this and Ava had her attorney do a quick deed shortly after the purchase converting the property to herself. Now was as good a time as any to stake her claim.

"They want to come by this afternoon and see it. Can we bring them by?"

If they were to buy it, where would Ava stay? She'd be homeless, and although she never thought it possible, that would be a worse situation than being in prison. The husband who'd divorced her while she was incarcerated had made it quite clear Ava wouldn't be welcome at his door. Thinking fast, she answered, "No. This afternoon isn't good."

"May I ask why?" The assistant sounded annoyed.

"Because I'm stepping out," Ava said quickly.

"That's no problem, we have a key."

"No. Let's just schedule it for another day, shall we?"

"Ms. Braxton, we're talking over two million dollars. This is a tough market. The Povliks are only in town for another two days. If we can't see your apartment today, I'm going to have to show them something similar in the area."

"Then maybe that's what you should do. Besides, I'm seriously considering taking it off the market," Ava said.

"Are you sure?" the woman asked in disbelief.

"What part of that don't you understand? Good day, Sharon."

About an hour later, Ava found herself on the corner of 86th and Lexington Avenue at the boutique grocer Euperican. It feels good to be back, Ava thought as she strolled the aisles of the store that carried the freshest fruit, seafood, breads and fine wines — in short, everything Ava was accustomed to and missed.

As she slowly and carefully walks down the narrow aisle of well-stocked domestic and imported food from all over the world, Ava doesn't know what to put into her cart first. She decides on a nice bottle of Pinot Noir and a box of crackers.

By the time she reaches the checkout counter, there are two bottles of wine, champagne, a jar of inexpensive caviar, block chocolate, strawberries, fresh prawns, two very lean medium-size filets and a chocolate truffle that Ava knows will melt on her tongue like butter on a warm biscuit.

Ava takes each item from her cart and places it carefully on the conveyor belt as the smooth-faced checkout girl scans the items.

"That will be $282.95, ma'am," the girl said with a smile.

Ava pulls money out of one of Yancey's designer handbags she's borrowed. She starts counting the bills, laying them flat on the counter's surface. "That's two hundred and ten, two hundred and twenty," and then Ava lays her last bill down. "Two hundred and twenty-five dollars." She looks up at the girl. "How much did you say it was again?"

"It's 282.95, ma'am."

"I see," Ava said, more embarrassed than she'd ever been on New York's East Side.

"You want to put this on a credit card?" the cashier asked.

"Don't you think that if I had a credit card I would have given it to you?" Ava snapped.

"I'm sorry. It's just that . . ."

"Yes, you are — very sorry," Ava said as she sank her hand back into her purse, fishing around for more money. When she found nothing, she became friendly once more. "Just put back one of the bottles of wine, hon."

Once back at Yancey's residence, Ava takes a warm bubble bath using Yancey's best bath salts. She washes her hair with a shampoo she has never seen before, and it is in such a beautiful muted gold bottle, Ava knows it had to have cost big money. It left her hair feeling cleaner than a visit to the famed Mr. Jason Salon in Beverly Hills.

She smooths an orange-ginger lotion over her body, paints her toenails with a pale peach polish, her fingernails with clear polish, then sifts through Yancey's drawers and finds a long, flowing, whore-red nightgown with a Saks Fifth Avenue tag still on it. It looks a little small, but Ava tells herself she is wearing this gown.

She squirms into it, removes the towel from her head, blow-dries her hair, leaving it wild and soft about her head and neck. Then she applies a light, age-defying cream to her face.

She stands in the large marble-floored bathroom, with its huge mirror and bright, circular dressing room bulbs all around it, and gazes at herself. She is back, she tells herself. Gone is the life from behind bars, the faded denim jumpers with her inmate number stenciled across the left breast. No more trying to be beautiful with nothing more than a plastic comb and a bottle of drugstore foundation, attempting to apply it in a mirror that was nothing more than a thin square of very shiny reflective metal. No more of that. Ava is back to the life she is used to.

Ava goes to the kitchen, pulls the steak from the broiler, sets it on a tray along with a bottle of wine, a beautiful glass, and colorful steamed vegetables and brings it into the living room. She sets the tray on the coffee table, before the sofa and in front of a fifty-two-inch Sony LCD HDTV, then grabs the remote and turns to the Fine Living Channel. She then thumbs the volume to a perfect level.

Half sitting, half lying across the sofa, her hair as silky as the red gown draped over her shoulders, Ava pours herself a glass of wine. She closes her eyes as she takes her first sip and then raises the glass before her and makes a simple toast.

"To me and revenge, baby."

CHAPTER 5

The last night of the tour was a good night. A very good night. I smiled brightly as I bowed before another standing ovation at the packed house at the Raleigh theater. I almost broke out in tears. Not tears of joy, because I would now have to return to New York and my mounting money problems. I knew if this was Broadway, and I had ripped it the way I had, I would've been getting seriously paid and most likely auditioning to do other shows. But all I would be getting for my Tony-worthy performance was a check barely enough to get me through a week in New York.

I sat in my dressing room, staring at myself in the mirror as I took the stage makeup off my face. My cell phone sat just to the side of me, but it hadn't rung in days and there were no missed calls or texts. This was starting to piss me off. S. Marcus hadn't called in a couple of days, and I was beginning to worry that he'd already moved on. I needed him for two things: the good loving he could deliver and to see if he could really help me get a reality show of my own.

I smeared some more makeup off my cheek with a cotton puff, and angrily threw it on the dresser, forcing myself to admit why he hadn't called. I must have appeared too desperate. I was acting like some dumb schoolgirl and I knew better. This man had fucked me one good time, and I was acting like I was sprung. Granted, it was some of the best sex I'd ever had, but still I needed to pull myself together.

A knock came at the door. I ignored it, not wanting to be bothered. It was most likely some castmates with their best friend from Bumpfuck, Arkansas, who wanted to take a picture with me and get an autograph so they could post it on their MySpace page.

Another knock. "Please, not tonight. Go away!" I shouted, looking at the door through the reflection in my mirror. After a moment of silence, I went back to my makeup, figuring they got the message, but the knocking came again.

I shot up from my stool, stormed across the room, and flung open the door. I was met with a wall of roses. I couldn't see the face of the fan who held them, but roses always made me feel better. Most times.

"Look!" I said, no longer controlling my anger. "I appreciate the roses but —"

Before I could finish my sentence, my fan brought the flowers down, and I gasped when S. Marcus appeared behind them with a broad smile on his face.

"You going to talk to me like that?" he joked, stepping into my dressing room. I took a step back, allowing him in. "After I take off from work, fly all the way over here, trying to surprise you, this is the reception I get?" He walked me backward across the room until my back was pressed against the wall.

"I'm so sorry, baby," I said, my voice sounding like a little girl.

He looked at me for a moment with those dark, hypnotizing eyes, as if he was trying to decide what to do with me. Had I messed this up for good? I wondered.

Without saying a word, he dropped the roses onto the sofa beside us, grabbed me tight, and then pressed his open mouth to mine. His lips were softer than I remembered. His tongue slid into my mouth, and it was full, sweet and playful. I kissed him back, sucking his tongue like it was his dick.

"Oh, baby," I said, slowly releasing one of my naked legs from the robe. He took hold of the other, lifting me up, spreading them open, and pressing his throbbing manhood against my now moist center. "Can we . . . can we?" I tried to say, digging my nails into the back of his jacket. "Can we get out of here?"

He pulled his full lips from mine and said, "Let's make it happen."

An hour later, we were in a suite on the concierge level of a hotel that had to be the best in Durham, North Carolina. S. Marcus was on his hands and knees, stark naked. I, too, was naked, on my back, my knees bent, my legs open like butterfly wings. S. Marcus's head was buried, can I say, in the dead center of those wings, and he was making them flap.

I didn't know what he was doing to me, but I was moaning his name one minute, and screaming, calling him all kinds of "motherfuckers" the next. This man was making me feel so good. He scooped up the back of my knees, looping them over his shoulders, opening me all the way. He rose up to look at me, the candlelight hitting his face so I could just see those shiny lips of his, and his penetrating stare that had my heart racing.

"I want you to relax, okay," S. Marcus said in a soothing voice. "Because I'm about to make you come, but not just once, baby. I'm going to make you keep coming till you tell me to stop. Is that okay with you?"

I tried to speak, but I was breathless from all the attention, so I just nodded my head.

Before he went back down, he said, "This is going to feel like nothing you've ever experienced before, so don't hold back on me. Scream if you feel the need. Dig your fingers in my back, but just enjoy yourself. Will you do that for me?"

I swallowed hard and nodded again as I watched him slowly lower his head between my thighs. A moment later, I felt his warm, wet tongue enter me, followed by one of his fingers. My eyes rolled to the back of my head, and even though I tried to stop myself, for fear of looking silly, I screamed out, coming immediately, it felt so incredible.

Afterward — I don't know how long, because I had totally lost track of space and time while Marcus made me come five times — we lay in bed. Although I felt like never before lying there in his arms, I was still feeling anxious about going home to New York.

"What's bothering you, Yancey?" S. Marcus asked.

"I'm okay."

"I'm sure you're not but you will be soon."

"You sound sure of yourself."

"I'm always sure of myself."

I decided to be honest. "I was just thinking about tomorrow. Getting back to New York."

"Are you excited?"

"I have mixed emotions," I admitted. "It's back to unemployment unless I can get a gig."

"Well, if it helps brighten your spirits, I talked to one of my boys and he is interested in looking into a reality show." He gave me a look of curiosity. "I googled you and you've done some things. In fact, why didn't you tell me? I think we got enough to make it happen."

I sat up suddenly. "You do?"

S. Marcus smiled. "Yep, I do. We just need to get some upfront capital and shoot some episodes and get a network like Bravo or VH-1 to do a deal with us."

"I love Bravo. What kind of deal can we get?"

"We're looking at one where we would get a percentage of the commercial time sold. It can be very profitable. But we have to get the right producers onboard."

"That sounds wonderful."

Then he turned serious. "Can I ask you

something?"

"Sure," I said, unable to guess what he was about to say.

"Were you able to forgive your mother?"

My heart dropped through the floor. My mother? Like my mother who was in jail?

"What are you talking about?" I asked.

"Come on, Yancey. It's all out there on the internet. Every story that's been written about you and then some. I read the reports about her shooting someone at a deposition and you testifying against her. Do you go and visit her in prison?"

I kept my eyes averted. "I went a couple of times, but prison depressed me. I could never stay longer than an hour."

"So you do talk to her?"

"She's my mother and I have feelings for her," I said defensively, "but our relationship is complex. It always has been but I wish it was the typical mother-daughter bond. I guess not every woman is cut out for motherhood."

He hadn't sounded condemning. If anything, he seemed amused. "She sounds like a character."

I shook my head and smiled. "You don't know the half of it. Can we can talk about something else? Please."

He pulled himself out from under me,

then turned to face me, leaning up on one elbow. "We can talk about whatever you want or we don't have to talk at all. Is that cool?"

I was happy for a chance to change the subject. "Do you really think we can get them interested in me?" I asked, having a moment of insecurity. This incredible man had thrown me a lifeline, but as hopeful as I'd felt, I'd seen similar prospects come and go.

"Girl, if they are foolish enough to pass on this, then I'll take my own money and make it happen. I haven't known you but a little over a week, but I'm already a big fan."

"For real? You would do that for me?"

"What did I say?"

All of a sudden I was so excited I wanted to burst. No, cry. No, jump on top of this man and fuck him like he'd never been fucked before, but I didn't have any more energy. All I could think about was if this god, in the mortal form of S. Marcus, delivers on what he's saying now, I won't have to live in damn near poverty anymore. I won't have to worry about the money to pay my mortgage, voice and acting lessons, eat and get new headshots. Life will be the way it once was, the way it is supposed to be.

I threw my arms around S. Marcus, pulled

him down on top of me, gave him a long, passionate kiss. "You just met me, and I don't know how I will ever repay you."

S. Marcus smiled slyly, his dimple showing deep in his cheek. "There will be ways."

CHAPTER 6

It was day three and Yancey still had not come back home, nor had Ava had any luck in trying to contact her. She knew from the yearly letter Yancey sent her that she might be doing a bus-and-truck Broadway show but couldn't remember which one.

Ava sat at the bathroom mirror, in a thick white fluffy bathrobe, and applied more of the aloe vera–cucumber facial cream to her cheeks.

It was midafternoon. She had taken another long, warm bubble bath, complete with a glass of wine, classical music playing softly throughout the house.

This had been Ava's life in the days since she was released from prison. Not rushing, not worrying, just taking time to pamper and treat herself to all the comforts that she had been accustomed to in her previous life.

What else was she expected to do? Ava thought, turning on the warm water in the bathroom basin. She hadn't money to do much else but occupy her time with leisurely, in-house activities. And since Yancey was probably traipsing about some white Mediterranean beach, or some European countryside, enjoying the spring with some rich young millionaire, Ava would just enjoy her time here till her daughter decided to reappear or the money ran out.

Ava lowered her face into the bowl, cupped the running water, and splashed it on her face, washing the cream away.

As she pats her face with a white face towel, she is happy that prison had not aged her as much as she knew it could have. On the day she had arrived, she took a look at the women with their split ends all over their heads and their bad haircuts and dye jobs. Many of those girls were Ava's age, but with their skin wrinkling like the leather on an old Coach purse, and them carrying weight like a head chef of a Fifth Avenue restaurant, Ava was determined not to allow the same fate to befall her.

Looking at herself now, she faked a smile, which became a real one when she noticed the very few smile lines at the corner of her eyes and mouth. Her skin was still relatively tight.

Sure, she had put on fifteen pounds, but

she wasn't worried about that. Ava knew she could drop those. But you can't drop age, and today she realized she needed her youthful appearance now more than ever. She had to get back on a twice-a-week facial regime once she got some money.

Pulling a bath towel that matched her robe from the rack, she wrapped it around her still damp hair. Ava grabbed her half glass of wine from the vanity and headed into the living room.

This morning, Ava had woken up with purpose. As much as she had enjoyed the last three days of watching soaps and relaxing, she could not escape the reality that her money was running out. Ava had a plan — two plans in fact, plan A and B. She cooked up plan A in prison while plan B had come to her only that morning.

With her little black book of names and numbers of everybody she knew, both in the business and on a personal level, Ava started calling folks.

It didn't matter who they were, close girlfriends from the past whom Ava loved, or individuals she may have met only once and never wanted to speak to again — she greeted them all the same way.

"Heeeyyyyyy, girl. It's been too long. How you been doing? Yeah, I've been fine . . .

Yeah, I've been away awhile . . . Oh, you heard I was in prison . . . Well, shit happens. What I was calling about is . . . uhm . . . times are a little hard, and . . ."

Right then is when whoever she had on the line suddenly remembered an appointment they were late for. Ava had spoken to half a dozen "friends" this morning, mostly actors and singers she'd worked with, but also a couple of guys whom Ava had dated and dumped when she found out they didn't have the money they said they did.

She would've lied to the people she called about her jail stint, told them she was out of the country for seven years, working, but it seemed as though everybody and their mamas knew that Ava had been sent up. What did they do, she thought, skywrite the news, put it up on billboards, run commercials?

She made several more calls this morning, but nobody was feeling her plight. Ava wondered if this had something to do with her all but laughing in people's faces when they'd turned to her for help, but decided no one would go so far as to hold that against her.

Sitting comfortably on the living room sofa, her bare feet kicked up on the coffee table, wineglass in hand, Ava again thumbed through her little black book. She told herself the problem was she'd picked the wrong people to call. Many of them were friends, but she hadn't spoken to any of them in at least the seven years she was away. Why would she have expected them to have any loyalty to her? Why would it matter to them that she was struggling now?

Ava needed to contact people who cared about her, loved her, or at least once had. That narrowed the list considerably.

Her finger landed on ex-husband Jacob Comstock. He was an exclusive art broker, and she knew he would have the money to help her out. However, when she called his work number, his secretary, a woman with a 900 sex-number voice, said he wasn't in.

"Can I take a message?" she asked.

"Yes. Tell him his ex-wife called, and that he needs to call me back ASAP."

Ava hung up, imagining the girl tearing the sheet she had written the message on from her notepad, balling it up, and tossing it in the trash can, because she was probably screwing Jacob and didn't want any other woman getting a piece of his wallet.

Ava tried his cell number, and when she got his voicemail, she said, "Hey, Jacob. It's been a long time. Was thinking about you, and just called to catch up. Give me a call when you get a chance. My number is the same. I got a little favor to ask of you."

She hung up, regretting telling him the last part. Knowing Jacob, he would figure out she meant money, and there was no way he was calling her back.

After that, Ava dialed David Middlebrooks, her second husband. But all the numbers she had for him were either changed, leaving no forwarding number, or disconnected. There was no way she could get hold of him, and by the sound of it, he might be broke, in which case Ava had nothing to say.

This left her with one last hope in the ex-lover department. Hector, her last. He was a wonderful, handsome, gentle man, and the only reason he and Ava didn't work out was because both of them had a problem with being faithful. But she had always been able to count on him, at least then. As she dialed his number, she hoped he would be able to do the same now. Hector, Ava thought, could serve a dual purpose by giving her money and great sex as well.

After the third ring, Hector picked up, and Ava was almost surprised to hear his voice.

"Hello, Hector," Ava said, "it's been too long."

"Who is this?"

"Now, Daddy, don't tell me you've forgotten me too?"

"Ava?" he asked with pronounced disbelief.

"I knew you wouldn't forget me, Hector."

His disbelief now turned to worry. "Where are you?"

"I'm in New York with my daughter."

"You're out of the joint?"

"Free as a bird," she sang. "I can't wait to see you. We got some business to talk about." Ava paused, considering the best approach now that she had him on the line. Never one to beat around the bush, she plunged right in. "Hector, I need some money."

There was silence and Ava thought he might be dead until she heard him whisper in the background, "I'll be there in a minute, baby."

"Who are you talking to, Hector? Listen, I'm serious, when can we talk about the money?"

"How about you text me a number where I can reach you?"

"Text you a number? Fool, are you crazy? I want to talk now," Ava demanded.

"I got a better idea. Why don't you call Steve or whatever his name was. Bye, Ava."

Ava looked at the phone when she heard

the dial tone. "This motherfucker has lost what little mind he had."

Later that afternoon there was a knock at the door. Ava looked out and saw a brown-clad delivery man. Was this the package she had been waiting for?

"Can I help you?" Ava said as she started to pull her robe together but decided maybe the handsome young man could use a cheap thrill.

"I have a package for Mrs. Ava Middlebrooks."

"It's Ms., sweetheart. Where do I sign?"

He pointed as he handed her the electronic tablet. "Right here."

Ava signed quickly and almost jerked the package from the man. She quickly shut the door and ripped the box open. Inside was a note that read: *Please call me as soon as you power this on. We need to get started with our plan.*

Ava pulled the BlackBerry out of the plastic wrapping, turned the power on and immediately dialed the number listed on the card. After a few rings, the familiar male voice answered.

"So I see you got the package."

"Just a few minutes ago. What took so long? I've been here for days."

The voice was brusque, in a hurry. "I've been busy. So are you ready to start?"

"I am. What do we do first?"

"She's coming back tomorrow, you know, but you need to gain her trust before we start anything."

Ava flashed a grim smile. "That part will be easy. I'll make her feel like I owe it to her since she's letting me stay in this dump. But how long do I have?"

"We can't move too fast."

She didn't like the sound of that. What, she was supposed to wait around forever? "Then can I get an advance of what you promised me?"

"No," he said firmly.

"Why not?"

"Because I said so, that's why. Remember what I told you in the joint. You will follow my orders or else the deal is off and you might find your ass back in the slammer."

"That's not going to happen," she said matter of factly. "But I don't see how a little money is gonna hurt our plan. Damn, you promised me five million when we get her. So I don't see why I can't get a little now. I can still act like I'm poor when I'm around Yancey."

"Ava, I said no. So just drop it. We need to complete our mission. As soon as you finish our little task, I'll take care of you. But I have to make sure I can really trust you and that you're doing what you promise. I don't need you to suddenly develop a case of motherly love."

Ava let out a surprised laugh. "That isn't going to happen. Yancey never showed any daughterly love when she testified against me. Any motherly love I felt for her went out the window of that courtroom," she added, with a growling edge entering her voice. "Your timing in approaching me couldn't have been better. A chance to get back at Yancey and get rich? What a golden opportunity."

"Yeah, for the both of us. I can't tell you how many nights I've sat up thinking of ways to get revenge on Yancey Braxton for what she did to me and my family."

"You're almost as sinister as me."

"I do what I need to do. Getting revenge on Yancey has been on my to-do list for a long time."

"So what do I do first?"

"Just enjoy your little family reunion. Make sure you hide this device but check it regularly. You never know when I will call you with further instructions. But be careful and make sure she never catches you talking to me or reading any of the texts I will be sending. We both know Yancey is no dummy."

Ava scoffed at that idea. "She only thinks she's smart. When we finish with her, she will understand what a silly little girl she really is."

"Hey, I got to run. I will talk with you real soon."

"I'll be waiting."

Chapter 7

I returned to New York on a sun-splashed spring day. I couldn't remember feeling so happy to be anywhere. The taxi let me off in front of my town house and I noticed the For Sale sign was missing. Did my real estate agent have some good news and hadn't been able to reach me? If that was the case, then the first thing I was going to do was to draw a bubble bath and just soak for hours.

I hoped whoever had bought my house didn't need to move in right away. S. Marcus was coming to New York and I really wanted to spend some time with him in my town house.

I entered my home expecting it to feel somewhat stuffy from being closed up, but it smelled as fresh as just-rinsed fruit. Maybe the real estate agent had cleaned the place for prospective buyers. I dropped my suitcases by the door and walked over to the sofa table to look through the mail I'd brought in. I was surprised when there were only a few pieces.

I walked into the kitchen and noticed a champagne glass and coffee cup in the sink. Had I left those there? I was going to look in the refrigerator for a bottle of water but figured I needed to go grocery shopping first. I only hoped I had some of my Carol's Daughter bubble bath and body lotion under the sink because I didn't feel like trekking to the West Side to my favorite perfume store.

I went back to the door to get my suitcases when I suddenly heard movement in the next room. Before I could turn around I heard a loud, theatrical voice say, "Welcome home, Yancey."

Like the clown in the horror movies, my mother stuck her face into the doorway. "Ava, you scared the shit out of me. What are you doing here? How did you get in?"

"Is that any way to greet your mother?"

"How did you get in?" I demanded to know. Not only that but what the hell was she doing there? I wouldn't have put it past the woman to tunnel her way out of prison.

"I used my key, sweetheart. I was praying all the way here that you hadn't changed

98

the lock. Remember who paid the down payment on this villa. I always had a key."

"What are you doing out of jail? Why didn't you tell me?"

"They let me out early. I don't know if it was for good behavior or good pussy," Ava said with a laugh.

My eyes narrowed as I noticed her robe was a color I knew very well. Plus, she was too thick to wear it. "Is that my robe?"

"It sure is. I almost couldn't get in it. And before you say anything, yes, I'm aware I picked up a few pounds, but we didn't have Jenny Craig meals in the joint. Nothing but greasy shit that went straight to my stomach and hips, so I got to join a health club quick. Which one are you a member of?"

I ignored the diva act. "Why didn't you call me and tell me you were coming to New York?"

"I could only call collect. The last I checked you can't call collect on a cell phone," Ava said, annoyed. "Come here and give your mama dearest a hug. I've missed you, pumpkin."

I reluctantly moved close to Ava and gave her a limp hug. I had missed her and I did feel sorry for her. She had gained some weight, I thought, as I felt a lot of loose fat around her waist. Ava looked older and her skin looked like it missed her twice a week facials.

"And don't worry," Ava said brightly. "I'm no longer upset with you for testifying against me and sending me to jail. It was good for me and I met some interesting people."

I crossed my arms defensively. "I only told the truth, Ava. I had to."

"Step back and let me take a look at you," she said, sailing right over my last comment. "I see you still got that size-two figure. I hate you. You know I'm kidding, girl," she added with a playful slap. "Where you been? Out in Hollywood working on some fabulous new television show or movie?"

"I wish."

"So where have you been? I've been here a couple of days waiting on you. And hon, we need to go to the store and get some vittles, quick, fast and in a hurry. Ain't shit to eat in this house."

I was still so stunned by finding her so unexpectedly that I hadn't given a thought to her staying with me. I waved my hand distractedly. "We can order takeout tonight. I'm tired and I want to take a bath. There are some menus in the kitchen. Figure out what you want and I'll order it when I get out of the tub."

"Aren't you going to tell me where you've been?"

She was in her mother full-bore mode, and I sighed. "In every podunk town in this country in a bus and truck of *Dreamgirls*. Didn't I tell you that in my last letter?"

"You mean, your annual letter?" Her mouth twisted, and her tone turned nasty. "I don't remember a mother role in the play. What role did you have?" Ava asked with cool sarcasm.

There it was, out in the open. The Ava I knew so well. She hadn't changed a bit. "Deena Jones," I snapped. "Who else would I play?"

"Touchy, touchy, aren't we?" she said, light as pie. "But don't forget I birthed you, so I know how old you are, Yancey. I must say, you look good for someone in her forties."

"I'm not in my forties!" Ava and I hadn't been in the room together for more than fifteen minutes, and she was already coming for me. I wondered how long she planned to stay, and if I was going to have to move S. Marcus's trip back for a couple of days.

"Chile, please, I know better. But that's cool because it would be hard to explain how a mother and daughter can both be in their forties. Now, where are those menus?

101

And is there a liquor store around here that delivers? I need a stiff drink. The champagne and wine has been cute, but your mother needs a good swig of something golden brown."

I could feel a familiar tension in the base of my neck. "Let's order our food first. I might have something in the bar."

"You don't. I've already checked."

I wasn't putting up with her demands anymore. I picked up my suitcase and said, "Let me take these in the bedroom and then we can catch up."

As I started down the hallway to my bedroom, Ava called my name. All the sting had left her voice. I turned around to see a sad smile on her face, which touched me and made me blink back tears. As crazy as she was and as much as she deserved everything she got, I'd missed her more than I was willing to admit to her or myself. Here I was almost forty, still longing for a mother who would never show up.

"I've missed you, boo," she said tenderly.

"I know you're glad to be free once again."

"I sure am, baby. Jail ain't for no punk bitches or deluxe divas."

A week passed and Ava showed no signs of leaving or heading back to California. As a matter of fact, she seemed quite comfortable in my guest suite on the first floor. I don't know what I should do, since it is only a couple of days before S. Marcus is coming to New York. When I entertain, I certainly don't need my mother close by. Plus, I am trying to figure out what Ava is really up to. She'd been pretty mad when they took her out of court after the jury convicted her. Ava shot me a look that I would never forget. Our relationship had never been a typical mother and daughter one, and we'd enjoyed only fleeting moments of true affection.

I hate to admit it but whenever I think about seeing Marcus again I'm as excited as a high school girl on her first date. I find myself smiling at the mere thought of him. S. Marcus sends flowers almost every day and I'm always getting texts from him telling me how much he misses me and how he can't wait to see me again. I would text back *k* or *me 2* because I didn't want to seem too desperate or let him know how much he'd rocked my world during the time we'd spent together.

I have to dazzle Marcus when he comes to New York, so I'm doing Pilates in the morning and going to the gym every afternoon. I'd packed my gym bag with a change of clothes and was on my way out the door when the phone rang. I look at the call identification and see the name of my real estate agency and pray it's good news. My funds are almost depleted and having to feed and take care of Ava is putting a further strain on my resources.

"Hello."

"Ms. Braxton, please," a perky female voice said.

"This is Yancey Braxton."

"Great. Ms. Braxton, this is Linda Huber, Ms. Weeks's second assistant. She wanted me to see if you were at home this afternoon."

"I'm on my way out. Why, does she want to show my place?"

"No, I was going to drop off your keys."

I removed the phone from my ear and looked at it in puzzlement. Am I hearing this dizzy bitch correctly?

"Why are you going to do that?"

"Ms. Weeks told me you'd taken your town house off the market."

I placed the bag on the floor in disbelief. "Where did she get an idea like that? I still want to sell my house."

"Hold on one second."

A few moments later Amy came on the line. "Yancey, how are you doing today?"

"I'm fine, Amy. What is your assistant talking about?"

"I was told you were taking your property off the market."

"Let me ask this question again. Where did you hear that?"

"About a week ago I had a buyer for your town house. A Russian couple, and I had my other assistant call to arrange a visit. He was already sold, having seen the property online. When my assistant called, she said you told her you weren't interested in selling. He was willing to pay the 2.3 that we were asking for. Instead, I sold him something similar to your home but cheaper in Harlem."

"What!" I screamed into the phone. "Are you fucking kidding me? Does your assistant smoke crack?"

"Yancey, no, she doesn't," she said in an attempt to calm me, "but that's what she was told. Is that not true? You didn't talk to my assistant about a week ago?"

"No, I was still on the road." Just then I saw the front door open and Ava walked in, wearing big dark glasses and a too-tight purple velour sweatsuit. "Amy, let me call you back. I need to check something out."

"Okay, then I'll hold up on sending your key back, but please let me know what you want to do. I feel like the market is going to heat up very soon."

"I will. Thanks, Amy."

Ava was sweating like a pig, obviously back from a run. "Girl, I'm tired. I forgot how hard it is working out. I might need to see if I can get me some diet pills or something to get rid of this weight. I need to get me a trainer too. What do you have to eat?"

I got right to the point. "Did you tell my real estate agent that I wasn't selling my house?"

"Did I what?" Ava asked, looking away. I knew this meant she was getting ready to tell me a big fat lie.

I walked over and directly confronted her. "You heard me. Did you tell someone that I didn't want to sell my house?"

"Who told you that?"

"Ava!" I screamed, stomping my feet. "Just answer my question."

"You don't need to sell this house. This is a nice place, and since I gave you the down payment, I felt like I had a say. It's as much mine as yours."

"I paid you back. How dare you do that without my permission?"

She mumbled, not meeting my eyes, "They wanted to bring someone over to see the place and I needed a bubble bath.

Besides, where are we going to stay?"

"*We?* Ava, we don't do well together for long periods of time. I figured you were going back to California. I'm going to find me something smaller, maybe in Harlem."

Ava wiped sweat from her face with the towel she held. "You know full well I can't move back to California."

Was I losing my mind? "Why can't you go back to California?"

"Because they would only release me if I had a place to go," she confessed. "The prison officials think you called them and said I could live with you."

At last we were getting to the truth. "Now, how did that happen? I never agreed to that."

She looked at me like I was dumb. "I got one of my friends to call and act like you. I guess she did a good job." Ava laughed.

I groaned. Why didn't I guess she'd pull some stunt like this. "I wish you would stop using my name in vain."

"Besides, how are you going to buy another house? I bet your credit is worse than mine."

"Let me worry about that," I said sharply. "And in the future if you're going to answer my phone, don't pretend you're me. Just take a message and write it down. Do I make myself clear?"

"Honey, you must have me confused. I would never pretend to be somebody else, especially you," Ava said.

"Whatever. Need I remind you some years ago you went to an audition with Robert DeNiro pretending to be me?"

"And your point is?"

She was deliberately playing stupid. "I will make this simple: just don't answer my phone. Also, I'm having company in a couple of days, and if you're not going back to California, then we're going to have to find you a hotel."

"I'm sure the Four Seasons has plenty of rooms."

"Who's got Four Seasons money? You told me you lost all your money to your lawyer filing appeals."

"Maybe your visiting friend has money. Is this the guy who's been sending you all these flowers and texting you every five minutes? You need to tell that nigga to send us some food and drink."

When in doubt, Ava copped an attitude. "That is none of your business. Look, get on the computer right now and check ho-tels.com. Nothing over two hundred dollars a night," I said.

"Where in the hell am I going to find

anything decent in New York for fewer than two hundred dollars? I know it's been a long time since I've been in a hotel but they were way more than that before I went to the joint. Otherwise, I'll just be quiet as a church mouse when your company comes."

"Oh no, you won't. I want my house empty."

"Then get me some suitable accommodations."

I'd had enough. I know how she played, and I wasn't going to be drawn into her game. "I'm going to the gym."

"Bring me back a chicken sandwich with some curly fries," Ava said.

"Is that on your diet plan?"

"It sure is, darling. Why don't you bring me a milk shake, made with skim milk, of course," Ava said.

Exasperated, I shook my head and went out the door. My mother was back and already wearing my nerves thin.

CHAPTER 8

Ava is not feeling this at all. She is hanging
on to an overhead rail as the subway train
bumps quickly across the tracks, tossing her
this way and that, practically sending her
falling to the floor. She had not traveled by
public transit in decades, when she, too, was
a struggling actress looking for jobs. She
heard how terrible it had become, how dirty
and unkempt the trains are now, but she
had no idea it was this bad.

The plastic seats are filthy. The windows
are coated with such a thick film of dirt and
dust, she can hardly see through them, and
the floors . . . she doesn't even want to think
of all the germs crawling around down
there. Isn't there a cleaning service that
could be called? Where are city tax dollars
being spent?

Ava averts her eyes from the many stares
she is getting. Stares from men and women
in cheap work outfits, carrying poorly made

briefcases and purses. They had to know that she doesn't belong here among them. She is special, above having to wait at subway stops, above having to tolerate the kids at the back of that subway car, wearing baggy jeans and hoodies, cracking vulgar jokes and acting ghetto. People can look at her and tell by the expensive jewelry she wears, the sparkling gold bracelet that hangs from her wrist, the watch her last husband had surprised her with that cost more than ten thousand dollars, the huge diamond ring she bought on Rodeo Drive, that she isn't one of them.

These people don't know that I was once damn near royalty, Ava thought to herself. Then why haven't any of the men jumped up, quickly offering their seat when they saw a woman of her stature step through those sliding subway doors? Maybe it's the fifteen pounds she put on while she was incarcerated. No, she isn't a perfect size four anymore, but she still has the body of a woman half her age, or she will very soon.

If this was Rome or Paris, even Beverly Hills, she tells herself, the men would've behaved as gentlemen, begging her to take their seats. But these workday commoners act like they haven't seen her in the social pages in newspapers across the world. By the vacant looks on their faces, and the time of day, Ava knows they are heading to jobs they hate. Poor trash, she thought. Ava is so thankful she has never had to live that life.

Yes, over the last seven years she had lost touch with many of her social connections, hasn't been to a dinner party or high tea, but she is free now. It is only a matter of time before her wealthy friends learn of her release and begin calling her for brunch and vacations. Maybe she can even revive her show business career.

She'll do one spectacular performance, then another, and another, and her phone will never stop ringing. She'll be back on top, and this momentary misstep will be a thing of the past.

The conductor's voice came over the train's speakers: "Harlem, 125th Street."

The train lurched to a stop, and Ava thankfully prepared to deboard behind a wall of other riders.

On the subway platform, she pulls out the slip of paper she had written her parole officer's address on. She looks left, then looks right at the signs pointing up toward two separate sets of stairs. This is the stop where she is supposed to get off, but she has no clue as to which direction to continue in. People busily crossed back and forth in front of her, still paying her no mind.

"Excuse me," Ava finally said to a man wearing a T-shirt so long it looked like a nightgown. "Can you tell me where to find the Adam Clayton Powell Building?"

The man looks at Ava like she is crazy, hunches his shoulders and says, "Lady, quit playing. Everybody knows where that building is." He turns and keeps walking.

Fine, she thought. Ava decided she'd find it on her own. How could she expect to get any useful information from anyone making minimum wage?

Half an hour later, Ava steps off an elevator into a long, sour-smelling hallway of the Powell Building. She passes several open-door offices until she finally reaches her destination. She enters an office with drab walls, a split-pea soup color, a ratty sofa in one corner and in front of that, a chipped and marred coffee table covered with outdated magazines fanned across its top. Ava can't believe this is the building that houses the offices of former president Bill Clinton.

"Can I help you?" a squeaky-voiced woman said from behind a high counter on the other side of the room.

"I have an appointment with a William Lomax at ten A.M."

The overly made-up middle-aged woman

chewed a wad of gum like a cow munching on cud, occasionally popping it between her teeth, much to Ava's disgust. "Let me see, let me see," she said, dragging an index fingernail that was painted bright red down an appointment list. "You Ava Middlebrooks?"

"That would be me," Ava replied, suppressing her impatience.

"And you said you're here to see Mr. Lomax?" the woman asked, looking up at Ava with a crooked smile, her two front teeth smeared with lipstick.

"Yes, that's exactly what I said," Ava said, becoming annoyed.

"Okay, that's what I thought you said. Have a seat over there," the woman said, gesturing toward the sofa. "And I'll let Mr. Lomax know you're here."

Ava glanced at the soiled sofa and said, "Thank you, but I'd rather stand."

"Suit yourself, but he might not be ready for you right away."

"I'll take my chances."

Ten minutes later, Ava heard a man yell from down a hallway to the side of the receptionist's counter. "Send my next parolee in."

The receptionist giggled and said, "You can go in now. Right down there, last office on the right."

Ava started down yet another hallway, a thin, dirty, worn carpet that exposed the hardwood underneath. A bare bulb hung overhead, and chipped paint flaked from the walls around her, making her ask herself, wasn't there a nicer office they could've sent her to, maybe in midtown Manhattan?

Ava approached the last office on the right. The door was open, and she stepped into the small room. A large, round man sat at a desk, his back turned to Ava, as he searched through a file cabinet.

"Have a seat, Middlebrooks," Mr. Lomax said, without turning around to address her properly. Ava continued standing until he pulled a file from the drawer, slammed it closed, then swiveled around to face her.

"I said have a seat," Mr. Lomax said.

"The name is Mrs. Ava Middlebrooks. And *please?*" Ava suggested coolly.

"What?"

"I would appreciate you calling me by my given name and asking politely."

Mr. Lomax is a fat man. His skin is the color of an eggshell, and his body is shaped like one. His head is bald on the top, and long strands of hair grow out from the side of it. In Ava's opinion, he is dirty and unshaven, and it looks like he still has food crumbs on his mouth from the breakfast he must've eaten not long ago. He's wearing a brown tweed jacket that appears too tight for him over an open-collar shirt that exposes a white V-neck undershirt. A man like this has no business talking to someone like her the way he had.

Mr. Lomax looks Ava over a moment and then starts to laugh. It sounds more like a series of coughs. "Did the warden call you Mrs. Ava Middlebrooks in prison?"

"Excuse me," Ava says.

"Did they say please in prison?"

"No, but this isn't prison," Ava says, looking around his mess of an office.

"Then I ain't calling you Mrs. or saying please now. Get it straight, Ava. You're an ex-con, and I'm a parole officer. My job is to tell you what to do to keep you from going back inside, and make sure you do it." He looks Ava up and down again, taking in the expensive jewelry, her clothes and her bag. She looks like she is going to a Junior League meeting. He probably has no clue what it is all worth, but she is sure he isn't fool enough to think it was cheap.

Mr. Lomax leans forward on his desk. "See, let me explain something. I'm not your personal assistant, your therapist, and I'm definitely not one of your suitors. So if you're looking for compassion, or under-standing, or a shoulder to cry on, you're definitely talking to the wrong man. But since you have no choice but to be here, you need to do exactly what I say. Now let me repeat myself, which, for further refer-ence, I don't enjoy. Have a seat, Middle-brooks."

Angrily, Ava took a seat, placed her purse in her lap, folded her hands on top of it and watched as William Lomax typed a few keystrokes on the computer in front of him. After a few minutes he looked at Ava and said, "So, the obvious things you can't do, unless you want to trade in those fancy clothes you're wearing for another prison uniform, go as follows: You can't do drugs. You can't associate with any other known felons. No stealing, no firearms, or commit-ting any other crimes."

"Who do you think I am?" Ava gasped, offended. "Some common street criminal?"

"You might not be common, and you might not be street, but you are definitely a criminal. I'm sure Raymond Tyler, the man you shot, would concur," Mr. Lomax said with a straight face. "And that brings up our next issue. You got an address, a place to stay?"

"For the record, the shooting was a simple

accident and yes, I'm living at my daughter's town house on the Upper East Side. She's a big Broadway star, you know."

Mr. Lomax pushed a notepad to the front of his desk, set a pencil on top of it. "I'm sure she's a *big* star. Write down her address and a number where you can always be reached. You know you're going to have to remain at that residence for at least six months."

"What?" Ava said, surprised. "I don't plan on staying there that long. It's just temporary."

"Yeah. If you consider six months temporary, or have you forgotten that this is a condition of your parole and early release?"

"Why do I have to stay there? What if I find housing of my own, like back in California?"

Mr. Lomax took off his glasses in a no-nonsense manner. "Look, these are the rules, Middlebrooks," Mr. Lomax said. "This isn't hard. You do what you're supposed to do, keep your nose clean, and you won't violate your parole and I won't have to send you back to prison. Understood?"

Seething through clenched teeth, Ava said, "Understood, Lomax."

His face remained entirely bland. "You also need to get a job and I'll need the name of your supervisor."

"A job? Tell me you're kidding. Ava doesn't work."

"Well, if Middlebrooks wants to stay out of prison, Ava will work. Tell her that if you talk to her soon. Will you?"

"You think this is funny, don't you?"

"No, funny is the Soul Circus. I take my job very seriously. Now, unless you have any more questions, I need to get ready for my next appointment. I'll see you in two weeks. Have a good day, Middlebrooks."

Ava gave Mr. Lomax her best raised eyebrow, got up and stomped out of the office, mad as she had been the day the judge sentenced her to prison.

An hour and a half later, standing in front of a corner pawnshop in lower Manhattan, Ava is still incensed by the grimy fat man who is her parole officer. On the subway ride home, she realizes that the fare she paid was just about all the money she has left. Although Yancey hadn't said so, Ava had determined she didn't have much money either. Ava desperately needs money.

As she stepped through the pawnshop door, a bell rang, announcing her entrance. She had never been in one of these places before, but this one looked straight out of *Law & Order.* Ava had become hooked on that show while in prison, hoping for clues on how she might get out early.

The shop is long and narrow, with a floor-to-ceiling gate to her left. Behind the gate is all the merchandise — boom-box stereos, flat-screen televisions, small kitchen appliances and lots of jewelry, mostly watches.

A square is cut out of the gate; a wood counter protrudes from the opening. A brown-skinned man with straight black hair, a beard, and an East Indian accent asks, "Can I help you, ma'am?"

Ava stood with her back against the wall behind her, almost afraid to approach. This is nothing that she wants to do, but after considering all her options for making money, fast money, this is the only one available. She steps up to the counter cautiously and says, "I need to pawn something."

"Okay. What do you have?"

Ava had thought about this on the subway ride back. She is wearing four pieces of jewelry. She was especially proud of the watch, a gift from her former husband, so she simply would not sell that. The ring is too beautiful to ever part with; it was off limits. The thin gold eighteen-inch necklace, with the tiny gold cross charm around the neck, she has had since forever. Besides, she knew it probably wouldn't fetch any real money. "This bracelet," Ava said, unclasping it, pulling it from her wrist and handing it to the man.

"Real?" he asked, examining the jewels.

Insulted, Ava almost snatches it back from him, but she needs the money so badly she controls her temper. "Of course," she says politely.

He studies it closely.

"I paid over five thousand dollars for it some time ago. I expect it would be worth at least —"

"Nine hundred dollars," the pawnbroker said, interrupting her in midsentence.

She flashes him an incredulous look. "Are you crazy? What kind of scam joint is this?" Ava said, no longer able to control her outrage. "Did you hear what I just told you? I paid over five thousand dollars for this."

"Then take it back to them," the man said, holding the bracelet out to her.

Ava forces herself to calm down again. "Please," she said. She hates herself for behaving like this. Having been forced into this situation. This is worse than sitting with her mother in the welfare office as a child begging for more food stamps and government cheese. Lower than helping her mother clean wealthy white folks' homes in

Jackson, Tennessee.

"Look, I've run into some hard times. This economy is kicking my ass. I have no money. Can you give me a little more?"

The broker looks down at the bracelet again, then back at her.

"Please," Ava says again, looking for something that resembled sympathy in his flat eyes.

"One thousand, then. That's my final offer. Take it or leave it."

Ava is getting one-fifth the value of her bracelet that today is surely worth more than she paid for it ten years ago, but considering she is flat broke and has no immediate means of changing that, she sighs deeply, then says, "Give me the money."

CHAPTER 9

I got home around eight o'clock after a very productive day of meeting with potential investors for my reality show. S. Marcus said that I should meet with them before he arrived in New York because it would speed things up. One of the men, Ron Preston, told me he liked the idea for the show but felt I needed a hook to make it successful. When I asked what he meant, he simply said, "Something exciting happening in your life in addition to your show business comeback."

I didn't know what that was but figured the producers and show runners would come up with something even if we had to make it up or, as the industry calls it, pollute reality.

I went into the living room to find Ava in burgundy silk pajamas carrying a tray with food and drink. Her hair was tied up in what looks like my Louis Vuitton silk scarf.

"Just in time," Ava said in a very cheerful voice. The evening before my mother had been clearly depressed about her first meeting with her parole officer. I guess the meeting had gone better than she had anticipated.

"For what?" I ask, prepared for her to tell me anything.

Nodding to the tray, she said, "For caviar, crackers, imported cheese, some dried fruit and Veuve Clicquot."

"What are we celebrating? And I thought you said you didn't have any money. Did one of your ex-husbands have a change of heart about loaning you cash?"

Ava set the tray on the coffee table and announced loftily, "There is always money for caviar and champagne, and fuck my exes and their new wives too." She picked up the remote control and flashed on the television. After flipping through several channels, Ava stopped on a show that really gets on my last nerves. *American Star,* a reality show that has become the launching pad for non-talent teens aged fourteen to twenty. How dare they leave out talented people like me?

"What's this?" Ava asked as several teenage girls and boys, black and white, pranced on the television show that reminds me of a Disney stage show and America's Junior

Miss pageant rolled into one — and I don't mean this in a good way.

"*American Star.* Please change that," I said as I plopped down on the sofa and went straight for the caviar on toast points.

"This looks interesting. I heard about this show, but I was never able to watch in prison because all the bull dagger inmates want to watch *Survivor* and shit like that. Let's watch it, Yancey. If it's not good, I will change it," Ava said.

"Okay," I said, not knowing if she really wanted to watch it or was looking for a chance to get another dig at me. "But I'm telling you, this is going to be painful."

"I'm sure it will be fine. Can I pour you some champagne, my dear?"

That "my dear" sounded no more real than the first one she used the night I found her in my living room. But I was in no mood for a fight, so I let it pass.

"Just a little," I said. "How did your meeting go with your probation officer?"

"Oh, let's not talk about that, love. I want to end the day on a good note. How was your meeting?"

"It went okay."

"What are you meeting about? Shouldn't you be trying to get an agent and some auditions?"

125

"I'm talking with people about getting my own reality show," I said, pleased to be able to impress her.

"Oh, that would be great!" she exulted. "Us having our own reality show. I'm going to be even more famous."

"Us?" I said, shooting her an "are you crazy" look. "Ava, nothing is certain yet and I'll be damned if I'm going to let you upstage me. Are we clear on this?"

"Yes, my dear. I can understand why you'd be afraid the television cameras would fall in love with me." She shook her head. "Honestly, Yancey, I thought when you got older, you'd get over the jealousy you hold for me."

I played that off, light as air. "Ava, darling, I'm not jealous of *you*. Trust me on *that*."

Disappointed I hadn't played along with her game, she changed her tune. "Whatever you say. You need to get that show so you can hire me. I have to get a job soon."

"Hire you for what?"

"I can be your personal assistant or stylist. Production assistant or whatever but you need to put me on payroll, show or no show."

"How am I going to pay you?" I asked. The woman's gall was unsurpassed. "If the show goes through, it will be the producers who call the shots."

"We will think of something, my child. We always do."

I let that pass. I knew what her *we* meant. It meant *she* would soon be causing *me* trouble.

She turned her attention to the TV, and for the next fifteen minutes, she became totally enthralled with *American Star*. She sat quietly, sipping her champagne as one no-talent teen followed another no-talent teen, singing off-key and doing dance moves that showed their lack of professional training.

American Star contestants sang all different types of music, from rap to Broadway, and did live photo shoots to test their marketability. Now, why didn't they have something like this when I was coming up? The only way some ordinary small-town girl like me could become a celebrity overnight back then was winning a beauty title like Miss America or Miss USA, which I'd tried, becoming first runner-up for Miss Tennessee. So without the national exposure of the pageant I had to get into show business the old-fashioned way, knocking on doors, knocking people out of the way at times, and knocking boots if it would advance my career.

When I'd finally seen enough, I announced I was going to bed. Engrossed, Ava didn't respond. But just as I stood up the host announced a special performance by the biggest talent ever seen on the *American Star* stage. The blond-haired host went on to say that her debut album had been certified triple platinum and she'd just signed a multimillion-dollar deal with Disney for a television series and feature films. Call it masochism, but for some reason I had to see what this little rich bitch looked like.

Out walks this young lady who seems to have the confidence of a seasoned Broadway star. This girl is totally at ease surrounded by crowds and bright lights but still manages an expression of wide-eyed innocence. She is a pretty, almond-colored girl with long black hair and bangs that could use some scissors quick. Her smile is inviting with teeth so white they could outshine a lighthouse. From the huge diamond studs in her ears you knew where the money was going. As much as I want to hate her and leave the room, I can't take my eyes off her. The host says, "Ladies and gentlemen, welcome back a true American star and a young lady who has made us proud, former winner and American star

Madison B. Lewis."

The crowd went wild, as my mind suddenly scrolled back to my senior year at Howard University when my boyfriend, Derrick, and I found ourselves in trouble. I'd gotten pregnant. Ava had told me to get an abortion, but Derrick talked me into having the baby and giving her up for adoption. That's what I did or at least thought I'd done.

About ten years ago, while performing the lead in the musical *Chicago* in Las Vegas, Derrick showed up in my dressing room with some disturbing news. My child hadn't been adopted, but raised by Derrick and his sister. He said it was time to share in her life if I was interested. Derrick told me that our daughter's name was Madison.

As I watch this young lady with an achingly beautiful voice totally kill Stevie Wonder's ballad "Blame It on the Sun" like a seasoned veteran, I tell myself this can't be my daughter, but the cold chill running down my spine says something different.

Moved by her talent, I can't help but say out loud, "She's fabulous."

"You think so?" Ava asks, never passing up a chance to contradict me. "If you ask me I'd say she is a whole lot of nothing special. How dare she sing a Stevie Wonder song?"

There is a catch in my voice when I say slowly, "Ava, I think that's Madison. *My* Madison."

"Who? What are you talking about, Yancey?" She noticed my awe-struck expression and didn't pass up the opportunity to pounce on me. "I think you've been drinking that champagne too fast, honey."

"No, I think that's my daughter," I said as the television camera panned her beautiful face and then pulled back, causing her to disappear like a ghost.

The next morning I'm sitting at the butcher block table in the kitchen drinking a cup of coffee when Ava walks in humming a tune. She is in a very good mood for someone broke. I couldn't get my mind off the previous night when the baby I'd given up at birth had suddenly reappeared.

"Good morning, sweetheart."

"Good morning, Ava. You sure seem chipper this morning. What are you up to?" I asked only half jokingly.

"I was thinking about last night. That little girl who you said was your daughter."

Taking a cup and pouring some coffee, she said, "I'm not sure, Ava, but I'm going to find out by calling Derrick. But I'm pretty certain it's her. Her last name was Lewis."

"I think she's too cute to be your girl, but I did some checking. I spent half the night on the internet doing a little research on Miss Madison B. It seems her daddy's name is Derrick. She was raised in California by her daddy and aunt. She never knew her real mother. That would be you, darling. And get this . . . she's going to be richer than God very soon. All our problems are solved," Ava announced.

I wasn't following her train of thought. "What? If Madison is doing well, that's her fame, and her money. Not ours. No one's entitled to it, but her and maybe Derrick. Even though he's not the type of person to live off his daughter." Derrick was always so sweet, and in this case, a nice guy had finished first.

"My sweet child," Ava said in a condescending voice. "Has your cheese slipped off your cracker? If it wasn't for you, that little girl wouldn't be alive. If there is anyone she owes, it's you and, uh, me. Because if it wasn't for me, you wouldn't have given birth to her. That's what's right."

This was too much. "Ava, stop it."

"Yancey, we're both broke. We have no money and not a lot of potential. Do you understand that? We can barely afford food without one of us having to pawn something. You're about to lose your house because you can't sell it."

"Well, I have you to thank for that. But it's going to sell. Besides, I'm going to make money when my reality show takes off."

"What if it doesn't come through? Do you know how much money that little girl is making or going to make? Millions," she said with a wave of her hand. "I read up on her and they say she's like a black Miley Cyrus. They say Miley Cyrus is almost a billionaire. I read somewhere that Madison is already bigger than some teen rappers called Lil Mama and Teyana Taylor, who both are millionaires." She opened her arms wide, as if to take in all her future money. "A couple million for her birth mother and grandmother would hardly be missed."

I sipped my coffee, trying not to lose it. "Ava, I will make my own money. I had a chance to become involved in Madison's life and, following your advice, I passed. She owes me nothing."

"I'm going to call her and see if she wants to meet us."

"Ava, don't you dare!" I yelled. "Do you hear me?" I said, raising my finger to Ava's face. "Promise me you won't try to contact her."

She looked right through my warning finger. "She's going to be in New York today doing a signing at a record store. Don't you want to go?"

"No, I *don't* want to go. And *you* better not either. Are we clear on this?"

Ava sighed deeply, lowered her face, and said, "Yes, we're clear."

But this is Ava, my mother, who I know doesn't take orders from anyone. I'm the daughter who has suffered from her capers most of my life. Ava, the devious diva. I know I have to come up with a plan to protect Madison long before Ava implements her own scheme.

CHAPTER 10

It was a beautiful day outside of Virgin Records, located in the heart of Times Square. The sky was painted a pastel blue, and not a single cloud dotted the luminous canvas. Ava wore a flowing red and yellow sundress, an off-the-shoulder design she'd found in Yancey's guest room closet. It didn't look like anything Yancey would have worn, and Ava figured it most likely belonged to a friend or former roommate. As she stood outside the record store, the dress fit more snugly than Ava thought appropriate, and the first thing she planned to do when she lost some weight and got some money was to go shopping. Still, Ava knew she looked cute with the matching red pumps and her huge, dark Donna Karan sunglasses covering her eyes.

Ava caught her reflection in one of the store's windows, and thought, I'm as broke as a joke, but I could still pass for a movie star. She knew she was about to do exactly what she had been instructed not to do. But Yancey didn't understand nobody told Ava what to do and what not to do. Those days for her were over.

Turning the corner, Ava was rudely halted by a long line of teenage girls and their mothers. The line stretched completely around the block.

"What is this line for?" Ava asked the blond-haired teen girl at the very back of the line. The girl turned to Ava, wearing a Madison B. T-shirt. She looked at Ava as though she didn't have the sense of a first grader, pointed to her shirt and said, "Duh, hello, lady."

"Are all these people here to see Madison B.?"

The blond girl's mother looks at Ava and nods her head. Eyeing the line of girls giggling, laughing, listening to iPods and practicing dance moves, Ava thinks about possibly waiting her turn in line. But then tells herself no way. If she believed in waiting her turn, Ava would never have reached her social standing.

She moves past the line and takes purposeful steps to the front door of the record store. She reaches out to grab the handle when a well-built man in a white shirt and black tie says, "Excuse me, ma'am, but you'll have to wait in line for your turn like everybody else to see Madison B."

The man looks like he is in his thirties, which makes him young enough to be her son, but Ava doesn't care. She enjoys the company of younger men.

Ava eyes him up and down while licking her lips lightly. "Young man, does it look like I'm here to see, who did you say, Madison B.?"

"I'm sorry, ma'am. It doesn't matter, you'll have to wait. We don't want the fire chief to close us down."

"It's that many people in there?"

"Yes, ma'am. We haven't had this many people since Hannah Montana. Madison B. is huge."

Stronger measures were clearly called for. "Oh shit!" Ava faked, grabbing her stomach with both hands. "You have to let me in." She balled her face into a grimace.

"What? Is there something wrong?" the man asked.

"I'm in pain," Ava said, not knowing exactly where she is going with this, but hoping it will work. "I'm having female problems and I need to get to the ladies' room so I can take my . . . my injection. Please be a doll, young man."

The man looks over his shoulder, then into the store, as if he is uncertain of what he should do.

"I'm on your property, young man," Ava said with attitude. "If I collapse, I'll sue, and you'll be the first one they fire. Believe that."

"Okay, okay," he said, concern now on his face. "Go and come right back out. Besides, you're too old to be a Madison B. fan."

"You don't know how old I am," Ava muttered, still holding her stomach as the door is opened for her.

The store has the atmosphere of a high school pep rally. Girls, a few boys, and mothers and daddies packed in, all holding copies of Madison B.'s new CD.

Ava sidesteps gleeful, excited fans, heading toward the rest rooms. She looks over her shoulder at the man at the door until he is out of sight. When she is sure it's safe, Ava turns left and heads straight for the customer service counter, where she sees a graying, smart-looking woman wearing a dark blue blazer and an earpiece.

As she pushes her way through a throng of bubble gum–popping teens, Ava is able to spot a long table with a huge banner over it reading Welcome to New York, Madison

B.! Ava guesses that's where her alleged granddaughter will be greeting her fans and signing CDs.

Madison B. hasn't arrived. Ava assumes she is in some back room, surrounded by flunkies of every sort, plotting the grand entrance the teen star will make when the time comes.

Ava approaches the smart-looking woman. "Excuse me, are you the manager of this store?"

"Yes, I'm Mrs. Sutton. How may I help you?"

"Hello, Mrs. Sutton," Ava said, extending her hand, a bright, confident smile on her face. "My name is Ava Middlebrooks. Maybe you remember me from some years back when I signed my CD here."

"I'm sorry, but I don't. I've only been manager a year or so," Mrs. Sutton said sharply. "But Ms. Middlebrooks, as you can see, we're very busy. So how can I help you?"

"I need to speak with little Miss Madison B. I'm her grand . . . I mean, we're related. I haven't seen her since she was this big," Ava said, holding out her hands like she was holding a loaf of bread.

"Do you have a card? I can give it to her people. I don't think she can be bothered right now. She's getting ready to meet her fans."

"Surely you're kidding me. Are you saying relatives have to take a back seat to these people?" Ava said as she looked at the anxious mob with disdain.

"Let me see if I can get someone to help you," Mrs. Sutton said, and then hurried away, zigzagging through the maze of adoring Madison B. fans.

A few minutes later, a nattily dressed young man approached Ava. She took one look at him and said to herself, this poor child is gay as a goose.

"Hello, Mrs. Middlebrooks. I'm Thurston Rogers, Madison B.'s publicist. May I help you with something?" His voice is lilting, and rises up a note at the end of each word, as if everything is about the dramatics.

"Yes, you can, young man. I need to speak with Madison before this little shindig gets started."

"May I ask why?"

"You may. I'm related to Madison B."

He gave her a probing look. "That's funny. Madison B. was telling me on the flight here that this was her first trip to New York. She didn't mention any relatives. Can I just take your number and give it to Madison B.'s father? I'm sure when he gets some time, they will give you a call."

"Well, that won't do," Ava said, taking offense. "You might lose your job if you keep me away from my kinfolks."

He struck a bored pose. "That's the last thing I'm worried about. What did you say your name was again?" he asked, eyeing Ava with suspicion. Thurston tapped an index finger, painted with a shiny clear polish, against his chin, looking as though he was in deep thought.

"Ava Middlebrooks. Maybe you know me from some of my stage and cabaret appearances."

A light went on in his eyes. "Were you in one of Stanley Bennett Clay's productions more than a decade ago?"

"Yes, I was. How nice of you to remember."

"I remember now," he gushed, coming to life. "It was one of the first musicals I saw at the Apollo."

"Those were the days."

"Girlfriend, you were fierce. You had me singing and hummin' for days after the show was over. Can I get a hug?"

"Of course you can, love," Ava said, thinking this might be easier than she thought.

Thurston held her tight, patted a number of times and then after the embrace said, "I have to run. It was so nice meeting you."

"But what about Madison B.?"

His eyebrows twinkled in concern. "Oh Ava, write your number down and I'll pass it on."

"I need to see her now," Ava demanded. She usually loved the gays but realized at times they needed to be put in their place.

"Well, that's not going to happen today. Write your number down on my clipboard and I'll pass it on," he said while checking his expensive watch. Ava wondered if her granddaughter paid for that.

Ava looks at him, obviously disturbed, and said, "Mister Thing, you must know that a diva like me just doesn't go around writing her number on clipboards. That's way too common. Good day."

Ava headed toward the door, pushing through the thousands of fans waiting to meet her granddaughter.

CHAPTER 11

I was watching *Paula Dean's Party* on the Food Network and the doorbell rang just as Paula was getting ready to pull a casserole out of the oven. I found myself watching a lot of cooking shows just in case that was the reality show route I had to take. I was an actress, so surely I could pretend I knew how to cook. A part of me wanted to see how the casserole looked and then another part wondered who was ringing my bell unannounced. Perfect solution to the problem; I put Paula on pause and went to answer the door.

"Yancey, it's me."

"Dalton, what are you doing here and how did you get my address?" I asked.

"Danni, remember; we're friends," Dalton said as he walked into my living area uninvited. He had a sling on his arm but it didn't seem to slow down the pace of his walk.

"Danni, what happened to your arm?"

"Can you believe that I fell on it trying to learn a new dance in this musical I'm working on? I might be a dancer slash actor but I'm still very clumsy. Wow, Yancey B., this sofa is nice. I guess you've already moved on up but I should have known from the address alone," Dalton said as he surveyed the living and dining area.

"So you didn't say where you got my address, Dalton . . . I mean Danni."

"It was on the cast list from *Dreamgirls* just as plain as day. I was going to call you and see what you thought of the songs I'd written but I said to myself, *Danni,* why don't you just go and see Yancey and find out what she thinks. I told you I was going to be living in New York working on this new musical. That's how I got hurt."

"What musical?"

"It's called *Claudine,* based on the movie starring Diahann Carroll and James Earl Jones. Remember?"

"Yeah, I love that movie. Have they cast it yet?"

"We're in the process. I'm assistant musical director and I was dance captain but I lost that job when my spin went out of control and I fell on my arm," Dalton said as he took a seat at the bar. Again without an invitation.

"You think you can get me an audition?" I asked, thinking this might be great for my reality show and even better if I didn't get the show.

"I'm sure I can but I really think you should be working on your music. With some of my songs we could make a bangin' CD," Dalton said.

"I haven't had a chance to listen to your songs," I said, looking around the room as if the CD was there when I knew I'd left it in the dressing room back in Miami.

"Do you still have the disc?"

"I'm sure I do."

"Well bam, here is another one if you don't have it, Yancey," Dalton said as he pulled another CD from his bag.

"Oh thanks," I said.

"Can I have a glass of sweet tea or something? I feel a little parched," Dalton said as he fanned his hand toward his mouth.

"I don't know if I have sweet tea but I'm sure I have some water and maybe some cranberry juice."

"That will be fine."

I walked into the kitchen with the CD. I placed it on the counter and when I laid it down I noticed a very nice headshot of Dalton with the name Homer House Productions splashed across it. I got a bottle of water and was heading back to the living area when I heard Dalton shouting, "So I guess you got all this when you had a recording career?"

"What did you ask me?" I asked as I handed Dalton the bottle of water.

"Thank you, Yancey. Now don't lose this CD, baby. Those blank CDs cost a pretty penny."

"I won't. Where did you come up with the name Homer House?

Dalton bowed down his head and whispered, "It's a long story."

I was now officially intrigued and I crossed my legs and placed my hands over them and said, "I've got plenty of time."

"I think I'm most likely being overdramatic but it's really very simple," Dalton said as he crossed his legs too.

"I'm listening," I said, suddenly wishing that I'd gotten some water for myself and hoping Ava didn't show up before Dalton finished his story.

"Homer is my birth name. Now do I look like a Homer to you? How country is that? It's not enough that I was raised in Bumpfuck, Georgia. I remember the casting director looking at me like I was a country-fried fool when I told him my name was Homer. The first thing I did when I moved to

Atlanta was to change my name. There is a secret about it, though, and you look like the kind of girl who would enjoy a good secret," Dalton said with a devilish giggle.

"Oh honey, you know me too well," I said as I playfully slapped Dalton on the knee. "Tell me the secret."

Dalton leaned over still laughing and whispered like we were in a public place and said, "My family doesn't know that I changed my named. They still call me Homer."

"Haven't they seen you perform?" I asked.

"Yeah they have but I told them that everyone on Broadway has a fake name. And they believe me. One night after a performance, they had me going through a *Playbill* telling them the real name of every cast member."

"What did you do?"

"I made them up. Had a new name for every one of them."

I started laughing so hard my sides were hurting. I really liked Dalton because he made me laugh and there's a sinister glint in his eye that I like.

"You're bad, Dalton, Danni, Homer or whatever your name is," I said.

"Yeah, I'm so bad that I'm good," he said.

Dalton and I were having a good laugh

146

between friends when suddenly I heard a key in the door and Ava popped in. She looked at Dalton like she knew him and said, "Somebody has a hen party and I wasn't invited. Now Yancey, is that any way to treat your dear mother?"

"Hey Ava. Where have you been all day?"

"Minding my own business, suggesting you do the same."

Dalton gave me a quizzical look and then glanced at Ava, who wouldn't look at him.

"I'm going to my room and get some beauty rest," Ava announced.

"I have someone I want to introduce you to," I said.

"Save it, Yancey. It's obvious he's on the boys' team, so don't waste my time," Ava said as she waved one hand in the air in a dismissive gesture.

When she left the room, Dalton looked at me and said, "Now isn't she special."

"Not special but touched," I said as Dalton and I burst into laughter.

CHAPTER 12

Ava walked through her bedroom and headed straight for the shower. She turned it on and removed her clothes, put on her robe and a shower cap, then picked up her cell phone to see if he had called. He had not.

"Oh, I can't wait to get this bitch out of my house," Ava said to herself.

She picked up her phone and hit speed dial.

"Hello."

"When are you coming here?"

"What's going on, Ava?"

"We just need to speed this up."

"Why?"

"Because this girl is getting on my last nerve."

"What's new about that? That's what daughters do or so I heard."

"And that's the main reason I never wanted one of those bitches."

"Statements like that will get you nominated for the Joan Crawford Mother of the Year Award."

"Joan Crawford ain't got shit on me. I bet she couldn't work an iron extension cord like me. Wire hangers my ass."

"What's the real reason you want Yancey out so quick? I mean you own the house. You could make it happen today."

"Well, I hope to start dating soon and I don't want to have to put up with her. I'm ready to move into the master suite. Besides, I don't want to show my hand just yet."

"Good thing you've decided to listen to me, Ava."

"Whatever, dude," Ava said as she clicked off the phone and headed to the shower.

Ava went into the bathroom and stared at herself in the mirror. She picked at her shapeless tangle of hair and suddenly imagined herself as a beautiful, sophisticated socialite wife. That's where she belonged, Ava told herself. That would be her first project once she took care of Yancey.

Just as Ava prepared to turn on the cold water a familiar voice intruded into her thoughts with a self-fulfilling prophecy. She heard her mother's voice with its patent gut-bucket southern accent saying, "That gal ain't gonna do nuthing but bring you trouble, Ava. Every female got a little bitch in 'em."

Ava splashed some cold water on her face and mumbled to herself, "Not anymore, Mama. That bitch is going down for good."

■ ■ ■ ■

PART TWO

■ ■ ■ ■

CHAPTER 1

Sixteen-and-a-half-year-old Madison Belisa Lewis is lying across the bed in the Presidential Suite of the Four Seasons Hotel. She's wearing her favorite pink pajamas with matching robe and reading a copy of *Teen People* magazine, on which she happens to grace the cover.

Her father walks into the room and announces, "It's bedtime, little lady. We have another busy day tomorrow."

"I know," she whines like the teenager she is and not the multi-millionaire star she has become in a very short time. "I just want to finish this story about Chris Brown. Do you think he's really dating Rihanna, Daddy? I mean Rihanna is pretty and she can sing."

Derrick smiles and pulls back the spread on the leather-and-metal king-size bed. "Madison, I don't care who Chris Brown is dating, just as long as it's not you, young lady. You remember our agreement; no dating until you're eighteen."

"I thought we said after I graduate from high school."

"Eighteen, Madison."

"But Daddy, he's so cute. I want to do a duet with him. Do you think you could talk to the producers of my CD about that?"

"Sure, baby. I'll check it out as long as it's strictly business. Now under the covers."

Madison follows her father's orders but holds on tightly to the magazine, like it is a prized childhood toy. Her father leans over her and kisses her on the forehead. "Don't stay up too late reading that magazine; you've got a very busy day tomorrow, Miss American Star."

"Daddy, one more thing I was thinking about. You remember Aunt Jenny's favorite saying, don't you?"

" 'To whom much is given, much is expected,' " Derrick says.

"I was thinking about what you said about taking some of my earnings and starting a foundation. I know what I want to do now."

"What, Madison?"

"I want to start an after-school arts program up in Harlem or over in Jersey City and call it Jenny's Place. We could have people teaching low-income kids dance, acting and singing. Won't that be cool?"

"Sounds like a great plan, Madison. I'll have the lawyers look into it."

Madison can't help but smile wide, and before her father closes the door, she says, "Thanks, Daddy."

He pauses. "For what, sweetheart?"

"For everything. Just everything."

"I didn't do anything. It was all you, Madison," her father replies, then closes the door gently.

Madison rolls onto her back and crosses her arms behind her head, knowing if it wasn't for her father, she wouldn't be where she is. He was the one who not only paid for but also took her to singing and dancing lessons when she announced at age seven that she wanted a career in show business. She closes her eyes and replays in her head the night that had changed her life.

"America has voted," the host, a slight-built man with a head full of hair and a five o'clock shadow, declared. Madison could feel her heart start to race. A cold, clammy hand slipped into hers, and she realized that Cody, the blond, ex–boy band rocker, must've been as nervous as she was. He was gripping her for support. Madison squeezed his hand back. Although they'd been competitors the competition had actually brought them closer.

When the host announced that Cody had received more than twenty million votes, Madison felt her heart sink. With his throngs of young teenage girl fans, Cody had been the favorite all season. Madison knew she had some skills, talent, looks and all the ability in the world, but felt she needed an angel if she had any chance of beating the popular Cody.

After all the cheers had died down for Cody, the host looked at her as though he felt sorry about her pending defeat and said, "Madison B., you're the new American Star."

Madison gasped, almost choking as Cody's arms wrapped around her neck, his body pressed into hers, giving her a big hug. The lights seemed to get brighter, the screams and music louder, and Madison felt as though she was floating through the clouds to personally thank her guardian angel.

Instead her eyes met her angel here on earth, her father standing among the thousands of people in the audience, clapping and crying joyously. He was smiling and mouthing the words, "You did it!" and "I love you, baby." Madison smiled back and her own tears started to roll down her cheeks.

It was an amazing night, one that Madison would never forget. She was overcome with a deep love for her father. He had given up so much for her, foregoing his own love life to make sure that Madison knew how blessed and loved she was.

In Madison's eyes, he is the greatest man in the world. He helps her with her homework when she needs it, watches her rehearse songs and dance routines and even goes clothes shopping with her if she asks him to. He would do anything for his daughter. Right after Madison was selected for *American Star*, Derrick broke off with his long-term girlfriend Shanice, who wanted more of his time. He even left his job as a lead engineer to travel the world with his pop star daughter, insisting that he be paid not a penny for his efforts. That is real love, Madison thought. She figured God had given her a special father because she deserved it after being born to a mother who didn't want her.

Her father never spoke much about Madison's biological mother, even when Madison asked him about her. He would just shrug and say they were better off alone. But Madison knew that she was out there and often wondered if she ever regretted giving her up. Now that she was becoming rich and famous would this so-called mother suddenly pop up? What would Madison say to her? Would she accept her mother, welcome her back with open arms, or reject her for abandoning her?

Madison reaches over, turns out the light and tells herself not to worry about such a thing, because that day will never come.

Madison stood on the set of *South Beach Dream Teen,* a pilot about a motherless sixteen-year-old teenager, a rich, pretty and popular high school girl living in South Florida. Madison hoped it would become a hit sitcom for the Disney Channel and be even more popular than Raven Simone's popular series *That's So Raven.*

After the *American Star* win, doors were opening up everywhere. She was the first to be considered for the lead role of Austen Simmons in the pilot, and after reading the script, Madison told herself she had to have it because it resembled the life she dreamed of. Although Madison at eighteen would be older than the part she played, she was always a popular girl at her private school right outside Los Angeles. Her family wasn't wealthy, but her dad made sure she didn't miss anything without totally spoiling her.

Madison was pulled from her afternoon disco nap by her daddy's deep baritone voice. "Maddy, wake your behind up." At first she thought she was dreaming. When she opened her eyes Madison didn't realize where she was.

"What? Is there something wrong, Dad?" she asked, lifting her head from the pillow.

"Wake up. I need to talk to you."

Madison rubbed her eyes and looked at her daddy with his arms folded over his chest and a stern look on his face. She had seen that look before and knew this can't be good.

"Who do you think you are, making Caressa cry and feel worthless," he demanded.

"What are you talking about, Daddy? Caressa is my girl. I would never do anything to make her cry."

"Well, you did. She came back to the hotel and asked me to get her a ticket back to Los Angeles. Caressa said you'd changed and weren't her best friend anymore. Maddy, I told you before we did that *American Star* show, the moment I saw a change in you I was going to stop it. I won't have you treating friends like servants and you know my sister and I didn't raise you that way."

Madison regretted her behavior immediately. "What did she say?"

Before Derrick could answer, his phone

rang. He looked at it and then clicked it on and said, "Hello, Shanice." Madison looked at her dad with concern. She knew Shanice was not going to take the demise of her relationship with her father lightly.

"Now is not a good time."

Thinking her presence might limit the conversation, Madison started to leave the room. She also hoped to avoid the tongue-lashing she knew she was in for.

"Madison, don't leave this room. Shanice, I have to go. I will try and call you later," he said and clicked off his phone.

"We're not done yet, young lady."

"Why are you mad at me, Daddy?"

"I'm not mad at you, Madison, but you know what you did. Don't play dumb with me. You're acting like a pint-size diva. For all we know the Disney executives could come in here tomorrow and kick our butts out on the street. Remember, what goes around comes around."

"They're not going to do that, Daddy," Madison said as she stood. "Besides, I think it's Caressa who's being the drama queen. I just asked her to do what we're paying her for. What's wrong with that?"

Derrick takes a seat on the arm of the sofa. "Madison, who do you think you're talking to? I love you but I know you. Some of those traits you were sadly born with, but I'm not having it. You need to get yourself together and get back to the hotel and apologize to Caressa. I never thought it was a good idea to hire her as your personal assistant. If she is your friend then that's the way it should remain. If you want her to share in your success, you give it to her without strings. Hire someone you don't know who's cut out to be a personal assistant rather than a family member or friend. Why do you think I didn't want to be your manager or agent? I'm your daddy and that's all I want to ever be. Do I make myself clear, young lady?"

Madison looks down at the hardwood floor and tries to conjure up her best hurt look, hoping her daddy will feel sorry for her. Sometimes it works and then there are times when it doesn't. She didn't mean to hurt Caressa's feelings but was trying to establish who the boss was.

"I didn't hear you," her father said.

"Okay, Daddy, I will go and apologize. But I think you're right. Maybe I need to get an assistant who's not so easy to upset. Maybe I do need someone I don't know."

"I agree. But you need to let Caressa know why you're making a change. And if she is your friend, and I do believe she is, then you guys will find a way to keep it that way."

Madison runs to her daddy and jumps into his arms, hugging his neck and kissing him on his plump cheeks as she says, "I love you, Daddy, and I promise I'll never be a diva, because I was raised right. I'll make you proud."

"I know you will, Maddy. I know you will," he whispered tenderly.

CHAPTER 2

"I tell you it's not a good idea," I said firmly.

"I don't understand why you're so against this. Your mother sounds perfect to include on the reality show."

What did Andrew Hart, one of the investors S. Marcus wanted me to meet, know about my mother?

"Trust me, Ava is not worth the trouble. Let's think of something else," I said.

"Most successful reality shows have some kind of eccentric characters and sometimes they become even bigger than the stars," Andrew said.

That's precisely what I was afraid of. "We can't let that happen. This is about me and *my* comeback," I protested. I started to pick my purse up and leave the dimly lit bar a couple of blocks from Times Square, but Marcus had told me Andrew is not only a big money guy but is also one of the major players behind the popular reality series

Run's House. If anybody could make the show happen it is Andrew. I pretended to peer inside my purse instead, then snapped it closed.

"Then tell me how you see the show, Yancey."

"It would just have the cameras following me as I go on auditions, take acting and dance classes." I could tell from his stony demeanor that he wasn't thrilled about that idea at all. "Maybe we can get the show to hire me an assistant, and he or she could be a wild and crazy character. Maybe we could get some flamboyant gay guy, maybe a white guy who could do a lot of my errands. Or I could ask my friend Dalton, who's a fabulous songwriter, to act like he's my assistant."

Andrew was unimpressed. "I think that's already been done. I remember the girl from *I Love New York* having a gay sidekick and it just didn't work. Now that I think about it, her mother, Sister Patterson, stole the show and was great for the ratings."

I could only imagine what Ava would do. She'd hang me from a coat rack if that's what it took to upstage me. "I don't want that. Why don't you like the gay assistant idea? Did I mention that Dalton is gay and he has one of those down-low boyfriends?"

"It doesn't matter, Yancey, it plays into stereotypes."

"And the problem with that would be?"

"Been done," he said as if to end the discussion.

"So has the mother thing."

"Well, we need to come up with something. I got a meeting with MTV, VH-1 and Bravo in the next couple of weeks, and I want to have a solid plan. What about a younger girl to serve as your assistant?"

That could be trouble all on its own. "Would she be in the business?" I asked.

"I hadn't thought about that. If she was, it could make it interesting."

"Could she be fat? And dark."

"Why?"

This was difficult territory for me, and I didn't know how to talk about it without sounding, well, difficult. "Because it's about me, and I can't run the risk of having some young pretty girl upstaging me. I was once young myself and I know how these so-called actresses will do anything to get a gig." I took a sip of my cranberry juice with club soda. It is just a little before three and a little too early for a drink. Well, unless you are an alcoholic.

"Do you have any other relatives or old friends besides your mother who you've been out of contact with?" Andrew asked. "Reunions are always good for ratings and big hits with sponsors."

I felt a cold jolt race up my back. "What are you talking about? Have you heard something?" I asked. I know it is impossible for Andrew to know about Madison. Ava is the only one who knows. Still, curiosity got the better of me and I'd gone to visit Madison's website and even signed up for her fan club. She is a pretty girl, but I'm still not sure how much talent she has.

He was oblivious to the sudden fear gripping my insides. "Have I heard something like what? I was just thinking about Keyshia Cole and how she and her mother reconnected on her reality show. One of the producers from that show is a friend of mine and sent me over several episodes. At first it was like watching a train wreck, but then I really found myself touched by some of the moments between the two of them."

"I heard about the show but never saw it. I think Keyshia Cole is a great singer but rather low class," I offered, attempting to make the point that I wanted my show to have class.

Andrew finished the rest of his Coke. "Well, we got a couple of days to think of something. I got a call right before I came over here from Lyfe Jennings, the singer who did some real time in prison. It seems he's interested in doing a show as well. They want me to be a part of their team."

Was he dismissing me? "Please don't do that. Marcus tells me you're the best, and if this is going to be successful, then I've got to have the best."

"Then we've got to come up with something," he said pointedly. "And sooner rather than later, Yancey. You feel me?"

"Yeah, I feel you."

I lie in bed beside S. Marcus, the stark white sheets entangling our bodies like satin ribbons. Both our chests are heaving from the marathon sex we just had. I turn my head, and stare at S. Marcus, wet strands of hair clinging to my face as I smile.

That man knows he can lay the hammer down with the best of them. So whenever he calls I'm there. I'd left my meeting fully intending to have Chinese food with Ava and call it a day. But as I looked over the takeout menu, my cell phone rang and it was him telling me he was in town for a meeting. I asked where he was staying, and before he could get "Seasons" after the word "Four," I was hailing a taxi on the way to his suite.

He turns, looks at me, his face not two inches from mine. "What?" he asks, still slightly short of breath, smiling.

I'm all smiles right back. "It's not going to work, so stop trying."

"What's not going to work?"

"Trying to make me fall in love with you and that thing you do."

"That's what's up?" S. Marcus said, lifting himself up, on top of me, a confident smirk on his face. "I'm not trying to do that anyway."

"And why is that?" I say, half playful, but the tiniest bit serious at the same time. I really had no clue as to where this relationship was heading.

He lowers himself, gives me a quick kiss on the lips. "Because I know you're already in love." He laughs as he rises up off me and jumps, naked, out of bed. "And very soon you won't be able to deny it," S. Marcus says, not turning around. As he walks to the bathroom, his sculpted, curvaceous ass entrances me so much that I don't really hear what he said. He stops at the door, turns around, and leans against the bathroom doorway. I try not to look down at his manhood, which is still semi-erect, but I can't help myself. He notices and says, "Yeah, just what I figured."

168

"Boy, take your shower," I laugh, throwing the pillow across the room at him.

I flop back onto the bed, feeling spent yet rejuvenated, giddy like a teenage school girl. Yet I knew to remain cautious from my years surviving in the romance jungle.

In the bathroom, I hear S. Marcus slide open the glass shower door and turn on the shower.

Not yet, I tell myself. Wait until he's all the way in, washing his face, has soap in his eyes and can't come out and bust me.

I count to ten and then spring out of bed. I don't throw on my panties and bra, because although I know he likes long showers, I won't take any chance at getting caught.

I go to his slacks first and, unlike most men who just throw them to the floor while getting undressed before sex, S. Marcus folds his neatly, along with his shirt and underwear, and then rolls his socks into a ball before climbing naked into bed.

He is a neat freak, plain and simple. Not just with his clothes, but with everything. His business papers are always stacked neatly. I remember how I didn't seen the faintest hint of dust on any surface in his house when I first met him. His face seems always clean shaven, his hair always cut crisp and his lining always razor sharp. His manicured fingernails are short and clean and look polished, although a closer inspection reveals they are not. All this had me wondering could he be one of those down-low guys who I'd found myself dating in the past. It didn't matter how many times you asked the questions "Are you married?" or "Have you ever been with another man?" Some men could lie so easily.

I almost married a man like this once and also dated a man who I later discovered was married. For that reason I am up searching through S. Marcus's pants pockets, then the dresser drawers and the shelves of the entertainment center, looking for his wallet.

I need to get his Social Security number, and somehow find the funds to do a background check and make sure that he isn't another John Basil Henderson who — while he was doing those wonderful things he did to me in bed — was thinking about some other man in sexy underwear, and how they would get together later that night.

Minutes later, I still haven't found his wallet, and realize that he has to be at the end of his shower. I turn in a circle, looking, wondering where he could be hiding it. Then it hits me. I forgot to check the nightstand drawer. That's where it is. It has to be.

I race back to the bed and nightstand, but before reaching it, I hear the water stop and S. Marcus humming loudly.

"Hey Yancey, how did your meeting go? We got busy so quick last night I forgot to ask you about it," S. Marcus calls through the bedroom door, making me jump. His voice sounds closer than the shower, like he is standing just on the other side of the door.

"It went well, but I want to talk about it when you got some time," I yelled back.

Is it worth it? I thought. Should I risk getting caught, just because the man is neat? I'm staring right at the bedroom door, knowing S. Marcus could walk back in at any minute. But then again, I was holding his wallet in my hand. Sifting through its contents would only take a second.

"Would you like to order some room service?" S. Marcus calls out.

"Whatever you like, Marcus," I said, trying to keep my voice from sounding different. Then I find his Florida driver's license. I yank it from the wallet, hold it right up to my face, my hand shaking slightly. I don't see his Social Security number, but I do see his first name Seneca and his birthday, which actually seemed to jump out at me:

8/12/1983. He told me he is in his thirties, so that makes him a liar. Guard up. This man is really just a boy, I thought. How could he be so young and yet so confident? And if I ever considered being truthful about my age, this child could be my son. But I guess I'm getting ready to enroll at Cougar High. But I hadn't reached cougar status yet, so I'll leave that to Ava.

I quickly shove the license back into the wallet and drop it into the drawer. I leap back in the bed just as S. Marcus is opening the bathroom door.

He walks over, a snow-white towel wrapped loosely around his narrow, flat waist.

He leans over me again. "You still breathing so hard, baby. You been playing with that pussy while I was in the shower?"

"Why I need to do that?" I said, playfully pulling him on top of me. "I got the real thing."

"Yeah, you do," he said. "And you can have it anytime you want it."

Chapter 3

Ava stood in the kitchen, about to pour herself a cold glass of white wine, even though she knew drinking alcohol was against her parole. But she needed a drink after dealing with that damn probation officer of hers. He had threatened her that she would go back to jail if she didn't get a job. He had even suggested she work at McDonald's. Who did he think she was?

Ava tilted the bottle, about to pour the golden liquid into her glass, when she heard a knock at the door. She set the bottle down, wondering who would show up unannounced.

She asks, "Who is it?"

There is no answer.

Ava steps closer to the door, wraps her hand around the knob, and peeks out of the peephole. A black woman was standing out there, but her back was turned to the door.

"I said, who is it?"

The woman turns around, and Ava sees a distorted, fun-house image of a young woman the color of a brown crayon. "What's happening, Ava?" she called out.

Just when Ava thought her day couldn't get any worse, it was about to. It was Lyrical, and Ava had no choice but to open the door.

"Bitch, I thought I wasn't ever gonna catch up with your ass." The tall and slender African-American young woman slid into the foyer. "Shit, this is a motherfuckin' nice-ass neighborhood and house."

After a few moments a speechless Ava regained her composure.

"Lyrical, what the hell are you doing here? How did you find me?"

"I figured you'd forgotten about our little motherfuckin' deal. Did you lose a bitch's number?"

Lyrical Chante Sanders was a twenty-two-year-old from Harlem who had befriended Ava while in prison. While Ava looked to Lyrical as a friend, Lyrical saw Ava in a strange way as the mother she had never had, being raised by her grandmother. She had been let out on early release, about six months before Ava.

Lyrical was tall for a girl, and she was dressed in jeans, with men's boxers and a wife beater. Lyrical struck fear in most of the inmates, which Ava recognized during the first week, and a friendship was born. She was serving time for transporting drugs, which Lyrical said she had done without her knowledge for a no-good boyfriend who only visited Lyrical a couple of times while she was in the joint.

Ava owed her a debt. Lyrical made sure nobody messed with Madame Ava, as the other prisoners called her, and in return Ava promised to help Lyrical with her music career and change her decidedly masculine style. She had a cute shape, a perfect size four, Ava guessed. She is wearing a ratty denim jacket and dirty cloth tennis shoes. Her hair, which is shoulder length and black, and could've looked nice with some more attention, is parted on the side. It is broken off on the ends, and looks like Lyrical used her fingers to rake through it instead of a comb.

"I didn't lose your number, girl," Ava lied while giving her former friend a half hug. "I was going to look you up when I got settled."

"Yeah," Lyrical deadpanned, not believing Ava for a second, "I figured as much. That's why I followed you home. I thought we might report to the same probation office, and I just asked a couple of those bitches up there if you were reporting and they said yes. It didn't take long to get one of those bitches to sing and tell me what day you report to your parole officer, so I just hung around and it was like, bam, there you were. I just followed you home. Pretty smart for a dumb bitch like myself, huh, Ava?"

"Yeah, that was really smart," Ava said warily, unsure where this was headed. "Can't pull anything over on you. Did you get an early release? I thought you had at least five more years."

"Yeah, you ain't the only bitch who knows important people."

"Well there you have it."

Looking around the elegant room, Lyrical asked, "You got anything to play music in this joint? I brought you one of my demos. I put that rap that I did for you on it."

The very thought horrified Ava. "I think so, but I don't know how to operate it."

Ava had to think fast. She knew the way Lyrical operated, and it was best to nip things in the bud before they got out of hand. She had heard enough rap music during her prison stay to cover her for a lifetime.

"Let me take a look at it. I can figure that shit out."

"Just leave the disc with me and I'll listen

to it a little later. You know in private. That will be better."

Lyrical nodded in response. She had more street smarts than Ava did. "Okay, that's what's up. You got anything to drink in this motherfucker? A bitch be thirsty like a motherfucker."

"Yeah, I think we got something to drink. What would you like?"

"You got any malt liquor?"

"I doubt it."

"What about some fucking Red Bull?"

Ava gestured to the kitchen, leading the way. "What's that?"

"Damn, Ava, I thought you'd learn a little bit from me while we was in the joint. It's an energy drink. My brother Conroy — the one who I told you was a truck driver but I think he's doing some illegal shit 'cause the nigga always got a pocket full of cash. Well, he turned my ass on to them. He said they give you energy and keep him from falling asleep when he driving that big-ass rig of his. Now, I don't drive no trucks, but I like to stay up late because that's when my inspiration for my beats come. You remember, don't you, Madame Ava? Are you still gonna help me with my music? You know, help me get a deal with some of the people ya know."

Ava neatly evaded the questions. "How about some lemonade or sparkling water?"

Lyrical reeled back. "Lemonade? Are you serious, bitch? Just forget it if you ain't got no beer or Red Bull." She leaned her arm on the refrigerator door. "So what we gonna do first?"

"About what?"

"When you gonna call some them motherfuckers you know in the music industry? When they hear my shit, they gonna want to sign up a bitch to a multirecord deal. Don't you think, Ava? That's what you told me."

It was rare for Ava to be caught so off guard. Lyrical was a wild card whom Ava had to play carefully. "Of course, just like I said in the joint, but I haven't had time to call any of my contacts yet. Why don't you write your number down and I'll give you a call when I get in contact with them?"

Lyrical looked suspicious, but finally she backed off. "Okay, but this time don't lose it. And give me your number so I can lock it in my phone."

Ava gave Lyrical her number as she tried to think of an excuse to get her out of the house before Yancey returned. She thought about what her probation officer said about the type of people she associated with and wondered if Lyrical had been told the same thing by her probation officer.

"Lyrical darling, it's been so good seeing you. Wow, look at the time," Ava said with a quick glance at her watch. "I've got to meet one of my gentlemen friends for drinks before the theater tonight." To make her point clear, Ava gave Lyrical a quick peck on the cheek.

"That's what's up, Ava. I need to get to the studio my damn self. Oh yeah, when are we going to start our classes?"

Ava could feel her jaws clenching like iron. "Did I promise some kind of classes too?"

"Damn, bitch, you forgetting everything we talked about in the joint. Remember, you said you were going to teach me to be more like a bitch, or how you say it, more ladylike. I don't know how my nigga gonna like that, but shit, he might dig it." Despite her masculine looks Lyrical was definitely heterosexual, a fact that surprised Ava, who wondered if Lyrical was fooling herself about her sexuality.

"So you're back with your boyfriend after what he did to you? What was his name again?"

"You remember. And Donnie Ray swears he didn't know that there were drugs in the bag when he asked me to take it to Jersey

179

City. Funny thing is, he asked about you and I told him I was going to find you. His name's Donnie Ray Johnson. He lives up in the Bronx and most of the time I'm with him at his place, but his motherfucking bitch-ass mother moved in with him. Old granny don't like my ass, but who gives a fuck what she thinks. I ain't got to sleep with the wrinkled-up bitch. Maybe that old bitch needs some dick. She reminds me of my old mean-ass granny. But I ain't going anywhere as long as Donnie Ray is laying the pipe like he do." Lyrical let go a big smile. "He also makes sure a bitch got a few coins in her purse and a blunt every now and then."

It occurred to Ava that Lyrical might be useful after all. "Do you think he knows where I might be able to buy some weed if I need it to calm my nerves? My daughter is still a piece of work."

"Hell yeah. Donnie Ray can get anything you need, Ava."

Ava led her guest to the door. "Well, tell him I said hello. Okay, Lyrical, I will call you soon. I need to start to get ready. Bye-bye, sweetheart," Ava said as she opened the door.

"Maybe I'll bring Donnie Ray with me the next time. You know, I'm going to let him manage me when I get my record deal. What do you think about that, Ava?"

The last person Ava wanted to meet was Lyrical's drug-dealing boyfriend. "That's fine. Have a nice evening, Lyrical. Take care of yourself."

"Okay, but give a bitch some love," Lyrical said, wrapping her long arms around a very surprised Ava. After a few moments Ava gave her a few gentle pats on the back as she wondered, How am I going to get rid of this crazy bitch?

CHAPTER 4

I sat in the 112 restaurant, a popular steak house that used to be an old hotel on South Beach. The lights were dim, and the music was up-tempo jazz, loud enough to be heard, but not so loud as to intrude on people's conversations. Suntanned beautiful people sat all around.

I sliced another corner from my filet and popped it in my mouth. The tender meat practically melts like butter. The lobster that comes with my meal is succulent, and the California Merlot is superb. I heard about this restaurant but didn't have the clout to get in, never mind afford it, so when S. Marcus called me out of the blue and said he wanted to fly me via private charter to Miami for dinner here, I jumped at the chance. "But don't tell me you want me to come all the way to Miami just to have dinner at 112?"

"I got a little surprise for you. Someone I

want you to meet."

"Who?" I said. I love being surprised and had a feeling this would be a big one.

"Pack a bag and get your beautiful butt down here."

Excited, I trusted what S. Marcus told me. Anything for S. Marcus, especially if it means getting my own reality show.

The person he wanted me to meet was sitting across from me now, enjoying baby back ribs. He wore a beautiful blue light-weight Sean Jean suit, with a white shirt that hung perfectly off his broad shoulders. I can't help but smile as I watch him with that napkin stuffed into the front of his shirt as he attacked those ribs. He ate them with his hands, and the sauce covered his fingers, the napkin and his cheeks.

S. Marcus introduced Jeff Porter as his business partner and best friend. I'm kind of surprised that S. Marcus's friend happens to be a white man. But this wasn't your everyday, proper-speaking, button-down, Polo shirt and penny loafer–wearing white guy. He has nicely chiseled, European facial features, and would be considered by most women, white or black, to be quite hand-some, almost *GQ* handsome. Two diamond earrings pierce Jeff's ears, one in each lobe. He sports a short-cropped Caesar cut, and

I can see a tattooed name on his neck, written in cursive, peeking up over the collar of his shirt. When he extended his hand to me, I noticed another tattoo of the head of a snake, slithering out from the cuff of his sleeve and stopping on the back of his hand.

"What's up, baby girl?" Jeff said, taking my hand and kissing me lightly on the knuckles. "My boy S. has told me a bunch about you, and best believe it's all good, girl. And my boy wasn't lying when he said you were all that."

I smiled, looking at S. Marcus, trying to decide if this is a joke or who Jeff really is. A combination of K-Fed, Puffy and Eminem all rolled into one, his speech filled with ebonic flavor.

"How did you two meet?" I asked.

"Our dads were in business together when black and white men didn't do that type of shit," Jeff said.

"What type of business?"

"Now, come on, Yancey, stop grilling my man. We didn't come here to talk about our parents," S. Marcus said in a somewhat nervous tone.

I tried to laugh it off. "Oh, I'm sorry. Well, I guess we'll have to go back to talking about me."

"Yeah, that's better," Jeff said.

In the middle of the dinner, S. Marcus explained another reason for the meeting.

"My man Jeff here is a producer and the main investor for a number of people in the music industry. He's the one who discovered Lil' Max and put together the reality show that brought together the girl group Dynasty Girls."

"That was you?" I asked, sincerely impressed.

"That's me, love," Jeff said as he sucked the rib sauce off his fingers and thumb.

"Both of those acts went platinum," I said.

"Double platinum, babe," Jeff said and he picked up another rib bone.

"I've been telling Jeff about your background and how you see the reality show going, and I think he likes what he's heard." I look at Jeff and smile, noticing the large diamond-encrusted Rolex on his wrist and the band ring loaded with small diamonds. He nods at me in approval. I suddenly realize that all of the other meetings had been building up to this one, and Jeff will be the one to make it happen. But I also had a dilemma on how I should handle Jeff. Should I treat him like the white businessman he is, or the brotha from the 'hood he aspires to be? I suddenly wished S. Marcus had warned me, but now there was no time for that.

"So Yancey, you got any kids?"

"No," I said, quickly wondering why he'd asked the question.

"It would be cool for the show if you had some bratty kid," Jeff explained. "Wouldn't matter if it was a girl or a boy."

"Sorry I can't help you there," I said quietly, raising my hand to my lips. "No children living here."

"You sure? Those look like child-bearing hips to me, baby girl. Maybe we can rent a kid from central casting," Jeff said with a laugh.

Seeing how uneasy I was, S. Marcus jumped right in. "We can still make this thing work without kids."

Jeff nodded, burping lightly from the ribs. "So tell me about yo peeps, Yancey. Who you hang with?"

"What do you mean?"

Jeff continued eating without pausing to look up from his plate. "Who are your girls you hang with?"

"I don't really hang with females. They deal too much with petty jealousy."

"My boy here told me about your mama, and she sounds like she is off the chain."

So this is where he was heading. "Yeah, but I told Marcus that I don't want her in

186

the show," I said quickly. There was no way in hell I was going to let Ava anywhere near the camera once we started shooting.

Jeff shrugged. "Okay, we don't have to have her, but you got any fags or, excuse me, 'gay boys' you hang with?"

"Fags?" I asked. Jeff's charm was wearing thin quick. I didn't consider Dalton a fag.

"Don't pay him any mind, Yancey," S. Marcus said with a slap on Jeff's shoulder.

"What's the politically correct term these days? Meat packers?" Jeff asked. "I know they don't like homo."

"I know some gay guys from some of the shows I've done and a couple who do my makeup. I have a gay friend Dalton but he won't do the show because his boyfriend is on the low."

"That's cool. But who's your BFF?"

"My what?"

"Your best friend forever, Yancey," S. Marcus said with a smirk in Jeff's direction.

I thought about Jeff and S. Marcus's question and realized I don't have an answer for them because I don't have a best friend. Damn, I don't even have anyone I can call a friend. I was suddenly confused for a moment by the feeling of loneliness, but I know I can't let those feelings last long. I might need to go into the rest room and give myself another pep talk. But if I need to have a best friend for the show, I will get one.

"Well, I guess you could say I'm a loner, but there are some girls and gay guys from the cast of the show that I was just in that I hang with. I don't know if I would want them in the show but let me think about it."

"What about your personal assistant?" Jeff asked.

"I don't have one."

"You need to get one. We got to show you living large. Nobody wants to watch somebody living like them. They want over the top. The higher we can take you from the common folks, the better. We'll make it seem like you got paid back in the day and you held on to some of your coins. We gonna make those women from Atlanta and Orange County look like welfare moms," Jeff said.

My heart sank at the callousness of his unthinking comment, but I kept up a strong front. "That may be tough. Some of those women seem to be doing pretty well."

"They just married well," Jeff responded in a blink.

"So you think we should do this?" S. Marcus asked Jeff.

He stared at me for a few moments like he was sizing me up, and I pasted a confident smile across my face. I decided to play it cool to go along with his playfulness. "So what's it going to be, Jeff? Am I going to be the new *it* girl of reality television?"

Jeff looked lost in thought. He turned to S. Marcus and said, "If we going to make it seem like our girl here got funds, then she should have two residences. Let me check and see if I can get Kat, my real estate boo, to find us some furnished place on the beach. I'll tell her we'll give her lots of free press if she gives us a good deal."

"Yeah, my nigga, I should have thought of that. That would make everything look real chill," S. Marcus said.

Am I hearing things? Had S. Marcus just called Jeff a nigga and had his own dialect suddenly gone street? What happened to the clipped, prep school voice he used to order five-hundred-dollar bottles of wine?

"That why we a team and nobody can beat us, S. man. 'Cause you my nigga for sho. I think we got us a hit with this lovely lady you discovered," Jeff added with a wink.

I could barely contain myself. "Great," I said, clapping my hands in delight.

"I think this deserves some champagne to celebrate," S. Marcus said.

Jeff turned and snapped his fingers in the air and suddenly two waiters were standing front and center at our table. I am back to living the high life, and it feels good all over.

CHAPTER 5

Madison felt like she was basking in her own success, literally, as a bright beam of sunshine shot like a spotlight through the warehouse-style windows of the midtown studio. And her voice teacher's eyes, sparkling with so much pride, only intensified the feeling that Madison was on her way to becoming a superstar.

"Great job, Madison," said Nicole Springer-Stovall, whose words sounded so smooth and deep as they echoed off the golden brown hardwood floor of the stark rehearsal room. "Your voice is lovely and strong."

"Thank you, Ms. Stovall," Madison said, enjoying the down-to-earth warmth that she felt from her teacher. Now that their first session was over, Madison realized that for the past two hours, she'd felt like her instructor really cared about helping her learn and reach her highest potential. "You were very helpful."

Madison caught a reflection of herself with Ms. Stovall in the mirrors behind the ballet barre in the enormous room. As they sat on the bench behind the gleaming black baby grand piano, the whole scene made Madison feel like she was at the center of the best that New York could offer young talent.

And hearing compliments from this elegant lady whose upswept black hair, satiny-smooth voice and ageless, deep caramel complexion reminded her of Diahann Carroll only made Madison grin with the thrill of it all.

For that, she could thank the producers of *American Star.* They had suggested Nicole Springer-Stovall to Madison's father as one of the best voice and acting coaches in the business. They felt that private lessons would help Madison adjust to the rigors of using her voice every night once she went on tour.

"Now I see why you won that show," said Ms. Stovall, wearing all black, from her high-heeled sandals and slim-fitting slacks to a sweater with shimmery beads around the neckline. "By the way, my kids are big fans of the show and you. They thought I was big time when I told them I was going to be working with you."

Madison suddenly liked this lady even more, now that she was bringing kids into the mix. "You have children? How many?"

"I have four," Ms. Stovall said in a regal way that made her raise her chin slightly, like a queen. "My oldest is fourteen and I have one twelve and twins that just turned eight. One boy and three girls." As Ms. Stovall beamed proudly, Madison admired her teacher's beautiful and sophisticated profile. Her skin was smooth and tight. Her cheekbones and chin were sculpted and sharp. She sure didn't look like a woman who had borne four children.

Madison tried to imagine all those kids around her teacher. "It must be cool to have so many brothers and sisters."

Ms. Stovall turned to face her with eyes that radiated a caring, motherly softness. "You must be an only child."

"Yeah," Madison said, wondering what it would be like to have a woman look at her like this every day. "It's just me and my daddy."

"Oh," Ms. Stovall said softly. "Do you mind if I ask what happened to your mother?" Madison appreciated the sensitive way that the teacher raised her eyebrow and asked the question as if she didn't want to bring up any bad memories for her new student.

"My mother gave me up at birth," Madison said with a matter-of-fact tone. She glanced down at her blue jeans, her favorite pair of True Religion with the white stitching. "Oddly enough, so that she could pursue a show business career. I don't think she ever wanted to be a mother."

Sympathy warmed Ms. Stovall's eyes. "How sad. I wanted my career, but I always knew I wanted children. I'm so happy the good Lord was great enough to give me both."

Madison was intrigued. She wanted to envision what this beautiful woman had done on stage and on camera. "What did you do in business? I mean you look young now, but when you were, say, my age."

Ms. Stovall told Madison how she had started in the Miss America system, won a state title and then came to New York and appeared on Broadway. When Madison asked her what shows she had done, the only one Madison recognized was *Dreamgirls*.

"Which role did you play?"

Excitement beamed from Ms. Stovall's face as she remembered her time in the spotlight. "I played several roles in different companies but mostly I played Deena Jones."

"Oh, the role Beyonce played?"

"Not Beyonce, but more Sheryl Lee Ralph," Ms. Stovall said with a smile. "Many, many years ago."

Madison tried to picture her teacher in a starring role. "Was that a movie, too?"

Ms. Stovall shook her head, making the diamond solitaires in her ears sparkle in the sunlight. "No, there was always talk about a movie back in the day, but it never happened until Jennifer Hudson and Beyonce came along."

"Oh," Madison said. Now it was her voice that rang with a bit of sympathy. "So did you do movies and television, too?"

"Lots of commercials, small roles in films." As Ms. Stovall spoke, she glanced down at her elegant manicure and the wedding ring on her left hand. "Have you decided what you want to do with your career? Have you thought about doing Broadway? You have the voice to be able to give a winning performance every night."

"You think so? That's so nice of you to say that." Madison smiled at her teacher, thinking how lucky Ms. Stovall's kids were. She would have done anything to have a mother like her. If Nicole weren't married,

Madison would call herself Cupid and introduce this lady to Daddy. They were even around the same age.

"Strong pipes and sweet sound," Ms. Stovall exclaimed. "I'm going to teach you how to protect it like the instrument that it is so that you can have a long career. Here, drink this." Ms. Stovall handed Madison a bottle of water. Then she reached in her purse, pulled out a packet of honey and instructed Madison to pour it into her water.

"So this is good for me?" Madison asked as she followed her instructions.

"Very good for you, Madison. You're a very pretty and talented young lady. I think your mother might be sorry she missed this." Ms. Stovall pushed back Madison's hair from her face with a motherly touch.

Madison, her eyes round with the wonderful feeling, simply mouthed, "Thank you."

Madison bounced into the hotel suite and did a not so perfect ballet leap across the living room floor.

"Daddy," she sang, "I'm home!"

"I see, Miss Dance Theatre of Harlem," Derrick said as he walked out of his bedroom. With his dark chocolate complexion and rugged coolness, Madison thought he was the most handsome man in the world.

"How was your day?" she asked.

"It was great," he said. "I take it the voice lesson went well."

"It was amazing!" she said. "Ms. Springer-Stovall was wonderful and really loved my voice. I'm so glad we hired her. She was in the *Dreamgirls* from a long time ago." Madison gave her father a speculative look. "Nicole is her first name and she is gorgeous and seems like a perfect mom. I can't wait for you to meet her, Dad. I wish you could find a woman like that to marry. Too bad Ms. Stovall already is." Madison plopped down on the sofa. "Ms. Stovall, this is my dad, Derrick. He's the most coolest in the world."

Her father shook his head. "Stop playing matchmaker, Madison." He walked over to the desk where they kept not only the hotel room service menu, but several takeout menus from nearby places that delivered. "What do you want to eat for dinner? I feel like some real good sushi."

"Sushi would be good," Madison said, not to be distracted from her subject. "I'm just saying, if you're not going to get back with Shanice, we gotta come up with another plan."

"I told you to leave my social life alone, Maddy." Derrick felt a surge of protectiveness toward his daughter when she met a woman she liked or when he introduced her to someone he was interested in. Of all the gifts he could shower on his daughter, there was no way he could give her the one thing she longed for the most — a mother who would love her as much as Madison was capable of loving in return.

While Derrick was dialing, Madison leaped up from the sofa.

"I know what I'm going to do," she announced. "I'll google Ms. Nicole and see if I can pull up a picture of her, so I can show you, Daddy."

Derrick smiled with amusement as Madison sashayed like a Broadway star to her bedroom where her laptop awaited.

CHAPTER 6

In her quest to meet Madison, Ava turned
to the computer again. The little money she
had was steadily shrinking, and soon
enough, she feared Yancey would sell the
house and she would be homeless before
she could complete her mission. It was
imperative that Ava get in touch with the
golden child.

She spent an hour sifting through several
Madison B. fan websites, reading the childish mess that was written on different blogs
about Madison and the *American Star* show.
Finally Ava found a site that listed Madison's booking information and manager —
she was being handled by the Thurston Silas Agency. Ava scribbles the name and
number at the bottom of her notepad, then
punches it into the phone. She's trying to
think of what approach she should take with
the manager. She remembers when she was
in show business, her manager was always

protective of her and wouldn't give out information to people just wanting to meet her. This was going to take some skill.

The phone rang once, then twice, and then during the third time, Ava told herself she had to make something happen. She was a talented actress. She hadn't used her skills in years, if you didn't count all the performances she'd put on trying to get her way while in prison. If her skills worked in the joint, there wasn't any reason Ava couldn't fool some talent manager.

"Good afternoon, Thurston Silas Agency," a pleasant-sounding voice answered.

Ava decided on a tone of authority. "Thurston, please."

"May I ask who's calling?"

"This is Ava Middlebrooks, owner of the Parker Agency of Beverly Hills."

"May I tell Thurston what this is in reference to?"

"Is she in?"

"I'll first need to know what this call is regarding."

"I'll tell Thurston myself."

This girl was no dummy and knew how to handle the strong come-on. "Why don't I take your number and have her call you?"

"Is she there?"

"Is this your number that came up on our

caller ID? The area code is 917. I thought you said your company was in Beverly Hills."

"We are bicoastal, little girl. Your agency manages Madison B., doesn't it?"

"Yes, we do."

"I need to get in contact with Madison," Ava said.

"Is this regarding a booking?"

Ava thought for a minute and then answered, "Yes."

"Do you have a date? I would need to give that to Thurston."

"I need to speak with Madison directly."

"I don't think that's possible. We handle all of Madison's booking ourselves."

"Well, I have a very rich client whose daughter is having a sweet sixteen party. She is Madison's biggest fan. What is her booking fee?"

"A sweet sixteen party?" the girl asked almost incredulously. "Can you hold on for a second?"

"Yes, but be quick. Ava doesn't have all day."

A few seconds later, Ava heard the voice from the phone talking to someone else in the office. "There's some crazy woman on the line wanting to book Madison for a sweet sixteen party. Should I tell her that's impossible or just take her number?"

Crazy? Who did this bitch think she was talking about? Another female voice said, "Yeah, take her number. We got bigger problems than some birthday party. I just got off the phone with Madison's dad. Her assistant quit and we got to hire one quick before the tour this summer. Call some personal assistant employment firms."

When Ava heard that, she thought the perfect plan had just landed in her lap. She hung up the phone before the young lady came back.

She smiled a big, self-satisfied grin. "I think it's time for the Ava Parker Personal Assistants Agency to open for business," she announced, writing the name of her new company on the pad just to see how it looked in print.

Ava went to her purse and pulled out her cell phone, looked up Lyrical's number and pressed Talk.

After a few rings Lyrical answered. "I thought you were trying to trick a bitch and not call a muthafucker."

"Now, why would I do that, darling? I've just been real busy. Listen, I have something important to discuss. Can you meet me at the bar at the W Hotel in the theater district?"

"What's the theater district?"

Ava closed her eyes in disbelief, wondering how this child could have lived in New York all her life and not know about the theater district.

"I mean Times Square," Ava said with emphasis.

"Oh shit, why didn't you say that?"

Ava shook her head. "Can you meet me around six-thirty?"

"Is this about my music career?"

Ava paused for a moment and said, "Yes, Lyrical. It sure is."

"Then a bitch will be there with bells on, Ava."

"Great! See you then."

A little before seven, Lyrical walked into the midtown bar and spotted Ava sitting at a high corner table by a window. Ava took a sip of her drink and waved at Lyrical to join her. When she approached the table, Ava looked at her watch and asked, "Why are you late?"

"I was trying to figure out how to record my favorite show. Have you seen *Housewives of Atlanta?* I love those crazy bitches." Lyrical laughed.

Ava was offended by the trifling show. "Why are you wasting your time watching that show? Those women are so fake. Trust me when I tell you real society women don't act like that. I bet they are up to their elbows in debt in those cheap-looking houses."

Lyrical took a seat facing the window. "I don't care. I want to be like that one day. NeNe is my favorite and I even like her husband the best. Now, her son, he is ghetto, but I like that. Can't stand Kim and Sheree. They are so fake."

"Whatever, Lyrical," Ava said with a knowing smile. "You know I didn't come here to talk about wannabes. I came here to talk about me. I want to open my own business and I want to hire you as my personal assistant."

"What kind of business?"

"I don't know yet, but it will deal with the entertainment area. Have you heard of this Madison B. girl?"

Lyrical sat up straight. "The one who won *American Star?*"

"Yeah, that's her. What do you think of her?"

"I don't know much about her. I don't like that pretty black girl trying to be white type of music. That ain't my thang," Lyrical said.

"I'm trying to get in touch with her

management because you make a valid point. Maybe she needs to be marketing to black people only. This is our time, you know."

Lyrical got right down to business. "How much are you going to pay me?"

"I won't have a lot of money at first, but my train is coming in soon, so you're going to have to trust me," Ava said.

"What about what you promised?"

"What are you talking about?"

"About teaching me how to be a lady and shit." She pounded the table with a solid thump. "You promised. Since I never had a mother to teach me those things I'm depending on you, Ava. If my own mother had lived, I wouldn't be in this position," Lyrical said.

"I know, boo," Ava said, picking up her drink. How was she going to avoid this conversation? The one she'd had with Lyrical many times while they were in prison. How Lyrical had lost her mother to AIDS when she was ten, when her mother got mixed up with the wrong guy and became hooked on drugs. If Ava had to hear that story one more time, she was going to scream.

"So when are we going to start our lessons?"

"Very soon, hon."

Lyrical didn't sound happy being put off like that. "What will I do as your personal assistant, and will I have time for my music?"

"You will do a little bit of everything, and sure, you'll have time for your music. Besides, you work on that basically at night. Am I right?"

Lyrical nodded grudgingly. "Yeah, that's right. Let me think about it for a couple of days."

"Okay. Do you think I can meet your boyfriend Donnie Ray?"

Lyrical appeared crestfallen. "What do you want to meet him for? I thought this was about my music career and your new business."

"It is but I think he might be able to help me do a favor for a friend, who will in turn do a favor for me and you. Do you get my drift?"

"Oh, I see that's how it works. Sure, I can make the hookup. When do you want to meet him?"

"As soon as possible. Do you want a drink?"

"No, honey," Lyrical said, looking around the room. "No telling who might be in this joint scoping us bitches out. If I were you,

I'd be more careful."

"Ava is always careful," she said with a sip. "Trust me on that one. So suit yourself. I'm going to get my drink on."

CHAPTER 7

It had been five days since I'd returned from Miami and still no word from S. Marcus about whether he'd found the financing for my show. Things were getting tighter by the minute. Every time my cell or land line rang and an 800 or unfamiliar ZIP code flashed across the screen, I grew agitated that yet another bill collector had learned how to get in contact with me.

My mortgage company was trying to goad me into a quick sale of my town house, but I wasn't going to do that because then there wouldn't be money to buy something cheaper in New York or even Florida, where I had now decided I wanted to live if something didn't come up acting-wise. And if the auditions I'd been going to were any indication, that wasn't going to happen soon. I'd gone on several national commercial castings but wasn't called back. There was one soap opera audition that

I really wanted, but they decided to go with someone older. It seemed I couldn't win.

So the reality show would serve two purposes: bringing me back into the public eye and shoring up my finances. S. Marcus told me that a lot of people with financial problems looming always bought property in Florida because of more lenient bankruptcy laws. I had to admit that as long as it was taking to get my show going, I liked being around S. Marcus. His age or lack of honesty at times was of no concern to me. If it was good enough for Demi Moore and Cher then it was good enough for me.

Just as I'm finishing the first half of my sandwich, my cell phone rings. I see it's S. Marcus. I use the linen napkin to brush the side of my mouth and smile as I answer.

"Hey, baby girl. What's shaking?"

"Just having myself a little lunch my housekeeper fixed for me," I lied.

"I didn't know you had a housekeeper."

"Oh yes. Her name is Tilda and she's been with me for years. She must have been off when you visited me." Sometimes when I make up these quick stories I think maybe I should consider writing a novel like Kimberla Lawson Roby, an author I started reading on long bus rides.

"Well I guess I'll be seeing a lot of Tilda in the future."

"What do you mean?" I asked. Having to hire some imaginary housekeeper was the last thing I needed to add to my woes.

"Are you sitting down?"

"Of course I am."

"It looks like Jeff is going to finance your reality show. It certainly will get green-lit with financing. You brought your A game, Yancey, and he was impressed just like I knew he'd be."

"You're kidding," I said as I jumped up from the table, spilling the cranberry juice and lime onto the tray. Now I really did need a maid to clean up this mess.

"Nope." He laughed. "We even thought of a catchy title."

"You did? What?"

"*Diva-Tude.* I love it, but I can't take credit. It was Jeff's idea. There are still a few things to work out, like with the cast. But I think since we're not going to use your mother, your housekeeper might be an excellent replacement. Is she foreign?"

"Yes. Hispanic," I lied quickly. I started to add that she spoke with a German accent but stopped myself.

"Okay. I have to check her out even though I like the idea of getting a quirky assistant like the one in the *Kathy Griffin Show,* maybe even two. We could have a guy and a girl."

"Two," I squealed. "That would be fierce, Marcus. Trust me, I can find plenty of stuff for them to do. Maybe one of them can be gay. Most likely the guy because a gay girl would surely spend her time trying to hit on me, which is understandable but not cool."

"That might be cool. We'll talk about all that when I come to New York and scout some locations."

"I thought we'd film it here," I said, hoping that part of the budget could be used to pay my mortgage and back taxes. I realized suddenly that I also needed a severe wardrobe makeover. It had been years since I was able to buy a nice dress or a pair of good shoes.

"Do you really want to do that? I mean if people found out where you live you might open yourself up to stalkers and the crazies."

"Trust me, I'm not afraid of any stalkers. All I've got to do is put my mother on them." I laughed.

"Let me talk to Jeff and see what he thinks. There are plenty of places in New York we could rent and shoot the show. I even like the idea of finding a place in Harlem."

"I know what we can do," I said, wanting to tell him that the doll wasn't doing Harlem, no matter how trendy it became.

"What's that?"

"Maybe we could find me something nice and small in Florida. You know if I'm really making a comeback, then I need to have a second home."

"We can look into that but what might be cool is to show a softer side of you and get something in New Orleans where you could do some charity work in your spare time."

"New Orleans? Do those people still need help down there?"

"Yes, Yancey," he said as if he were talking to a child. "There is still plenty of work to do in New Orleans."

I thought about it for a minute and said, "Okay. Look, I'll do whatever I have to do but I'm sure there are some charity things I can do on South Beach as well."

"We got plenty of time to decide, baby girl."

"Marcus, you have made my day. No, my year! Remind me that when I see you in the flesh that you deserve something special."

"No doubt, baby girl. No doubt."

Just as I hung up the phone, it rang again;

it was Dalton.

"Hey Boo."

"Yancey, what's shaking?"

"Nothing much, just got off the phone with the boyfriend."

"How's that going?"

"Umm . . . it's okay."

"I thought you were pretty excited about him."

"I am but you know men. Don't get me started," I said, not really wanting to get into the subject any deeper.

"Listen," Dalton said, "I got some exciting news for you."

"What?"

"I talked to the director of *Claudine* and they're interested in having you come in today to sing for them."

"Are you serious?"

"Yes ma'am. I told them how fabulous you are. The casting director said she knew of you."

Was that good or bad? "And they still want to see me?"

"Yes!"

"Will you be there, Dalton?"

"No, I'm nursing a little neck injury."

That was a tune I'd heard before. "Neck injury? Child, I hope you have good insurance because there's always something wrong with you."

"Thank God for SAG."

"Do you need anything?"

"I need you to go in there and sing your face off, bitch!"

It was a little too forceful, but I smiled. "Oh, I'll do that. Do you think they will let me bring cameras in for my reality show?"

"These are show business people, Yancey. You know they want a camera anytime they can get one."

"Okay. Where do I go?"

"The Michael Bennett Studios on Sixth Avenue and 56th Street."

"What time?"

"Six o'clock."

"I'm there, thanks, Dalton. I'm so glad you're in my life. Oh, by the way, I listened to your music when I was working out. You really are a great songwriter."

He was very pleased to hear that. "Thanks, Yancey, I'm glad you liked it. What did you think of 'Dearest One'?"

"I loved that one! That's the one where you had a female singing with you."

"Yeah, I see it as a duet."

That was the sort of song I loved to sing, back in the day.

"Great song."

"Thank you. I hope one day to hear you

singing it."

"With a guy?"

His voice sounded thoughtful. "I think two females can sing it. Maybe a younger singer because I wrote that as a tribute to my mother."

"You're probably right," I said as I looked at my watch. It was a little past four and I needed to get dressed.

"Good luck with the audition. I'm sure you'll be perfect."

"Let's hope so. I need to get ready."

"Bye, sweetie."

"Bye, Dalton. I'll text you after the audition."

"Do that."

Ava walked into the living room with her robe still on and a sleeping mask resting on her forehead. She looked like she was sleepwalking on her way to the kitchen.

"Good afternoon, Ava," I said, practically bursting inside with my fabulous news. This was going to kill her but good and I couldn't wait to tell her.

"Is it that late already?" she asked as she twisted off the top of a bottle of water. "I see the food fairy hasn't paid a visit overnight."

"I just got some incredible news so that might be changing soon," I said, but regretted telling Ava this as soon as the words left my mouth.

She was suddenly wide awake. "What? You contact that daughter of yours?"

"No, Ava. I told you I'm not interfering with Madison's life."

"I'd think about it if I were you. It would solve a lot of problems for the both of us. That little bitch is rich."

"That's her money and I'm happy for her. Madison made her money and I'm going to make mine again. Oh, am I going to make mine."

"You talking about that man who's promised you a reality show?"

"It's going to happen and you better believe that shit," I said firmly. "And I have an audition this evening for the lead in a Broadway show."

"What show?"

"I'm not telling."

"Why?"

"Just not. I shouldn't have said anything to you about my reality show."

Ava tried to suppress a laugh but couldn't stop herself. "Yeah, if you believe that I got a condo in Florida I want to sell you." She walked out of the kitchen back toward the guest room.

CHAPTER 8

Madison couldn't believe her ears.

"So they really want to give me a reality show, Daddy?"

"It sure sounds that way, sweetheart. Your manager called me a few hours ago and said VH-1 gave the project the green light. They want to follow you as you pick a new assistant and record your first album."

She took a bite of her turkey club sandwich from room service and shot her father a playful look of exasperation.

"CD, Daddy. It's a CD, not an album. Album is old school," Madison joked.

He laughed. "Whatever. Should I tell them you want to do it?"

"But what if the series is picked up?"

"Who said you couldn't do them both?"

"Nobody, but you know I have to do some dates with the *American Star* tour. Is there any way we can get out of that?"

"Now Madison, we made a commitment,

so no. But if you think it's too much, I'll tell VH-1 no. There's plenty of time down the line for some of the other projects."

"I don't want to wait. VH-1 will be important for my career. Especially when my music drops. I don't think it would be wise to make them mad at us."

"So I'm telling them yes," Derrick said. He picked a cold French fry from Madison's plate. "You're not going to eat those, are you?"

She put a hand over her belly. "No carbs. I have a photo shoot in two days," Madison said.

"So I don't guess the bread counts."

"Daddy, are you saying I'm gaining weight?"

He leaned over and kissed her on the forehead. "Sweetheart, I didn't say that and you know how I feel about diets. I just want you to eat healthy."

"You don't have to worry about me looking like Nicole Richie. I love my body."

"Good, and you should, no matter what. So we're telling VH-1 yeah."

She nodded her head brightly. "I think so."

"Now, you know they will want to be privy to every part of your life."

"They won't be following me into the

bathroom, will they?"

"You know I wouldn't let that happen."

"And never without makeup."

"I'm not going to promise that. I still can't get used to you wearing makeup anyway."

"Daddy, I'm growing up. I'm almost a full-fledged woman."

"I know but not too soon," Derrick said as he leaned over and kissed his daughter on her forehead again.

"Have you talked to Shanice lately?"

"Madison, what did I tell you about dipping into grown folks' business?"

"I'm almost a grown folks myself." Madison laughed.

"But not too soon, little girl."

CHAPTER 9

Hendrick Ramsey, Ava's dark-chocolate, exquisitely built personal trainer, stood behind her in the reflection of the floor-to-ceiling mirror, spotting her as she tried to complete her third set of squats.

He was the reason Ava had lost those fifteen-plus pounds, and she was grateful. She fought him at first, whining and complaining every time he urged her to "Push it! Give me just one more rep!" But she realized now that's what really made the difference in her fat loss and muscle gain.

Before Ava knew it, she was looking more like her old self again. Soon she found herself looking forward to seeing Hendrick's straight white smile, his cleanly shaven face and head, and of course those pectorals of granite and those buns of steel.

While in prison, Ava had all but lost her sexual appetite. She never thought about the act because all she had around her were women and male corrections officers. Despite how good-looking some of those officers were, Ava just couldn't get with that captive/prisoner sex thang. Sounded like the basis for a bad porno movie.

But now that Ava was out, her appetite was back. She was like a wild animal held captive for seven years, then turned loose in a jungle filled with delicious prey.

As Ava lunged deeply, the bar of weights across her shoulders, she noticed how much she was sweating — and how Hendrick was sweating too.

"Come on, baby. One more!" Hendrick's body was contoured to hers, his pelvis almost touching her behind, his strong hands on her waist, making sure she did the rep correctly. At twenty-seven years of age, Hendrick was young enough to be her son — no, make that her grandson — even though his thick mustache made him look years older.

Ava breathed through her mouth as she was taught, heaved the weight all the way up and, with Hendrick's help, set it on the squat hooks, then stepped out from under it.

"Girl, you are sweating something fierce," Hendrick said, smoothing a hand across Ava's forehand and showing her his palm coated with her perspiration.

Ava didn't know why, but that turned her on.

"Yeah, I sweat when I'm excited," Ava said, smiling, hoping he'd pick up on the flirtatious comment as she dabbed the crook of her neck with her towel.

Hendrick paused for a moment, as if to gauge the remark for its double meaning and then laughed it off.

Ava didn't know if that line was direct enough, so she told herself to try another.

"Okay," Hendrick said. "You're ready for the leg press." He walked the ten feet over to the machine. Ava followed behind him, appreciating how well he filled out his warm-up pants and imagining how he must look without them.

"So have a seat down there, and I'll start you out with a couple of ten-pound plates."

"Only if you sit with me," Ava said, a bit more aggressively this time. She took a step closer to Hendrick, a sensual look in her eyes. She knew she was crossing the line. But back in the day when Ava wanted a man, all she had to do was blink a single eyelash, and he would be drooling and stumbling over his own feet to get to her. In spite of her age she knew she still held some of that allure.

Hendrick gave her another weird look, then said, "Are you trying to —"

Ava stepped right up to him this time, not caring about the other people working out right next to them.

"Look, Hendrick. We're both very good-looking, consenting adults. And I have to be honest. I haven't had sex in dog years. But after working out with you all this time, I'm ready to remedy that." Ava slid her fingers down the length of one of his muscled arms. "And believe it or not, I think you're the lucky man I'd like to share that with."

Hendrick flashed that wonderful, bright smile of his and seemed to blush a little. "Ava, I'm flattered that you'd find me attractive, and chose me to be the one to . . . to . . . well, you know. But I'm a professional personal trainer, not an escort or a boy for hire. If you'd like to continue being trained by me, I can oblige you, but if you need more, I'd suggest you hire someone else."

His candor wounded her already vulnerable pride, but she laughed it off as if it meant nothing to her. Lowering herself onto the leg press machine, she said, "I was just testing you, you know that. I saw the way you've been looking at me, and I just wanted to make sure you weren't the type

223

to cross any lines, you understand."

Hendrick humored her. "You know, I thought that's what you were doing. I'm glad I passed the test."

"Me too. Now go over there and get those twenty-five-pound plates so we can continue my workout. I haven't forgotten I pay you by the hour, mister."

Ava's bat phone rang just as she got out of the shower after her workout. She flipped it open. "I was wondering when I was going to hear from you. I think I found a contact for those drugs you were looking for. But I'm going to need some big money."

"Find out how much you're going to need and we can get started. See if your person can get some weed and crack."

"I'm pretty sure this thug can get whatever we want," Ava said.

"You remember when you were in the joint, you told me that you thought Yancey kept all her love letters and emails from her lovers. Have you been able to locate them yet?"

"Uh, no. I didn't know you still wanted them," Ava said. "You haven't mentioned them since I last brought them up."

"I just want to make sure I got all the proof I need before we go in for the kill."

"I have to see if I can pick Yancey's brain to find out where she might keep them. She's been at home a lot lately so I haven't been able to snoop like I need to."

"So we're all set?"

Hendricks and all the money she was spending on her training popped into her head. "Can you send me some more money? I need to pay someone for his time."

"I can send you another thousand."

"I guess that will do." She sounded like that was barely sufficient, then pressed him on another matter. "Before you go, have you talked to your person about getting them to relax my parole yet? As soon as we finish our deal and I get my money, I want to head back to California."

"I haven't yet, but once we're close to finishing, I will get it done, Ava. I just need you to get those letters or any other evidence that proves Yancey was the one."

"Oh, she was the one, all right, but I will see what I can find out. You know we can get copies of her texts during that time."

"I know that but those letters and any pictures you can find will help as well."

"I know she keeps all her pictures especially when she's in them," Ava said, being evasive. That way she could explain her way out of it when no pictures in fact showed up.

"Has she made a move on her daughter yet?"

"I'm not sure, but if I know Yancey, she has some plan in her tiny little mind."

"Well, we have to make sure that the first meeting of mother and daughter is a bust. Yancey doesn't deserve a daughter like Madison."

Ava thought about how pure and noble Yancey was being about her daughter, and her lips twisted in disgust. "You got that right. I didn't deserve that bitch as a daughter. I can't tell you how many times I've rued the day that backstabbing child was born."

"Okay, Ava, get to work. Let me know when you get the stuff."

CHAPTER 10

I flung open the door of my town house, expecting to find S. Marcus standing there, but instead was greeted by a tall girl who was dressed like a reject from the WNBA.

"Can I help you?" I asked cautiously.

"Yeah, girly. Where is my boo Ava?" she said, walking into my house like she lived here. "You must be Yancey."

Raising a finger, I said, "Excuse me. Did I invite you in and how do you know my mother?"

Lyrical cocked her head, surprised. "Ava didn't mention me? She sure in the hell ran her trap about your ass a lot. Did she give you a copy of my disc?" She leaned down in my face. "Maybe you can help a bitch get a damn record deal? I heard you used to be in the music industry."

I backed away, outraged by her strong-arm come-on. "First of all, you need to stop all that damn cussing in my house. Who in the hell are you?"

"Bitch, don't speak to me like that. You might be Ava's daughter, but you don't mean shit to me. Besides, Ava told me she gave your ungrateful ass the money for the fuckin' house, so technically that makes it hers." She moved in closer again. "Now, miss high-and-mighty, would you like to start this introduction all over?"

She was breathing hard like some kind of wild animal. I needed to get to my phone so I could call 911 and get this crazy bitch out of my house.

"What is your name?" I said flatly.

"It's Lyrical. What about it?"

"And you met Ava where?"

"You call your mama by her first name? My mama would have knocked my ass into next week if I tried some shit like that," she said with a slight laugh. "But I met Ava — and I can call her that, because she ain't my mama — at the joint. She didn't tell you about me?" Lyrical went over and took a seat on the sofa. "I thought Ava would, since I've already been up in your crib several times since Ava and me got out."

She sat with her legs wide apart like a boy and looked like one, too, with her jeans and two white T-shirts and backward baseball cap. I hoped Ava hadn't been carrying on some lesbian prison affair in my home, but I put nothing past her.

Now I was ready to put my foot down. "That's real nice. What did you say your name was again, honey?"

"It's Lyrical, not honey. If I can remember your name, why can't you remember mine? I kinda got from Ava that you think you better than everybody. But I also know you a broke bitch just like me, so don't act all grand with me, *Yancey!*"

My fingers were itching to punch in digits on my phone. "Look, Ava's not here. I will tell her that you dropped by, but I'm going to have to ask you to leave because I'm expecting my boyfriend."

"Boyfriend accounted for." I turned around when I heard S. Marcus's voice. He walked into the town house carrying a black leather duffel bag.

Lyrical gave him a hungry once-over. "Aren't you a little old to be referring to a dude as your boyfriend, Yancey?"

S. Marcus came over and gave me a kiss on the cheek. He took a long, hard look at Lyrical and whispered, "You ain't been hiding nothing from me, Yancey?"

I laughed. "You don't think she's here to see me, do you? This is one of Ava's friends."

Lyrical leaped up from the sofa and gave

S. Marcus a handshake usually reserved for two men. She even gave him a brotha man hug. He looked surprised but he was smiling.

"Are you the record company guy that's gonna help me get a record deal?" Lyrical asked.

"I'm not in the music business. What are you, a rapper? What's your name?"

"Not really. The name is Lyrical. And I guess you could call me a little bit of hip-hop with neo-soul thrown in for good measure. What is it you do besides bone prissy Miss Yancey here?" Lyrical asked as she eyed me with a look that could best be described as leering.

S. Marcus went wide-eyed with a grin almost as wide. "You got any of your music on you?" he asked Lyrical. I couldn't believe he was still talking to this child.

"Oh, snaps," Lyrical said, snapping her fingers in anger. "This would be the one goddamn time I ain't got none of my music on me."

S. Marcus was smooth as he said, "I'm sure I'll see you again. I'm not in the music business, but I know people."

"I bet you do. Well, I'm going to dash so you two can get your mingling done." Lyrical gave me a knowing wink.

S. Marcus extended his hand. "Nice meeting you, Lyrical. I look forward to hearing some of your tracks."

"You're going to dig the hell out of my shit. Listen to what I say, dude. Yancey," she said, pointing, "don't forget to tell my girl Ava that I stopped by. I won't be happy if you do."

Crazy as the girl was, I was starting to warm up to her. In your face was just the way she was. "I will tell Ava you dropped by, sweetie."

"The name is Lyrical. But I'm sure that's your way of making me feel small. Trust me, Yancey. It takes a little more than that to make a bitch like me feel low class."

Lyrical popped out the door, leaving me standing in front of S. Marcus completely flabbergasted.

"Can you believe her?" I asked.

"I like her. She was cool."

"Cool?" I pulled back and looked at him. "You're kidding me. Aren't you? I didn't know you were into lesbos."

"Looks like your mother is or maybe it's a prison temporary thing." He glanced around the place. "So, when am I going to meet this Ava?"

"Don't talk like that. And you will meet her soon enough. Besides, Ava would never do something like that. If she did, it would be one of those lipstick lesbians." I gave him an assessing look. "I still can't believe you would say something like that."

S. Marcus wasn't paying any attention, though. He nodded his head in contemplation. "She might be just what we need."

"*We?* Marcus, what in the *hell* are you talking about?" I asked. I hoped this boy wasn't having some kind of sick threesome in mind with Lyrical and me performing some sex act for him. I was a lot of things, but having sex with my man and a female was not in my plans.

"We should see if she's working. I think she'd be fascinating as your assistant for the show." He turned to me, swept up in his idea. "It would be great to see the two of you interact. It could be great television. A gay woman would be so much better than a gay man. Everybody has done that already."

I was appalled. "I won't have that *thing* working for me. Matter of fact, as soon as Ava brings her ass back home, I'm telling her don't ever have that thing in my house again."

Marcus took the tips of my hands and tickled the tops of them. "Come on, Yancey. Don't make a rash decision. Think about what I'm saying. This could be one of the hooks we need."

"Stop. That tickles," I said with a light slap.

"I know." He kissed me quickly on the lips.

I pulled back. "Marcus, please tell me you're not serious."

"Then I'd be lying and I told you I'd never do that."

I took a deep breath in an attempt to calm my nerves. For the first time I noticed he'd brought a black bag. "What's in the bag?"

He instantly looked uncomfortable. "Oh, nothing really, but I need to leave it here for a minute. I got a meeting when I leave you."

"That's cool. I will keep it for you."

"So what about our girl Lyrical?"

"Damn, you remember her name. What is that about? So you think she could help?"

"Seriously, Yancey, I think it would be the most brilliant casting in reality television. There's never been anyone like her. I want Jeff to meet her. If he feels the same way, then I think we got to do it."

"Jeff won't like her," I protested weakly, afraid he in fact would.

"How about a deal? If he doesn't, then I'll drop it, but if he does, will you promise me you'll ask her to come work for you?"

I hated this idea. Still, I was aware that I had to appear reasonable, or the show would be called off before it started. "Only if Jeff agrees, and I need to be there when he meets her or 'him.' Shit, you're going to leave me alone with a thing like that? Aren't you worried she might try to turn me out?"

He pulled me in close. "If I do my job, then that won't ever be a problem." S. Marcus kissed me again, this time deeper, causing me to pull him by his expensive tie toward my bedroom.

"I think it's time for a little afternoon delight."

CHAPTER 11

Ava glided into the restaurant at the Four Seasons on 57th Street as if on air. After losing fifteen pounds, she felt light as a feather.

She stepped to the host's podium, wearing a beautiful peach knee-length silk dress that clung to her newly visible curves. The shoulder straps were sparkling sequins that matched her diamond earrings, and a breathtaking tennis bracelet was draped on her wrist. She was clearly overdressed for the dinner crowd at the popular restaurant.

"Table for two, madam?" the host, a tall, thin man with a pencil mustache and a very bad fake French accent, asked.

"Does it look like there are two people here?" Ava said, catching an attitude because she felt the host was making a smart remark regarding her single status.

"So sorry. Obviously." He grabbed a purple velvet-covered menu and led Ava to a table. She rejected it, saying it was close to the kitchen, and asked to see another.

When they stopped at a table Ava found acceptable, she stood motionless beside one of the chairs. He paused as if expecting her to seat herself, but Ava nodded her head at the chair. She then cleared her voice, waiting for the host to pull the chair out for her. When he finally got the clue, she gingerly took the seat. "Thank you," she said in a dainty voice, and then accepted the menu.

"Your waiter will be right with you, madam." The host bowed slightly and disappeared.

The elegant golden room was dimly lit by candles that danced in the center of all the tables. Most of the parties were small, couples leaning across the white cloths, holding hands and sneaking kisses and drinking wine.

If Ava weren't so confident, she might have felt a little self-conscious about being alone in a restaurant so obviously made for couples and powerful business moguls closing deals. But she was the new Ava, and not the old patronized one who dragged her fat, broke, tired ass out of jail four months ago. No, she was the new, fit, spectacularly made-over, not as broke Ava, and there was no way she was feeling the slightest bit of shame. She was going to have herself a nice meal, and a wonderful time by herself tonight, and if anyone glanced her way, she'd look them in the face like, "What!" then tip her glass of wine and continue eating.

Ava opened the menu, even though she didn't need to. She had never been to this restaurant, but if the *New York Times* food critic was right, she was in for a treat. The writer had said the filet was to die for, and the prawns were so succulent they'd bring you right back to life.

The waitress, a beautiful, young, cinnamon-colored girl who reminded Ava of Yancey when she was younger, approached the table smiling. "Would you prefer sparkling water or flat tonight, ma'am?"

"Oh darling, sparkling, of course," Ava said, raising her arm in the air so the waitress could see her expensive bracelet.

"Okay, I will get that for you. Would you like to order a drink? Maybe a glass of wine."

"In a moment. Tell me love, do you have a tasting menu that comes with wines?"

"No, ma'am."

Ava acted put off. "Well, you should. All the top restaurants are doing that."

The waitress blinked in hesitation, not used to anyone criticizing this fabulous place. "Would you like to hear the specials this evening?"

"No, thank you, sweetie. I know exactly what I want. The filet, medium well, not one degree warmer, and the prawns — the biggest ones you got — with asparagus, and hold the rice. If I never eat another grain in my life, it'll be too soon."

The waitress laughed, writing down the order. "And to drink?"

"Wine. White. The best you've got. Surprise me," Ava said. "And bring the bottle, baby."

"Yes, ma'am," the waitress said, then left to place the order.

Ava made herself comfortable. When a basket of bread and butter was set before her, she simply pushed it away and took a sip of her water.

She felt a staring eye on her, and when she looked up, she noticed a man at a corner table sitting by himself. His face was so wrinkled, it resembled a road map, and his hair implants were so bad that Ava could almost see each individual hole the strand of hair was plugged into.

Ava quickly looked away, but when she glanced back, he smiled with a mouth of what looked like fake teeth and raised his wineglass.

Okay, she was hard up for money, Ava reminded herself, taking another sip of her sparkling water. But even if she were living on the street, with nothing but a loaf of white bread to last her a week, she didn't think she would give that guy the time of day.

Ten minutes later, Ava's wine and her meal came. The waitress happily placed it down in front of her. "Does everything look okay?"

"It looks perfect," Ava said.

"Enjoy."

"Oh, I intend to." Ava surveyed every morsel on the beautiful white china with the gold band surrounding it. She didn't know where to start, so she speared a single piece of the grilled asparagus with her fork and bit off the end. It tasted fabulous. Next was a small slice of the steak. Ava was certainly going to eat it all but maybe not tonight. She thought how the succulent beef would make the perfect addition to a salad the following day. Besides, she didn't want to gain back an ounce of the weight she'd lost until she'd found a new husband or mate.

About fifteen minutes later, the waitress

appeared and asked again if everything was to her liking.

"Yes, it's wonderful," Ava said, starting to regret what she knew she would have to do to the sweet girl. But Ava pulled her mind off that as she took in the sweet aroma of the steak and shrimp wafting up from the plate. She was grateful that no one was sitting across from her, because her stomach growled like there was a bear inside, trying to get out.

Ava motioned for the waitress to pour a glass of wine almost to the top. She gave her knife and fork a rest, but only for a minute. She kept telling herself, Take small bites, hon. Small bites.

Twenty-five minutes later, Ava's belly was comfortably full, and she had a buzz going. Ava was twisted quite nicely, and she smiled wide as the attractive waitress came back to check on her.

"Was everything okay?"

"Wonderful!" Ava said, smiling, composing herself in such a way that the woman could not tell she was a little pissy. "May I have the check now, please?"

"Sure," the waitress said. She set a small leather-covered binder in front of Ava, who opened it and tried to focus her drunken eyes on the tiny numbers on the check.

When she did, she saw that she had eaten and drunk $163.54 worth of food and wine.

Ava smiled again, looking up at the waitress, who was smiling back. "I can sign this to my room, correct?" Ava asked.

"Of course," the waitress said. "Just put your room number there, and signature there."

Ava grabbed the pen, did as she was told, writing in the huge tip she would've left the woman if she were staying in that hotel and did have money. She handed the binder back to the waitress, her heart beating quickly now.

"I'll just go run this and bring you your receipt," the waitress said.

"Okay," Ava said, her heart beating even faster now, already preparing to make her getaway.

Ava kept her eye on the woman. When she disappeared behind two swinging kitchen doors, Ava was up, throwing the cloth napkin out of her lap onto the floor, snatching her purse from the seat beside her and scrambling away from her table.

As she turned, she caught a glimpse of the old man who had been eyeing her. He had a repulsed look on his face, like he knew what she was doing.

But Ava thought, The hell with him. If he

wanted the bill paid so much, he could hobble over there on his cane and pay it himself.

Ava blew past the host, saying, "It was wonderful. I'll see you again soon." She didn't wait for his reply, just looked over her shoulder, hoping she didn't see her waitress as she pushed her way out the restaurant's front door.

On her high heels, Ava did more than glide through the hotel lobby. She was practically jogging. If she got caught, it would be theft, and a sure violation of her parole. She would go back to jail, lose everything she had been working so hard to get.

No, she couldn't let that happen, and she realized maybe that's what made this escape so exciting. Maybe even why she pulled the stunt in the first place.

Once Ava had broken through the hotel's exit, hurried down the street, and turned the corner, she stopped and leaned against the brick wall of a jewelry store to catch her breath. Her chest heaving, her body tingling, Ava, a huge smile on her face, had to admit that was the most exciting thing she had done in quite some time.

CHAPTER 12

As Madison sang in the rehearsal room for her teacher, she imagined the windows behind her were a glamorous stage and that she was performing for a huge, cheering audience. She tingled from head to toe, feeling the flow of silky-smooth sounds flowing all around her.

"Bravo, girl!" Nicole Springer-Stovall cheered. "Sing out!"

Madison hit the last notes and held them, making her voice echo off the shiny wood floor. Then, as her teacher pushed away from the piano, she took a swig of water from the bottle she'd set on the window ledge.

"Great job, Madison," Nicole said, turning on the piano stool, pushing up the sleeves of her soft brown sweater. "I think you're ready to start recording that CD. I plan to be the first one in line to buy it."

Madison grinned. "Thanks, Nicole. I

couldn't have done it without your help. Now all I need is to get some songs that will be hits."

Nicole walked over to Madison in the warm sunlight. "I'm sure you'll have your choice of songwriters, Madison."

A worried look twisted Madion's face. "Thank you, but all the songs my producers have brought to me are bubble gum stuff, like what Miley Cyrus sings. My daddy always had me listening to Marvin Gaye and Stevie Wonder. I grew up with old-school R & B and I'd like to add youthful twists to some of the classics or something new."

Nicole shrugged. "Like I said, you won't have any problems."

Madison wished she could be as confident as the wonderful woman at her side. "You know the day I first met you, I was so excited that I went home to google you. It said you were directing and teaching voice in Atlanta at Spelman College."

Nicole gazed down at the bustling Manhattan street. Taxicab horns and screeching bus brakes punctuated the silence. "I did that for a while, but my husband, Jared, got promoted to headquarters here and suddenly the family was living in New York." Her tone turned wistful as she added, "I loved living in Atlanta and didn't think I'd ever live in New York again."

Madison had found out so much about Nicole, including one piece of information that interested her very deeply. "I saw where you were in a lot of musicals besides *Dreamgirls*."

"Yeah, I was blessed. I had a great career," Nicole said as she took the stool near the piano again.

Madison stepped closer, resting an arm on the piano. "Can I ask you something?"

"Sure."

"Do you want your children, I mean like your daughters, to follow in your footsteps by going into show business?"

Nicole, smoothing her sleek brown skirt, shrugged. "I just want my children to be happy, Madison. I think that's what all parents want for their kids."

Madison looked at the floor and said with a soft, sad voice: "I wish that were true."

Nicole saw the tears glazing the teen's eyes. "What's the matter, Madison? You sound sad."

Madison wiped her eyes and hardened her voice. "No, I'm okay. Maybe I'm just a little melancholy about not really knowing my own mother, but I have the greatest dad in the world and he more than made up for my not having a mother."

"God always equalizes things, Madison. I hope you know that," Nicole said as she gently brushed her hand across Madison's smooth cheek.

The girl stared up with curious eyes. "Can I ask you one more question?"

"Sure, Madison. Ask me whatever you like."

Madison paused, not sure how to ask her next question. Not sure if she wanted to know the answer. Would Nicole even give her an honest answer?

Her teacher spoke softly, "Madison, you have something you want to ask me, sweetheart?"

Madison's heart pounded as she forced the words from her mouth: "What did you think of Yancey Braxton? I read on Google that she once was your understudy but later took your role."

A sudden jolt of surprise shot through Nicole, making her cast a quizzical look at Madison.

"Yancey Braxton. Now that's a name I haven't heard in a long time." Nicole laughed as if she were enjoying a private joke.

"So you remember her?" Madison asked eagerly.

"Oh yeah, I remember Yancey. Trust me,

Madison, you don't forget a person like Yancey Braxton."

Madison couldn't figure out whether the name was bringing back good or bad memories for her teacher. "So what did you think of her? Was she talented?"

A faraway look swept over Nicole's face. "Oh, yes. Yancey was talented and very beautiful. She was headstrong and always knew what she wanted when it came to her career."

Madison studied her teacher's face and said, "So definitely not the mother type."

Nicole shrugged slightly. "I don't think any of us were thinking about being parents at the time. We were too busy worrying about the next gig."

Nicole studied Madison's intense expression, trying to find clues about where this conversation was going. Why did the girl care so much about Yancey?

"But I bet if you had a child," Madison said, "say when you were young, I think you would have given up your career."

"Thank God that wasn't an issue for me." Nicole exhaled with relief. "But I did have friends who had kids early and still managed to have successful careers."

An *aha!* look flashed in Madison's eyes. "Exactly, so it could be done!"

Nicole focused hard on the girl's curious eyes. "Is there any particular reason you're asking me about Yancey Braxton, Madison?"

Madison opened her mouth to answer —

"Are you two finished?" A deep voice boomed through the room.

It was Derrick.

"Oh, Daddy!" Madison exclaimed. She walked briskly over to him and pulled him by the hands toward her teacher. "I want you to meet the wonderful lady I've been telling you about."

He chuckled, allowing her to tug him across the shiny floor. "Okay Madison, I'm following you."

They stopped by the piano, where Nicole stood, looking up at this man who gave tall, dark and handsome a whole new meaning.

Madison could barely contain her excitement. "Daddy, this is my voice teacher, Nicole Springer-Stovall. See? I told you how pretty she is."

Nicole blushed and patted Madison lovingly on the shoulders. She then extended her hand and said, "Madison has been bragging on you ever since we met. It's so nice to meet you, Derrick."

Madison searched their expressions for clues about how they were reacting to each other. Her father had to see how amazing her teacher was.

"Nice meeting you, Mrs. Stovall," Derrick said.

"Please," the teacher said warmly, "call me Nicole."

Derrick smiled. "Tell me, Nicole, how did Madison do today?"

Nicole cast a happy look at her pupil. "She's doing great. Your daughter has major talent."

Madison blushed.

"I think you're right," Derrick said, beaming at Madison. "You ready for some lunch, Madison?"

Madison looked back and forth between her father and her teacher. "Sure, can we get some sushi? Nicole, why don't you join us?"

Nicole smiled but shook her head. "Thanks, Madison. I wish I could, but I promised to meet my daughters at their school for lunch. But please give me a rain check."

Madison looked at her father and said, "See, Daddy? I told you what a great mother she is."

"Yes, you did, Madison," Derrick said, flashing a broad smile at the teacher as he wrapped his arms around his daughter.

Feeling all this love right after an excellent

performance in her singing lesson, Madison felt like she could become the biggest superstar ever. Better yet, she could stay right here and feel this happy forever.

CHAPTER 13

I was spending my evening watching an *I Love New York* marathon thinking, if this simple bitch can get a reality show, then certainly I can. I mean, this crap was barely watchable and it was clear to anyone with half a brain that this chile wasn't looking for love but a career as a D-list actress. This shit made *Charm School* look like *Masterpiece Theatre.*

Just as I was getting ready to turn to Bravo, Ava walked in with a satisfied look on her face, wearing one of my dresses.

"Where have you been? And what are you doing with my dress on?" I asked.

"Hello to you, too, darling. Doesn't this look lovely on me?" she said, spinning for my approval.

She looked better these days. I was willing to concede that point. "Where have you been?"

"So are you my probation officer now?

I've been out, darling, enjoying the city. I think it's time for me to reclaim my place in New York society, so I've been out scouting." Ava went over to the bar and started to make herself a drink.

"Isn't that against the rules?"

"Yancey, please mind your own business, love. I don't see that horrid man until the end of the week. This will be out of my system by then." She picked up the bottle and poured herself a tall glass. "Have we gotten the final word on our reality series?"

"You mean *my* series," I said, folding my arms. "Not a final word. Have you ever seen *I Love New York?*"

"Oh, yes. That was a popular show in jail. I love Mother Patterson. Can't you see me playing that role in your little show? That is *if* you get it."

"No, I can't," I said quickly. That was the main reason I didn't want Ava anywhere near the cameras, mugging and taking time away from me. That New York child was crazy for letting her overbearing mother steal the show right from under her.

"Now, Yancey, I know you're not afraid of me being the star of your show. Are you, darling?"

Both of us knew full well what the answer to that was. "Fix me a drink."

"Do I look like your maid or bartender? I think not. You better bring your ass over here and fix yourself a drink."

I didn't feel like fighting or talking with Ava, and so I just got up from the sofa and went into my bedroom, shutting the door behind me.

The next afternoon S. Marcus came by the town house with some not-so-good news. Jeff thought Lyrical absolutely had to be a part of my show as my trusty assistant.

I shook my head but kept my cool. "I have said this before and I'll say it again. This is a bad idea. That girl is nothing but trouble." We were sitting at the end of my dining room table, and I still had on my black nightgown. Was I going to have to do S. Marcus right on the spot to get my way? I didn't have to worry about Ava walking in because I knew she had a meeting with her parole officer.

"Come on, Yancey. I tell you, the contrast between you and Lyrical will create drama people want to see. You see, with you being so pretty and feminine and Lyrical being kind of hard will be just great. Jeff liked her as well. I knew he would."

Something was up. No one told me about this face to face. "When did he meet her?"

"A couple of days ago."

"Why wasn't I told?"

"We just flew her down for the day and she was back home before dinner," he said, trying to play it down. "Can you believe she'd never been on a plane?"

"Not hard to believe at all. So has she agreed to do it?"

"Not yet, but I think you can convince her. If not, maybe your mother can help us out."

I shook my hands, indicating a complete rejection of that notion. "How many times do I have to tell you I don't want Ava involved in any way?"

"Then you need to close the deal," he said firmly.

So now it was up to me? What happened to Mr. I'll take care of everything?

"Can I get something to drink?" I asked, changing the subject. "What do you want? Do you want something clear or dark?"

"Just a bottle of water."

"How long are you going to be here?"

"I'm going back to Miami as soon as I leave you."

I went to the kitchen and got a bottle of water for the both of us. I opened a button that held my nightgown together. If S. Marcus had time, I would start my plan to keep this girl out of my life. When I walked back into the dining room, I saw S. Marcus looking at the cleavage now peeking out.

"Damn, girl, you look good in that. Have I seen it before?"

"I don't know," I said with a sexy smile. "I have several of them in all different colors. But this silk is feeling warm on my body. Do you mind if I take it off?"

"What do you have on under it?"

"Nothing," I replied.

"Then I don't think you should do that, because my flight leaves in a couple of hours." I was surprised by the rejection, and his face darkened into a frown. "Besides, I have something else I need to talk to you about, and I don't think I can stand the distraction of you sitting at the dining room table naked. But I will keep that in mind for future nights of pleasure."

"Are you sure?" I asked coyly.

"Yancey, you know there isn't anything I like better than making love to you, but I got something to talk to you about."

Now I was concerned by his mysterious tone. "Does it have to do with my show?"

"Not really. Well, sort of."

"What?" Please don't let this fall through, not after we got so close.

"Let me go get my briefcase."

S. Marcus walked from the dining room and returned moments later with the black bag. He sat it on the table and snapped it open. The bag was filled with money. There stacked neatly beside each other were hundred-dollar bills. I don't think I've ever seen so much money at one time.

Alarmed, I asked, "Marcus, what are you doing with all that money?"

"I took it from my bank account."

"Why are you carrying it around like that? That's dangerous."

He tried to make light of my worry. "It's fine. But I need you to do me a favor."

"What?" I had no idea where this was going. Was I about to lose my show *and* my man?

"I need you to keep this for me. You can take some to buy yourself some new clothes for the show," he offered.

"Like a wardrobe allowance?" I asked, hoping this was legit.

"Yeah, that's what we call it."

"But in cash? Why don't you just give me a credit card?"

S. Marcus looked at me in exasperation. "Yancey, come on and just do what I ask."

"I don't know if I feel safe having that amount of money just laying around the house." Suddenly I had an image of Ava finding the money in my closet and stuffing her bra with as much as she could get inside and then denying she knew anything about it when I confronted her.

"Don't you have a safe here?"

"Yes, but it's a small one. All that money wouldn't fit in there. I have a safety deposit box at the bank. But if I'm going to do that, I might as well put it into my account."

"Why don't you open another account, so it won't get mixed up with your funds?" S. Marcus suggested.

This whole thing bothered me, but I didn't want to screw up my chances with the show. "Don't worry. I don't have that much money in my Citibank account, but if you like I'll open a new account and put it in there. How long do you want me to keep it?"

"For a couple of months. By then this mess will be over."

My barometer shot up a few degrees. "What mess?"

"Well, I got a little problem," he explained, looking sheepishly at me. "It's a young lady from Michigan I use to kick it with. The bitch ain't nothing but a gold digger. She claims I'm the father of her little girl, but that shit ain't true. I took a paternity test and it came back negative. Now she's claiming I had one of my boys take the test and she's suing me for child support. That little girl is almost four years old. Do you know how much back child support that would be?"

My heart dropped at the thought of S. Marcus possibly hustling me. "Could it be your child, Marcus?"

"Hell, no," he scoffed.

"Then take the test again. Prove to her it's not yours and this mess will be over."

"Look, are you going to do this or not? My lawyer told me she might try to get my bank records to see how much I'm worth. I promise you, Yancey, soon as this is over I will take the money back and never get you involved with my problems. It's only temporary."

S. Marcus gave me a puppy-dog pleading look. He'd done so much for me and I wanted to help him out. Besides, having a bank account with a bunch of zeros behind it would be nice, even if it weren't mine. Maybe I could leverage a line of credit using Marcus's money as collateral. Yeah, I should do this, I told myself. I've done crazier things.

"Okay," I allowed, still not feeling right about it, "but you're sure this is on the up-and-up?"

"I promise you, Yancey. Besides, you're going to be a big star and make me even more money. Why would I do anything to harm you? Baby girl, you haven't been anything but good to me ever since we met."

His look was so sincere that I accepted his flattery. "Okay. Give it to me. I'll take it to the bank first thing tomorrow."

"Thanks, baby," S. Marcus said, then checked his watch. "Damn, I need to get moving so I won't miss my flight. Give Daddy a kiss."

I kissed S. Marcus gently on the lips and I felt his huge hand caress my left breast. Damn, that felt good.

I took hold of his hand and held it in place. "You sure you don't have time for a quickie?" I asked.

"I would love to, baby, but I got to get back to the city tonight. I've got a lot going on, including a meeting that starts with breakfast in the morning." He gave me a wink. "Just put it into my pussy account alongside my money."

"I can do that," I said. I gave S. Marcus a quick kiss, and before I could blink, he was out the door.

Early evening Dalton showed up at my apartment with a guest. I opened the door

259

and said, "Dalton, what a pleasant surprise."

"Hey girl," he said as he walked in and gave me a kiss on the cheek. A tall, well-built dark-skinned guy followed in silence.

"What are you guys up to?"

"Yancey, this is Anderson, my friend I've been telling you about."

"Hi Anderson," I said as I extended my hand toward him. He didn't reciprocate. He was well dressed in a houndstooth jacket, black turtleneck and white gabardine slacks. He had a neatly groomed beard and mustache and his hair was cut low. He could have easily passed as a model or an Ivy League scholar.

"Hello," he said in a deep voice. Nothing else.

I turned my attention back to Dalton and couldn't help but notice that there was something wrong with his lips. He was trying to hide it with an excessive amount of Vaseline but it was clear something had gone wrong. Did he have some kind of disease like herpes or had he been stung by a bee? I didn't want to ask because I didn't know how much information he'd shared with Anderson.

"Why don't we go in the living room and take a seat?"

"We don't have much time, darling, we're

on our way to the movies, but I thought I should come over here and tell you this myself."

"Tell me what?"

"You didn't get the job."

"What?"

"They wanted younger and went with some girl who got kicked off *American Star* during the second week."

"You're lying!"

"Young and pretty will do it every time."

"Damn, I really wanted that job."

"Would you take an understudy role?"

"Hell no!"

"Just what I thought. But there will be other jobs, sweetie," Dalton said as he leaned over and kissed me. A closer look at his lips clearly told me it wasn't a bee sting and I wasn't feeling this Anderson character.

When I shut the door on Dalton and his friend, I leaned my back against the door wondering if Dalton was in some kind of trouble.

CHAPTER 14

Ava sat before Mr. Lomax's desk watching his tilted bald head look down at her file. She knew what he was going to say before he opened his big fat mouth with his fat, stubble-covered cheeks.

"Sorry you had to wait so long. I had a little backlog today."

"Why should today be any different?" Ava asked, wanting so badly to chastise him for keeping her waiting for over two hours, but she knew better than to cross him.

"We discussed how important your getting a job is, didn't we?" Mr. Lomax said, looking up and pulling off his reading glasses. They hung around his neck by a chain.

"Yes, and I've been trying."

"Trying," Mr. Lomax said, closing the manila folder and pushing it aside on his desk. "You've been sent to several temp centers that had open positions. When I called to follow up, they said you either didn't show or declined the jobs."

"I'm a stage actress, not a receptionist; a singer, not a secretary," Ava said.

"You're an ex-con, according to the state of New York, Middlebrooks."

"That's a mean thing to say, Mr. Lomax."

"You don't turn down jobs like you have a choice in the matter. I think I'm going to have to show you I mean business," Mr. Lomax said, raising his voice, his face starting to turn red.

"Look," Ava said, scooting to the edge of her seat. "If they could just find something a little more suited to my liking —"

"What!" Mr. Lomax said, shooting up from his chair, leaning over his desk, giving Ava an incredulous look. "Do you understand what could happen here, what's most likely about to happen?"

"Uh, no," Ava said in a way that suggested whatever it was, it couldn't be that bad.

Mr. Lomax lowered his big body back into his chair and then slid open one of his desk drawers. He pulled out a sheet of paper, grabbed a pen and started writing.

Ava tried to get a look at what he was scribbling on the page. "Um, what are you doing?"

"It's clear that you're violating the conditions of your parole," he said calmly, not looking up.

"What! Does that mean what I think it does? You trying to send me back to —"

"That's what I'm going to recommend."

Ava had to think quickly. There was no way in hell she was going back to that place. She wouldn't survive that again. She had just found a wonderful stylist. Didn't this man understand that?

Ava stood from her chair and approached the side of the desk. The dress she wore only showed the tiniest bit of cleavage, but Ava leaned forward to expose as much of her breasts to the fat man as she could. "Mr. Lomax, please."

He looked up from the paper. "It's too late," he said, then looked back down, but only after taking a longer than normal glance at Ava's plump twins. "I'm tired of wasting time with you. You obviously think this is a game."

"No, Mr. Lomax," Ava said in the sweetest dumb-blonde voice she could create. She shuffled farther around the desk until she stood in front of him. "I promise I'll never waste your time again if you just give me one more chance."

Mr. Lomax looked up and over his glasses at her. Ava could tell he was giving it a little thought. She just needed to give him a nudge.

Ava placed her hand on his thigh, just above his knee, squeezed it a little, and said, "I swear, if I don't get a job in the next two weeks, you can do whatever you want with me."

Mr. Lomax looked down at Ava's hand on his knees, then up at her with narrowed eyes. "Don't make promises you know you won't keep."

"No, Mr. Lomax," Ava said suggestively. "I'll bend over backward before I break a promise."

Mr. Lomax gave Ava another long look, then balled up the form on his desk and pitched it into the wastepaper basket in the corner. "Okay. You're free for right now, but let me say this, you don't want to try me."

CHAPTER 15

"OMG, Madison, OMG! Are you serious?" Caressa squealed like the last girl selected for the varsity cheerleader squad.

"So do you want to do it?" Madison asked. She was holding Caressa's hands to keep them from shaking as the two of them sat on the edge of her bed. Madison was thrilled to make her best friend so deliriously happy.

"Be on your show. Are you serious? What's my character's name?"

"Caressa, silly. It's a reality show. You'll be playing yourself."

"Oh, I'm so slow," she said, shaking her head. "A reality show. That's even better. But what about the show for Disney?"

"I'm going to do that as well. The cameras will follow me as I shoot the series. So you'll be on the set with me, only this time not as my assistant but as my best friend."

Caressa threw her arms around Madison's

shoulders. "Madison, you're the best. This is going to be so great." She pulled back and said with a wide smile, "Now people will know me just like you."

Something about that didn't sit right with Madison. It felt a little too fast, too complete before they'd even started. But Madison let go of her suspicions. "I'm sure you're going to have a lot of fans, Caressa. You're so beautiful and nice. But I warn you, you will have your share of haters as well."

"Who cares about haters? I can't wait to tell my parents and Wallace."

"Are you still talking to him?" Wallace Davis was the blue-eyed basketball star who Caressa had a mad crush on. The only problem was, he was a ladies' man and didn't treat Caressa in a manner that made either her or Madison happy.

"Well," she said, coming down from her high long enough to explain, "he calls sometimes. But since he's been away at college, I don't hear from him as often."

"Where did he end up?"

"Auburn University."

"And that's where? Down south?"

"It's in Auburn, Alabama. He asked me to come down for a visit, but since I'm doing the show, I won't be able to do that." The somber tone that suddenly came on suggested that Caressa was weighing her options.

"Do you think he'd let us film the visit?" Madison asked. "That would be a great episode. The two of us visiting a college campus. I have a lot of fans in college. They all watch *American Star.*"

Caressa brightened, and Madison felt like she had come to the rescue once more. "That would be so cool."

"And the producers would pay for our trips. When are you going to talk with him again?"

"I can call him tonight. I texted him this morning, but I haven't heard back yet. I don't see any reason why he wouldn't want us, though."

"So just ask him," Madison suggested with a shrug. "If he doesn't, I'm sure the producers will come up with several other things for us to do."

"You know what would be cool for them to film on the show? You looking for your birth mother."

"What? Are you crazy? I don't want to do that." Madison had resigned herself years ago that she would never meet her birth mother. From all that her father had told her, the woman wasn't likely to be responsive even if Madison took the trouble to locate her. Not that she hadn't thought about this before. "Besides, who needs her now that I'm famous?" Madison said. She got off the bed and went to her dresser, picked up a brush and slowly stroked her hair.

Caressa knew that's what Madison did when she didn't want to talk about something. "Sorry that I brought it up, Madison," she whispered.

Madison didn't respond but continued to brush her hair and mouthed the number to each stroke.

Derrick walked into the room and exchanged a small smile with his daughter while she continued to brush her hair.

He thought for a moment. "They asked me about your mother."

"Who asked?"

"The producers." Derrick kept his eyes fixed on the floor, unable to talk about the topic any better than his daughter.

"What did you tell them?"

"I told them you don't have a relationship with your mother."

"Why didn't you just tell the truth? That my real mother is dead," Madison said as she turned away slightly.

"Your aunt died, sweetheart. That's the truth. Your mother, I mean your birth mother, is still very much alive and while they didn't say so, I think they know Yancey Braxton is your mother."

"Who told them that?"

"I don't know, Madison, showbiz people have a way of finding out things. Besides, don't you remember how I told you that when you turn eighteen, if you want to meet Yancey, I will make it happen."

"But I'm not eighteen yet, Daddy."

"You will be soon. Why are you scared to meet her, Maddy?"

"I'm not scared."

"I think you are."

"I'm scared I might grow up to be like her."

"Your personality is already clearly defined, Maddy, you don't have to worry about that."

"So the producers brought this up?"

"I guess they think it would be good for the show."

"Absolutely not."

"See what I mean? Doing this show is not as simple as it seems."

"I thought they were just going to concentrate on my show and my music. They have no right to pry into my personal life like that," Madison said.

"And they haven't yet, sweetheart, but I'm

just telling you they might."

"I don't want to talk about this again. Have you thought any more about me getting my own place? It's time for me to have my own life."

Derrick stood up from the sofa and walked over to his daughter and put his arms around her. He whispered, "I think it's too soon for you to be living alone, Madison. Your daddy is not ready to let go of his little girl."

She sighed, sad at the thought of leaving her father's house, but excited by the prospect of independence. "I know, Daddy, but it's time. And it's not like I'm going to be living alone. I'll get a roommate and a dog."

"Let me think about this some more. I don't think I'm going to change my stance."

"Why not?"

"I don't know, Madison. I need to pray on this."

"But it's my money," Madison pouted. "Can't I buy a place of my own with my own money?"

"You're a star out there," Derrick said pointing to the door, "but in here, I'm still your father."

"What if I agree to meet Yancey? Then will you let me get my own place?"

"Are you trying to bribe me? "

"Not really, but just let me know what you decide," Madison said and grabbed her keys off the counter.

"Oh, Madison, I forgot to tell you the real estate agent did find an old brownstone in Harlem that she thinks will be great for Jenny's Place."

"Cool beans. When can we see it?"

"I'll find out."

"I was thinking about asking Ms. Nicole to help out with the voice lessons."

"Let's do it!"

"Okay, Daddy. See you later."

"Where are you going, young lady?"

"I'm going to the studio to redo some of the tracks for my CD. I'll be back."

"Make sure you're back in time for dinner."

"Daddy, you know I would never miss a chance to spend time with the best daddy in the world," Madison laughed.

"You think you're slick, don't you, little girl?"

"Not slick, just smart, Daddy."

CHAPTER 16

"I only have ten minutes, Ms. Middle-brooks." TV director Cole Cantwell was a no-nonsense type, and Ava for once had something besides pure nonsense to feed him. Cutting to the chase, he asked, "Can you tell me why it was so important that you meet with me?"

Ava took a seat in his midtown office. She adjusted her jacket and turned her knees toward the desk as if presenting an invitation.

"Thanks for seeing me. That little assistant of yours told me eleven o'clock sharp and then had me waiting for almost an hour." Cantrell shifted in his chair. As the director of Yancey's reality show, he had more to concern himself with. Seeing his impatience, Ava rushed ahead. "Now, I realize you're a busy man being a director and all, but I'm a busy woman and my time is important too. If you need to get a new assistant, just let me know because maybe I can help you with that."

He gave her a cold look. "I'm sorry, but I had a conference call that went a little over and thanks, but I'm perfectly happy with Liz. Now, how can I help you?" he asked, taking a swig of his Gatorade.

Ava returned his look with an even cooler smile. "It's more how I can help you. You're a director and one of the producers on my daughter's reality show, right?"

"Who is your daughter?"

"Yancey Harrington Braxton, of course. I know we look more like sisters, but I had her really young." Now it was Ava's turn to cut to the chase. "I understand you did the Salt-N-Pepa reality show, which I really like, but I don't think you're going to have as much to work with when it comes to my daughter. I don't know if it's my place to tell you this, but she can be so secretive and fake. I mean, it is called a reality show, right? So she should be real. Don't you think?"

"I've met Yancey, and she's really beautiful and charming. We will be just fine. I'm really looking forward to shooting the show," Cale said, as if that were the end of the discussion.

"Well, she is a fairly decent actress, but I have some information that I think might make the show more interesting for the audience."

Cale frowned, as much out of annoyance for being forced to defend his star as over the time Ava was wasting. "What are you talking about?"

"Did Yancey tell you she has a teenage daughter who she gave up at birth?"

"No," he said, stiffening.

"So I guess you didn't know that her daughter is now a big star."

"What are you talking about?" Cale asked with a puzzled look on his face. "Is this for real?"

Ava leaned in closer. "Does the name Madison B. ring any bells?" He looked both dumbfounded and overjoyed at this news. "Oh, I could tell you all sorts of interesting things about my daughter. Did she tell you that she once almost married a pro football player who was really gay and wrote a song about him, then took money from him so she wouldn't tell his secret to the press?"

"Mrs. Middlebrooks, what are you talking about?"

"Then surely she didn't tell you that she once put a laxative in the coffee of a young lady she was understudying in *Dreamgirls* and then went on to steal the part from her?" She had his complete attention now.

"Cale love, you got yourself a sick, confused diva on your hands, and I think the public should know."

He paused for a moment, overcome by these revelations. Finally Cole asked, "How do I know you're really Yancey's mother? Anyone can walk in off the street and pass themselves off as someone else."

"Of course I am. I just want the show to be a success, and I think if you revisit some of Yancey's past, people might understand her better."

"And what role would you play in this? I understand from one of the producers that she was firm about you not being a part of the series. Is this a little case of payback? Are you jealous of your daughter?"

Ava let out a scream of laughter and slapped the desk. "Me, jealous of Yancey? Cale, tell me that you're joking. Yancey has nothing that I want. I have tried all my life to get my daughter to tell the truth, and she just doesn't understand the concept. But think about it. How great it would be if you reunited her with her daughter, ex fiancé and some of her ex castmates. What great television that would be. Your ratings would go through the roof."

He shook his head. "That's not the direction we're taking. We're concentrating on

Yancey's comeback in regards to her acting and recording career. I don't think she wants to revisit her past. Now if you don't have anything else I have another conference call in ten minutes," Cale said as he stood up and extended his hand toward Ava. "It's been nice talking with you."

Ava remained seated, her mouth open in disbelief. "Is that it? Are you dismissing me, Cale?"

"Don't look at it that way, Miss Middlebrooks. Let's just say we have a different direction for the show." He opened the door, a less than subtle invitation. "Have a nice day."

"Who's financing this joint? They might be interested in this information."

"I'm not at liberty to say."

She stood and walked toward the door. "I think you're going to be sorry for not taking my information. But I guess you know best," she said, ignoring Cale's extended hand.

CHAPTER 17

Even though I knew my life was about to be turned upside down, I was a little startled on the first day of shooting when I awoke to find three men in my bedroom. Cale and two cameramen were there with a bright light greeting me as I woke up.

I got out of bed in a black-and-burgundy short teddy and my hair all over the place as I went into my bathroom to brush my teeth. I made them leave as I took my shower. As much as I wanted to shock the television audience, I was only going so far.

I put on my pink Juicy Couture warmup suit with a white Gap T-shirt and pulled my hair back in a ponytail. This was going to be a busy day. When I walked into the living room, the first person I saw was Lyrical, who was talking with Cale. When he saw me, he whispered something to her, and in a very loud voice she replied, "You want me to do it now?" Cale nodded his head and

Lyrical walked toward me with a paper cup in her hand.

"Here is your coffee, Ms. Yancey," she said with a smirk. "Do you need anything else?"

"Thank you and no," I said, looking at Cale and the cameraman out of the corner of my eye. I took a sip of the coffee and almost spit it out because it was cold and tasted horrible.

"Is something wrong?" Lyrical asked, knowing full well the answer.

"This coffee is cold."

"I'm not surprised," she said, "I got it about an hour ago, but your ass was still in the bed."

"I thought we talked about your language," I scolded her, "and I want hot coffee."

She waved her hand dismissively. "Then you better get it yourself. I'm out of money, honey."

I looked at Cale, who had a puzzled look on his face, and then back at Lyrical. I knew with her I was going to have to pick my battles wisely. And I really didn't need any coffee, I told myself.

Trying to regain lost ground, I asked, "So what's on my schedule today?"

"You have an audition and a doctor's appointment at three."

"A doctor's appointment?"

"Yes, with a Dr. Kym Z. I guess it's your annual pussy check."

"Cale!" I screamed as I closed my eyes so that I couldn't see this girl.

"Yes, Yancey. What's the problem?" he asked as if he hadn't been in the room.

"What's the problem? Did you hear what she just said?"

He giggled. "I thought it was funny, but we will most likely have to cut it out."

"Both of us have told her that her language has to be clean, and already she's said two cuss words."

"Don't act like I'm not here," she called to both of us. "Those words just slipped out. I will get better."

I looked across the room and saw the camera coming closer to me. I placed my hand over the lens and yelled, "Stop it. I need to pull myself together."

Cale stepped in and put a reassuring hand on my shoulder. "You look great, Yancey. And this exchange can be edited. But I think one of the big reasons we got Lyrical is so you two can play off each other, to show the difference between you and her. Now, why don't we go into your office and talk again about your schedule. I will speak with Lyrical and make sure she tones down the language."

Maybe my nerves were getting the best of me. I took a deep breath. "Okay," I said, then went into the kitchen. I grabbed a bottle of water and headed to the former den that the producers had turned into an office. There was a glasstop desk with a pink computer for me and several of my head-shots on the wall. I took a seat in the black leather chair. When the cameramen came in, I called out for Lyrical to come in.

"Do you need me, Miss Yancey?" she asked sarcastically.

"Yes, I do. What's on my agenda today?"

"Agenda? What in the hell . . . I mean, heck, is an agenda?"

I rolled my eyes and took a swig of water. "My appointments. What do I have to do today?"

"Oh, that." She took a pocket-size note-pad from her jeans and opened it. "You have a session with your trainer in thirty minutes. Then you have lunch with some girl named Rochelle. You have an audition at two and then an appointment with Dr. Kym at three. Where would you like to have lunch?"

"I don't care. Make some suggestions."

"I know this great place up in Harlem. They make some great fried chicken and rib tips."

I smiled to show that I knew her game but wasn't going to let her get to me. "I don't eat fried foods."

"You don't? I think you might be the first black person I ever met who don't eat fried chicken. What's up with that?"

I ignored her question and looked over at Cale, who had a hand over his mouth in order to suppress his laughter.

"Forget about the restaurant, I'll find one. Where is my audition?"

Flipping through the pad quickly, she finally landed on the information. "It's in midtown, on 46th and Sixth Avenue."

"What's it for again?"

"Your agent said it was for some show called *Ugly Betty,* whatever that means. Is that a television show or movie?"

"It's a television show. Fabulous show. Did they send over a script?"

"Yeah," Lyrical said, plopping herself in the white leather chair in front of my desk. For a moment I just stared at Lyrical, wondering how big a pea she had for a brain. She simply stared back at me.

"Well, where is it?" I almost shouted.

"Oh shit, it's over here," Lyrical said as she jumped up and picked up a manila envelope from the loveseat. I wanted to snatch the package from her hands, but the cameras were rolling. As I pulled the pages out of the envelope, horror filled my face. The character I was auditioning for was to play Vanessa Williams's mother. Are you kidding me? No way, no how, I thought and knew I had to get another agent. He should have told me this information personally.

"Is everything okay?" Lyrical asked.

"Get my agent on the phone."

"Who is that?"

"Just push four on my cell phone and give it to me."

"Where is your cell phone?"

"Lyrical, that's your job. Find my phone."

"Okay," Lyrical said huffily as she left the office. As soon as she left, Cale came closer and said I needed to loosen up and not let everything Lyrical did get to me.

"We're just starting and it's going to be a headache for everyone if you don't chill."

"But she is so stupid," I said in almost a whisper.

"You're playing off each other. It makes great television. Look, she won't be in every frame. We will be shooting you without her when you work out and go to the audition."

"I'm not doing the audition."

"Why not?" he asked, surprised by the news.

"The freaking script calls for me to play

Vanessa Williams's mother. Can you believe that shit? Do I look old enough to play that role? That's something my real mother should be doing."

"Speaking of real mothers, where is Ava?"

For the first time that morning, a true smile lit my face. "I sent her to Naples for a week or two," I said.

He looked at me skeptically. "And she went without a fight?"

"Of course," I said. So what if I had to use some of the money S. Marcus had given me to find Ava a five-star hotel and give her some money for new clothes? I was hoping that Ava might get lucky and snag herself another rich old husband. I had my fingers crossed when I didn't hear from her the first three days. When she did call, it was for more money, naturally, for spa treatments.

"So what are you going to do?" Cale asked.

"About what?"

"The audition?"

"I need a new agent," I said as much to myself as to him.

"Do you have any prospects?" Cale asked.

"Not really."

He was quick on his feet, and sure enough, in another moment he suggested, "I think you need to come up with three agents you'd like to represent you, and then we could follow you while you meet with them. I think that would be great."

"Good idea," I said. I was thinking that maybe with cameras following me around, maybe some of the top agents might reconsider representing me. This was a great plan.

"Hey, why don't you give me a list of five, and I will have my assistant contact them and we'll film three?"

"That sounds like a plan," I said, finishing my water. I swiped the cold, sweaty bottle across my forehead and thought how I couldn't wait to immerse myself in the pool at the new health club I was going to join as soon as the money started rolling in.

I was a little surprised when Cale showed up at my town house the next morning without his two cameramen. The scowl on his face told me that something wasn't right.

"Cale, where are David and Billy?"

"I need to talk with you, Yancey." His tone was serious. "Where can we talk?"

"Let's go into the office. No, wait, let's just sit here on the sofa," I said. I figured Lyrical would be arriving shortly and I could just send her to the office. I didn't want her around if I was about to be handed bad news.

"Yancey, I think we got a problem," he said, raising a finger, "but it's one I think we can solve and make into a win-win situation for the both of us."

I didn't like the sound of that. When had anything ever been a win-win for me? "What's wrong? Oh my, where are my manners? Can I get you something to drink?" I asked nervously.

"I've been looking over the footage we shot, and I showed some of it to one of the producers and Jeff. Let's just say they were not impressed. They're talking about pulling the plug."

"What!" I jumped up from the sofa.

"Yancey, sit down. We can work this out," Cale said calmly.

"We can't let them do that. Why are they talking about stopping the show before it even goes on the air? I need this show, Cale."

Cale grabbed my hand and gently pulled me back to the sofa. He told me we could make sure they didn't stop production of the show. He went on to inform me they had been unimpressed with my daily routine, and the only thing they liked about the show was Lyrical. I scowled at that news. I knew it was a bad idea to hire that bitch. Just like Ava, I knew she'd try to steal my show, but I wasn't going to let that happen.

"How can we stop them? What if they've already made up their minds?"

"We just make it more exciting. Put more focus on you."

"What are we going to do?"

He looked away — a bad sign. "I've thought of a couple of things. Besides focusing on your career and your comeback, I think it might be a good thing to show some of your past. But you'd have to agree to help me."

I didn't know exactly what he meant about my past, but if talking about it would save the show, I was ready to listen. "Tell me how I can help."

"I think we might need to bring your mother into the picture. I think she would add a lot."

I groaned loudly. "Why? I don't want to do that. Ava will try to upstage me. She always has."

"I also want to explore some of the things that have happened in your past and use them to show how much you and your life have changed."

My antenna immediately went up. Changed? How much did Cale know?

"I want you to revisit some people from your past."

Confused, I turned my head slightly to

287

signal for him to explain.

"I want to set up meetings with Nicole Springer and Basil Henderson, and I want you to try and reconnect with your daughter."

Had Cale thrown cold ice water in my face, I could not have been more shocked. The mere mention of those names left me speechless.

Cale placed a hand over mine to help calm me. "Those are a few of the people I think we should visit, but I think the real focus should be on reconnecting with your daughter. I understand she's in the business as well. I think the ratings will go through the roof."

I stood up and paced the room, searching for the right words. "Who told you about Basil and Nicole? Who told you I had a daughter? That's a lie, Cale. I don't have any children. Who have you been talking to?"

He remained utterly calm, a director used to handling divas. "Now, Yancey, if we're going to continue to work together, you have to trust me. Don't you want to get to know Madison better?"

"Madison. I don't know a Madison," I said firmly.

"Yancey, I've checked it out and it's all

288

true and you know it. First, tell me about this Basil Henderson guy you almost married. And you can't deny that, because I searched the web pre-production and saw all the gossip columns talking about the wedding and when you recorded that song, the speculation was on if it was about the former football star. Is he out now and do you think he would let us tape the two of you meeting?"

"I don't know what Basil is doing," I said, my arms crossed as if to block my memory. "I haven't talked to him in a long time. Why do you want to do that?"

"Imagine it like a forgiveness tour, if you will. Every week you could visit someone who's hurt you or who you've hurt, and seek forgiveness. Let's start with Nicole Springer. When was the last time you talked with her?"

"It's been a long time. I don't even know if she's still alive."

"She is. She has children and lives in Atlanta. Is it true you once poisoned her to go on in her place in a company of *Dream-girls?*"

"Hell no! Who told you that? Cale, you're tripping. I would never do something like that."

"Come on, Yancey. I've done some things

I'm ashamed of as well. We all have. But just think how great it would be for your audience and your fans to see you've learned from your mistakes and are willing to admit them." His eyes were blazing. I could tell he had a glorious vision for how the series would unfold. The series that now would embarrass the hell out of me. "Those would be mini episodes," he went on, still dreaming, "but the meat of the show would be trying to establish a relationship with your daughter. I think the fact that she's a big star now makes it even better."

I was still not willing to confirm Cale's information. These were secrets that were best kept that way. Why would I open old wounds like that in front of the world? I continued pacing as images of Basil, Nicole and Madison danced in my head. It suddenly dawned on me that Ava had something to do with Cale finding out this information. What a bitch she was. Ava had used my past to parlay her ass onto my show.

I went to the window and stood there, attempting to gather my thoughts. "Let me think about this, Cale. I don't know if I want to do this. Even if it means saving the show, you're asking a lot from me."

"I understand, but I think if we told the producers what we're going to do, they might not only keep the show in production but also give us a bigger budget to work with."

I couldn't bring myself to face him.

Cale approached me, remarking gently, "Trust me on this, Yancey. We will still follow your day-to-day activities related to your career, but I think this gives the show more than a one-season run."

My shoulders slumped, already starting to give in. "So what are you suggesting?"

"We can do it like a little confessional. Just you sitting on a stool with a black backdrop, talking to the camera about some of the things in your life that have brought you deep pain. I think it will endear you to the audience. They will feel for you and also feel like they can relate to you."

"So it's just me on camera by myself?"

"Yeah, I will be shooting you questions off camera. They won't see me, but they will hear my voice."

If I could tell my side of the story, I might be able to make people see I wasn't a horrible person. "Let's try it. But if I don't like it, then we won't use it. Okay?"

"That's fair enough." He pulled away, and instantly his voice gained about fifty decibels. "I was hoping you'd say yes, so I've already set up something in your bedroom.

291

We will make it a closed set. Just one cameraman, me and you," Cale said.

Why wasn't I surprised he'd already counted on me to say yes? "Okay."

I followed Cale to my bedroom, where he had a mirror covered in black fabric behind a stool. A bright light hung overhead.

"Sit on the stool, Yancey."

I looked into my dressing mirror to make sure my hair and makeup looked okay. I was wearing a white man's oxford shirt, which I thought would look dramatic. Right before I sat down, I pulled out a pair of black pearls from my jewelry box and held them up for Cale to see.

"By all means put those on," he said.

I put the pearl earrings on and then took a seat. Cale checked to make sure the lighting was okay and asked me if I was ready. I nodded my head.

Off camera, sitting in a chair near me, he started shooting questions.

"Tell us your name."

"Yancey Harringon Braxton."

"What is your occupation?"

"I'm an actress and recording artist."

"Have you had any hits?"

"I had a song that was number one on the *Billboard* charts for nine weeks."

"What was the title?"

" 'Any Way the Wind Blows.' "

"Has that been the best thing that has happened to you?"

"That was good. But I've had other highlights."

"Like?"

"I've had some love in my life."

"Anyone you want to talk about?"

I paused for a moment and said, "Maybe later."

"Okay. Where were you born?"

"Jackson, Tennessee."

"So you're a southern girl."

"Southern born but not southern bred."

"What do you mean by that?"

"That I'm not a southern belle."

A note of humor entered his voice. "So you see something wrong with that?"

"I'm more sophisticated."

"Okay. Tell me about your mother and father."

"What about them?"

"Whatever you want to tell us."

"My mother was an actress and singer." With a measure of satisfaction I added, "She didn't meet with a lot of success in the States, but she was popular in Europe and Japan."

"So she was your role model?"

I didn't have to pretend my ridicule of

such an idea. "Oh hell no! She was hardly in my life."

"How do you feel about that?"

"What do you mean?"

"Did that bother you?"

I thought for a moment and looked in the camera dead on and said, "You know that line in the movie *A Chorus Line?*"

"What line?"

" 'I felt nothing,' " I sang.

"So is she in your life now?"

"She's around but not really. I come from a long line of bad mothers and most likely the reason I was so afraid to be one myself."

He paused, as if deciding whether to press on, but said instead, "Let's talk about Madison."

I started to fidget on the stool, suddenly fearful of what Cale was getting ready to ask me.

"What about Madison?"

"Do you ever hope to meet her?"

"I don't know."

"Tell us who Madison is, Yancey."

I looked over at Cale and rolled my eyes at him. I suddenly had the urge to tell him this wasn't a good idea, but if this was going to sell my show, then I had to go for it.

With a sigh I said, "I gave up Madison when she was born. I had her while in college. I thought I'd given her up for adoption, but later I learned that her father, my boyfriend at the time, had prevented the adoption and raised her by himself."

"How did you feel when you found that out?"

"I felt betrayed."

"Why?"

"Because that's not what we agreed on."

"But that makes it pretty easy for you to get in contact with her. Have you ever thought about doing that?"

I paused for a minute and lowered my head. Finally I lifted it toward the camera and said, "Maybe someday I will."

"How do you think she might feel about that?"

"I have no clue about how Madison might feel," I said. As soon as the words left my mouth, I felt an intense rush of emotion gush out of my body like I was giving birth again. I got off the stool and rushed past Cale toward my bathroom.

"Yancey, are you okay?" Cale asked.

With tears streaking down my face, I mumbled, "I will be fine, but you need to leave."

CHAPTER 18

Ava crossed her legs and tightened the belt of the white terrycloth robe. She pulled her cell phone out of her beach bag and realized she had fifteen minutes before her massage at the Boca Day Spa. She picked up a *Florida Homes* magazine off the table and was thumbing through it when she heard a loud female voice. Ava looked up from the magazine and saw a somewhat attractive black female walk into the spa talking on a jeweled cell phone. She had on big black sunglasses, and Ava remembered seeing her with an older white man at the beach bar a couple of days before.

She was talking so loud that Ava couldn't help but overhear some of her conversation.

"Girl, Dennis is driving me crazy with his old ass. Can't keep his hands off me and so I made an appointment to get a wax just to get some rest . . . I know, girl, but this was not a part of the deal or my plan. I don't think he's sick at all."

The lady, who looked to be in her early thirties, sat down next to Ava and continued her conversation as if alone.

"Well, at least the place is nice. Strictly five-star. The food is off the chain, and it's money people at every turn. You should come down here when you start looking for another husband."

Ava made eye contact with the lady and then looked away. As she did, her own cell phone rang and she saw Yancey's name cross her screen.

Ava knew it was only a matter of time before Cale dropped the news on Yancey. In fact, she had been expecting this call. "What's going on, Yancey?" she asked sharply. "I'm just getting ready for a massage."

"Did you go to my director and tell him some stuff about me?" Yancey yelled.

"Now, why would I do that?"

"Come on, Ava. I know you told him about Nicole, Basil and Madison. It couldn't be anybody but you. Now they want me to revisit these people." Yancey sounded like she wanted to reach through the phone and strangle her. "Why can't you just mind your own business?"

"That's what I'm trying to do, sweetheart.

I told you, I'm getting ready to get a massage."

"I know you, Ava, and nobody did this but you, and if it causes me to lose my show, then you're going to have to deal with me. Do you understand?"

"Yancey, stop tripping," Ava said in a motherly voice. "So what if I did? I was only trying to help you. I knew before they started filming the show, you needed something to make it pop. I'm glad to see that the director took my advice."

"Well, you better find you a rich husband at that damn spa because you're going to have to pay me back every penny for this trip, since you can't stay out of my business!"

"Now, Yancey dear, I thought this was a trip for you to show your wonderful mother how much you love her."

"You just wait and see."

"I love you too, Yancey," Ava said. As she clicked off her phone, a self-satisfied grin appeared.

"Are you still reading that magazine?"

"Excuse me?" Ava said, looking at the woman who had been talking so loudly on her cell phone.

"Are you finished with that magazine? I think my new home is featured in it.

Can I see it?"

"I'm not finished with it," Ava said coldly.

"Okay, well let me know when you're finished. I'm dying to see the house." The woman glanced around. "Are you down here with your husband?"

"Don't you see I'm reading?" Ava said.

"Sorry, I was just making conversation." The woman leaned in and confided, "It's always good to see another sister at places like this. Me and my new husband, Dennis, come here all the time. Maybe you've heard of my husband. Dennis Meyers of Meyers Homes. He built all these retirement homes and condos in Tampa and right outside Miami. I'm Sonja Meyers of Palm Beach. And you are?"

Ava didn't answer but simply gave Sonja the side eye that said *okay bitch that's enough.*

That didn't stop the woman for a second. "How long are you going to be down here? Maybe you could have dinner with Dennis and me?"

A plump white lady in a white coat appeared and called out, "Ava Middlebrooks."

"I'm Ava Middlebrooks."

"Ava. What a beautiful name," Sonja said. "You look like an Ava."

"Are you ready for your massage, Mrs.

Middlebrooks?"

Ava got up from the chair and was escorted to her massage. Just as the attendant opened the door leading to the dim hallway, Ava heard Sonja's booming voice call out, "Nice meeting you, Ava. See you around."

Once inside Ava whispered to the attendant, "Some people have no class at all. I thought this place was exclusive."

When Ava returned to her room, she was thinking how much she had missed pleasures like a ninety-minute rub down. She was looking forward to a nice room service meal with an expensive bottle of wine and then maybe a walk along the beach before sunset.

She walked over to pick up the room service menu, but before she reached for it, she stopped at the computer that the resort provided and punched in the name *Dennis Meyers.* A few seconds later, up popped a picture of an older white man and a complete bio. Ava started to read the information on this wealthy real estate mogul, who had made his name with properties all over Florida. Ava learned that he had boosted his net worth by cashing in on the tough market buying foreclosed homes in exclusive areas like Star and Fisher Islands.

"So that cheap ghetto bitch wasn't lying," Ava said to herself.

At that moment Ava's plans suddenly changed. She wasn't going to order room service. No, she was going to take a shower, put on her best dress, shoes and jewelry and figure out at which restaurant her new best friends the *Meyers* were having dinner.

CHAPTER 19

"This was such a great idea, Ms. Nicole," Madison said as she dipped the golden brown French fry into the pile of ketchup on her plate.

"You've been working so hard and I always loved having lunch at Bloomingdale's when I first moved to New York. It's like something out of a movie," Nicole said.

"Who knew that there was a restaurant in this fabulous store," Madison said, gazing all around.

"Yeah, my girls love it here too. They make a mean hot fudge sundae."

"I love hot fudge but I have to watch my weight."

Nicole didn't approve. "Now Madison, I hope you're being smart about that. You're a growing girl and you should eat what you like in moderation. I know this business can be very cruel to young girls about weight issues."

"I know you're right Ms. Nicole, but my daddy is on me about that all the time."

"Your father seems like a really smart and nice man," Nicole said with a warm smile.

Madison returned the smile and said, "Yes, my daddy is all that and a bag of chips."

"You sound like my daughter now," Nicole said with a laugh.

Madison wanted to say that she wished she were Nicole's daughter but only if she could keep her real daddy. She was certain that Ms. Nicole was married to a nice man, too, but nobody was like her daddy and she wasn't willing to give him up even for a mother as nice as Nicole.

"I want to meet your children someday. Maybe we can come back here," Madison suggested.

"That would be nice. I'll make sure that happens." A cloud settled over her features as a new thought came to her. "Madison, there is something I needed to tell you."

"Yes, ma'am."

"I'm going to be out of the country for about a month starting next week. My husband has an extended business trip in London, so the kids and I are going to meet him there. We'll have to miss a few lessons but you'll be fine."

Madison tried to hide her disappointment. She looked forward so much to her lessons. "London, that sounds exciting, especially for your children."

"Yeah, we're taking them out of school and will home-school them for a month. The trip to London will be educational, we think."

"I'm sure it will be." Once the news had settled in, Madison realized she should bring up a plan she'd been thinking of on her own. "Ms. Nicole, I have something to ask you."

"Sure, Madison."

"I'm starting this foundation named after my aunt Jenny. She raised me since I was a baby but died of breast cancer. I'm starting an after-school program for kids in the area that's arts related and I wondered if you'd consider coming by maybe once a month and teaching voice lessons."

"Oh, Madison, that's wonderful and sure I'd come by maybe even once a week if you'd have me."

"Thank you . . . thank you. Come as often as you like."

Nicole appraised her in this new light. "I know your aunt Jenny and father must be so proud of you for giving back. Most young people in show business aren't as generous

304

as you. I can tell that you were raised right."

"That means a lot coming from you, Ms. Nicole."

Nicole picked a slice of buttery avocado from her Cobb salad and took a bite. She washed it down with the sweet tea the waiter had prepared just for her. Since moving back to New York from Atlanta, Nicole knew she had to make a special request to get the drink she missed so much from her days of living down south.

The thick-waisted waiter with dirty brown hair approached the table and asked if he could talk the ladies into dessert.

"What do you think, Madison? We've got plenty of time."

"Could I have some strawberries and blueberries mixed together?"

"Sure, would you like some whipped cream with that?"

"I better not," Madison said. Nicole raised her eyebrows but didn't say anything. Madison saw the question mark, though, and quickly told the waiter she changed her mind and to pile the whipped cream on high.

When the waiter left, Nicole had a question for Madison.

"Madison, why were you so interested in Yancey Braxton?"

Feeling unexpectedly defensive, Madison said, "Oh, no reason."

"Really?"

Madison didn't answer because she liked Ms. Nicole and didn't want to lie to her.

"Did I say something wrong, Madison? You know you can talk to me."

"It's really nothing, Ms. Nicole. I'm really interested in anybody who reached a certain degree of success in this business. Especially African-American women."

"Okay, I can understand that."

Silence hung like a curtain for a few moments. Both Nicole and Madison avoided each other's gaze and moved their eyes all around the bustling café. When Madison's eyes finally met Nicole's, slow, small tears began to fall.

"What's wrong, Madison? And please don't say nothing again."

"I need to wash my face," Madison said as her voice dropped to a whisper. She rushed from the table, leaving Nicole dumbfounded.

CHAPTER 20

I opened the sack with my salad in it and discovered that once again, Lyrical had gotten the wrong salad dressing.

"Lyrical!" I yelled out.

No answer.

"Lyrical!" I screamed at the top of my lungs. Where in the hell was she?

I got up from the dining room table and went to my office, where I discovered Lyrical at the computer with headphones on. When she saw me, she rolled her eyes and slowly took the headphones off.

"Did you hear me calling you?"

"What's up, Yancey?"

"I said, didn't you hear me calling you?" I was still trying to get over the idea of meeting Madison face to face.

"I guess not, 'cause I didn't answer, now did I," Lyrical said as she began to put the headphones back on her ears.

I held out the yellow salad dressing.

"What is this?"

"Salad dressing."

"What did I ask for?"

"You asked for a salad."

"But what kind of salad dressing did I ask for?"

"I don't know, but I got you honey mustard."

"I asked for ranch. Why can't you just do what I ask?" I asked wearily. "It was a very simple request."

Lyrical said, "Where is Ava, by the way? I haven't seen her in a couple of days. I want to talk to her about something. I want to make sure she doesn't forget what she promised me."

"She's not here."

"I can see that," she said, looking around the house in an exaggerated manner. "Where is she?"

"Out of town."

"What is she doing out of town? She's not supposed to do that. Did she get permission to leave town?"

"Permission from whom?"

"From Mr. Lomax, her probation officer. She can get in big trouble for leaving the city without his approval. She is still on paper, and they could send her grand ass back to jail if they found out about it."

A magnificent thought popped into my head. I almost could have hugged Lyrical. "Are you serious? They can do that?"

"Damn straight. Now, I'm going to go back down to this damn deli and get your salad dressing, princess, but the next time, get your order straight," she said with a downward glance at her own body. "I got better things to do than to be carrying my ass back and forth to that deli. Look at me. I don't need the exercise."

When I heard the door close, I smiled to myself and said, "Well, well, Ms. Ava, look what information just fell into my hands. Let's see what lessons I can teach you about interfering with my life. Can't say I didn't learn from the best."

"This hot chocolate is to die for," Dalton said as he took a long sip. "It's like someone melted a Hershey bar into milk."

"Would you like another one?" I asked. I'd invited him to have tea with me at the chic Lowell Hotel on the East Side. Dalton told me he wasn't a tea drinker so I suggested the hot chocolate. I wanted to make sure he gave me his songs and didn't go dig up one of those old divas like Angela Winbush or Regina Belle. Dalton could be my way back to the top.

"I don't think so but thanks. This place is nice," Dalton said as he looked around the exquisitely decorated café. We were seated at a sofa in the corner with a glass-topped table. On the table was a crystal vase filled with elegant white flowers, surrounded by lavender candles. I loved this café, and even though it wasn't in the budget I thought it would be the perfect place to close the deal with Dalton. I had even dressed like I was going on an interview or audition.

My hair was in a tight chignon and I wore a white sateen high-collared blouse, a black pencil skirt with pleats in the back and a simple pair of low-heeled black Chanel pumps. On days like this I was happy I'd invested in expensive shoes and bags when I had money.

"Yeah, this has always been one of my favorite places," I said as I finished the last sip of my tea.

"I can see why. Maybe I will bring Anderson here sometime. He would like this place."

I kept my face carefully neutral at the mention of Anderson. "How long have you guys been a couple? I always thought you were dating someone in the cast."

"No chorus boys for me, hon. I've been dating Anderson about two years."

"What does he do?"

His friendly smile instantly shut down. "I can't speak on it."

"What?"

"I'm not allowed to speak about Anderson's private life even with someone I really adore and trust."

"Is he in the closet or one of those down-low brothers?" I wondered what he meant by not being allowed to talk about his boyfriend's life. What kind of shit was that?

"Yancey, I can't speak on it," Dalton said in a voice that almost sounded like he was singing.

Sensing an opening, I plunged ahead. "Where did you meet him?"

"You gonna make me get up from this table, Yancey."

"I was once in love with one of those down-low brothers," I explained, "and I could never understand why he couldn't just say it."

"Maybe because he knew you'd make a hit record out of it," Dalton said with a giggle.

I shared a smile, tipping my spoon at him. "Okay, you got me on that one . . . hon. I like gay men like you, Dalton. I like my gays, gay gay so I know what side of their bread is buttered. You know?"

"Yeah, Yancey, you like your gays to do your hair and make your dresses. I totally see where you're coming from."

I looked at Dalton to see if he was serious and realized how stupid I sounded. I need to get back to the task at hand, getting those songs.

"Let's talk about your music," I said.

He, too, seemed relieved to change the subject. "Yeah, let's get down to business, Miss Yancey. When do we go into the studios and record my songs?"

"Do you really think I'm the one to sing them?" I asked in that sugary voice that suddenly sounded so fake.

"Come on now, Yancey, cut the crap. You know I want you to sing the songs. That's why I gave them to you. Don't be coy, hon."

"So you're saying I don't have to kiss your ass," I said. I really like Dalton, with his dazzling charm and wit and the way he always seemed in control.

"Like my mother always said, 'Never kiss anyone's ass to get along with their face,' Dalton said with a hearty laugh. Taken by surprise, I started laughing so hard that I quickly grabbed the glass of water at the table and took a sip to avoid choking.

"Are you okay, Yancey? We're going to

need those vocal cords. Let's not damage them."

A few moments later I felt back to normal. Dalton and I talked about the songs and some of his ideas for arrangements. This boy was not only a talented songwriter but also knew more about music than anyone I'd met in a long time. He shared with me that he also wrote Christian music and a couple of those songs were being considered by Heather Headley for her gospel CD. Maybe now was the time to bring up my God question.

Dalton and I decided to order a glass of champagne to celebrate our new collaboration and while we were waiting I asked him why he started the Bible studies every other day when we were on tour.

"Because I think prayer changes things. My faith is very important to me."

His response startled me and I found myself studying him so intently that I could tell he was growing uncomfortable.

"What, Yancey? Is my wig not on straight?" Dalton acted like he was fixing an imaginary wig on his head. Leave it to Dalton to turn my serious question into something funny.

"I was just wondering because you know I've had a lot of gay friends but never one who was so into the church and God," I said. Maybe my question had been thought-less.

"Yancey, because I'm gay doesn't mean I can't believe in God. That I can't love him like straight people. My faith is the most important thing in the world to me and I couldn't imagine my life without God."

"But you know what the churches and the Bible say about homosexuality." It wasn't like I knew this for sure since I'd never picked up a Bible in my life unless I was using it as a prop in some play I was doing. Neither my grandmother nor Ava had ever been high on the church but I thought it was because most of the church ladies didn't like my mother and grandmother. The reason being neither had a problem dating married church folk.

"I know what it says but I know how I feel. God made me in his own image and loves me no matter what, Yancey. He loves me just like he loves you. Once I was in doubt and I talked to Nicole Stovall about it and she assured me that God loved me no matter what."

"Oh, I forgot she has a direct line to God," I said curtly.

"I get the feeling you're not as big a fan of Nicole as she appears to be of you."

"No, we're cool. Perfect people just bother me," I said. My fears about Dalton's loyalty had all but disappeared. This child really *got* me.

The champagne arrived and I made an announcement that seemed to surprise Dalton.

"I don't think God loves me, knows where I am or cares," I said as I took a quick sip of champagne. Dalton didn't say anything but just gazed at me in puzzlement. An agonizing silence stretched between the two of us until finally Dalton leaned over and put his arms around me, bringing me close to him and then hugging my neck. I pulled back and looked into his eyes. It was the first time that I'd noticed how beautiful they were, dark brown with a deep gold circle the color of clover honey. They were now glistening with tears and I realized Dalton was crying for me. I felt like he really cared about me, might even love me like a close friend.

"Who hurt you, Yancey?"

"What?"

"Somebody hurt you bad, baby girl. I can see it when I look into your eyes. I can also tell you that God will never hurt you."

"I'll be okay, Dalton. The past is just that, the past," I said.

He pulled me close again and gently butted his forehead against mine. Low and intimate he said, "God loves you just as much as he loves me, Yancey. So trust me when I say he always loved you. Always will. One day whoever hurt you will have to answer to him."

CHAPTER 21

The limo pulled up at the service entrance behind the building. Mike, the driver, got out and opened both doors for the excited teenage girls.

"I can't believe this is happening to me," Caressa said. "This is so exciting."

"Believe it, Caressa," Madison said, stepping out of the car. "I think you better get used to this because this is going to be happening a lot."

"They closed the entire store for us?"

"Yes, they did." Madison was pretty amazed herself that they had done it, but she wasn't going to let on to her friend. "I can't wait to see what kind of new party dresses they have in. We have to get you a wardrobe for when you go to Auburn."

"You're going with me, aren't you?" Caressa asked, sounding concerned.

"I think my schedule will permit it," Madison said, and then both girls broke out giggling. She walked up to the back door and knocked a couple of times and a young lady opened the door.

"You must be Madison B. Come on in. We've been waiting for you," she said.

"Thank you, and this is my best friend, Caressa. My daddy told me I could bring a friend."

"That's no problem at all. We're happy to do it. We've already pulled out our best dresses for you. Some of them haven't even been put out yet."

Madison and Caressa followed the lady through the door and into a back space covered with boxes, gift wrap, ribbons and dresses in plastic bags.

"This is our shipping area for online orders," the woman explained, more out of nervousness than anything else. "Are you going to wear these dresses on your tour?"

"Maybe, but these will be for my two television shows," Madison said.

"OMG. You have television shows too?"

"Yes, she does," Caressa stepped in proudly. "Madison B. is going to be bigger than Hannah Montana and Raven Simone."

"Sounds that way," the woman said, smiling as she led them into the showroom. "Okay, where do you want to start? Pants, skirts or dresses?"

"I don't know," Madison said, having not given it much thought.

"Then why don't we start with some of our new party dresses."

Madison and Caressa followed the straw-thin young lady with brunette hair to the front of the store, where several strapless dresses in different colors hung on a metal rack.

Madison raced toward a short dress with pink chiffon on the top and black silk on the bottom. She caressed the fabric and said to Caressa, "This will look beautiful on you."

"It is pretty," Caressa replied. "But are you sure you don't want it?"

"Not if you do."

"You pick first, Madison," Caressa said.

Madison paused and stared at Caressa for a moment in an exaggerated manner. Finally she smiled. "Look, Caressa, this isn't all about me. I want you to get some nice things as well. Go try it on," Madison said as she took the dress and handed it to Caressa.

"Oh, thank you, Madison. You're the best friend in the world."

"She sure is," the young lady said. She smiled at Madison and said, "I think I have a pink and green dress over here that you might like. It's made by the same designer as the dress you picked out for your friend."

Two hours later, both Madison and Caressa left the store with two bags of new dresses, skirts, blouses and shoes. When Mike saw them coming out the door he leaped from the car and raced to the young ladies to assist them.

Caressa slipped her arm in Madison's and whispered, "Thank you for the best day of my life, Madison."

"No problem, and I hope you know this is only the beginning, girl. Only the start."

CHAPTER 22

Ava finally spotted the power couple enjoying lunch at the beach bar. Perfect timing, she thought as she whisked by the hostess and headed straight to the table in the private dining area.

"I'd been hoping I'd run into you," Ava said, kissing a startled Sonja on the cheek.

Regaining her composure, Sonja said, "Ava, right?"

"Yes, love, and this must be the handsome man you were telling me you were lucky enough to marry. I'm Ava Middlebrooks of Palm Springs, California," she said, extending her hand to Sonja's husband. "You must be Dennis. What a pleasure to meet you."

"You're from Palm Springs? I've been thinking about building out there," Dennis said.

"Then we have to talk," Ava said, pulling up a chair.

"Would you like to join us?" Sonja asked.

Ava patted her on the arm and said, "I already have, love. Pay attention." She zeroed in on Dennis. "What are we drinking?"

"Champagne," Dennis said.

"But of course," Ava replied, "Dom in the middle of the day sounds wonderful. And I'm famished. I think I'll order a steak. Medium rare, of course, and a baked potato."

"I don't think they offer baked potatoes during lunch. I tried to order one the other day and I had to wait until dinner. I just love baked potatoes with cheese," Sonja said.

"Nonsense, child. It's all in how you ask, and if they tell you no, then you ask somebody else. Isn't that the way you do it, Dennis?" Ava asked with a smile. She was wearing a snow-white wrap dress with a plunging neckline. Her hair was pulled back in a bun and covered by a bright yellow hat with a polka dot band. Ava had on gold open-toed mules and carried a matching bag. Her eyes tilted down as she sourly examined the bright orange shorts set Sonja wore.

"I like the way you think, Ava," Dennis said, smiling back. "Do I know you from somewhere?"

"Most smart men do." The waiter appeared and handed Ava the menu. "Now, let me see what kind of salads they have. After a workout and a swim I have quite an appetite. I guess I can always go back to my diet when the vacation is over. A diet I will be happy to share with you, Solange, when you decide to get rid of those pesky ten pounds. Potatoes can be fattening, you know."

"It's Sonja," she corrected gently.

"Of course it is, sweetie." Ava turned her full attention to Dennis. "Now, when do you think you might be building in California? I have seen some of your homes and they are something else. I think they will be a big hit in Cali."

"What kind of business are you in, Ava? I think we met with Seneca on his yacht on Fisher Island."

"Oh, you name it and I've done it," Ava said, ignoring the Fisher Island statement. "But basically I'm a woman who aims to please her man. I know you can appreciate that, Dennis."

The older man was enthralled by her flirting. "Are you married, Ava? You look so familiar."

"Maybe you know me from my show business career. I was a huge cabaret star. Cur-

rently I'm between husbands. I'm a widow."
She looked away misty-eyed. "I lost my
husband at a very young age. But I'm always
looking. You'll have to introduce me to some
of your business associates."

Charmed by her directness, he asked,
"Sonja, who do you think might be good
for Ava?"

"I have no idea," Sonja said flatly.

"Now don't tax yourself thinking about it,
sweetheart. I'm sure if Dennis puts his mind
to it, he will think of somebody. Sonja tells
me you have a home in Tampa Bay. I was
thinking of visiting there in the fall. I'm a
big Tampa Bay Bucs fan. I bet you even
have a box. Maybe I can be your guest at
one of the games."

Sonja jumped in, "I'm in charge of the
guest box. That's my job."

Ava turned a tolerant smile on her, like a
mother with an awkward teenager. "Oh
well, great. Let me look at the schedule and
I'll tell you which games I can make." Ava
looked around the restaurant and said,
"Now, where is that waitress? Good help is
so hard to find."

Just as Ava was preparing to get into the
limo for a trip to the airport, she heard a
female voice call her name. Ava turned and

saw Sonja walking toward her. She was wearing a tiger print swimsuit top and a see-through sarong. Ava imagined Sonja had missed the memo about no animal prints after age thirty. She figured Sonja had missed a lot of memos about taste and class.

"Sarita. How are you? I'm on my way back to New York," Ava said as she approached Sonja for a fake kiss. Ava was a bit taken aback when Sonja backed away.

"First of all, and for the last time, my name is Sonja. I don't want to have to tell you again."

"My, my, aren't we touchy, hon. But you know how it is. I've always been so bad with names. Where is that lovely husband of yours?"

"Dennis is getting a massage, but that of course is none of your business."

"Now, Sonja, why so bitchy so early in the morning? I guess you must have caught Dennis eyeing me like a Thanksgiving turkey with stuffing when we broke bread. Not to worry, child. If he makes a play for me, I promise you'll be the first to know."

"I'm not the least bit worried about you, Ava. If Dennis were to leave me, it would be for someone a lot younger and a lady with real class and not the fake shit you bring."

Ava was delighted to see Sonja's claws bared. How little this clueless wonder really knew. "Oh my, my, love. Is that the ghetto I hear seeping out? I must say, it did take a little longer than expected," Ava said with a satisfied smirk.

"Call it whatever you like, but I want you to know my husband told me all about you last night when we retired to our suite. So I don't think it would be wise for you to come and visit us. Football games or otherwise."

Ava reacted like she was speaking in tongues. "What in the hell are you talking about, and try not to use the ebonics? As you can see, I have a driver waiting on me, and I don't want to waste time with the translations."

"He told me about you and his friend, and I'm warning you, I will find him and let him know where to find you."

"Him? Does this imaginary friend have a name, love?"

"You know the name, bitch. So don't you forget that you've been warned."

As a parting shot, Ava decided to return the heat with a little fire of her own. "Sweetheart, dumb little no-class tramps don't warn Ava about shit. Now if you're finished,

I have a plane to catch," Ava said as she ducked her head into the backseat of the limo. But before she was almost in, Ava backed out slowly and turned toward Sonja. "And in case no one told you, it's never proper to wear open-toed sandals without getting a pedicure."

CHAPTER 23

I sat at a corner table of Blu, a popular midtown restaurant, nervously stirring my iced tea. I couldn't remember the last time I'd been so uptight about a meeting. It was an important meeting, one that could get my life back on its proper course.

The only way I was going to get my show and rid myself of both Ava and Lyrical was to bring Madison into the mix. I'd attempted to avoid involving Madison but I no longer had any choice. Derrick could make that happen. Which is why I phoned him. When I told him I wanted to fly to California to discuss an important matter he told me he was actually in New York and reluctantly agreed to meet with me the next day.

I got to the restaurant about fifteen minutes early to secure a table facing the door. I wanted to flash my winning smile the moment Derrick entered the establishment. I now sit there nervously anticipating his arrival. I look at the tea glass and see that all of the white crystals of the sweetener have dissolved. I pull out my compact to make sure that my bright red lipstick is flawless. I still had ten minutes before Derrick was scheduled to arrive.

Taking a sip of the sweet tea, I thought about Derrick and our relationship, and wondered if he had fond memories of me. We'd met during my freshman year at Howard University. I'd dropped my student ID card, and when I bent down to pick it up, Derrick beat me to the punch. Our hands touched and the feeling was electric. I knew I was going to fall in love with this man.

The first two years it was a perfect love affair and I thought I'd met the man I was going to marry. Derrick was in the ROTC with hopes of becoming a civil engineer. He, like me, was a first-generation college student. He had the most beautiful hazel-brown eyes and a boyish vulnerability that I found hard to resist.

Right before my senior year I discovered I was pregnant. My whole future was about to start and the timing couldn't have been worse. My first reaction was to get an abortion, but Derrick was adamant that we get married and have the child. A couple of months into my pregnancy, he started to waver about our future and I decided to give the baby up for adoption. After our daughter was born, Derrick double-crossed me and managed to adopt her without my knowledge.

We lost touch until a few years ago. Derrick showed up in Vegas to tell me that his sister Jennifer, who had raised our daughter, was dying of breast cancer and that he needed me to raise Madison. This was a time when my career was on the landing strip for a big takeoff, and being a mother was the last thing I wanted to do. But Derrick said that enough time had passed. If I ever changed my mind and wanted to be a part of Madison's life, he would welcome that.

My trip down memory lane was ended by a male voice. "Still just as beautiful as ever." I looked up and saw Derrick standing a few feet from me just as handsome as ever.

I stood up, took both his hands in mine and gave him a kiss on each cheek. "Derrick. It's so good to see you."

"Yancey Harrington Braxton. Man, was I surprised to hear from you."

"Have a seat," I said. "I hope this restaurant wasn't hard to find."

"No, my driver came right here," Derrick said, taking the opposite seat.

"Where is that waiter?" I asked nervously. Damn, I couldn't calm myself.

"Are you okay?"

"I'm fine," I said, forcing a smile on his behalf. "I just need to get the waiter so we can order you something to drink."

"I'm fine, but I must say, you seem a little nervous. Is everything okay?"

I slapped his wrist playfully. "Oh, it's fine. Tell me, are you still an engineer?"

"I still have my license, but for the last couple of years I've been managing a rising young star, who also happens to be my daughter," Derrick said proudly.

I didn't respond. Even though he had put the issue on the table, I still couldn't talk about Madison. I was getting ready to look over the menu when the waiter approached the table.

"Can I get the gentleman a drink?" the waiter asked.

"Just let me have a cranberry juice with Seven-Up," Derrick said.

With the sweetest smile I asked if they had any specials.

He warmed right up. "Yes, we do. Why don't I get the drink and then I'll go over them with you?"

"That will be fine," I said as I smiled a hundred watts at the waiter. When I turned toward Derrick, he was blushing like a boy.

"I see you still got that charm," he said.

"You think so?" I asked, fake eyelashes operating at full speed.

"You *know* so. Are you still in the business?"

"Oh yeah, and things are going well. Right now I'm looking over several projects trying to decide which one to take. There are television, stage and movie offers my agent and I are considering," I said.

"That's good to hear. I tell you I've learned a lot since Madison got in this crazy business, and I don't know how you all do it."

"I couldn't do anything else," I said.

He was fully under my spell. "You always were a star, Yancey."

"How is your mother Charlesetta doing?"

"She's doing fine. About a year ago she moved in with us in California to help with Madison."

There was my opening again, and this time I took it.

"I see Madison is doing quite well. I guess the apple doesn't fall too far from the tree. You must be so proud of her." I picked a piece of the rye bread from the basket and spread whipped butter across it. Just as I took the first bite, the waiter came over and set Derrick's drink in front of him. He rattled off several specials, and when he mentioned a broiled trout stuffed with spinach and rice, Derrick and I looked at each other and nodded our heads in agreement just like we were on a date. Some nice habits hadn't died, even though we had moved up a few stars on the restaurant scale.

When the waiter left, Derrick pulled one of the thin golden brown breadsticks from the basket and bit off the tip. He looked at me and said, "Yes, I'm quite proud of her, and I think you'd be, too, if you took the chance to get to know her."

"I'm sure you're right, Derrick," I said, not faking it. "Everything I've read about her makes Madison seem like the perfect child."

"She's not perfect, but Madison is a good girl."

I didn't respond, although I was proud of her too.

"How's Ava?" Derrick asked.

A dark cloud passed on my brow. "What can I say? Ava is still Ava."

"Is she still in jail?"

"You heard about that? Wow."

"Yeah, we heard about that. I wanted to

contact you, but since you hadn't responded to any of the notes I'd sent with pictures of Madison, well, I figured you had your hands full."

"I'm sorry, Derrick," I said, genuinely meaning those words. "I was busy, but I should have responded and thanked you for sending the photos. She is a beautiful girl. You've been an excellent father."

He looked down at the table and nodded his head. "No problem. So, tell me what you need, Yancey. I know you didn't want to meet with me to talk about the times we had back at old HU?"

The waiter brought out two small salads and suddenly I thought I might need a little help, so I ordered a glass of wine. I encouraged Derrick to do the same but he declined, saying he was meeting Madison and her producer at the studio later in the evening.

"Tell me what you need to talk about, Yancey," Derrick said, unfolding the napkin that held his eating utensils.

Time was running out so I got to the point. "I guess there's no other way but to come out and say it. I want to meet Madison. I want to be a part of her life," I said.

Derrick dropped his fork to the floor. Shocked, he asked, "Are you serious?"

"Yes I am, Derrick. I think it's time."

"But why do you want to meet her now after all these years? You didn't get news that you have some terminal illness, did you?"

"Don't be silly. Of course not. I just figured since we're both in the business it would be good for us to meet. I could help her out," I said.

"Is that the only reason? I mean, Madison has tons of people including myself looking out for her."

"I'm sure she does but certainly not someone with my knowledge. Have you thought about having her do Broadway? That is the best training for a young actress. Maybe you should see if they found someone to play Sparkle. I heard there was talk of finally getting that movie made," I said as I took the avocado out of the salad and placed it on my bread plate and sliced it in half.

"Like yourself, we're looking at a lot of things. Right now it's getting the first album in the can and filming this reality show that VH-1 is doing about Madison."

Shit, Madison couldn't do her own reality show if she was going to be in mine.

"A reality show? Are you serious? With VH-1? Have you thought about this clearly,

Derrick? Reality shows are going to be a thing of the past very soon," I said.

"Madison wants to do it. She's even bringing along her best friend Caressa."

"Who's the parent here? I hope you don't let Madison make all the decisions," I said.

"I'm the parent," he answered with emphasis. "Madison knows that."

"Does she have a boyfriend?"

"Not really. I just started letting her have boys over once she turned sixteen. Madison was seeing this young man but he dropped out of sight when she auditioned for *American Star*. Madison didn't tell me but I think he was pressuring her for sex."

"So she is still a virgin?"

"Of course she is, Yancey."

"That's good. We certainly don't want Madison to have a sex tape out before she's twenty-one," I joked. The waiter brought out our entrees and I gave him my patented dismissive smile.

"Did you say *we?*"

"I meant you."

"So why now, Yancey? And what does Ava think about this? Does she want to meet Madison as well? I'm not sure I'm prepared for that."

"Because I feel like I'm ready and no, I haven't discussed my plans with Ava. She is busy trying to stay one step ahead of her probation officer and find another rich fool to marry her before what beauty she has left fades."

Derrick considered the last statement as he cut into the fish. "I'm going to have to think about it before I talk to Madison."

"What do you think she might say?" I asked.

"She's a teenager, Yancey, so it's no telling. Since *American Star* her life has changed drastically. Madison has a lot on her plate."

"Okay, okay, but can you do it soon. I need to tell . . . ," I said stopping myself before I said producers.

"You need to tell who?"

"No one," I said. "I'm just anxious to meet my baby girl."

"This is so strange," Derrick said softly. He took the last bite of his fish.

"What's so strange about this? Why can't you see that I've grown wiser and realize what a mistake it was to never meet Madison?" I said.

"It that all it is? No other motives?" Derrick asked, looking at me the way he always did when he was trying to determine if I was telling the truth.

"No other motives but to do what I should have done years ago," I said.

"And what is that?"

"Be the best mother that I can be," I said, eyeing the dessert tray and avoiding Derrick's inquisitive eyes.

CHAPTER 24

When Derrick asked Caressa and the two producers to give him and Madison some privacy, Madison hoped it wouldn't be bad news like when he told her about Aunt Jennifer and her cancer diagnosis.

"I don't know how to tell you this."

"Tell me what, Daddy? You're making me really nervous."

"I can't believe this is happening now." Derrick went silent for a few moments and cupped his hands under his chin. His face looked pensive until he finally came to a decision.

"Your mother wants to meet you."

"My mother?" she asked, almost breaking into a laugh at the surprise. She half expected her father to say he was punking her. "Are you serious?" Madison leaped from the rolling high chair she was seated in and began pacing the control room repeating, "You've got to be kidding me."

"No, sweetheart, I'm serious. I met with her for lunch and she really seemed serious," Derrick said.

"Did she say why?" Madison raised her hand to her forehead in an attempt to collect herself. "I don't know, Daddy. I don't know if I want to meet her now."

"Well, it's totally up to you, Madison. I'm just the messenger. If you decide you don't want to meet her, I'll call her and tell her. But I thought you should know. I also think it's time you two met."

"What did she say? How does she look? Is she still pretty?" Madison's thoughts twirled back to her youth, when she'd found out her mother was the glamorous recording and Broadway star known as Yancey B. She had cut out pictures of her attending parties with handsome men and being seen with famous people. Madison had a scrapbook hidden in her room containing the pictures that nobody, including her dad, knew about. She thought about how many times she'd sat up in bed all alone wondering what she would say when Yancey and she met. Madison thought about it during her *American Star* audition and every time she competed. Secretly she'd wished her mother would seek her out once she became famous.

Out of nowhere flashed a memory of when

she was in the sixth grade. Despite her young age, she had been picked to play the lead role of Dorothy in *The Wiz.* The production wasn't polished, but people raved about Madison's powerful voice. Her castmate's mother, a beautiful socialite, gushed over Madison, her beauty and performance. When she asked Madison if her mother was proud of her, Madison announced that her mother had given her up at birth, one of the few times she'd ever said this. Shocked, the socialite said in a whispered tone, "She wouldn't have done that if she knew what a talent you'd grow up to be." And from that day on Madison often wondered if this could possibly be true.

"She looks great," Derrick said. "Just like the girl I fell in love with."

"Who looks great?" Madison asked as her daydream ended.

"Yancey. Remember you asked me if she was still pretty."

"So she's here in New York. I thought she was doing some road show," Madison said.

"Yeah, she's here. Yancey told me that she had a lot of projects upcoming, but she wants to take the time off to meet you. She could offer you advice on dealing with show business."

Madison wasn't convinced, though the

idea was growing on her with every passing second. "But did she say anything about why she'd waited so long? Did she say anything about being my mother? Did she, Daddy? Am I finally going to have a real mommy?"

"She said if you allowed her, she was ready to be a mother."

Madison felt a sharp pang of longing, but quickly forced it away. "Do you believe her?"

"I don't know, Madison. I just don't know."

"What about you and Shanice?"

"What about her?"

"If you two get back together, won't that make Yancey uncomfortable?"

"I don't think you have to worry about that, sweetheart."

"Are you sure?"

"Yes, I am sure. Stop worrying about your daddy."

Madison walked over to her father and put her arms on his shoulders as he sat quietly wondering how his little girl had become a woman without his knowledge.

Later that evening Madison, Caressa and Derrick were looking over the architect's plans for Jenny's Place in Harlem when the phone in the hotel suite rang. Derrick left the two girls scouring over the blueprints on the dining room table and went to the desk to answer the phone.

"Hello."

"Mr. Lewis?" the vaguely familiar-sounding voice asked.

"Yes, this is Derrick Lewis."

"This is Nicole Stovall, Madison's voice teacher. We met once."

"Oh yeah, how are you?"

"I'm doing fine. I just want to talk to you about something that's been bothering me and thought maybe you could give me some insight."

Derrick looked over at Madison and Caressa, who had now spread the blueprints on the floor.

"How can I help you?"

Nicole went on to tell Derrick about their lunch date and how Madison responded when Yancey Braxton's name came up.

"She was really sad, Mr. Lewis, and I just couldn't get it off my mind."

"What did Madison tell you?"

"That's it; she didn't. Madison told me it was nothing. Does she know Yancey?"

"Not really, but there is a connection."

"Oh, I see."

"Look, Ms. Stovall, I really appreciate your concern and I'll talk to Madison about this. What am I thinking? I'm the adult here. Yancey is actually Madison's biological mother."

There was dead silence on the phone line. After a few minutes Derrick called out Nicole's name.

"Yes, yes, I'm here. My God, I don't know what to say. I didn't know Yancey had a daughter. Is she in Madison's life now?"

"Not really."

"Oh I see then, that explains the tears. I wonder if Yancey knows what she's missing having such a beautiful and talented daughter," Nicole said.

"That's nice of you to say but if you know Yancey, then you know what her number-one priority is," Derrick said with a laugh.

"Well, I guess it's great you can laugh about it, Mr. Lewis. I don't know how I could live my life without my children," Nicole said.

"Madison said you were a great mom. Now I see what she was talking about."

"That's very nice of you and Madison to say that. So you're telling me she's okay and I shouldn't worry?"

"Always worry about kids, Ms. Stovall, especially in today's world. But trust me when I say I'm looking out for my daughter double time."

"I hear you. Please forgive me if I've overstepped my boundaries but I just think Madison is the best. You've done a great job of raising her."

"Thanks, Ms. Stovall. That coming from someone who Madison thinks so highly of means a lot."

"Have a good evening, Mr. Lewis."

"Derrick, call me Derrick."

"Only if you call me Nicole."

"You bet."

CHAPTER 25

Ava found Lyrical lying on the sofa in Yancey's office with a newspaper covering her face. Lyrical's high-top sneakers rested on the arm of the sofa. Disgusted, Ava was tempted to push them to the floor, but she needed some information and didn't want to get Lyrical riled.

"So what's the bitch been up to?" Ava asked.

Lyrical woke up and removed the newspaper. She was still sleepy and didn't reply.

"Surprised to see me?"

Finally Lyrical stirred herself and sat up. "When did you get back?"

"I've been back a couple of days."

"How was it?"

"What?"

"Your vacation, diva. What did you do?"

Ava was pleased to have an audience. "I did nothing but lay around on my ass and eat a lot of very fattening food with a bunch of boring rich people."

"Sounds like fun to me. You know, the lying on your ass thing." A street edge entered her voice. "When are we going to start my classes about how to be a lady, Ava?"

"You mean etiquette lessons, darling?"

"Yeah, whatever, Ava. You think I forgot, but I introduced you to Donnie Ray and it's now time for you to pay up."

"It's all so easy, my darling. There are just three simple rules you must follow," Ava said.

"What are they?"

Ava raised a finger, signaling the number one. "Stop cussing. It's so crass and juvenile. Learn how to express yourself without the use of those words." Up went a second finger. "Start wearing more dresses and bras. I'm surprised you're not mistaken for a dyke or young boy more often." She dropped her hand. "And finally, don't give out no pussy without rewards."

"Are you telling me to become a whore?" Lyrical said, suspicious. "I ain't selling no pussy, Ava, and I don't like dresses or bras."

"Who said anything about being a whore? There is a big difference. And I don't mean you have to get something every time you get down, but you need to keep a little tally running in your head and when it's time you cash in."

Lyrical didn't get her drift at all. "Donnie Ray ain't got no big money. He ain't paying for no pussy."

"Then you need to upgrade, my dear," Ava replied, as if that was the most obvious move in the world. "Now you asked and I've told you. Lesson over," Ava said. "It's time to answer my question. What has Miss Yancey Braxton been up to?"

"You mean besides getting on my damn nerves," Lyrical said crossly.

"That's just her style. But she gets on my damn nerves too. Has she gotten the final approval on her little television show yet?"

"I don't know. They started filming and then they just stopped. So I don't know what's going on." She sighed, not liking her new life as a reality show assistant. "She's been having me make a lot of calls and I don't really like harassing people on the phone."

"Like who?"

"Lots of agents who don't have a fuckin' clue as to who she is," Lyrical cried. Then she paused, considering something. "But I must give your girl credit. She is going to wear somebody down."

Ava sneered at that idea. "No agent worth his or her salt is going to represent a has-been. Trust me on that. When I came back from Europe, I couldn't get a decent agent and I was willing to pay some big money. So I guess somebody should tell Yancey to forget that. And she can forget television and pray to God that her reality show gets picked up." Venting about her daughter picked up her spirits, and she asked, "Who else has she been talking to?"

"There was a Nicole somebody in Atlanta, a lady named Windsor, some guy named Basil Henderson, and Derrick Lewis in California. I'm pretty sure it has something to do with her show. I overheard her talking to the Derrick guy. I even think she went to lunch with him a couple of days ago."

"Derrick Lewis?" Ava perked up. "What does she have to talk to him about?" she asked, but she already knew the answer. "I bet she's trying to get to the goose who laid the golden egg. I've got to find a way to beat her to the punch. Damn, I hate being broke."

"Did you see this?" Lyrical said, pointing to a picture in the newspaper.

Ava held up the newspaper for a closer look. "Who is that?"

"It's some count from Luxembourg. Didn't you tell me you used to be married to somebody from there? I thought you might know him."

"Yes, I was. That's my ex's brother-in-law, Duke Van Puttan. What is he doing in the newspaper?"

"The article says he and his wife have donated a lot of money for some cancer ward here. It seems like they are having some big gala at the new Plaza Hotel to celebrate. I heard that hotel was the shit in its day."

Ava scanned the article, then closed the paper. She looked at Lyrical and said, "I've got to get an invite to this party. It could be just what I need to get back on my feet. I'm just not good in this broke bitch role."

"So you know him?"

"Do I know him? Honey, please. Not only do I know him, but I know his secrets," Ava added with a smile. "And where I'm from, that's like money in the bank."

CHAPTER 26

"That is the most exciting news I've heard in a long time, Madison! You're finally going to meet your mother. Are you more nervous or more excited?" Caressa asked. The two of them were sitting in the middle of Madison's king-size bed decorated with pink and white polka dots and green pillows.

"Who said I was *going* to meet her?" Madison said firmly. "She *wants* to meet me."

Caressa watched Madison for a moment before choosing her words carefully. "How many times have we talked about this? Of course you've got to meet her."

"That's when I was young and stupid. What do I need with her now? I'm the one who's rich and famous now," Madison said.

"You don't really mean that, Madison. I think it would be great if you met your mother. What if you have some sisters and brothers? That would be so neat."

Madison shook her head. "Trust me, I don't have any sisters and brothers unless my daddy is hiding something." Then she voiced a worry she'd had ever since she talked to her father. "I don't understand it. Yancey isn't the mothering kind. I think she's up to something. I don't know what, but I'm going to figure it out."

"What do you think she is up to? Maybe she just came to her senses and realizes what a wonderful young woman she is missing out on."

That's exactly what Madison was hoping, and she flashed a broad smile. "Oh, Caressa, that's so nice of you to say."

The two of them lay back on separate pillows. After a few moments Caressa said, "You think she wants some of your money?"

"Everybody wants my money," Madison answered, pulling another pillow to her chest. "Not you, of course, Caressa. I would just hope that she is more original than that."

"So did she call you?"

"No, she called my dad and told him she wants to meet me." A slight burr entered her voice as she said, "I think he still has feelings for her."

"You do? Is there a chance they might get

back together?"

Madison stared at the ceiling. "Anything is possible when you're talking about adults."

"That would be so romantic," Caressa swooned.

"You've been watching too many movies, girl," Madison said.

Caressa popped up, bursting with energy. "What are you going to wear? I mean, with her being a diva and all, we have to pick the perfect outfit for you to wear. I'm sure the press will be all over this."

"I *told* you, girl, I haven't decided if I want to do it," Madison said. Still, she had been thinking hard on that very question. Crawling off her bed, she walked into her large walk-in closet. What *would* she wear if she granted her birth mother a meeting? Madison wondered as she looked at all the new clothes she had bought and been sent by various designers. Moments later, Caressa reached into the pink section of the closet and pulled out a sweater and skirt set.

"You should wear something like this, since pink is your favorite color. What if you guys look alike?"

Madison eyed the pink confection doubtfully. "I've seen pictures of her and I don't really think we look alike."

"I've seen pictures of Yancey and I disagree."

"Really?"

"Both of you are beautiful and you still got some more growing up to do, Madison."

"Are you saying you think I'll look more like Yancey when I get older?"

"That's not such a bad thing," Caressa suggested.

Madison's gaze swept down the long row of clothes. Finally she announced, "If I go — and I haven't decided that I will — I think I will wear pink."

Caressa smiled and said, "Good decision."

"You think this is going to turn out okay, Caressa?"

"Madison, I do. How many times have we talked about you one day meeting your mother."

"I know, but what if she doesn't like me?"

"You don't want her to like you, you want her to love you."

"Is that possible, Caressa?"

"Anything's possible, Madison."

The two girls embraced in a supportive hug.

CHAPTER 27

A New York number flashed across my cell phone, and I decided to answer because I was in the mood to give a bill collector a good cussing out.

"May I speak to Yancey Braxton, please?"

"Who's calling?"

"Regan Reynolds."

My demeanor switched to sunny like the flip of a switch. "*The* Regan Reynolds? I mean, with the Reynolds Agency?"

"That would be me."

"I heard a lot of great things about your firm, Regan. Is it okay if I call you Regan?" I asked, like a schoolgirl trying to impress her favorite teacher. I had read so many articles about her in the trades. This former actress now ran one of the biggest talent agencies in New York, with offices in Los Angeles and Miami. She had become a star with fashion spreads in *Essence* and *Vogue*. Her Central Park South apartment was featured in the pages of the *New York Times.* Needless to say, as an African-American woman I'd admired her from afar.

"Sure, call me Regan." She laughed at the sudden informality. "I must tell you, I was a big fan of yours when you were recording. 'Any Way the Wind Blows' is still one of my favorite songs."

I couldn't believe this was falling into place so smoothly. "Thank you, Regan. How did you get my number?" I had to remain cool and calm like I was expecting her to call. I mean, why wouldn't she? I was still Yancey Harrington Braxton with numerous stage roles and platinum-selling albums.

"Well, if I'm to believe my executive assistant, *you* called *me.* I usually don't return unsolicited calls for representation, but I recognized your name."

"Maybe it was *my assistant* who called you," I said. I didn't need Regan to feel that I was desperate.

"You've not released anything in a while, so what have you been up to?"

Keeping up a front was second nature to me. "A lot of work, mostly theater."

"Well, that's not what I heard, but that's neither here nor there. Are you still looking for representation?"

"I'm still interviewing agents," I corrected.

She didn't believe that for a second. "Listen, Yancey, let's cut to the chase here, girl, and not waste each other's time. Now, we both know your best days in the industry are behind you. Still, I think I can help revive your career, but only if you come clean and leave those tired diva ways at home. Do I make myself clear?"

I was stunned into silence. Who did this woman think she was, and who was she talking to in that "let's be real" tone?

After a few moments of silence Regan said, "Yancey, are you still there?"

"Yes, I'm here, Regan," I said coldly. "I guess I'm a little stunned here and don't know quite what to say."

"Let me tell you what you say, Yancey," she said with a new warmth in her voice. "You say, Regan, I want you and your firm to revive my career and take it to new heights, or you say, You so like a bitch and I don't think I can work with you. It's just that simple. Let's not waste each other's time. I'm sure we both have things to do if we work together or not."

Reality was settling in, and I didn't want her to hang up. "Okay, I understand."

"So is that a yes or no, Yancey?"

"That would be yes."

"Great. Let me have my assistant Corrie

give you a call to set up a lunch date for us to discuss a plan. I will have her schedule it somewhere close to our office so that we can bring you over after we eat."

"That sounds good," I said, feeling as though I was in great hands, but not knowing why. "I look forward to meeting you, Regan."

"And I look forward to meeting you, Yancey. Have a good day."

CHAPTER 28

Ava couldn't believe her good luck. While going through Yancey's good underwear drawer, she discovered stacks of hundred-dollar bills neatly placed beneath the silk and satin panties and bras. However Yancey had gotten this money wasn't legal, and Ava would use that if Yancey got upset with her.

So Ava counted herself thirty thousand dollars and took it to her room and placed it in her purse. She immediately called for a car service and then phoned Bergdorf Goodman, introducing herself as Lady Ava Van Putten and demanding a personal shopper in two hours. When asked if she had anything in mind, Ava replied, "Everything, love. It's fall, and time for a new wardrobe."

Two hours later, Lady Ava found herself in a private salon on the seventh floor of the Fifth Avenue department store. She sipped on champagne while her personal shopper brought items for her to look at.

Lauren, a tall, willowy blonde who looked like a runway model, suggested that Ava start with shoes. Ava agreed.

"What do you think of these, Lady Ava?" Lauren asked, offering a pair of purple crisscross platforms in violet silk.

"Oh, those are beautiful," Ava said.

"Yes, they are, and they will look spectacular on you. They're Brian Atwood."

Ava instantly went against the grain. "Do they come in any other colors besides purple? Is that the lesbos' official color? Ava don't play that."

"Yes, in red and black," Lauren said.

"Okay, I will take both in a size nine, and let's take the purple as well. You never know when you might have to do a lesbo charity event," Ava said. She knew from her days of money that you never ask a personal shopper the costs of items. If you had to ask prices then you couldn't afford the item. Ava would know when it was time to stop shopping.

"Got that. Now how about these? I think it's a great show for that St. James suit I'm sure you have and will go well with pantsuits as well," Lauren said.

Ava shot Lauren an incredulous glare. "Pantsuits? Tell me you're kidding, Lauren.

Lady Ava doesn't wear pantsuits."

"Oh, so you weren't swayed by the Hillary effect?"

"I love Hillary, but the only thing I want her to give me advice on is how to make more money. But I do like these shoes," she said, examining a pair of open-toe pumps with a beautiful rosette. "Who makes them?"

"These are Stuart Weitzman. It's satin, in chocolate or black."

"I'll take them in chocolate." She tore her eyes away from them and saw that her flute was nearly empty. "Before we go on to handbags, can you get me some more champagne and maybe some finger sandwiches?"

Ava had already bought up a storm, and Lauren was having a very good day. "Sure. Would you like some cucumber and tomatoes?"

"That sounds lovely. And maybe some smoked salmon as well, honey."

"I will get that right away and see if my salesclerk has pulled those bags I asked for. Why don't you look through these books and see if there are any dresses that catch your eye?"

"I will. Just leave them on the table," Ava said.

As Lauren prepared to leave the salon, Ava called her name. The mild frown on Ava's face suggested a problem.

"Is everything all right, Lady Ava?"

"Is this *it* with the shoes?"

Lauren was surprised by the question. Ava had bought six pairs in one sitting. "Yes," she said apprehensively, not wanting to lose her rich customer with the wrong answer. "Is there a problem?"

"Yes, Lauren, there is. I can't believe you haven't shown me any Christian Louboutins. You do have them, don't you?"

"We do, but when I checked, we didn't have any in your size. I would be more than happy to order them for you. It takes about two weeks, and I can show you a satin bow sling he made in pink. I think it would be perfect for you."

"No, I don't want to wait two weeks. And don't show me those shoes," she said, pointing to the pink Louboutin. "It's like teasing me. Just get the sandwiches and champagne."

"Are you sure?"

"Very much so. Scurry, Lauren," she said with a wave of both hands.

Three glasses of champagne and several finger sandwiches later, Ava's shopping spree was complete. Lauren arranged for two sales associates to take her packages to the car and Ava tripped out of the store carrying her new Bottega Veneta woven napa leather bag on her shoulder.

When she got back to Yancey's town house, she was happy to discover that her daughter wasn't at home. Ava immediately enlisted Lyrical's assistance.

"I need you to help me hide this stuff."

Lyrical was wide-eyed at Ava's purchases all lined up. "Where did you get all this from?"

"The department store, silly."

"Who are we hiding it from and why?"

"Yancey, because I don't want her to know I went over my budget or have her borrowing my stuff."

"You have a budget?" Lyrical asked as she opened one of the shoe boxes. "Oh, these shoes are tight," she exclaimed.

Ava took the box from her and closed it. "I guess I could put the stuff under my bed. Damn, I need my own place. I feel like a dumb teenager hiding something from my parents."

"Yancey is too self-absorbed to be looking for shit. I think you'll be just fine leaving it in your room."

"I know, but we still need to hide it,"

Ava said.

"What about your bathroom or the office? She never really comes in there unless to give me orders." Lyrical bristled at the thought. "I mean, your daughter is a piece of work. But then you know that."

"I'm too tired to think about this," Ava said, handing the bags to Lyrical. "Just take this stuff and put it under my bed. I need a drink."

"Me too," Lyrical said, not moving. She wasn't playing the family servant.

"I don't think it's a good idea for you to be drinking on the job, Lyrical."

"I didn't ask you, and it's after seven. I was just waiting on you to get back," Lyrical informed her. "I'll hide these packages while you go in the kitchen and fix us some drinks."

Lyrical was tough, and Ava lost the attitude. "Okay. I'm sticking with champagne. What do you want?"

"I've never had champagne," Lyrical said.

"Then I think it's time we change that. Champagne for everyone," Ava said as she snapped her newly manicured hand in the air with a haughty laugh.

CHAPTER 29

I met Cale at a crowded Starbucks across
from the Time Warner Building at Colum-
bus Circle. I felt great in the black-and-
white belted poplin shirtdress I'd recently
purchased at Bloomingdale's.

We were getting ready to resume filming.
The producers liked our proposed changes
to the show, and I filled Cale in on my meeting with Derrick. I knew this would score
major points for me.

Delighted by the news, Cale asked, "So
when are you going to hear from him?"

"As soon as he talks with Madison. You
know, Cale, I feel as though I ought to thank
you for pushing me to reunite with my
daughter. This could be a wonderful direction for all of us. And, oh, did I tell you I
got a call from Regan Reynolds about
representing me?"

"You did?" he asked, sounding a little too
surprised. "That's great. Do you think she

will give us permission to tape your first meeting?"

I played right along. "I don't see why not. I mean, it's her job to promote my career. I'm going to meet her for lunch, so we ought to plan what I should say."

"It looks like things are coming together. With Regan Reynolds representing you, it will mean that you'll be getting more auditions, and that will make the producers and investors happy."

I raised my latte in a toast to myself. "Yeah, things are looking up. It looks like Yancey Harrington Braxton is on her way back to the top."

"The haters better get ready," Cale laughed.

"Yeah, they better because I'm ready for them."

Talking about Regan Reynolds with Cale over coffee must have gotten her ears burning. No sooner had I walked through the door of my home than my cell phone rang.

"May I speak to Yancey Braxton?"

"Who's calling?" I asked.

"This is Gilliam James calling for the Regan Reynolds Agency. Is this Yancey?"

"Yes, Gilliam, this is Yancey."

"Hold for Mrs. Reynolds."

After a few moments of silence Regan came on the phone.

"Yancey," she said brightly, "how are you doing?"

"I'm doing well. How are you?" What I really meant was "find me some damn work."

"Everything is great. Look, I'll get right to the point. I have a couple of opportunities for you."

Those were the magic words. I quickly replied, "I'm listening."

"Well, Seal needs a couple of background singers for a recording session and for a party he is doing for Sean Combs. I understand Mary J. Blige is one of the hosts and will be singing." When I didn't respond right away, she added, "A lot of industry people will be there."

So this was her news? "I don't do backup," I said flatly.

I heard a sucked-in breath of surprise. When she spoke again, her voice was ten times harder. "Now, Yancey, what did we agree on?"

"What are you talking about, Regan?"

"The diva attitude and how you were not going to do that. This is a good-paying gig and a chance for some much-needed exposure." The phone went silent, and when she came on, she was reading some listing. "The only other possibility we have is a recurring role on *Ugly Betty.* You know they moved filming to New York."

"Yeah, I knew that, but I can't play Vanessa Williams's mother. I already turned that role down."

"That's not the role," she clarified. "It's playing opposite Vanessa, but it's not her mother. I would never send you up for a role like that."

"I'm glad to hear that, Regan," I said, thinking that maybe Regan Reynolds understood me better than my former agents.

"So are you on board? This would only be for two nights. Let's see what we can parlay those jobs into."

I liked Regan's direction. She spoke my language, and for the first time in a long time, I felt that someone other than S. Marcus had my back. "Yeah, I will do them," I said without the normal hesitation I would have put up.

"Great. Do you have a reel and a demo tape?"

"Sure."

"I will have Gilliam send over a messenger with the script and pick up those items while she's there. She'll let you know where you need to be for the rehearsals." She added a little pep talk. "I know you'll knock them dead."

"I will do my best. I'm really excited at the possibility of doing something involving the election," I said.

"These are some exciting times," Regan said, being genuine for a change. "Who would have ever thought we would live to see the day where we might have a chance at electing an African-American man as leader of the free world?"

"Who would have thought that would ever happen?" I chimed in. "Maybe if we're lucky we will live to see the same thing happen to an African-American woman."

"One thing at a time," Regan said.

Before I hung up the phone, I did something else I normally didn't do.

"Regan?"

"Yes, Yancey."

"Thanks for this. Thanks for giving me a chance and believing in me."

"Not a problem, Yancey," she said smoothly. "Just don't let me down."

"I won't. I promise."

His steel gray eyes were hard to ignore in the nearly dark BB King's Blues Club on 42nd Street. John Basil Henderson, a man I'd come oh so close to marrying, sat across

369

from me.

"You still look good, girl," Basil said, all smiles, the charm dripping from each word.

I couldn't help but return the smile. "So do you, Basil, but you already know that."

"Thanks, babe, but I know you didn't want to meet with me just to tell me how good I look. What's up? You said something about a forgiveness tour. What's that all about?"

Basil and I knew how each other played our game. So there was no fooling him. Even so, I tried to stall.

"How is your daughter?"

"Tally is fine."

"I bet she is beautiful."

"She'll be the Halle Berry of her generation," he said expansively. "So come on now, Yancey. What are you up to, and how does it involve me?"

I bowed my head, took a breath, then faced him. "Okay. I know you're busy. But I got this chance to do something big for my career. I'm shooting a pilot for a reality show, and the producers thought it would be great if I include some of my friends and boyfriends who knew me when my career was really smoking. So naturally I thought of you. But we've been out of touch a long time, and I don't know what you've been up to. Are you involved right now?"

"Come on, Yancey. You know me."

"Man or woman?" I just couldn't resist asking.

"Yancey," he said, looking off to the side.

"Just asking. Anyway, it would be what they call in the business polluting reality with us. We would pick some restaurant or public place where it would look like we ran into each other accidentally, and when I get back to my town house I would talk into the camera about our relationship."

"Kinda like what you did with your hit record."

I knew he would get around to that sooner or later. There was no way I could make that up to him. I'd hoped after all this time he might have found room in his heart to forgive me. It wasn't as if we both hadn't done hurtful things to each other.

Basil took a swig of his beer. "Thanks, but no thanks, Yancey. I don't need the publicity."

"I know you don't, Basil, and I promise you I won't do anything to embarrass you or make either of us look bad. You know how I feel about you," I said as sweetly as I could. That was the closest I'd ever come to an apology for how I'd exploited him. Basil could be tough, but I knew he had a sensitive side. I always viewed him as a male version of me when it came to getting what I wanted. Which is why we worked so well as a couple; also why we were so fucked up. It showed in the way he dressed and how people (both men and women) stared at him whenever he entered a room. I had become used to this when I was younger. I missed it and was determined to have it again.

"I don't know, Yancey. I know you and there's always an agenda up that beautiful sleeve of yours. Just like your mama. Is she still in the joint?"

"No, she's out for now. Didn't Raymond tell you? I'm sure the prison authorities notified him before they released her," I said. Raymond Tyler was the man my mother had shot. I was convinced he was also the love of Basil's life, even though he would never admit it.

His face had completely shut down. "I don't talk about Raymond with you, Yancey. You know better."

"You started it asking about Ava," I pointed out.

He took my point. Plus, he wanted to get off that subject immediately. "So that's it? No strings?"

"Yes, that's it. Simple as that. I'll make

sure the producers make you seem like the big balla you are, Basil."

He chuckled, spreading his arms out wide. "Can't keep that from happening, Yancey B. It is what it is. Anybody can see that." He regarded me curiously. "I don't know why, but I thought maybe you'd given up the acting thing and just married well and had some kids."

I leaned in toward him. "You know better than that. I still got to win an Emmy, a Tony, an Oscar, and a Grammy, Basil. Then and only then will I consider my second act."

"You mean your final act, don't you, girl? Neither one of us are spring chickens," Basil said with a sexy grin.

I flashed him a smirk right back. "Now, Basil, that's cold. Don't you know forty is the new thirty?"

"Yeah, that's true, baby girl, but you sure you want to spend the best days of your life messing around those phony people in the entertainment world?"

"Aren't you still an agent?" I asked, already knowing the answer to that question. I had contacted Basil through his agency, XJI, so I knew he was still in sports management.

"Yeah, I am," Basil said. "Keeps me living the life I've become accustomed to."

"There you have it. Same thing for me, Basil. Same thing for me."

My words must have given him food for thought, because for a long minute he just sat there. Finally he said, "So this reality show is really important to you, huh?"

"Yeah, it is, Basil," I said with full sincerity. "It's something I need to reclaim my place in the world."

"Who said you ever lost your place, Yancey? You struck me as a girl who would always land on her feet."

"And I will. That is, with your help, of course."

"Let me take a day or two to think about it. I will get back to you," Basil said. He leaned over to give me a sweet kiss on the cheek and then slid his amazing body from the booth and headed to the door.

CHAPTER 30

The security detail at the newly renovated
Plaza Hotel was larger than Ava expected.
Still, she looked like she belonged with the
well-dressed crowd in an eye-popping white
evening gown with sequined straps and a
low bustline. Was she going to get inside?
Ava wondered as she watched people line
up to get their names checked off and gain
entry into the party of the season in New
York. In other words, a ballroom full of
wealthy men looking on the sly for a woman
like Ava.

She had opened her small jeweled purse,
pretending to be looking for her invitation,
when she suddenly felt eyes on her. She
looked over her shoulder and found a tall,
handsome man staring at her. He was
broad-shouldered, with flawless dark skin
and wavy black hair. The only problem was
that he looked too young. Ava thought, That
boy could be my son and is probably an-

other broke brother with a good dick.

When Ava looked at him, he raised his glass of champagne and smiled at her. He had a perfect smile and his tuxedo fit him like a glove.

A waiter carrying a tray of champagne glasses passed Ava. She took one and winked at the stunned waiter. She turned to the handsome stranger, who was now having a good laugh at Ava's boldness. Making her way to the corner he was standing in, Ava stopped and said, "What's so funny, youngster?"

The man smiled, took a swallow of his drink. "I wouldn't call you funny. Maybe bold, but most definitely beautiful."

Ava tried to restrain herself, but a huge smile spread across her face. She suddenly didn't feel the need to get into the ballroom. Things were suddenly getting interesting in the lobby.

"I'm Houston Sturdivant," he said, sticking out his large, masculine hand.

"Ava Parker Middlebrooks," Ava replied as she daintily shook.

"Are you going inside the party?"

"I was thinking about it. I'm related to the family."

He drew back in surprise. "You related to Duke?"

"Yes, I am. How do you know Duke?"

"We went to prep school and Yale together."

"You can't be as old as Duke," Ava teased.

"Yes, I am. But you know what they say: black don't crack."

Ava liked that he was older. He was becoming more suitable all the time. "I know that's right. So are you here alone?"

"Looks like not anymore." Houston smiled.

"Now, Mr. Sturdivant, are you flirting with me?"

His eyes glittered like a tiger's. "What would make you think that, Miss Middlebrooks?"

"Let's just say I know men like the back of my hand. Especially those in heat," Ava said. She had turned to take in the rest of the party when she suddenly felt soft lips touch the side of her neck.

Houston whispered, "Let's blow this joint and go back to my suite at the Trump and have a real nightcap."

Ava couldn't decide if she needed to meet her future husband or have some headbanging sex with a smart young stud. Why couldn't she have both? she asked herself as she pictured Houston lying butt naked, his deep dark skin contrasted with the brilliant white of sheets. Just thinking about that brought tiny beads of perspiration popping across her forehead.

Ava leaned into Houston and said, "Why don't you escort me inside, have a drink, and talk a little more about your proposal, Mr. Sturdivant?"

Houston bowed and held out his arm in invitation. "Lead the way, Ava, and I shall follow."

CHAPTER 31

"I don't know why you're so keen on me meeting her, Dad," Madison said. Derrick had just returned to the hotel suite from lunch.

"Because she really wants to meet you, Madison, and it's long past time that she did."

The pendulum had swung for Madison all over again. Meeting her real mother was exciting, but it was scary too. What if Yancey decided she didn't like the daughter she'd never met? Madison plopped down on the sofa and grabbed the remote. She clicked on the flat screen and thumbed the volume up on the music video to level ten.

"Madison," Derrick called out, raising his voice in order to be heard over the television.

She pretended not to hear him.

He walked in front of the television, his fist on his hips. "Turn that down, young lady. I'm talking to you."

Madison huffed and clicked the flat screen off.

"What is your problem, little girl? You had always said you wanted to know who your mother was, that you wanted to meet her, and now —"

Madison turned to him, half in anger. "I simply changed my mind." She got up from the sofa, looking as though she was going to walk away into the bedroom. "I don't need her now. I have you and Ms. Nicole in my life."

"Sit back down," Derrick commanded. He walked around the coffee table and took a seat beside his daughter. "Nicole cares a great deal about you but she has her own family. Now tell me the real reason why all of a sudden you don't want to meet Yancey."

"Where has she been, Dad?"

"What do you mean?"

"All these years. When I was born, two, or five or even last year. Where was my so-called mother then? What if you had allowed her to have her way and give me up for adoption? Now I've got a little fame, making some money, she all of a sudden just pops up like 'Oh, I want to meet my darling daughter.'" She frowned deeply. "I don't think so, Dad. Something is not right about this."

Derrick rubbed his chin, giving it some thought. "But what if you're wrong? What if this is just your mother wanting to meet you? What if all those years she just didn't understand what a huge mistake she was making by missing out on your life? Then one day she did. Grown-ups sometimes take years to grow up, Madison. Yancey doesn't want your money."

Madison looked up at him in hope. She had always relied on her father's judgment. He was the one person she could count on in a business where no one could be counted on. Her meeting with Yancey clearly meant so much to him for some reason. What was the worst that could happen?

"I tell you what, Daddy, maybe you're right. I trust you. But I will meet her only on one condition."

"Name it."

"That we film the meeting for my reality show and that I get to invite Ms. Nicole. Talk about drama when Yancey sees her."

This was the last thing he expected from his daughter. "Why would you want to film something so personal, Madison?" He seemed appalled by the idea. "And surprising her with Nicole. I don't know if Yancey will agree to that."

"Then we won't meet," she said, firmly crossing her arms.

Derrick sighed heavily. "Yancey is not a bad woman. She's a little different, to say the least, but she's not a bad person. You might even learn to love her if you get to know her."

Madison was unmoved. "I will meet her if we film it. And maybe you're right about not inviting Ms. Nicole." That was best, she thought, nodding. That way she could protect herself. If the meeting turned out badly, well, it would at least help her ratings.

"Let me give her a call and find out what she says."

"I hope she says yes."

Derrick sighed. "Women. Can't live with them and can't live without them."

CHAPTER 32

"Now remember to wait ten minutes before you come in. I want to make sure I tell Madison that I want to film some of this for the show," I said to Cale and the camera-man.

"Do you want to have some kind of signal or maybe text me?" Cale asked.

"Just time ten minutes from the time I walk in the door."

"Okay Yancey, good luck," Cale said.

"Thanks," I said as I made sure my blouse was properly tucked in my skirt and the thin red belt was in place as well. My cell phone rang and I saw it was Dalton. I still hadn't told him about Madison or meeting her. I planned to as soon as the timing is right.

"Hey honey, I don't have much time. What's going on?"

"I need to talk to you, Yancey," Dalton said. He whispered and it sounded like he'd been crying.

"I promise to call you once I finish the shoot. Bye, Dalton," I said as I clicked off my phone and the power.

Right before I opened the door I was struck by the strangeness of the moment. I was suddenly very afraid. It was like I was going on the most important audition of my life and I so needed this role. Here I was meeting my daughter in some fancy hotel that she was able to afford but I couldn't afford to buy a bottle of water in. Was this God's sick sense of humor, giving Madison everything I'd longed for even before I was her age?

I pushed open the door and walked into the suite. I saw Derrick looking out the large picture windows and spotted Madison coming from a door on the left side of the room. Our eyes met and there was suddenly a moment of silence and stillness and I felt like I was standing in wet cement pumps. I couldn't move. I was struck by how beautiful she was in a young sort of way. When I was her age I was awkward in my beauty.

Madison's gaze remained fixed on me and I stared back. She was wearing a form-fitting cotton candy pink sweater dress with dark brown trim and looked poised and confident as a seasoned performer. She didn't look like a teenager. I noticed her light eyes with a rim of darkness around the pupils and long hair that cascaded in soft waves right below her shoulders. Madison was really a beautiful girl.

"Yancey, you're here," Derrick said as he walked toward me but stopped and put his hands on the small of Madison's back and pushed her toward me. She was smiling and there was no look of forgiveness in her high-cheekboned face.

"Hello Derrick," I said. My first words were easy but I felt on the verge of nervous laughter. Not that there was anything funny about this situation but I didn't know what to do. When my eyes met Madison's again, I felt them drop down and focus on the expensive Persian rug in the middle of the room.

"Yancey, I have somebody I want you to meet. This is Madison."

I nervously stuck out my hand toward her and said, "It's very nice to meet you, Madison. I've heard a lot of good things about you. Congratulations on your success."

"Thank you," she said in soft sweet voice. Her eyebrows expressed a skeptical arch.

"Why don't we sit down? Yancey, would you like something to drink?"

"Just some bottled water will be fine," I said as I spied the sofa and the two chairs facing it. Should I sit on the sofa and hope Madison joins me or take a place alone in one of the chairs?

Madison settled my dilemma when she sat on the sofa and then patted the spot next to her and said, "Daddy, sit here."

"Let me get Yancey's drink, darling. Would you like something, Madison?"

"No, Daddy. Thank you," she said politely.

Just as I was getting ready to tell Madison that I'd bought her CD and really enjoyed it, two cameramen came from the bedroom. I heard the door open from behind me and I turned to see Cale and my cameraman walking into the suite.

"Excuse me but you must have the wrong suite," Derrick said.

"We're with Yancey," Cale said.

"Yeah Derrick, I forgot to tell you I would be bringing them. We've been shooting all day for my reality show that I told you about," I said while eyeing Madison from the corner. I saw her leap from the sofa and rush toward Derrick, shouting, "What is she trying to do, Daddy? She's using me for herself. Don't let her do this, Daddy."

"Madison, calm down. I'm sure we can solve this and finish our meeting."

I moved toward Madison and Derrick, reaching toward them as I said, "I'm sorry.

I didn't think this would be a big problem. You will get to approve the footage."

"Yancey, you should have told me," Derrick said sadly.

"Then you should have told me that you guys were going to have cameramen as well, Derrick. What's with the double standard?" I said.

"Get her out of here," Madison said as she looked at me in pure disgust. The first meeting was not turning out like I expected.

"Don't worry, I will leave," I said. I was a little sad but I suddenly thought what great television this would make and I hoped Cale was getting shots of Madison and me at all the right angles.

I heard Madison mutter, "I can't believe this." Derrick was telling her that everything would be okay as I headed toward the door with Cale and the cameraman still filming the look of disappointment I felt this moment deserved.

CHAPTER 33

"So I finally get to meet the infamous Donnie Ray," Ava said as she slid into the booth of Wilson's Restaurant.

"Don't you mean famous, Ava?" Donnie Ray eyed Ava like she was a plate of Sylvia's fried chicken and waffles with syrup dripping all over it. "Lyrical told me you were an older lady, but she didn't tell me about them hips you got there. You look like you could teach a young gent a few things in the bedroom."

"You know that's right, Donnie Ray, and flattery will get you everywhere. I see how you got Lyrical to do your dirty work for you." Ava was a bit surprised how attracted she was to Donnie Ray. He was dripping in thug-boy sex appeal with heavily muscled arms. Donnie Ray was dark as a Tootsie Roll with multicolored tattoos mapped over his neck and arms. The contrast of his white T-shirt with matching du-rag and baggy jeans completed his thug ensemble. "I hear you packing too. A girl could do a lot worse."

"Let's get to business before I have to get one of these famous biscuits they make in here and slop you up, Ava. Tell me, what you need?"

Just like that, Ava was all business. In a hard prison tone she informed him, "I need enough drugs to get somebody sent up for a long time. What would that take?"

"So, you want to make it look like they dealing big time?"

"If that will get them sent up for a long time."

"Then I think we ought to do some crack or liquid cocaine," Donnie Ray said as he peered down over his dark glasses. As he came closer to Ava, the smell of his body aroused her. The smell of musk and cheap cologne created the sweet aroma of sex, and Ava thought she might arrange a private visit with Donnie Ray after her vaginal rejuvenation. Ava had researched several doctors who could perform the procedure that would tighten and enhance her vaginal muscle tone. As she gazed at Donnie Ray intently she bet he could make her pussy hum like it belonged to a sixteen-year-old girl.

"Liquid cocaine? That sounds dangerous."

"It's cool, but it's just an easier way to transport it before you turn it into the hard stuff. Turn that shit into lil rocks."

"Oh, I get it. Is that expensive?"

"Let's just say it's higher than giraffe pussy," Donnie Ray said with a husky laugh.

This was a world she knew nothing about. "How long you been dealing drugs?"

"Now, Ava, you know I can't answer no questions like that. How do I know you're not wearing some wire between those beautiful legs of yours? You might have a wire hugging those plump titties I see."

Ava tilted her head with a haughty diva air. "Why would I do that when you're trying to help me?"

"I don't know, but I don't trust anyone completely. Lyrical will tell you I might look dumb, but I'm a long way from it. I'm a biz-ness man."

"I'm sure you are." When he turned on his thug persona, he gave her the chills. He was a lot tougher than she thought. "So, you say this shit is expensive. How much is this going to cost me?"

"I don't know yet, but I know you'll come up with whatever I need."

She read his doubt right off, and answered it. "Yeah, money is no problem with my business partner. When can you get it?"

"Whenever you need it."

"You won't tell Lyrical about this, will you?"

He gave her a penetrating look. "No, I don't tell that girl all my business. How did you get her to introduce you to me?"

Ava laughed carelessly. "I knew from your pictures that you were a muscular guy, and I told her when I get my fortune back, I might need a bodyguard. It didn't take much. Lyrical is pretty simple."

"That's my boo, but you right. She's a couple sandwiches short of a picnic basket."

"I think Lyrical might be missing some pickles, too, but I think she means well."

He leaned back, spreading his arms across the back of the booth. "So, when you gonna let me show you Harlem, Ava?"

"Show me what?" she asked, startled by the change in subject.

"What you want to see?"

"Are you flirting with me, Donnie Ray?"

"I'm just doing my thang, girl."

"I bet you are, but you don't have to show me Harlem if you're trying to get a little piece. I might give you some of that as a little bonus," Ava said with a sinister smile.

He wasn't impressed. "That ain't no bonus, girl. Donnie Ray gets plenty of pussy.

But it's something about you that makes me want to give you a shot. You remind me of this lady I used to lay the pipe on when I was thirteen. That old girl taught me some tricks."

She shot back sternly, "First of all, Donnie Ray, don't use terms like that old girl, and second, you ain't been taught no tricks like I teach tricks. You ain't had no cat as tight as Ava's pussy."

He laughed uproariously. "Now, that's what Donnie Ray is talking about."

A glint of gold sparked in the back of his mouth, turning her off. He was just a low-life thug, she reminded herself. "So, text me on the number I gave you when you get the stuff."

"So you tryin' to make this happen fast?"

"As soon as you can make it happen," she growled. "The sooner I can get this bitch off the streets, the better."

"Sounds like somebody really pissed Miss Ava off bad."

"And it isn't good to ever make Ava mad. But I'm sure you know that, Donnie Ray."

He flashed another shark smile. "Donnie Ray only wants to make Ava happy. You look like a lady that know how to take a nigga if he treat her right."

"For the record, I don't date niggas,

Donnie Ray. You think I could dress like this if I was hanging with the homeboy?"

"Now, Ava, you know us thug boys know how to lay pipe right."

He slid his hand right next to hers on the table. The sweat on it made her recoil. "This conversation is veering in a direction I don't need it to go in. Just text me when you get the stuff. Then we need to get a less conspicuous place to make the deal."

"Less what?"

"Less conspicuous, Donnie Ray. It means not a place like this out in the public for all to see," Ava said.

He bobbed his head, grinning. "Oh, I see you like to drop those two-dollar words every now and then, but that's cool. I'm always interested in learning new shit. Never know when I might need it."

"Well, you'll have to get somebody else to tutor you, sir, because when I get through with this deal I'm heading to the West Coast."

"Cali. I love Cali. Every time winter hits this motherfucker, I say I'm going to move out there."

"You should do that. That might make Lyrical want to move out there."

"Who said anything about Lyrical? I'm going to Hollywood and I don't need some female tagging along. Besides, Lyrical can't leave New York without permission of the state." He pulled himself upright at that thought. "Hey, don't you have the same rules?"

"What are you talking about?"

"You're on parole. How you gonna leave the state?"

"I know people," Ava said as she scooted out of the booth.

He slouched back down again, watching her as she marched to the door. "I bet you do, Ava. I bet you do."

CHAPTER 34

"Can you believe she did that?" Madison asked Caressa as the two of them thumbed through a stack of pastel cashmere sweaters at the Ralph Lauren store on the Upper East Side. The manager had closed the store to the public for a half hour so that Madison could pick up a few items as a limo driver waited outside.

"I don't quite understand why you're upset, Madison. I think it's great that both of you are going to have reality shows," Caressa said.

"But she didn't ask my dad's permission." Madison got upset every time she thought about those big camera lenses sticking in her face. "I thought this was about meeting me, her daughter, but it was clear to me that it was all about her and how she can use my fame," Madison said as she moved toward a rack of plaid skirts.

"I don't know what the big deal is, Madison. We know that your show is going to be better. I think you should have let her do it."

Madison put down a skirt on the counter and put her hands on her hips. "You're supposed to be on my side, Caressa. Stop taking up for her."

"I'm not taking up for her, Madison. I'm just pointing out that you missed a great opportunity to start a relationship with your mother. That's something you've wanted for a long time, and I just want you to have that."

"Maybe it's not all that it's cracked up to be," Madison said as she picked up a navy blue leather belt.

"I don't think you should give up so quickly."

"That's easy for you to say. You already have a mother who loves you. I try to meet mine and what happens? I find out she's a user." Despite her best efforts, tears were forming in her eyes.

Madison stormed into the room. "Can you believe the nerve of her, Daddy?"

Derrick looked up from his computer. "What are you talking about, Madison?"

"Yancey bringing a camera crew to our first meeting. What kind of woman is she?

First she wants to meet me, and then she wants to use me."

"Well, you had a crew there as well. Sounds like a case of like mother like daughter."

Madison took a seat in the chair next to his desk. "She's *not* my mother. Yancey Braxton is just the woman who gave birth to me. I know now she is not interested in getting to know me but just trying to save her sinking career."

"And you're trying to build yours. Sounds similar to me, Madison."

Madison crossed her arms, annoyed that her father was not taking her side. "She should have asked me if she could bring cameras."

"Did you ask her if you could tape the meeting?"

"No, I didn't and I don't see why I had to."

"I suggest you guys try and meet again. Without cameras."

"I don't ever want to *see* Yancey again!" Madison shouted.

"Bring your voice down, young lady," he said, reminding Madison who was really in charge.

"I'm not going to do it, Daddy. And you can't make me!" Madison said.

"I'm only suggesting that you owe it to yourself to hear what she has to say. Yancey is a decent woman. She's been through a whole lot in recent years, things you don't even know about and even if you did you wouldn't understand. That's why I'm asking you to give her another chance."

"Decent? Another chance? Do you know how that sounds, Daddy? This is the woman you said you once loved dearly."

"I did once love Yancey. I've always told you that you were conceived out of love. That was the truth. Someday, when you have children you might regret not getting to know your birth mother."

"I met her and I immediately knew I didn't like her. She was such a phony, more interested in talking to the camera than to me. I'm so happy that I got all of my traits from you and not some spoiled over-the-hill actress. Why couldn't I have a mother like Ms. Nicole? She really loves her children and I can tell that when she talks about them."

Derrick knew better than to press the issue further. Nothing would be resolved at this rate. "Let's go get something to eat. We can discuss this later."

"We don't ever have to talk about this."

"Whatever, Madison," he said, switching

off the computer. "What do you want to eat?"

"Chicken strips and fries."

"Okay, grab your jacket and I'll call for the car."

"Can we bring Caressa?"

"Sure, honey. That's fine."

"Great," she said, returning to her bubbly self, "let me call her."

CHAPTER 35

I was going to do a little shopping for fall and the show, so I went to my closet to get some cash from the bag Marcus had asked me to keep a few days before. I loved having this cash at my disposal.

While I was getting a couple of stacks of money, I couldn't help but notice a little plastic bag with white stuff in it. I picked it up and inspected it in puzzlement. Then I saw many more of them. My first thought was that this couldn't be what I thought it was, but how could I be certain? I decided to go straight to the source.

I located my cell phone and pulled up S. Marcus's name and hit dial. After a couple of rings he picked up.

"Hey, lovely lady, would you believe I was just talking about you? That means you're going to live a long time."

I didn't respond to his pleasantry at all. "That's good to know. Marcus, I think we have a problem here."

"What kind of problem, sweetheart?"

"You know that bag you asked me to keep?"

"Of course."

"I was looking through it because I was going to put some of the money in my bank account and pick up a few items, when I saw these little plastic bags with white stuff in them." My tone was curling like barbed wire. "Can you tell me what it is? What is going on?"

For a moment there was dead silence on the phone. I called out S. Marcus's name to see if he was still there. When he answered, I could tell there was a difference in his voice, like he'd been caught.

"What is this in the bag?" I demanded.

"Don't worry about that, Yancey," he said quietly. "I need to get the bag back ASAP."

"Marcus, please tell me that you didn't leave some drugs in my house. Are you dealing drugs?"

"Hell no, and don't ask me questions like that. Stop tripping and bring the bag to me."

Did I hear that right? I was the one who was tripping? "No, you need to come and get it."

"It's not drugs and I can't come right now. I'm in an important meeting."

"Where are you?"

"In New York."

Something was definitely up. "When did you get here, and why didn't you tell me you were coming?"

"It was a last-minute thing, Yancey," he explained. "I need to talk to the network sales force about your show. I was going to call you when I finished my meeting."

"Are you staying with me?" I asked, looking around. The house was a dump, thanks to my mother.

"No, you're staying with me. I'm at the Four Seasons. So close the bag back up and meet me at the hotel in two hours. Don't say anything to anyone."

The Four Seasons sounded nice, but not if I was going to meet some drug dealer. "Who am I going to tell? Why are you being so weird about this? This looks like drugs to me and to be honest, I'm a little nervous about having this stuff around."

"Yancey, damn it. Stop asking so many questions and just do what I say." His voice was so loud and forceful it scared me. He had never talked to me this way.

"Look here, S. Marcus Pinkston, don't yell at me that way and you better not be lying. I don't play that shit. And I mean with men yelling at me *and* with drugs."

"I'm sorry, baby," he said softly. "I'm just a little upset that you don't trust me."

"I trust you," I said, although I didn't really. "Marcus, listen, I'll see you in a couple of hours. Let's talk then."

"That's a good girl."

"Bye, baby."

I hung up the phone and found my eyes fixated on the bag on my bed. Should I trust Marcus and follow his instructions, or should I ask Ava what I should do? No, I didn't want Ava involved with this. S. Marcus was a legitimate businessman and wouldn't be involved in drugs, I told myself. I hadn't seen any signs which would suggest otherwise. The strangest part of it was, I didn't remember seeing any bags before.

I looked into my closet and pulled out one of my pink warm-up suits and a white Gap T-shirt. Instead of going shopping, I was going to take a shower and get this bag out of my house as fast as I could.

After I finished my shower and put moisturizer over my body it suddenly dawned on me that I hadn't talked to Dalton in a few days. I located my cell phone and dialed his number. After a few rings Dalton picked up but he really didn't sound like his chipper self.

"Hey, boo, why haven't I heard from you?"

"Hey Yancey, so sorry I've been a little under the weather."

"What's wrong? You got a cold or something?"

"Not really. I'm in the hospital."

"What hospital? What happened?"

"I fell down the stairs in Anderson's building."

"You did what?" Something didn't sound right about this. Dalton was trained as a dancer and wouldn't be falling down a flight of stairs. I needed him to tell me the truth.

"But don't worry, I will be okay."

"I'm coming to see you right now," I said.

"No Yancey, don't do that. But there is something you can do for me."

"What's that?"

"I need you to call Nicole and tell her I'm going to miss my voice lesson. If I don't show up, she'll be worried about me."

I didn't answer right away. Could I do that? I mean, talk to Nicole Springer after all these years?

"Yancey, are you still there?"

"I'm here, Dalton. Give me her number," I said. This wasn't about Nicole and me but about Dalton. He was my friend and I would do whatever he needed.

"It's 555-9910."

"Got it," I said as I wrote the number on a yellow pad.

"Thanks, Yancey."

"I still think I should come and see you now," I said.

"Not now. I don't want you to see me this way."

"What way?"

"I'm pretty bruised up but the doctors say I will be just like new in no time."

"Dalton, are you being honest with me? Does Anderson have anything to do with all your untimely injuries? Tell me, Dalton. You can trust me," I pleaded.

There was no answer and the silence between us was haunting. After a few moments of silence Dalton whispered that he had to go and simply hung up without even telling me what hospital he was in.

I took a deep breath and looked at the pad with Nicole's number. I picked up my phone and slowly dialed the number, allowing seconds, almost minutes to elapse between each number. Finally the phone rang. It rang again and then I heard Nicole's voice.

"This is Nicole Stovall. I'm not in right now and I'm sorry I missed your call. But please leave a message and a number even if you think I have it. Have a tremendously blessed day and keep singing."

When I heard the beep I released another deep sigh and said, "Hey girl, long time no hear from. This is Yancey Braxton and I understand we share a good friend, Dalton. He asked me to call you and tell you he needs to cancel his lesson today. He said he would call as soon as he got well . . . I mean not got well but got back in town. Bye Nicole. Sorry I missed you and you keep singing, too, girl. Smooches."

CHAPTER 36

As Ava walked into Harry Winston jewelers to do a little rehearsal shopping, her phone rang. She'd not heard from him in over a week and was growing impatient. She clicked on the call.

"Ava. Are you ready to collect your money?"

"Funny you should ask that. I'm getting ready to make some big purchases," she said.

"It's going down today. You'll have the place all to yourself tonight."

"What's going down?"

"Payback for Yancey. We won't have to deal with her after this evening."

That was exactly the news she wanted to hear. "Are you serious? Hell yeah. What's going to happen?" Ava didn't really care as long as it got rid of Yancey for good. She had a good mind to call Sturdivant and see what he was up to. A nice meal and a handsome young man would be the way to spend a glorious evening.

"Just don't answer your phone later on today. I'm sure you're going to be getting a call from your lovely daughter this evening. But make sure you don't take the call."

"Great. Maybe I'll just look around today. If you're sure I'm going to have my check, then I might be able to hold old Harry off another day."

"It will be there tomorrow."

Finally, sweet revenge. "You've made my day, Steven Pinkston III. You've made my day."

CHAPTER 37

The fall sky was a deep blue, and a cool breeze caressed my face as I turned the corner on 57th Street. This was when I loved New York the most. I was about four blocks from the Four Seasons Hotel, and as I passed the chic stores, I thought how lucky I was to have a man like S. Marcus in my life. I would be back to shopping in those stores, spending up a storm like the old days, in no time. All thanks to S. Marcus. I was wrong to think that he would be involved with drugs.

A couple of blocks away my thoughts turned to Madison and how stupid I looked with my camera crew following me to record my first meeting with my daughter. I knew that I was wrong and hoped that one day Madison would give me another chance to get to know her. But it had to be for the right reason and not to advance my career. I would do that with my talent.

I was near the entrance of the hotel when my cell phone rang.

"Yancey. This is Regan. I have some exciting news for you."

"I'm listening," I said, praying she'd finally gotten me more than backup work.

"We got a callback for the recurring role on *Ugly Betty.* The casting director said that everyone really liked your audition."

"They did? That's great! Will they let me bring the crew from my reality show?"

"Yes, they will, and to be honest, I think that's going to end up helping you get the job. They asked me a lot of questions about the show."

"And this is for the role of Vanessa's nemesis and not her mother, right?"

"Yes, that's right," she said, enjoying my concern. "You will play a magazine diva who works at *Mode* and is trying to get Vanessa's job."

Finally, the sun was shining on me. "Oh, Regan, this is so wonderful. You're the best."

"Well, we don't have the job yet. You need to go in there and knock them dead. Make sure you dress the part," she advised. "Wear something real high fashion. Casting directors love it when you do that."

"Oh, I know, and trust me when I say I will be ready. I might even go out and get me something new that will leave their mouths hanging open."

"That's what I want to hear. Call me when you leave the audition," Regan said.

"I will." I shut the phone with a pleased snap. I had to restrain myself from dancing the whole way to the hotel, I was so happy! My life was turning around all at once. I couldn't wait to tell Marcus.

Just then I heard the call-waiting beeper go off. It was Dalton, who I hadn't heard from since he hung up on me. I called several times but it always immediately went into voicemail.

"Dalton, are you okay? I've been worried sick about you," I said.

"I'm better, Yancey, and I'm sorry I didn't call. I had to work out some things," Dalton said.

"What kind of things?"

"Like what I'm doing with my life," Dalton said sadly.

"Where are you? I need to see you, Dalton."

"I'm at the airport."

"Where are you going?"

"I don't know. I just need to leave here for now. But I'll be back. We got a CD to make."

"Dalton," I said and then I paused.

411

"Yes."

"You know I love you, don't you," I said as I fought back tears.

"I know, Yancey, and that means the world to me."

"And you know you deserve someone who loves you just as much as I do. As God does. Don't you?"

Dalton didn't answer right away but after a few minutes he mumbled yes.

"And it needs to be someone who doesn't think they can control you by beating you, Dalton. I know what Anderson has been doing to you."

"He says he loves me and it won't happen again."

"And you believe him? Don't take that, Dalton. If you need me to get somebody to scare him I will. I can't let anybody treat my friend like this," I said.

"Yancey, believe it or not I know what I deserve. I just got caught up but old Dalton is going to be just fine. I just want you to know that I love you very much and your friendship has been awesome."

"Really?" I asked.

"You sound surprised," Dalton said.

As the tears continued to roll down my face I realized I was surprised. No one had ever called me an awesome friend.

"Dalton, that's the nicest thing anyone has ever said to me."

"Then I'm glad it was me. I need to go, Yancey, but I promise to call real soon. I love you."

"I love you too, Dalton. Take care of yourself until we see each other again."

"I will."

I clicked off the phone and the river of tears continued.

The tears during my conversation with Dalton were good for me but left my face and makeup looking a mess. I stopped at a deli and went into the bathroom and washed my face and reapplied my makeup. I had taken my phone in with me in case Dalton called again. Just as I put a new coat of lipstick on the phone rang. The name John B. came across the screen. It was Basil.

"Is this who I think it is?" I asked.

"What's up, Yancey? You got a minute?"

"Always for you, Basil," I said, though I was hoping he wasn't going to make me late for meeting Marcus.

"I'm not going to hold you long, but I wanted to get back with you. Look, I talked this over with my better half, and I think I'm going to have to say no to doing the re-ality show. I hope you understand. I know it will be great without me."

I could afford to be magnanimous. "I understand, Basil. Not everybody wants to live their life in public. Thanks for getting back to me and it was good seeing you."

My backing down so easily surprised him. "Same here, Yancey. It was good seeing you."

"Let's try and keep in touch," I offered.

"I would like that."

"Basil, can I ask you something? It's what I wanted to ask you when we met the other day. Are you really happy now?"

"Extremely," he said.

"I'm glad to hear that."

"I hope you know you deserve the same thing, Yancey."

"I'm finally getting there, Basil, and I know what you're saying is true."

"I hope so. Take care and have a nice evening."

"I will and you do the same."

I smiled to myself, thinking how great it was that Basil and I were becoming friends because that was missing while we were dating. I also hoped that he was right when he implied that I could be happy too. Maybe I would really talk with S. Marcus tonight and find out where he thought our relationship was going and not just the business side. Maybe little pieces of me always feel like I need a man.

I reached the front entrance of the Four Seasons Hotel on the 57th Street side. I smiled at the doorman as he opened the door for me. As I entered the spacious lobby, I looked for the front desk. I'd been in the hotel several times, but for whatever reason I didn't remember where the check-in was from the 57th Street side.

As I turned around, looking for someone who might help me, I heard someone yell, "Hey, miss."

Two white men were staring at me and then began to approach. When they finally stopped directly in front of me, a wave of fear overcame me. Who were they and what did they want?

The taller one asked, "Can we talk to you for a minute, miss?"

"About what?" I asked.

"About what you have in that bag," the other one said.

"That's none of your business," I snapped.

"I'm afraid it is," the shorter man said as he flashed a badge that read New York Police Department. Drug Enforcement.

"I'm Officer Daniels and we'd like to inspect your bag."

Fear was screeching in my mind like

fingernails on a blackboard. "What are you talking about? Drug enforcement. Is this some type of joke?"

"No, it isn't. Now, please follow us. Let's go over here," he said, gesturing to a remote section of the lobby.

Frozen by fear, I remained motionless. Officer Daniels took this to mean I was being uncooperative and took me by the arm.

At last I reacted. "You better let go of me."

"Let's not make a scene, Miss Braxton."

"How do you know my name? Do you have a search warrant?"

"We don't need a search warrant," Officer Daniels said, suddenly jerking the bag from my hand.

This smelled to high heaven, and I wasn't going quietly. "Stop it. You can't pull on me like that. I want my lawyer. What in the hell is going on?"

"We are just going to check the bag, and if nothing is in there, you're free to go."

Passersby had begun to notice the commotion and stopped to watch. The two officers took me to a corner of the lobby. Officer Daniels opened the bag and began pulling out the stacks of money. He then pulled out one of the plastic packets with the white powder. He looked at the other officer. "Look what we got here." In reply the officer simply smiled.

Officer Daniels took out a pair of handcuffs. "Yancey Braxton, you're under arrest for possession with intent to distribute cocaine. You have the right to an attorney. If you can't afford an attorney, one will be appointed for you. Do you understand your rights as I have explained them?"

I stared at him in shock. Officer Daniels took both of my arms and forced them behind my back. Moments later I felt the cold metal of the handcuffs. S. Marcus's face flashed in my head and the only words I could think of was *that muthafucka.*

Officer Daniels spoke in an earpiece I hadn't noticed, and moments later I was back into the cool evening air, being pushed inside a waiting police car, tears streaming down my face. Over and over I said, "This is some type of mistake. This bag doesn't belong to me."

I was sitting in the waiting room of the jail when he walked in. Raymond Tyler looked as handsome as I remembered. I still couldn't reach Ava or S. Marcus, and when I realized I still had my cell phone, I'd called Basil and told him I needed his help in getting an attorney. It didn't dawn on me that he would send Raymond or that he was practicing criminal law now.

I stood as he entered. "Raymond, it's good to see you. Thanks for coming," I said, nervously shaking his cold but strong hand.

"Yancey, it's been a long time. Basil tells me you might need my help," Raymond said. He took a seat on the bench in front of me.

"Yes, I do. I think I'm in big trouble and I still don't know what happened."

"Basil didn't give me a lot of information. He told me you were bringing a bag that belonged to your boyfriend to a hotel where he was waiting. Have you heard from this guy?"

"No, I called but got no answer. I gave the policemen his cell number. They now tell me the number is no longer in service. I can't reach my mother either."

His eyebrows rose at the mention of her. "Yeah, I heard Ava was out of jail. I was notified before her parole. Where is she staying?"

"At my house the last time I checked, but I told her not to answer my home phone."

He turned his attention back to my mysterious man. "Did you check to see if your friend had registered in the hotel?"

"I didn't have the chance. But when he called me, he said he was already there."

"What's his name? I'll follow up."

"S. Marcus Pinkston is the name he would be registered under."

"Okay. I will follow up on that. Do you want me to check up on Ava?"

I looked around the bleak room, thinking of what she had gone through. "Yeah."

"I will get your address before I leave, and I will send one of my assistants over to your house to see if she is there." He pulled out his BlackBerry and made a quick notation. Looking up again, he asked, "How long have you known this Pinkston guy?"

"About four months," I said.

"Where is he from?"

"Miami, I think." I was feeling like such a fool now. Obviously he had set me up. What I couldn't understand was why.

"Do you think he was a drug dealer?"

"No," I said, dismissing the idea outright. "He told me he was in finance. He was backing my reality show."

"Reality show?"

"Yeah, S. Marcus was shopping a reality show for me. We'd already shot a lot of film."

He looked as puzzled as I felt. "I need to find him. Do you have any other numbers for him?"

"No," I said, realizing for the first time how strange it was to have only one phone number for a businessman.

"Are you sure that was his name?"

That question had never occurred to me. "Why would he lie about his name?"

"First we just need to find him, Yancey. Also, I might have to bring somebody else in. It's been a long time since I've worked a criminal case, but Basil just wants me to let you know that we are working on this. We need to see if we can get bail and worry about finding this mystery guy later," Raymond said.

"Just do whatever you can to get me out of this place." My mind raced over what to do next. Then, of all things, it occurred to me that it was Election Day. "Can you believe I didn't get the chance to vote? Of all the years not to have that chance. I'm heartbroken."

"It doesn't seem like President-elect Barack needs your vote," Raymond said.

"I also missed a callback and a chance to sing at a victory party. Can you call my agent and tell her what's going on?"

"Yeah, I will. What's your agent's name and number?"

"Regan Reynolds and I don't know her number off the top of my head. I just signed with her agency, but I'm sure she's listed."

"Okay, I will look it up."

"Thank you, Raymond," I said, taking his hand in mine.

He gave it a slight squeeze. "Don't thank me, Yancey. I haven't done anything yet."

"But you will," I implored. "I know you can prove that I'm not dealing drugs. This is a horrible mistake."

Raymond looked into my eyes as if he was trying to figure out if I was telling the truth.

"Let me get out of here and get started. I will work on bail and then see if I can find this S. Marcus character."

"Please hurry. I don't think I can last a night in this place."

"I'll do what I can, Yancey."

I watched Raymond being escorted out by a guard. I was feeling so abandoned that I might have welcomed seeing even Ava, wherever she was.

CHAPTER 38

The lead detective had been questioning Ava for an hour. "Why do you think your daughter would be dealing drugs, Ms. Middlebrooks?"

"Because she's broke and spoiled. Those two don't go together," Ava replied.

"She lives in this big town house in the neighborhood and she's broke?"

"Looks are deceiving. The bitch has no money and no career and no husband. I was a much better actress and singer. But I always married well. I think you guys should nail her to the cross. Selling drugs to our youth." Ava shook her head in disgust at the thought. "I'm ashamed of her."

"So you're saying most of her customers were young people?" the second detective asked.

"That's who used to show up here," Ava lied. Yancey hardly had visitors, especially young ones, but that was what Steven told her to say. He'd come up with a brilliant plan, and now Yancey would know how she had felt when Ava spent so many nights in a dingy jail cell. Serves the bitch right, Ava thought.

"Lots of traffic?"

"You got it. She told me she was mentoring these kids. I should have known. Yancey doesn't care about anybody but Yancey. Do you know that big teen star Madison B.? Well, that's her daughter. She gave her up at birth because she was too selfish and self-absorbed to be a mother. I should have done the same thing. My daughter plays the blame game."

"The blame game?"

"Blames everything on someone else. Doesn't take responsibility for shit!" Ava caught herself. "Oh, excuse my language. But this upsets me so bad. Think of how this is going to damage our family name. Think about poor Madison B. She will have to learn that her mother is a liar and a drug dealer. My Lord."

"Who is Madison B.?"

Ava glanced at him like he was the stupidest man on earth. "That's the daughter she gave up at birth who's now a bigger star than Yancey ever was. What a shame."

"Are you willing to testify at her trial?"

423

"Tell me where to be and I'm there," Ava said eagerly. "We can't have people, especially Yancey, bringing drugs into our community."

The detective scratched his head, as if something wasn't adding up. "Do you know how long she's been dealing drugs?"

"Who knows? I just got back to New York a couple of months ago. I was out of the country." For a moment she thought maybe the policemen knew she'd been in jail and immediately regretted the lie. But both the officers stood up and told her that they would call her if they had any further questions.

"Has bail been set for Yancey yet?" Ava asked.

"I'm not sure. But with the amount of drugs and money involved, bail will be high. We're talking liquid cocaine," the first detective said.

"Good," she snapped, "because I'm sure she should be considered a flight risk. Who knows how much money Yancey has stashed away? You officers know how easy it is to get a private plane to take you out of the country these days. Oh, you should take a look in her room at all the stuff she has in there."

Sensing more drugs, the detectives asked

in chorus, "What kind of stuff?"

"Clothes. Expensive ones, designer dresses, shoes, purses. About a month ago, I guess when her business got going, she started spending money like it was water. When I asked her where all the money came from, she told me the producers of her alleged reality show gave it to her. Gave it to her, indeed," Ava scoffed. "Shouldn't that stuff be confiscated since it was bought with drug money?"

"That will be up to the prosecutor but most likely. We will come back and take a look."

"Suit yourself because you don't have to worry about me touching any of it. I'm not that type of woman."

"Is this your daughter's home?"

"Not anymore. I paid the down payment and right now I'm in the process of getting it changed back to my name."

"If she makes bail, will she be able to live here?"

"I don't think we have to worry about that. Yancey won't make bail," Ava said, pleased at the prospect. "She doesn't have her own money, and I'm sure any friends she has left will be as disgusted with her as I am."

The first detective nodded. "Thank you

for your time, Mrs. Middlebrooks. You've been very helpful."

"Any time, Officers. Let me know if I can help."

CHAPTER 39

"Come here, Daddy! Come look at this!" Madison yelled. A few moments later Derrick walked into Madison's bedroom, where she was sitting on the bed with her legs crossed, staring at the flat-screen television on the wall.

"What are you yelling about?"

"Can you believe this? It's on the news. They are saying that Yancey Braxton has been arrested for drugs. Did you know she used drugs?"

Derrick's face went ashen. "Are you sure it's Yancey?" he asked, moving closer to the television. "This must be some kind of mistake."

Madison didn't think so. "OMG. This is crazy. Yancey Braxton will do anything for attention." She turned to her father in horror. "Can you imagine if I'd let her into my life? This could ruin my career. There's no way in the world Disney would pick up my show if they knew my birth mother was a drug pusher."

Derrick snapped, "Madison, this isn't about you and don't convict Yancey before she's had a trial. I'm sure this is some mistake."

As she suspected, her father was still in love with his old college flame. "Like I said, Daddy, maybe you don't know Yancey Braxton like you think you do."

■ ■ ■ ■

PART THREE

■ ■ ■ ■

CHAPTER 1

I found myself lying on a ratty, nasty iron cot in an eight-by-ten-foot jail cell, not believing all that had happened to me today. As I looked up at the mattress above, waiting for lights out, I tried to stop myself from crying. This had been the worst day of my life.

After I explained to my stupid public defender I wasn't able to post my own bond, I was told I would have to be processed and thrown in jail. A pair of corrections officers came over to the courthouse and marched me and some other women in handcuffs back to the jail across the street.

There, the most humiliating things were done to me. We were corralled like livestock and then marched down a hallway.

"Okay, take off your clothes," a very large woman, who looked more like a man, said.

"Excuse me?" I said.

"Take off your clothes. All of you!" Almost

six feet tall, the woman wore a dark blue uniform and had hair braided back in corn-rows.

The other dozen female inmates started disrobing quickly. I still hesitated, folding my arms over my breasts.

The officer walked over to me, smiling meanly. Her name tag read Jenkins. She had skin the color of a shelled almond. She could've been pretty, I thought, with a little eyeliner, maybe some lip gloss. But she wore nothing, so she looked like a man.

"Problem, missy?"

"I'm not accustomed to just stripping off my clothes in front of people like this."

"Aw, that's sweet. Miss Thang is shy," the officer said over her shoulder to another mannish female officer, standing in a corner.

"If you could point me to a private dress-ing room, I could —"

All the officers and even some of the new inmates burst out laughing.

"Ain't no dressing rooms! This ain't The Gap, missy. Take off all your shit, or I'll take it off for you," Officer Jenkins said, looking me up and down. She licked her lips. "And I might just enjoy that."

Moments later, standing naked, the other twelve women and I were strip-searched. We were told to squat and cough. We had to open our mouths, and move our tongues around, so the officers could make sure we weren't hiding anything there.

After that degrading session, we were given back our clothes, and each of us was given an inmate number.

This was when it really started to hit home that this was real. I felt like I wanted to cry, and I did my best to hold back my tears.

I felt a hand on my shoulder, and I jumped, startled.

"It's okay," the woman standing behind me said. She was a thin, petite, mildly attractive Latino woman. "Everything's going to be all right."

"And how do you know?"

" 'Cause I been through this more times than I wanna admit," the woman said with a Puerto Rican accent. She held out her hand. "Marcella."

"Yancey," I said, shaking her hand. "What happens next?"

"We're going to be separated now, depending on what you're being charged with. Some of us will go to minimum security, some medium and some maximum."

I shuddered when I thought about being sent off to some little room with some huge woman. I felt someone's eyes on me. I turned to see a very large white woman star-

ing at me. She was squat and broad shoul-
dered, like a defensive linebacker. Her short
red hair was parted down the center and
twisted into two pigtails that sprouted from
either side of her head.

"Why is that woman looking at me?" I
asked Marcella.

Marcella turned in her direction. "She's
choosing."

"What do you mean, choosing?" I said, a
chill racing up my spine.

"Not that I'm a lesbian, but you're kinda
hot. That woman is sizing you up. Hopefully, you didn't commit a crime that puts
the two of you in the same division. And if
so, you better hope you don't get the same
cell as her. Unless you find her equally attractive."

The idea totally repulsed me. "I don't!
And how will I know what division I'm going to?"

"They about to tell us now," Marcella
said. "What you charged with anyway?"

"Drug possession, with intent to distribute. But they weren't my drugs. I'm not
guilty."

Marcella smiled, and then broke out
laughing.

"What's so funny?"

"Ask any of these women. There's not a

guilty person in this entire jail."

After our charges were read off to us, we were separated and taken to our divisions. There were four women in the group I walked with. Marcella was one of them. There was another black woman. And then there was the big, white woman who could not keep her eyes off me.

All during the rest of our processing, while we were having our clothes taken from us and given the jail uniforms, I was praying that I would not be put in a cell with that gigantic woman. But each time I looked at her, she seemed to be licking her chops like she was a dog and I was some meat-covered bone.

The heavens must have heard my prayers, because when all was said and done, I stood in a small prison cell and Marcella was on the bottom bunk.

"Are they fucking kidding?" I practically screamed, looking at the toilet. It was a weird, stainless-steel thing, and the sink was actually connected to it. The sink and the toilet were actually one piece. "I'm supposed to wash my face and shit in the same place. This isn't real!" I said.

"Pinch yourself. It's real," Marcella said.

"Don't they know who I am?"

"They don't care, but who are you,

honey?"

"I'm Yancey Harrington Braxton. I have been on the Broadway stage, movies, and I had a big, big hit song."

She started to look more interested. "Oh yeah. You do look kind of familiar. You ever been in any Tyler Perry movies?"

"No."

"What about Spike Lee?"

"No, I haven't."

That seemed to be the limit of her exposure to actresses. "And you say you're a big star. Well, I ain't never heard of you. What about BET?"

"Some time ago, but mainly I was onstage. Have you ever heard of *Dreamgirls?*"

"Of course I've heard of *Dreamgirls.* You were in that? Tell me, how is Beyonce really? And Jamie Foxx? Girl, I loved it when he used to play Ugly Wanda on *In Living Color.* He was so funny. He played that role well. So, how were they?"

"I wasn't in the movie," I had to admit. "I was in the stage production. It came out before the movie."

She made a face like I was an impostor. "I never knew it was a play. If you're such a big-time star, why didn't you get a private suite? I'm sure that if you tell them, they might move you." She saw how doubtful I looked, and she added, "But I wouldn't tell them you haven't been in any Tyler Perry movies."

I smiled politely and walked over to the mirror. It was nothing more than a square of reflective metal. I looked in it, and it looked as though I was staring at myself in a funhouse mirror. "How the hell am I supposed to do my makeup?"

Marcella laughed, like I was her private jokester. "Which bunk you want? Top or bottom?"

"It doesn't matter. I won't be sleeping."

Marcella climbed to the top bunk. She lay back, comfortable, like she was returning to her childhood bed back home. "Relax. It gets easier. You'll make friends, get used to things. You'll see. It's not all that bad."

I turned and looked at the woman, thinking what a sad, sorry life she must've led up till now if she thought this wasn't that bad.

"Okay," was all I could say.

"So get to bed," Marcella said. "Lights out in about half an hour."

As I lay in bed, staring up at Marcella's mattress, I felt the warm tears slide down the side of my face. I didn't bother to wipe them. They were tears for Marcella, but mostly for me. How did I get myself in here?

But the more important question was, how would I ever get out?

CHAPTER 2

"Well, looks like Yancey got what she wanted. Publicity," Ava said. She had been watching the news unfold all day. The coverage was giving the election returns a serious run for their money. She had been on Entertainment Tonight, E and CNN and not in a good way. " 'Former Broadway and recording star arrested for distribution of drugs.' I couldn't have planned it better myself. Steven, you're brilliant," Ava said, raising her wineglass in a toast.

Steven smiled at Ava across the table. "I told you to trust me." He reached into his pocket and produced an envelope. "Here is your check. Certified, of course."

Ava quickly ripped the envelope open and eyed the check that read 2.5 million dollars. Her smile instantly turned into a frown.

"This is not what we agreed on. You promised me *five* million. What the fuck is this?" Her rage gathered steam the longer she eyed the check. "Are you trying to mess me over, Steven? I did what you asked me and I want my money. All of it!"

Her outburst didn't faze him in the least. "Calm down, Ava. This is only a down payment. Once we get that bitch of a daughter of yours convicted, you will get the balance."

"But you didn't tell me that," she cried. "Don't change the rules in the middle of the game. That's bullshit! I'm not the goddamn prosecuting attorney. It's out of my hands." His face remained blank, and she waved the check at him. "I've made plans for this money. Do you realize the chance I took getting those drugs and dealing with that low-life Donnie Ray?"

Steven sat there unmoved. "I realize you don't run in Donnie Ray's circle and you took a big chance, Ava. But business is business, and I'm not going to give out a large amount of money until I get my desired result. By the way, how did the interviews with the blue go? Did you put the nails in Yancey's coffin?"

She nodded firmly, happy to have hoodwinked them. "I did what you said. I think they believe me and I know the jury will believe me too."

"Don't worry about the small shit, Ava.

You will get the rest of your money. Just chill and spend the money you have." Steven looked at his gold watch with the blue face, as if that was settled.

Ava wasn't letting go that easily. "I don't want my fate to be resting on twelve idiots making sure that Yancey goes to the prison for more years than I did. That's not the program I signed up for."

"It's not a program, Ava," he said dismissively. "Look, I got another meeting to make. You've trusted me up until now and I don't think you got much of a choice but to continue to do so."

Ava sat fuming, her hands tied.

"What do you think Madison thought of her birth mom being in jail?" Steven asked as he stood.

"If she's like me and Yancey, she didn't give a damn, because narcissism runs in the family. We're all bitches. Even though I don't know Madison, I could tell the minute I saw her that's she got the bitch switch."

Steven slipped his arms through his overcoat. "I've got to go. Enjoy your renewed wealth. I'm sure black society awaits you once again," Steven said.

"Black society? Child, please. The whole world awaits the return of Ava."

The doorbell rang, and Ava thought, About damn time. She opened it to find Lyrical. "What took you so long to get here? We got work to do."

"What are you talking about? You only called me about two hours ago," Lyrical protested. She was pretty much through with Ava and her attitude. "And what's all this talk about a big party? Does Yancey know you're giving a party at her house?" Lyrical asked. "She's pretty strict about who she lets in here."

"*My* house, darling, and we don't have to worry about Yancey anymore. She's going to be busy for a while." Ava led Lyrical to the dining room, adding, "I need you to call a locksmith to get all the locks on the house changed."

Lyrical stopped in her tracks, sensing trouble. "Does Yancey know you're doing this?"

"Yes, of course, dear."

When Ava got that purr in her voice, Lyrical knew she was lying. "Where is she?"

"You ask a lot of questions. Here," Ava said, placing a pen and notepad in Lyrical's hands. "Take this so we can start writing down what we need to do. I want to have a fabulous dinner party that will be the talk of the town."

"What are we celebrating?" Lyrical asked.

"We can celebrate everything. My return to Cali, the election, and the fact that we don't have to kiss Yancey Braxton's ass anymore. So let's get started. I want you to order two cases of champagne. Get Ruinart, which is wonderful. I need some Grey Goose, Crown Royal and Hennessy."

"You know we can't drink, Ava," Lyrical warned.

"Said who?"

"It's a part of our probation. Remember?"

"This is a private party, sweet one. Nobody will know. I want you to contact the executive chef at the Trump and ask him to come up with a menu. I want a beef dish and a fish dish. Tell him I also want an assortment of some of those desserts he's so famous for."

Lyrical didn't write any of this down. Instead she eyed Ava suspiciously, wondering what all this was about. "So where are you getting the money to pay for this? Did you hit the lottery?"

"There you go with those questions," she said airily. "I told you I was going to soon be in my rightful place in society. And this will be good for you as well, Lyrical. I'm going to hire you as my assistant and help you to get your record deal, honey. You don't think I've forgotten about that?"

"But you said you're moving to California. I'm not leaving New York," Lyrical said.

"But of course not, love. I will just have you manage my New York affairs. Now let's get busy," Ava said, clapping her hands twice.

Lyrical still didn't know what was going on, but she asked, "So when is this big shindig going to occur?"

"In forty-eight hours. I want to get to the West Coast this weekend."

"How are we going to make it happen so fast, Ava?"

"When you have money, Lyrical, anything can happen. And I have money. Those bitches on *Housewives of Atlanta* don't have anything on me." A snide tone entered her voice. "Don't you just love that show? Those poor girls actually think they have money and class. Child, please, that shows us what Yancey's little show would have looked like if it ever made the air. NCAA. No class at all."

Lyrical looked surprised. "What happened to her show and why is it not going to happen?"

444

"It was never going to happen," Ava informed her, patting her arm. "Yancey is delusional, honey. Like anyone would be interested in her pitiful little life."

Now Lyrical was getting worried. She knew how much Ava hated her daughter. "Where is Yancey, Ava? You didn't kill her, did you?"

"Didn't have to. Yancey took care of it herself." The lie hung in the air for just a moment, and then she said, "Now let's get busy. I'm going into my room to compose a list of who I want to invite. We need to find a service to hand-deliver the invitations." Lyrical was still looking at her funny. "Come on, let's get busy, dear. Ava's back and that's reason to celebrate."

CHAPTER 3

Derrick walked into her dressing room where the makeup artist was applying the last touches to Madison's face. "The director said they would be ready for you, Madison, in fifteen minutes."

"Thanks, Daddy. I see they made the changes you suggested." She was holding the script in her hand but laid it on the makeup desk as she took the earplugs to her iPod out of her ears.

Abby, the makeup artist, gave Madison a quick once-over and asked, "How is that, Madison?"

Madison moved her face close to the mirror and said, "Looks perfect as always, Abby. Thanks a lot."

The makeup artist smiled. The young star was a doll to deal with. "No problem. I will see you on the set."

"Okay." Madison turned for her father's inspection.

"You do look beautiful, darling," Derrick said.

"Thanks, Daddy. I'm so excited. Can you believe we've shot nine episodes?"

"And if the producers are right, looks like we'll be shooting many more. They are going to add a mother for you to the show. They are talking about some pretty big names, like Angela Bassett, Lynn Whitfield and Vivica Fox."

"Wow. I like all of them. Lynn Whitfield was the mother on the *Cheetah Girls,* but that doesn't matter." Then she paused, her excitement replaced suddenly by a somber expression. "Daddy, don't you think it's kind of funny and sad at the same time?"

"What is, darling daughter?"

"That I would have to wait to have a successful television show before I could agree to get someone to be my mother."

He quickly turned somber. He knew how hurt Madison had been at her first meeting with Yancey. "Don't think like that, sweetheart. God never shorts you on your blessings." He gave her cheek a light pat. "Besides, you got me. And even though I can't take the place of a mother, I try hard to be a great dad."

She leaned into his hand. "And you are. The best there is. I was just thinking, that's

447

all. Besides, whoever they pick, she won't really be the mother of my dreams. I've given up on that."

"Don't ever give up on your dreams, Madison. Please don't ever do that."

"I won't, Daddy. I got plenty of dreams left."

"Have you decided what you want to get for dinner, and please don't say chicken fingers."

"Why don't you decide? And, Daddy."

"Yes, Madison?"

"I want to get Yancey out of jail. I saw on the *Entertainment Tonight* website that she's been unable to make bail. I don't know her, but somehow I feel sorry for her. I mean, I don't owe her anything, but I feel obligated to help. It's nothing but nasty gossip all around."

He looked her straight in the eye. "Do you want to get her out because you feel sorry for her, or are you embarrassed by all of this publicity?"

"Do you want me to be honest?"

"Yes. Always, Madison. You know that."

"It's a little bit of both. I read where she doesn't have the money." She had an acute moment of doubt, and added a condition. "But if we do help her, I don't want her to know it was us."

"Why is that?"

"Because it's not that important, but also I don't want her to think I want her in my life."

"I don't know if I agree with you on that, Madison, but I'll talk to my lawyers and see what we can do. I heard her bail was half a million dollars. That's a lot of money."

"I know, but we can afford it. Right?"

"Yeah, Madison, and I think we only have to pay ten percent of that."

Madison jumped out of the chair and raced over to her daddy and kissed him on the cheeks. "Thanks, Daddy. I think this is the right thing to do."

"It is, Madison. I'm sure your mother will be real happy you did this."

She was instantly cautious. "You mean Yancey will be happy. My mother is dead."

"Whatever, Madison."

CHAPTER 4

On my third morning in jail I was greeted early by a prison guard. My appearances on entertainment television had earned me a private cell, which I was very happy about. I hadn't yet brushed my teeth or washed my face when I found her standing there staring at me in disgust.

"Yancey Braxton. Collect your stuff. Someone has posted bail. Let's go," she ordered.

I'd heard from no one but Raymond since I'd been arrested. I had all but given up on that bastard S. Marcus, who I now realized had some hand in setting me up, and I had a strong suspicion Ava might be involved too. What I couldn't understand was *why* anyone would set me up. That said, I couldn't begin to guess who would post bail. I jumped from the iron cot and looked at her like she was playing some cruel joke on me.

"Are you kidding me? Who?"

"They don't give me that kind of information, Braxton. Just get your stuff. Your lawyer is waiting on you."

I saw this was no joke. "Oh, my God. Thank you," I said. Basil had come through again, I thought as I looked for the prison-issue toothbrush and the bad-tasting toothpaste they issued.

"Hurry up, Braxton. I don't have all day. You're not the only prisoner getting sprung today."

I didn't want to look a wreck in front of Raymond. "Do I have time to wash my face and brush my teeth?" I asked.

"Hurry up."

"I will," I said as I moved over to the face bowl. Once again I tried to avoid the mirror. I knew I looked a hot mess. The first thing I was going to do when I was let out was go to the beauty shop and get my hair done and a facial. I hoped the press hadn't been alerted and weren't waiting outside to take snapshots of me looking my worst.

About thirty minutes later, I was given my purse, cell phone, earrings and the little money I had and released into the reception area. I was expecting to see Raymond Tyler but instead was met by Basil. He gave me a smile, one that was warm and caring, and I just lost it. Tears streaked down my face as I raced into his arms.

"Basil, thank you. I can't thank you enough. Please take me home and get me out of this place," I cried.

"I will, Yancey, but I didn't do anything."

"You got Raymond to come and see me," I said.

"I mean besides that."

I pulled away from him, confused. "Are you saying you didn't put up my bail?"

"No, I didn't. Raymond just got a call this morning saying someone had paid your bail but they wanted to remain anonymous. He's busy in a meeting and asked if I would come down here and make sure you got home all right."

"Maybe S. Marcus came through after all." It suddenly occurred to me that he might have steered clear of the press in order to protect me and the show. I'm sure it killed him to do that. But this would be his style. Could I have been wrong about him? Was somebody setting him up and I got caught in the middle? He was probably waiting at the house for me. "Let's go," I said.

"There's a car waiting. Raymond said he'd come and see you later this evening."

"Good, I can't wait to get home." Then a pang in my stomach reminded me of something else I had been dreaming about when I was stuck in that cell. "Can we pick up something to eat? I haven't eaten anything in days."

"What would you like?" Basil asked.

"I don't care. Just as long as it's not from this place," I said as I grabbed Basil's hand and led him toward the door.

When we got outside, a half dozen photographers were waiting. Basil tried to shield my face and I had on my big sunglasses, although it was an overcast day. One yelled out, "Yancey, why did you do it? Did things get so bad that you had to sell drugs to children?"

They had overstepped the boundaries and I stopped, went over to the photographer who hurled the question. I took off my glasses and looked him dead in the eye. "How dare you accuse me of something so low? I've never sold drugs to children or anyone else, for that matter. Let me have my day in court before you accuse me of something so classless. Do I make myself clear?"

"I was just asking you what we were told," he explained meekly.

I was preparing myself to read him the

riot act when I suddenly felt Basil pull my arm.

"Come on, Yancey, these guys aren't worthy of your time. Why don't I take you to my place to avoid the creeps that I'm sure are camped out at your house?"

I glanced at the reporter one last time and said, "You're absolutely right, Basil. Just get me away from this horrible place."

As soon as we reached Basil's car, I made the call I needed to salvage whatever was left of my career. I called Regan Reynolds. I knew she would be upset with me and most likely drop me as a client. She hadn't returned my calls over the past three days or maybe she had since my voicemail was full. I also needed to call Dalton because he had left several frantic messages saying he was worried about me. There was also a sweet call from Nicole Springer that almost brought me to tears. She simply said she was praying for me and told me she had come to know my lovely daughter. Nicole didn't have to do or say that. She really was a sweet woman and one day soon I wanted to tell her that. But right now my plate was full.

"Is Regan in? I need to speak with her urgently."

"Who's calling?"

"Yancey Braxton."

The receptionist made no reply for a pregnant moment, then said, "Let me check."

After a few minutes Regan came on the phone. She didn't sound cold as ice, as I'd feared.

"Yancey, how are you?"

"I'm fine. I was released this morning. The whole thing was a horrendous mix-up obviously. I don't know how I was included in it or why someone would set me up that way, but I'm in the process of clearing my name right now. I don't know what to say, Regan. I feel awful that one of your clients has put you through this." I added, dreading the reply, "I hope I'm still a client."

"Yes, Yancey, I'm still representing you." She sounded surprisingly pleasant. "I'm just glad to hear you're okay. We can try and get the *Ugly Betty* audition changed. I know for a fact they haven't cast it. I also got a call today from Disney for a part I think you might be right for." That explained why I was still alive with her. I was still a bankable commodity. "But the most important thing is your well-being. So when you're ready, then I'm ready. Are you at home?"

"No, I'm staying with a friend," I explained, reminding myself I had unfinished business with Ava, "but I'm ready to go to work whenever you have something for me. I'm not going to sit around and feel sorry for myself. I know that I will be cleared of this mess. Until then I want to work."

"Okay, let me make some calls and get back with you."

"Thanks, Regan. I really appreciate you not giving up on me."

She was all business. "I'm not doing anything that I should not be doing. Just don't let yourself down, Yancey."

"I won't. Thanks, and I'll wait for your call."

"Bye, Yancey."

I hung up the phone and stared at it for a second and then hit Dalton's speed dial number. He picked up on the first ring.

"Yancey, where are you? Are you okay?"

"I'll be fine. How are you doing?"

"I'm back home."

"Home? Where?"

"I'm back in Athens with my folks."

"Have you heard from Anderson?"

"No, and I won't because I told him if he contacted me I would file charges and I mean it!"

"Good for you."

"So what's gonna happen?"

"I have a good attorney and some good

friends. Everything will be fine," I said, not wanting to worry Dalton with my problems. He had enough of his own.

"Do you need me to come back to New York?"

"Only if it's to record some music, baby."

"Well, I'm there if you need me."

"I know, Dalton. I love you for that."

"I love you too."

"I'll call you later, I got some more calls I need to make."

"Bye now."

As soon as I hung up from talking to Dalton, my cell phone rang. I recognized Regan's number.

"Hello?"

"Yancey, this is Regan. Can you make an audition tomorrow morning?"

"That was quick, but sure I can," I said.

"Like people say, I guess publicity good or bad keeps your name out there. We've had several calls about your availability. But this casting seems perfect for you."

"What is it?"

"It's for the role of a mother of a teenager on a new show by Disney. They've already ordered a full season of episodes, so I think it will be a good gig."

"What's the name of the show?"

"Madison of South Beach."

My heart instantly sank. I knew that was the name of Madison's show. I started to tell Regan that there was no way in hell I was getting that job, but instead I asked, was she sure they wanted to see me? Regan told me they had specifically requested me.

"Okay, I will go, but I won't hold out high hopes," I said.

"Why is that, Yancey?"

I sighed. How much more complicated was a client supposed to be? "Regan, it's going to come out sooner or later, and this falls under information about me that I'm not so proud of," I said.

"I'm listening, Yancey. Tell me what's going on."

"The star of that show is actually my daughter, but I gave her up at birth."

I heard a gasp of disbelief. "Does she know that?"

"Yes, and I don't think she's a big fan of mine," I said.

She didn't seem so sure. "Do you think the director and producers know that?"

"I have no clue, but I would imagine any audition would also include a screen test with Madison."

"Then we just have to see, Yancey. I think you should still give it a try."

I wasn't sure if she was hoping against

hope, but in any case, we had nothing to lose. "Okay, if you think so."

"I do. I will send the script over right away."

"Send it to this address. Something is going on at my house so I'm crashing at a friend's," I said.

"Where do you want me to send it?"

"Send it to Eleven Central Park West in care of John Basil Henderson. It's a doorman building and they know his apartment number."

She sounded impressed. "Okay, I'll send it over right now. Let me know when you get it."

"I will. Thanks, Regan."

"Good luck."

CHAPTER 5

The day before her big party, Ava was annoyed. Kathleen Crowell of the Ebony Socialite website hadn't returned her numerous calls. The party wouldn't be a success if it wasn't written up in the popular website, which told the comings and goings of the black elite in New York City and surrounding areas. In fact, many of her expected guests were people Ava saw mentioned on Kathleen's site.

Ava decided to give Kathleen one more chance to do the right thing.

"ES for in the know and on the go with New York Society," the friendly female voice answered.

"Yes, Ava Parker Middlebrooks, of the Palm Springs Middlebrooks, for Kathleen Crowell."

"May I tell Ms. Crowell what this call is in regard to?"

"No, you may not. Just put Kathleen on

the phone."

"Excuse me?"

"Excuse me, hell. I have left more than five messages for this woman, and I won't stand for this kind of treatment. So if you know what's good for you and this little website, you'll put Kathleen on the line." Ava exhaled loudly, letting out a breath she felt like she'd been holding for days.

"I don't know who you are, but you need to sign up for some sensitivity training. Hold on."

A few moments passed and then Ava heard a slightly gravelly voice come on the line.

"Kathleen Crowell speaking."

At first Ava was shocked that she'd gotten through and stuttered for a moment but quickly regained her composure.

"Kathleen, my love. How are you?"

"Who is this?"

"Did your little assistant announce me correctly? This is Ava Parker Middlebrooks, formerly of Palm Springs, California, and now of the Upper East Side of New York City. I'm sure we've met at several affairs. I have your card in my Rolodex."

"I don't have cards."

"Then it must have been your assistant. I think we met at Sunday brunch at Lynn

Whitfield's, or was it the annual birthday affair of Reggie Van Lee of the Van Lees of New York and Houston?"

"I know both Lynn and Reggie, but I don't recall meeting an Ava Middlebrooks."

"It's Ava Parker Middlebrooks, and I'm sure when you see me tomorrow, you'll be the first one to give me a big old hug around the neck, sweetheart."

"Tomorrow? I'm going to the gala for the Alvin Ailey Dance Theater at the Met."

"Oh, I know, darling, and I was going to be there, too, but I had already scheduled my dinner party to celebrate the beginning of the New York social season. Everyone will be here — Flo Anthony, Reggie Van Lee of course, Susan Taylor, and Mikki Grant. It will be the best of New York. I mean, you must be here to get the proper coverage for your website. We're talking an opening-page event," Ava said.

"First of all, I have never heard of you, and I know that all the people you've mentioned will be at the Ailey event. And how do I know? Because, Ava darling, I'm the co-chair of the event and all of those people have RSVP'd to me personally. So it must be some mistake. I'm sure your event will still be successful," Kathleen said dryly.

"But you must be here," Ava said with

sadness and frustration in her voice.

"Ava, I'm sure one day you'll have the pleasure of really meeting me but until then, have a good day."

"But —" Ava said before realizing that Kathleen had already hung up.

CHAPTER 6

"I guess we can cross Angela Bassett off our list," Derrick said, setting a plate of scrambled eggs, toast and fresh fruit in front of Madison.

This was their Sunday morning ritual — father and daughter breakfast, prepared by Derrick for just the two of them.

"Why?" Madison asked.

"She's a regular on *ER* for their last season. Our producers moved too slow." He patted her back, knowing how much Madison wanted her. "But we're going to get somebody great to play your mother. They already talked to Lynn Whitfield's and Vivica Fox's people. But I don't know about them either. It seems they've both been working a lot."

"I know, Daddy. And thanks."

He was puzzled by Madison's bright expression.

"For what?" he asked with a confused laugh.

"I saw on the internet that Yancey got out of jail. I know it's because of you," Madison said.

"It's really because of you. It's your money and your suggestion, sweetheart. I didn't want to see her in jail as well, but I didn't think of bailing her out. Besides, sometimes I really feel sorry for Yancey."

"Why?"

"Yancey didn't have the best family life when she was your age. When she told me some of the stories of what her mother did to her, I wanted to protect her. That's one of the reasons I fell in love with her," Derrick said.

Madison set down her fork, lost in thought for a second. "I guess I could understand that but I don't know why I felt sorry for her."

"Because you're a good girl and have always thought of other people before yourself."

"I got that from you and Aunt Jenny." At the mention of Jenny, Madison shook her head. "Boy, do I miss her. She would be enjoying all that's happening to me. Wouldn't she be so proud?"

Derrick cut into his eggs and took a bite. He missed his sister too. "I got a feeling she knows what's happening to you long before we do."

"So you think she's in heaven looking down on us?" Madison asked.

"Where else is she going to be?"

"She was my angel here on earth."

"And will always be, Madison." He stopped eating and turned to her. "Now let's stop talking about this before I shed some tears. Did you look over the changes the writers submitted for the script? The ones around how your mother is introduced?"

"Yeah, I did and the changes are fine," Madison said.

"Okay, I will let the director know."

"Hey Daddy, I just had a great idea."

"What, Maddie?"

"Why don't we get Yancey to play my mother?"

Derrick looked at his daughter with a curious glance and then asked, "Are you sure?"

"It will be perfect casting. Talk to the casting agent and have him call Yancey's agent. But don't tell him or her that I was the one who suggested it."

"Why not?"

"If I know Yancey, and I'm not saying that I do, she might not want to be given a job because I suggested it."

"It sounds like to me you know your mother better than you're willing to admit," Derrick said with a smile.

"Mother . . . boy, does that sound strange."

CHAPTER 7

I put my key in the door, but for some reason it wouldn't open. Had the jail given me someone else's keys? Every time I tried to insert it, I felt resistance. I turned and looked at Basil. "That's strange. Something's wrong with the door."

"Your key's not working?"

"No, and something feels different with the lock."

"Why don't you ring the bell? Maybe your mother is here," Basil said.

She gave him a cold "are you kidding" look. "Are you sure you want me to do that?"

"Why you ask that?"

"We *are* talking about Ava. You two don't have the best relationship," I said, understating the obvious.

"Ava and I don't have *any* relationship. I'm just trying to help you get into your house. And I can deal with Ava."

"Okay," I said, ringing the doorbell. No answer. I pulled out my cell phone and tried Ava's number again, but it was still disconnected. I then called Lyrical's and the voicemail picked up immediately. I left her a message asking her to give me a call and if she had seen Ava.

"No answer?" Basil asked.

"No." I felt something was up, but what? In spite of all the publicity around my arrest, I hadn't heard from Ava. I thought that she, like Marcus, was steering clear of all the bad press. However, standing there at the door, locked out of my own house, I began to suspect more was at play. "Maybe I should just wait until Ava comes here or maybe get a locksmith to come and let me in," I said.

"You could just come to my place. You've been through a rough three days, Yancey. Just chill at our place until you figure out what's going on," Basil said.

That wasn't a bad idea. I sure didn't want to wait around for hours. "Are you sure that's okay?"

"Yeah, it's cool, and maybe if Raymond is there, you can talk about your case," Basil said.

"That's a good idea. But let me check something real quick," I said as I pulled out my phone to call my real estate agent. After a few rings Sharon picked up.

"Weeks Realty, this is Sharon."

"Sharon, is Matilda in? This is Yancey Braxton."

"Hello, Ms. Braxton. Ms. Weeks is on vacation. Is there something I can help you with?"

"I'm at my brownstone and it seems the locks have been changed."

"Oh yeah, the new owner did that."

"The new owner? What are you talking about?"

"Your mother, Ava Middlebrooks. The day of the little incident she brought a quick claim deed insisting we take the house off the market again. Before she left Ms. Middlebrooks asked me for the recommendation of a good locksmith because she was getting the locks changed. I thought you knew."

"Bye Sharon, I will handle this," I said.

I joined Basil at the bottom of the stoop. An alarm bell was ringing in my head. I was more and more certain that Ava was up to no good.

It was my first day on the set of Madison's Disney show, and I was more nervous than I had ever been in my life. I knew all of my lines and it was going to be great being in front of the camera again, but I couldn't calm my nerves. I didn't want to disappoint the director, Derrick, and most important, I didn't want to disappoint Madison.

I took a look at myself in the makeup mirror, dabbed on a final dash of orange-red lipstick and left the small dressing room that I was given. As I walked down the hallway, I came up to a door with a huge gold star on it with Madison B. right underneath it. The door was slightly ajar and I could hear voices inside, one which I immediately recognized as Derrick's.

I walked in and saw Madison seated in front of a mirror with a stylist putting the final touches on her hair. Madison at first didn't notice me enter the room. I watched for a moment in silence, admiring her beauty but also her incredible confidence for a girl so young. I had to admit, she reminded me of myself when I was her age. I was looking at a younger mirror image of myself in more ways than one.

But there was a difference. That being she had a loving, responsible parent guiding her along the way. It was easy to see Derrick had done an extraordinary job raising her, and suddenly I felt a deep inferiority to them both. Also a deep debt, which was why

I needed to speak to them both.

The stylist had finished and collected her gear when Madison saw my reflection in the mirror.

"Yancey. How long have you been standing there?" Derrick asked. I noticed Madison looking away. If she couldn't look me in the face now, how was it going to be once we hit the set?

"I'm sorry. I just want to speak to the both of you before we begin filming," I said nervously.

"What's going on, Yancey?" Derrick asked.

"I just want to thank you both for not vetoing my chance to get this job. I'm really grateful for the chance," I replied.

"This wasn't about old relationships, Yancey. It was about who was best for the job, and the director clearly thought it was you," Derrick said easily. Madison was still ignoring me and was now preoccupied with a script.

"That's nice of you to say, Derrick, but I know if you or Madison would have said something, this wouldn't have happened. Also, my lawyer finally discovered that it was you who posted bail for me and I want to thank you."

"You don't have to thank me, Yancey. It wasn't all me," Derrick said as he looked toward Madison.

"Madison?" I said. She didn't move and her eyes remained on the pages.

"Madison. Yancey is talking to you. Don't be rude, little girl."

"What?" Madison quizzed.

"You were the reason your father posted my bond?"

"What are you talking about?" Madison asked, clearly dodging my question.

"You were the reason I got a chance to audition for this role as well, weren't you?"

She pretended to be engrossed in adjusting her hair. "Stop talking crazy," Madison said. She was no better at lying than her father.

"Madison, tell the truth," Derrick said.

"What do you want me to say to her, Daddy? Do you want me to tell her that I thought that since she did such a rotten job being my mother in real life that we thought she might be able to do it in a make-believe world? Is that what you want me to say?"

"Is that how you feel, Madison? I wouldn't blame you if you did. Because you're right about me being a rotten mother because I was young like you," I said.

"So that's your excuse? You were too young? Do you know how many young mothers out there make it work every day?

473

Young ladies who didn't have the support and love of someone like my dad. Why don't you just tell the truth and say what's so? Your career was more important than being a mother. My mother. But looks like you get the chance, if only for a few hours a day."

"Madison, stop it. Don't talk to Yancey like that," Derrick said.

"That's okay, Derrick. Madison is right. I was selfish. She is telling the truth."

"That was a long time ago, Yancey. You've got to stop beating yourself up," Derrick said.

"Daddy, why are you taking up for her?" Madison asked with disappointment.

I looked at Derrick and saw the man I had fallen deeply in love with. The first person who I felt really loved me for me. Madison may have missed out on some things, but how lucky she was to have Derrick for her father.

"Derrick, would you give me a few moments alone with Madison? I promise this won't take long," I said as I looked at Madison, who was now looking down.

"Sure, I can do that. But both of you need to be on set in ten minutes."

"We will be there," I said as Derrick walked out of the dressing room, pulling the door behind him.

For a few moments the room was dead silent as Madison continued to look down and I glanced around the room searching for what words to say.

"Madison, I understand your feelings about me. You wouldn't be normal if you didn't harbor harsh feelings about me. What I did was wrong, but I didn't know better. Even though my mother was around, she was never a mother to me, and I now realize she never loved me. She left me helpless to love you. It wasn't until I met your dad that I knew what love was," I said.

"Are we running lines? Is this for the script of some movie you did?" Madison asked.

"This isn't a movie, Madison. This is life," I said.

"Yeah, right."

"Madison, I know I can't walk in here and ask you to understand. It looks like from the wonderful young lady you've become that Derrick did a great job," I said.

"How would you know that I'm a wonderful young lady? Don't believe the hype, Yancey. I could be a bitch just like you. We do share the same blood line," Madison said.

"You could never be the rotten woman I was," I said.

"Was?"

"It's never too late to change, Madison. You'll learn that as you grow older," I said.

"Maybe the next time we do a little scene like this, they will pipe in music," Madison said as she stood up and brushed past me, adding, "A real actress is never late to the set."

CHAPTER 8

Ava's first party back in society had been all she hoped. Over thirty guests arrived, all of them from, in Ava's words to Lyrical, "all the right places." Lyrical, however, was unimpressed. In fact, she was very upset over a slight confession made in confidence after too many glasses of champagne.

Lyrical had begun to suspect Ava had a hand in Yancey's problem, but never would she have thought she'd set up her own daughter for a drug bust. Although Lyrical knew Ava had a ruthless streak right down to her bone, and while she found Yancey a stuck-up bitch, it was a stretch for her to imagine a mother would do her own daughter so dirty. Her own mother had disappointed her so many times in her childhood, but even a crackhead wasn't this low down.

Lyrical had the whole night to mull over what she'd heard, and by morning she decided to confront Ava.

"How could you do that to your own daughter?" Lyrical asked.

"Do what, girl?" Ava was making a pot of coffee, pouring out little scoops into the filter.

"Last night when you told me you had helped set up Yancey with the drugs."

Ava's hand stopped dead. "I never said that. What kind of bullshit are you talking about?" Ava asked. She gave a brittle laugh as she looked into the cabinet for the bagels she'd purchased.

"Yes, you did. We might have both been a little drunk, but I remember what you said."

Ava's shoulders slumped. There was no way she was going to con an ex-con. "She did it to me and I was just giving her what she deserves. The little bitch."

Lyrical had already added up two plus two. "Does this have anything to do with you meeting with Donnie Ray? Did you get the drugs from him? I don't like it, Ava."

Ava stopped and faced Lyrical. "My business with Donnie Ray is just that. My business, Lyrical. Now, have you thought any more about moving to California to be my assistant?"

"I'm not moving, Ava. I've told you that a million times. You know what I think? I think you're trying to buy me off and keep me quiet or something by getting me out of New York. Why don't you go to the police and tell them that Yancey is innocent? And who is this guy that she keeps talking about but nobody can find?"

Ava gave her a long-suffering look. "Lyrical, you're bringing me down. All I want to do is have a cup of coffee and a bagel. I need to start packing my stuff. I will call you later on." She was talking fast, moving swiftly about the kitchen. "And let's just forget about last night. I mean the bad stuff. The party was a big hit, wasn't it?"

"I didn't like any of those people. Thought they were big shit. Are those the kinds of people you used to hang around with?"

"Some of those people were my friends. And I think you're the one that's being snooty, Lyrical."

She couldn't believe Ava was such a phony. "They weren't your friends, Ava. A lot of them had never heard of you. One lady told me she had met you over the internet when you read about her in some society blog. Is that what you're going to do the rest of your life, use your money to buy friends?"

"Girl, you're tripping me the fuck out," Ava said hotly.

"You're so fake, Ava. Listen at how you're

cussing at me. I thought you told me a real woman didn't need language like that to make her point."

"Whatever, bitch. Talk to you later."

"Don't walk out on me, Ava. I told you how my mother used to do that and how it made me feel. Don't do that to me," Lyrical pleaded.

"Oh shit, you're going to make me scream! You make my ass hurt. I'm so sick and tired of hearing about your dead drug addict mother," Ava said harshly. "She's dead, so build a bridge and get over it! I'm not your mother, Lyrical."

Tears rushed down Lyrical's face, and she felt like she'd been hit in the stomach with a baseball again. Still, she was determined to have the last word. "You're nobody's mother, Ava. Look what you did to your own daughter."

CHAPTER 9

I was zipping up the side of my black pencil skirt when I heard a knock at the door.

"Come in," I said.

Derrick opened the door and peeked in. "Are you decent?"

A part of me wished he had walked in a minute before. "Come on in, Derrick," I said as I located the red leather belt I usually wore along with a snow-white oxford cloth shirt.

"You did great today. The directors are really pleased with your work, Yancey," Derrick said.

Did he really come in just to tell me that? "Thanks, Derrick."

"It couldn't have been easy. Madison told me what she said, and I really got on her about being so grown."

"That's okay, Derrick, and Madison had every right." I held up a hand to stave off his protest. "She is quite the little actress.

481

You would have never known how much she hates me when we did our scenes."

"Madison doesn't hate you, Yancey," Derrick said, discouraged. "That's one thing I know about my little girl; she isn't capable of hate. Give her a little time and everything will be fine."

"I deserve whatever happens to me," I said solemnly.

Derrick was having none of that. "Do you deserve to go to jail for something you didn't do?"

"I'm hopeful that won't happen. My lawyer and a friend of mine are trying to help me find the guy who set me up."

"Is there anything I can do?" Derrick said.

If I didn't know how protective he was of his daughter, I would think he was making a play for me. "Thanks, Derrick, but you've done enough. A lot more than I'll ever deserve."

He was pleased by that remark, and he slapped his thigh, thinking of something else. "Say, Madison got some big news."

"What happened?"

"She's doing a concert for the president-elect's daughters. It turns out they're big fans," Derrick said.

"Oh, that's wonderful. I was supposed to sing at one of the victory parties, but my arrest messed that up." I didn't really mind, because I was only singing backup. "I sure would like to go to see Madison singing at the White House."

"Why don't you come?"

I drew back, immediately refusing. "I don't know. Madison might not like that. I mean, this is about her. Not me."

"You can come as my guest," Derrick said.

There it was again, that sparkle in his eye which I didn't know how to interpret. "Let me think about it. I don't want to do anything to upset Madison. This could be a really special night for her," I said.

"Okay, but I'm sure it wouldn't be a problem. Do you have plans for this evening?"

"Just to study my lines for tomorrow," I said, wondering why he asked.

"If you like, I will ask Madison if she'd mind if you joined us for dinner."

I thought about it for a moment and thought how uncomfortable I would be if I was in Madison's place, and so I told Derrick I would pass.

He seemed deflated. "Are you sure?"

"I'm sure."

"Okay, but this isn't the last time I will ask you."

"That's fair, Derrick," I said as I reached

up and gave him a quick peck on the cheek. He looked surprised but in a good way. He wasn't looking at me like a protective daddy.

I was standing outside the studio in Queens, trying to hail a taxi when my cell phone rang. I saw the 305 area code and thought it might be Marcus finally calling me to explain what was going on. Instantly I answered it.

"Hello."

"Yancey. This is Jeff. Steven's partner. We met when you came to Miami. Remember?"

What could he want? "Yes, Jeff, I remember." Then what he said registered with me. "But you said Steven. I know your partner as Seneca," I said.

He sounded fretful as he replied. "That was all a part of his plan. I need to talk to you and try and explain what's going on. Where are you?"

"Right now I'm in Queens on my way back to Manhattan," I said.

"Do you have plans this evening?"

"No, I don't."

"Then you should meet me and I can try and explain what's going on."

I would have preferred that S. Marcus do it face-to-face, but I would do anything to find out what had happened. "Sure, I can do that. Where do you want to meet?"

"How long will it take you to get to Manhattan?"

"About fifteen minutes when I get a taxi," I said.

"Okay. I'm staying at the Hudson Hotel. Why don't we meet there? I understand the restaurant there is pretty good," Jeff said.

I wasn't familiar with it myself, but Jeff seemed to have good taste. At least when he wasn't trying to act ghetto. "Okay, but why don't you give me an hour? I need to make a stop."

"Okay. Did my number show up on your phone?"

"Yeah."

"This is the number where you can reach me. Lock it in."

"Okay, Jeff. I will see you shortly," I said.

I walked into the dimly lit bar at the Hudson Hotel on West 57th Street and saw Jeff standing at the corner of the bar. He raised his ring hand in the air, motioning for me to join him.

"You got here really quick," Jeff said. He gave me a kiss on the cheek and I immediately pulled back. I didn't know what information he had for me or if I could trust him.

"How are you, Jeff? Where is your buddy?"

He saw the suspicion written all over my face. "That's what I want to talk to you about. I think I have some information you might need. Can I get you something to drink?"

"No. What information?"

"At least have a club soda or something."

He had offered to meet with me, I remembered. "Club soda with cranberry juice."

Jeff motioned to the bartender and patted his hand on the bar stool, which I took as his telling me to take a seat. As I did, he gave me an appreciative once-over.

"You look great, Yancey. How is the filming going?"

"Look, Jeff, I know you didn't invite me here to talk about how good I look. Are you and Marcus involved in some sort of drug trade? Is that why you agreed to finance my show, so that you could use me?"

He waved both hands, as if to signal cancel that. "No, I'm not involved in any type of drug trade, and I seriously doubt that Marcus is. I've known him since prep school and that's not Marcus. His family would be livid. Marcus comes from good stock."

"Then explain to me why I was arrested carrying a bag with drugs provided to me

486

by Marcus."

"I can't explain that, but I did find out a few days ago that Marcus and some of his family members are really upset with you."

That idea completely threw me. "For what? I only know Marcus. Why would members of his family be mad at me?"

"Come on, Yancey. I found out you were the one who took Marcus Senior away from the family some years ago."

The stern way he was looking at me was totally irritating. "What are you talking about?"

"Didn't you have an affair with Marcus Senior?"

I was trying to figure out what the hell he was talking about. "Are you talking about Marcus's father? Hell no! I've never even met Marcus's father. Matter of fact, Marcus and I have never even discussed his father. I just assumed he was either dead or they weren't close."

"Marcus and his father were always very close, Yancey," Jeff said.

"Were? So he is dead?"

"No, but he has a sickness that makes him no good to anyone. It's been that way for several years. I think that's why Marcus Junior was so hell-bent on getting revenge on you. He told me you were the reason his family is in such disarray. He blames you for his mother's death. He told me that he knew one day he would meet you and exact revenge." He must have seen how baffled I was by the accusation, and he backed off slightly. "I love Marcus, but I don't think he's going about this the right way. He didn't tell me until a couple of days ago when I asked about the show what he'd been up to."

"I don't know Marcus's mother or his father. This is crazy." Suddenly I had a flash of that first night, when his car pulled up to the curb. "So we didn't just meet innocently. This was all some plan to get back at me for something I didn't do," I said as I stood up from the bar stool.

Jeff said quietly, "You better sit down. There is more I need to tell you."

CHAPTER 10

"So, do you have the menu for my party, Chef Crenshaw?" Ava asked. After one successful party she was ready for something on an even grander scale. A party that, once word got out, Kathleen Crowell would be begging to attend. This party could put her dead center on the social map of New York society and provide entrée back into California's social movers and shakers.

"I do have it, Ms. Middlebrooks, and I hope you will approve," Crenshaw Roberts said. He was the former head chef for the South African cuisine in a popular restaurant in Harlem. Ava read an article on him in *New York* magazine and was delighted when he agreed to cater her going back to Cali party.

"What are you suggesting, Crenshaw? It is okay that I call you Crenshaw, isn't it?"

"That's fine, Ms. Middlebrooks."

"Call me Ava, darling," she said in a teasing purr.

"Okay, Ava. I thought we would start with fish sambal served on toasted bread. We will also have chicken satay and corn fritters with a sweet apricot sauce."

"Oh, that sounds wonderful. My guests will be so impressed," Ava said. "Do you know Kathleen Crowell of EbonySocialite .com?"

"Yes, I know Kathleen, and how many people are we talking about?"

"Between twenty-five and thirty," Ava said.

"Perfect number."

"I want you to make sure Kathleen's office knows that you're the chef of this party."

"No problem."

That was a key piece put in place. "So what will we have for dinner?"

"I suggest, with it being fall, that we start with a pumpkin soup."

"Again a perfect choice."

"Follow that up with a beet root and onion salad. I also want to have a platter of cold green asparagus with a spicy mayonnaise that I do."

"Is this popular in South Africa?"

"Yes, it is, Ava. I want to serve a braised lamb with apple mint relish and fish cakes. I will also serve pumpkin fritters with a coconut curry sauce."

"What's for dessert?"

"I have the perfect thing," Crenshaw said.

"I'm listening."

"Pears in spiced red wine with vanilla ice cream," Crenshaw said.

The spiced red wine part would be helpful. "Sounds delicious."

"I think we should serve South African wines with each course."

"Oh, honey, my guests are going to be so impressed," Ava said.

"I hope that you will be as well, Ava. I hope this won't be the last party that I do for you. Is this your only home?" Crenshaw asked as he looked around the living room.

"Oh, of course not, honey. My house in Palm Springs is being renovated. I will be back there in the spring. If this goes well, maybe I will use you for my housewarming. I will fly you out at my expense, of course."

"I would love to do that," Crenshaw said.

"Can I get a copy of the menu? Oh, and how many on wait staff?"

"I think four will work perfectly, and yes, I will have my assistant forward you a menu. I'm pretty sure we have your email address."

"Okay. That will be fine, Crenshaw. I hate to rush you, but I still haven't found the right dress for the event and I'm expecting my personal shopper any moment."

Crenshaw stood up. Ava looked up, briefly startled because she hadn't realized how tall Chef Crenshaw was when he came into the house.

"I don't want to get in the way of a lady looking for the perfect dress. It was nice meeting you, Ava Middlebrooks."

"Same here, love."

Ava picked up her cell phone and pressed the number programmed for Lyrical. It went right to voicemail.

"Damn," Ava muttered to herself.

"What up, ya'll? This girl Lyrical. Right now I can't chop it up with you 'cause I'm laying down some tracks on my music hustle, so just leave me a message and I'll get back witcha soon."

"Lyrical, girl, where are you? Are you all right? I haven't heard from you and I'm worried. I hope you're not mad at me. Call me or come by when you get this message. This is Ava."

Ava was waiting on some of her purchases to be delivered so when the doorbell rang she answered without hesitation.

"Yancey, what are you doing here?"

"I need to talk with you, Ava. What are you up to?" Yancey asked.

"I think I should be asking you that,

Missy," Ava said as she looked at Basil, who was standing next to Yancey, and gave him a dirty look.

"Why did you have my locks changed?"

"Because this is my house and I don't consort with drug dealers even if we are blood. And what are you doing with him?"

"Basil is letting me stay with him and you know I'm not a drug dealer."

"I don't know any such thing. So he's doing girls again. Can't you make up your mind, Basil Henderson, and Yancey, are you that hard up for a little dick? You're really a case."

"Do you know Marcus?"

"Who?"

"Marcus Pinkston. Do you know him?"

"Can't say that I do and if you two don't mind I have some beauty sleep to catch up on. Good day," Ava said as she slammed the door.

CHAPTER 11

"I told Yancey about your big news and she was really excited for you," Derrick said.

"She was? I bet she wishes it was her," Madison said.

"That's not nice, Madison. I thought you and Yancey were getting along."

"I'm fine."

"I think she wants to come."

"Are you surprised?"

"Would it be okay if I invited her to be my guest?"

"Daddy, whatever you want to do. Yancey being there won't upset me."

"Are you sure? I think it would mean a lot to her."

"Why don't we invite Yancey to move in here with us, Daddy? We've got more than enough room," Madison said.

"Are you being funny, Madison?"

"No, I'm very serious."

"What brought this on? I mean one moment you're questioning her motives and now this."

"She's been through a lot, Daddy. I don't have hard feelings toward Yancey."

"I don't know if that's such a good idea, Madison. And you're sending out mixed signals here, sweetheart. When you're around Yancey you act like you can't stand the sight of her but behind the scenes you act like her fairy godmother. What are you really trying to do, Madison?" Derrick asked.

"I'm not trying to do anything but what you've taught me, Daddy. We have more than enough of everything and I'm just trying to share."

"I understand that but Yancey will get back on her feet. Trust me on that. Besides, thanks to you she's working again and will be able to make something happen."

"I know and that's why it will only be temporary. She can stay in the guest suite."

"If that's what you want, Madison, then you'll have to make the offer and see what she says," Derrick said.

"Why can't you do it?"

"Because it's not my plan, Madison. You're becoming a woman who is responsible for your own decisions. It won't be long before you'll be running your own business and you won't need me."

"I will always need you, Daddy. Always."

"You know that's what I want to hear but we both know that's not true. Some day some little dude is gonna capture your attention and suddenly I won't be the only man in your life. I don't like it but I understand it," Derrick said.

"What about you?"

"What about me?"

"Are we going to find a wife someday?"

"Is that what you're trying to do with Yancey? Because if it is stop it right now. Yancey and I had our chance at love and we failed," Derrick said.

"So you're saying having me was a failure?"

"Now Madison, you know better. I would never consider you a failure. I love you and I know when Yancey gets the chance to know you she'll love you too," Derrick said.

"I don't think she wants to get to know me. But the feeling is mutual because I'm doing fine without her.

"Yancey is an actress, Daddy. Besides I'm grown and don't need a mother," Madison said.

"You could always use a mother, baby. Don't you think you're being a little tough on her?"

"What do you have up your sleeve, Daddy? Are you jocking for Yancey?"

"What's that?"

"You know, feeling her? Is that what's going on here?" Madison laughed.

"I don't know what you're talking about, little girl, but we did have a nice time. It's been a long time since I've been on a date like that."

"So it was a date. I thought you said it was a meeting? Meeting or date? Either way. If you're happy, then I'm ecstatic. Maybe it's time for me to get my Chris Brown thing going."

"I have told you I'm not letting you get anywhere near Chris Brown, Madison."

"I should say the same thing about Yancey Braxton. But I won't. I like seeing you like this."

"Like what?"

"Falling in love."

"Who said I was falling in love."

"I can see it in your face. But maybe you never fell out of love."

"No comment," Derrick said.

Madison folded her arms across her chest and cocked her head slightly left and smiled at her daddy.

CHAPTER 12

After a long day of filming it was nice to share a glass of wine with Basil at his apartment. A football game was playing on the flat-screen television, but to my surprise Basil was looking at me intently as I had remembered him doing all too well. He asked me how my filming had gone and about Madison. I told him they were both okay and I hoped things would get even better. I sipped my wine and asked Basil a question that appeared to catch him off guard.

"Are you as happy as you seem?"

"What are you talking about, Yancey?"

"Is Raymond the reason you're so happy?" He didn't answer right away. I figure he was trying to find a way to tell me yes without hurting my feelings. Although I hadn't seen them embrace, kiss or even touch each other in my presence, it was obvious they were in love.

"I'm not going to talk with you about that, Yancey."

"Why?"

"Just not. I try to keep my personal life private."

"That's cool," I said, feeling uncomfortable with his intense reply. "This wine is great. What's it called?"

"La Crema. It's a California wine," Basil said as his eyes were averted to the television set.

"It's very good. Do you have players who play for either of these teams?"

"A couple."

"Oh," I said.

Basil must have realized how flustered I was, because he turned and posed another question. "Yancey, how did you get mixed up with this crazy dude?"

"I didn't think he was crazy," I corrected him. "He treated me like a princess. He made promises. He had money and I need money to give my career one final shot."

His face scrunched up at that remark. "You're still young, so why do you say final shot?"

"No, Basil, I'm not as young as I'd like to be. There won't be many more chances. I just thought Marcus cared about me."

"How do you feel about seeing the old boy?"

"Who?" I asked, though I knew exactly who he meant.

"Derrick was his name, I think."

"Derrick's still pretty much the same. A really solid guy," I said.

"Any sparks? They say first loves are the only loves."

"I don't know if I believe that."

He gave me a catlike smile, then let it go. "What about Madison?"

"What about her?"

"Have you given any thought to being a real mother to her?"

"I don't think that's an option," I said.

"Why?" he asked, still with that easy probing.

"Because I don't think Madison needs or wants a mother. Especially me. I mean, this little girl is getting ready to sing for the president's daughters. She is going to be huge."

"Wow, that's great. Are you going to be able to go?"

"I doubt it. I'm just hoping that I'm not going to be sitting in a jail cell."

"Raymond is not going to let that happen," Basil said.

His certainty bolstered my spirits. "I hope

you're right, but even if I'm not, Madison doesn't need me."

"Has she said that?"

"No."

"I think you should go, Yancey. I think you've grown up a lot since I met you. I think you are ready to be a mother," Basil said.

I felt an upwelling of hope. Madison and I had been getting along really well onstage, and not just playing a role. We were starting to feel a real connection. "What makes you say that?"

"Just an observation. I think now that you're working with her, it might be a chance to get to know her. It doesn't sound like Derrick would mind."

"Are you still enjoying being a father?"

Basil broke out in a warm smile. "One of the best things in the world that ever happened to me."

"How old is Talley now?"

"Almost ten and she is going to be a diva. And I mean that in a good way."

"And not a bad diva like me," I said sadly.

He reached his hand out along the back of the couch and stroked my shoulder. "You weren't always bad, Yancey. There are a lot of good things about you. I don't think I could have fallen in love with you if that was not true."

"So you really were in love with me?"

His fingers gave me a squeeze that instantly turned me on. "Yancey, come on, girl. You know I was. But I was also very confused and self-centered. Parenthood changes that. It's not all about you but how you can be the best parent possible."

Basil sounded so wise. Then again, I reflected, if he had grown up, so had I. "If it were only that easy."

"It's not easy, Yancey, but it's not hard either."

"I don't think it's fair for me to get too close to Madison now," I said.

"Why not?"

"What if I can't prove that I was set up for the drug bust? I might be going to jail. Raymond said I could get up to fourteen years. How fair would that be to Madison?"

"See, you're acting like a parent already. Thinking of Madison instead of yourself. Plus," he said, "we're going to get to the bottom of why that dude set you up. You're not going to prison," Basil said confidently.

I didn't answer. Instead I just took a long, slow swallow of the wine and savored its taste as though it was for the first time.

The next day when I walked into the studio

my cell phone rang, and XJI rang across the screen. That was the name of Basil's company, so I answered.

"Hello."

"May I speak to Yancey?"

"This is Yancey."

"Yancey, this is Abigail Gatlin. I'm one of Mr. Henderson's assistants. He asked me to call and see if you have plans this evening."

I felt a flush of excitement. We had been so close last night. "Right now I don't. Why?"

"He wants you to meet him at Telepan at eight. It's on West sixty-ninth. Can you do that?"

"It shouldn't be a problem. Did he say why he wanted to meet me?"

"No, Ms. Braxton," she said flatly. "He just asked me to call you and that if you could, to make the reservation. I'm sure he'll be glad you can make it. I will text him as soon as I make the reservation. Do I need to call you back to confirm?"

"No, I'll be there. Thanks, Abigail."

"Have fun, Ms. Braxton."

CHAPTER 13

"Ava, what are you doing here?" Lyrical asked. She was surprised to see Ava standing outside her West 138th Street walk-up.

"Where is Donnie Ray?" Ava asked. She looked totally out of place in a St. John's knit suit covered by a knee-length fur coat.

"I don't know."

"What did you tell him?" Ava asked in an accusatory tone.

"What are you talking about?" Lyrical asked.

"I got a call from him saying he needed to talk to me about you. He hasn't called back. So what did you tell him?"

"I just told him about your party," Lyrical said. She noticed one of her neighbors coming out of the building, who smiled at Lyrical and Ava.

"I don't believe that. He left some cryptic message about how I needed to watch my back. What do you have up your sleeve,

Lyrical? Don't mess with me or you'll live to regret it," Ava said as she pointed her finger close to Lyrical's nose and then waved her hand in a dismissive gesture.

"Get your fingers away from my nose, Ava. You know I'm not scared of you," Lyrical said.

"That tells me how stupid you are. I got money now, which means I got my power back and you best not fuck with me."

Lyrical couldn't believe this woman was always running a con. "You really are a sad case, Ava. I actually feel sorry for you. But I feel worse for Yancey. What did she do to deserve you as a mother?"

"The bitch ended my career, that's what she did," Ava said savagely. "If I hadn't had Yancey, I would have been a big star."

"That's no reason, Ava, and you know it. Now I'm going inside," Lyrical said.

"Tell me where Donnie Ray is."

"I don't know where he is, so get out of my way," Lyrical said with a dead calmness in her voice.

Ava took a step closer. "Listen to me, Lyrical, don't mess up your life by crossing me. I've told you a hundred times, don't fuck with me."

Lyrical did some stepping up of her own. "I'm done with you, Ava."

CHAPTER 14

I paid the taxi driver as he pulled up in front of Telepan, an Upper West Side restaurant that Basil had raved about. I was a little surprised when I got the call to join him, but a free meal was a free meal. I didn't know what to make of him telling me to wear something hot and sexy. He had rejoined my team, and if so what did Raymond think about that?

I walked into the dimly lit restaurant. There was a bar to my right and a coat check to my left. After I checked my black cashmere coat, my tight-fitting black dress was revealed. A single strand of pearls hung just above my breasts, which swelled from the top of the dress. I went to the hostess station where two young white girls were enjoying their conversation, looking over a huge white reservation book. When I approached, the one with the brunette hair looked up and smiled before asking if she could help me.

"Yes, I have a reservation. The name is Henderson. Basil Henderson. Is he here yet?"

"Oh yes, John Basil Henderson. He and Mr. Tyler are two of our favorite customers. You must be Yancey Braxton. We've been waiting for you."

She sounded like she was in love with Basil. That figured. "I am Yancey Braxton. So, Mr. Henderson is already here?"

The young lady didn't answer. She simply smiled again and told me to follow her. We walked through the restaurant past several patrons who were enjoying dinner. The young lady opened a door that led into what appeared to be a private dining room. There was a table set for two with a huge display of white and yellow roses. Candles were flickering everywhere, and the smell of the flowers was intoxicating. But there was no Basil, and now I was really wondering what he had up his sleeve.

"Have a seat, Ms. Braxton. Can I get you something to drink before your dinner guest arrives?"

"Can I have a cranberry juice with club soda?"

"Sure. I will get that for you."

"On second thought, let me have a glass

of champagne," I said.

"Is there a preference?"

"I know you don't sell Dom by the glass. Do you?"

"We don't, but there are always exceptions, and Mr. Henderson instructed us to make sure you got whatever you wanted. Let me check with the bartender."

When she left the room, music suddenly began playing. It was Seal singing the Sam Cooke classic "A Change Is Going to Come." I walked over to the large window that looked out on Central Park West and thought how nice it was of Basil to plan such a special evening. A few moments later I heard a deep male voice say, "I was told to come back here."

I turned around and was surprised to see Derrick standing there, looking quite handsome in a black suit, white shirt and a rose-red tie. He smiled but looked surprised to see me.

"Derrick. What are you doing here?" I asked.

"I was getting ready to ask you the same thing," Derrick said.

"I thought I was meeting someone else," I said.

"Me too."

"Who were you meeting?"

"I got a call from your former guy Basil Henderson. He asked me to meet him here. Said he wanted to talk to me about my daughter's career and he was bringing some important people," Derrick said as he looked around the private dining room.

"I was expecting Basil as well but he just told me to meet him here."

"It doesn't look like this is set up for a meeting," Derrick said as he eyed the elegantly designed dining table.

The hostess walked in with the champagne on a silver tray. I immediately noticed two white envelopes. She handed me the champagne and one of the notes, then looked at Derrick. "You must be Mr. Lewis," she said.

"I am," he replied.

"This is for you." She handed him the other envelope. "Can I get you something to drink?"

Derrick looked at me and said, "I'll have what the lady is having."

"Let me see what is going on," I said as I tore open the envelope. There was a handwritten note in Basil's handwriting that read: *Yancey . . . life is short . . . choose happiness and forget about the past.*

I noticed Derrick reading his note and a smile breaking out across his face.

"What does yours say?" I asked.

509

"That's personal," Derrick smirked.

"It seems like somebody is trying to set us up," I said, flashing a delighted smile.

"Do you have a problem with that?"

I shrugged. "I don't if you don't."

"At least we'll have a nice dinner. I heard the place is very good," Derrick said.

"I heard the same thing."

Derrick walked to the table and pulled out a chair and said, "Have a seat, Yancey."

I took the seat as I smiled at him and mouthed *thank you.*

The hostess smiled at the two of us and informed us that the chef had prepared a special meal. All we needed to do was to let her know when we were ready for the first course.

Derrick and I sipped champagne and enjoyed the music. After a few moments of awkward silence Derrick grinned at me like a teenage boy and said, "I guess we're on a date."

"I guess so. It's been a long time since we've been on one of those."

"Do you remember our first one?" Derrick asked.

"I do." I blushed.

"Where was it?"

"You took me to eat hot dogs at Ben's Chilly Bowl in D.C.," I said.

510

That brought a fond smile to his face. "Boy, I miss those hot dogs and that chili. I wonder if it's still there."

"I don't know. I haven't been to Washington in a long time," I said.

"We had some good times there, didn't we, Yancey?"

"Yeah, we did." A picture of Derrick and me walking around the campus hand in hand popped into my head. When we first started dating, we spent every free moment together, even if it was in the library or the student union. We even took classes together, though we had entirely different majors. Derrick was majoring in Engineering and me in Theater Arts and Dance.

"That was a great time for me, Yancey. And I always hated the way it ended. Do you ever wish that we could go back to that? Be honest," Derrick said.

I thought for a moment, back to that time at Howard University when I felt love for the first time in my life. It was a special time that ended tragically when I got pregnant and gave up my baby girl for adoption. It was a painful time that I pretended never happened. I told myself if I wanted a career, having a baby wouldn't allow that to happen. I wasn't prepared to be a mother. Hell, I didn't even know what a mother was.

When I left Washington, I cried myself to sleep almost every night. I had given up the only person who ever loved me.

"I don't know if I would go back to that time, Derrick. I wasn't a good person then. I don't even know if I'm one now or if it's in my DNA."

"I always thought you were a great person," Derrick said.

"Why?"

"Because I saw through the shield."

"What shield?"

"The one you used to protect yourself, Yancey. You just needed to be loved."

"I felt you loved me," I said softly.

"I did," he said, and I felt just the same as I did when he told me he loved me decades ago. "Have you ever thought how ironic it is that Madison's first big hit is 'Blame It on the Sun'?"

"What do you mean?"

"I'm the one who suggested to the producers at *American Star* that she sing it. I always remember that song as our song." His face softened, and in that moment he almost seemed the same age as when I met him. "I remember one of the first times we stayed up all night in my dorm room, and you shared this really sad story about you growing up. Do you remember the story, Yancey?

It was one of the first times I think you were really letting me see inside your soul."

I didn't answer Derrick. Instead I stared at the tiny bubbles in the champagne and thought back to that night when I shared my life with him. I told Derrick that when I was fifteen, I was getting ready for one of my first teen pageants, Jackson Junior Miss. One of my rich classmates and fellow contestants invited me to her house to spend the day and get ready for the pageant. We had spent hours sunbathing at her pool. When I got home, I was greeted by a look of shock and disgust when Ava and my grandmother saw me. Ava screamed, asking me what I'd done. When I asked her what she was talking about, she screamed that I was too dark, and now I looked like all of the other nigger bitches in Jackson. I was always light brown, but on that day the sunbathing had changed my color at least three shades darker. I remember telling Derrick how Ava and my grandmother beat me as they told me how ugly I was now with darker skin. They forbade me from competing for Junior Miss. I ended the story by telling him how Ava said I never took responsibility for anything and that I was blaming the sun for my sudden change.

Weeks later, Derrick had brought me a

recording of Stevie Wonder's ballad "Blame It on the Sun," telling me to listen to the beautiful song with the haunting yet comforting words anytime I thought about that night. "Just tell yourself that Stevie Wonder wrote this song with you in mind because you're so beautiful and special," Derrick said after I listened to the song for the first time.

"Do you remember the first line of the song?" Derrick asked.

I thought for a minute and then quietly said, "No."

"It's 'where has my love gone.' So the song became my feel-sorry-for-myself song when you left me and moved to New York."

I was saddened by this revelation. "I never knew that. Why didn't you tell me?"

"You know us guys. We keep it all here," Derrick said while lightly tapping his chest.

"I will listen to that song again."

"Then listen to Madison's version. It doesn't make you sad. It makes me very happy."

I joined in the pride he felt for her. "It went to number one, didn't it?"

"On all three formats, pop, adult contemporary and R & B."

"You must be so proud."

"Every second of the day."

The memory of that time of my life brought a blur of tears to my eyes. Derrick smiled a gentle smile that seemed to hide nothing, and I suddenly felt special again for the first time in years.

After a wonderful dinner and great conversation, Derrick invited me back to his and Madison's apartment. At first I declined, but after he assured me that Madison was away in Orlando for a Disney photo shoot and that he wasn't looking for anything more than continued conversation, I agreed.

When I walked into the spacious apartment with a majestic night-time view of the city, I couldn't believe this was the boy I'd met at Howard University.

"Derrick, this is beautiful. What a view," I said.

"I wish it wasn't so cold or we could have a drink on the terrace," Derrick said.

"I think I've had enough to drink."

"Well, maybe if you come back, we can have some hot chocolate or something. Do you still like hot chocolate?"

"I do."

"Let me take your coat. I have something I want to show you," Derrick said with a sly smile.

I wasn't sure what that meant, but I felt a

flutter in my chest. "So, how long have you lived here?"

"For about three months. It's just a furnished rental that Disney found for us. Madison had to stay here once she found out Michael Jackson once lived here while recording an album."

"MJ stayed here? Wow."

"Come on, let's go in the media room."

I followed Derrick down a dimly lit hallway into a room that had about six movie chairs and a popcorn popper and an old-fashioned soda machine. At the front of the room was a huge flat-screen television, one of the largest I'd ever seen.

"Where do you want me to sit?" I asked.

"Take the chair right in the middle. Would you like some popcorn? I make a pretty good bag if I do say so myself."

"No, I'm fine. I'm still stuffed from dinner. Are we going to watch a movie?"

"Sort of," Derrick said.

He went in what looked like a production room I'd seen in some of the studios I'd worked in. Minutes later, he came out with a remote control in his hand. He sat down in the chair next to me and clicked one of the buttons. On the screen popped a little girl running through a field of beautiful flowers of all different colors. She had two long pigtails with pink and blue ribbons, but her back was facing us. The deceased singer Minnie Ripperton's "Loving You" was playing in the background.

"Who is that?" I asked.

Derrick looked at me with puppy-dog eyes and said, "It's Madison. I made this for her high school graduation. Just sit back and watch."

For the next few minutes I watched the screen as Madison grew up right before my eyes. One minute she was a precious little girl running through a field and playing with a dog that seemed to be enjoying his height advantage over what looked like an eight-year-old, with hair in a bun and a pink ballet tutu. There was Madison at a gym tumbling uncontrollably and giggling wildly as she tried to keep up with Derrick on a basketball court.

Madison singing in a youth choir at church and then being carried by Derrick when she had fallen asleep and Derrick whispered how she couldn't last through an entire middle school football game.

When the Madison I knew appeared on screen singing and dancing with obvious skills, I lost it. Tears ran down my face and I leaped from the chair and raced to the hallway. I leaned against the wall and cried tears of shame and disgust as my body shuddered all the way to the floor. The truth of what I'd done wrapped around me like a worn winter coat.

"Yancey, what's the matter?" Derrick asked.

"Why did you do that?" I cried.

"Do what?"

"Show me that? Are you trying to pay me back for leaving you? For leaving Madison?"

"Yancey, why would you say that? Heavens, no. I just thought you might enjoy it. I had no idea it would cause this reaction. I'm sorry," Derrick said as he knelt down and began wiping the tears from my face with his warm hands.

"She must hate me." I wept.

"Madison doesn't hate anyone, Yancey. Especially you. I just wanted to share a part of her that you didn't know about," Derrick said.

"The part where I deserted her."

"Yancey, you thought you'd done the best for Madison by giving her up for adoption. You didn't know that I'd changed all of that. But you must know how I loved you. It's a different kind of love, but I simply gave all the love I had to give to our little girl."

"She's not my little girl. I gave that up. My ass was too selfish to be a mother."

"Maybe you were scared and too young. But giving a child a chance at a better life is never selfish. You must know that."

I thought about what I was about to say. Something I'd never said to anyone ever in life. Something that I knew was the truth and if anyone deserved to hear it then Derrick was the one.

"Can I tell you something, Derrick?"

"Sure, Yancey. Talk to me."

"I think things would have been different for us if Madison had been a boy."

"What do you mean?"

"When I got pregnant I use to pray that I would have a healthy baby and that the baby would be a boy. If Madison was a boy then I would have felt that God loved me and wanted me to keep the baby and be a mother and possibly a wife to you."

"Why a boy, Yancey?"

"Because I was a girl born to a mother who hated me for that fact and I didn't want that to happen to our child. When Madison came I figured God didn't want me to be a mother. It was my answer. I just knew that I couldn't be a mother to a girl."

"Yancey, God sent us the child we were supposed to have. Trust me on that."

"Then why didn't I know that?" I asked as tears begin to stream down my face.

"We don't always know everything, Yancey. Stop blaming yourself for that. You wanted Madison to be adopted and that can be the most unselfish form of love."

I wouldn't be comforted, no matter how nice it felt. "I need to wash my face. I'm going home."

"Yancey, look at me," Derrick said as he cupped my chin up toward his face.

"What?"

"Yancey, you're not selfish. You gave me the best blessing in my life. I can never thank you enough for Madison. I wasn't trying to hurt you. I would never hurt the mother of my child."

He was being so sincere. What he didn't understand was how I felt about giving her away. "I know, Derrick. I want to go home."

"Okay," he said, resigned. "Go into the powder room and wash your face. I will have the doorman get you a car."

I got up from the floor and nodded toward Derrick. I was heading for the rest room when I heard Derrick call out my name. I turned to face him and he said, "I never stopped loving you. I hope you know that."

CHAPTER 15

"This girl, and I use the term lightly, said she won't leave until she speaks with you, Madison. She said it's real important. But we can call the police if you like," the studio security guard said.

"Where is my father, Joseph?"

"He's not here. Normally I would just go to him or Thurston, but I can't contact either one of them."

Madison could tell that something was different. "You think it's a fan?"

"It's hard to say, Miss Madison. I can just as easy call the policeman."

"No, I'll talk to her if you stay with me. Let's go to the conference room," Madison said.

She followed Joseph down the long hallway into the conference room. He instructed her to sit at the table, and he'd go and get the lady and bring her back. Before leaving, he assured Madison that he wouldn't leave her side.

A few minutes later, he walked in with an imposing young lady who looked scary and yet meek at the same time.

"Are you Madison?"

"Yes, I am. And you are?"

"My name is Lyrical. Thanks for seeing me," she said quietly. "I want you to know that I don't mean you any harm, but I have some information that I think you need to know."

"About what?"

"Your mother and grandmother."

"My grandmother?"

"Yeah, Ava Middlebrooks."

"I don't know my grandmother," Madison said.

"I know, but she knows you. I used to work with her. She's a real bad lady."

Madison's mouth twisted. "That seems to run on my mother's side of the family."

"This time it's not Yancey's fault. She is a real B, but even Yancey doesn't deserve this. She doesn't know what Ava did to her." Lyrical paused for a beat. "She is the reason Yancey was arrested."

Madison nearly jumped out of her seat. "How do you know this?"

"Ava got drunk and told me. Yancey

shouldn't be going to jail. It's all Ava's fault."

This should be interesting, Madison thought. "Sit down and tell me what you know, Lyrical."

For the next thirty minutes, Lyrical told a totally engrossed Madison how she'd met Ava in prison and in return for protecting her how Ava had promised to help her with a music career and teach her how to be a lady.

"Where is your real mother?"

Lyrical paused for a moment and looked around the room. She bit her lip to keep the oncoming tears at bay. "She died when I was a young girl."

"I'm sorry to hear that," Madison said softly. She gently touched Lyrical's arm to offer comfort, and Lyrical managed a small smile.

"So, did Ava do what she promised?"

"Not really," Lyrical said, scowling. "All she was really concerned with was having my boyfriend get her drugs."

Madison felt her spirits starting to brighten. She just knew that her mother wasn't the type of person who would do that. "Are those the drugs Yancey was caught with?"

"I'm not certain, but if I was a betting person, I would say yes."

"Then why not go to the police? Why did you feel like you needed to come directly to me?"

"I'm on parole," Lyrical explained, and then added, "They might not believe me and I know how two-faced Ava can be. The next thing I know, she will have me involved in some way."

That prompted the natural question, considering Lyrical was an ex-con herself. "Are you involved more than you're telling me?"

"Look, Madison, I'm telling you the truth. I have no reason to lie to you."

Madison considered that statement, then nodded. "Will you repeat this story to my daddy?"

"Why do I need to do that? Why can't you tell him?"

"I can do that, but I think it will make more sense if you did."

Lyrical stood up from the chair. The notion of squealing obviously made her very uncomfortable. "Look, I've done my part. I told you what happened. Do what you must, Madison. You have a chance at something I never will."

"What are you talking about?"

"Your mother is still alive. Yancey is still around. You could save her and maybe get the chance to have a mother."

"Who said I wanted a mother? Especially a mother like Yancey. I haven't been around either one of these women as much as you. Do you think I deserve to have these crazy women in my life?"

"I wouldn't trust Ava."

"Exactly, and I don't need a mother either."

"We all need a mother, Madison."

"So, do you think we should believe this girl, Daddy?"

"Well, it doesn't surprise me that Yancey's mother is behind this. They never really had a good relationship. Besides, I told you, Yancey is a lot of things, but selling drugs wasn't her deal."

Madison was so happy that her father had confirmed what she felt intuitively. "What do you think we should do? Tell Yancey?"

"We could. I'm sure this is information she and her attorney could use," Derrick said.

Madison had a sudden thought. "What if I had to testify? This can't be good for my career."

"Then you need to make that decision now."

Her father almost barked this out, and she knew instantly what he meant. He had raised her to be responsible for her actions. "What's the decision? I have to do what's right. But it's so hard for me to understand how a mother could do something so tragic to her own daughter knowing it would get Yancey in a lot of trouble."

Derrick was pleased by his daughter's reaction. "In the world we live in today, I guess you can't be surprised by much. Yancey used to tell me stories all the time about stuff her mother did to her, and it just makes your heart break. It also makes you understand why she was so afraid of becoming a mother herself."

"So you're saying because her mother was a B that she gets to be one too?"

"No, that's not what I'm saying. You think Yancey is a bad person because she made what she felt was the best decision for her."

"I think Yancey has gotten to you again. Will you ever get her out of your system?"

Derrick gave her a searching look. "I think she's gotten into your system, little girl. So what are you going to do?"

"What are you talking about, Daddy?"

"I see the way you look at her when you

526

don't thinking anyone is looking."

"It's contempt," Madison said quickly.

"Contempt? I'm not sure that is what I would call contempt, Madison."

Madison looked away. The one person she couldn't fool was her father. "Maybe I'm just checking out her acting skills."

"Or maybe how much alike you two are. How you look alike."

"We don't look anything alike," Madison protested.

"Whatever, Madison. Whatever," Derrick said as he started toward the door. "I just want to make sure you do what's right for your mother."

CHAPTER 16

Raymond walked into the conference room with a long, green folder in his hand. He took the chair in front of me and said, "This doesn't look good. It's going to be hard to prove your friend Mr. Pinkston set you up, Yancey."

"Why?"

"He has quite the impressive background. You never heard of the Pinkston family from Florida?"

"No, I haven't."

"Are you sure?"

"Yes, Raymond, why do you ask?"

"They are a powerful family from right outside Orlando, Florida. They are in the insurance and banking business. It seems his great-grandfather started the first black bank in Florida and then sold insurance door to door to black clients in the forties and fifties. They are a very wealthy and powerful family. They even have buildings named for them at FAMU and Bethune Cookman College. They have given a lot of money to the black community and several politicians," Raymond said.

"Well, I knew Seneca was wealthy, but he never told me that."

"It seems his name is not Seneca but Steven. Why do you think he lied about that?"

"I have no clue," I said, frustrated.

Raymond gave it to me straight. "Nobody is going to believe this model citizen tried to set you up, Yancey. And if so, why?"

"I don't know, Raymond. But I'm telling you the truth when I said that Seneca, or whatever his name is, gave me those drugs."

"And then we have the problem of the large sums of money that suddenly start showing up in your bank accounts when you'd gone years with almost no balance. That's why the DA is talking about adding money-laundering charges as well."

That's why the bastard gave me the money. "He told me he wanted me to keep the money to buy clothes for the show and keep it away from some young lady who had a paternity suit against him."

"And you just believed him? You didn't ask any questions?"

I tried to make him understand. "Raymond, I was broke and here was a man who I thought cared for me, offering me the chance of a lifetime. Why would I question him? Men for the most part have always treated me that way."

"I'm going to try and get in contact with his attorney and see if we can't set up a meeting with him. Maybe if you make a plea for him to tell the truth, he might explain to us what's going on. Are you willing to do that?"

"To get the charges dropped, I will do whatever you tell me to do, Raymond."

"Okay. Let me get back with you later on today."

"Thanks, Raymond. I really appreciate all that you're doing for me."

"I haven't done anything if I can't get the charges dropped and your name cleared. And I wouldn't be doing this if I didn't believe you were being judged wrong."

"Can I ask you something, Raymond?"

"Sure."

"Why do you believe in me?"

Raymond looked at me for a moment and said, "That's simple. Basil believes in you and I know how hard a task that is. That's all I need to know, Yancey."

I was looking over my script for the next

episode when I heard a knock on my dressing room door. I got up from the chair and went to open it. Dennis Wilson, the show runner, was standing there.

"Dennis, what can I do for you?"

"Can I come in? There are a few things I need to go over with you."

"Sure."

Dennis walked into the dressing room with a couple of scripts in his hands. He leaned on the dressing table and said, "Yancey, we are thinking about going on location in South Beach next week, and the writers want to make sure you can go before they finish writing. We had to make them aware of your legal troubles and how you might not be able to leave the state."

"I know. That might be a problem but let me check with my attorney. I do have bail, but I know I have to get permission to leave the state. How long are we talking about?"

"It will be for at least three days. We need to get some actual beach scenes, and that is not going to happen in New York in December."

"I completely understand. I will be meeting my lawyer tomorrow and I will get you an answer then."

"Great, because I'd really hate to go down there without you. We wanted to do some scenes with you and Madison walking along the beach."

"Sound good. I hope that I can go as well."

Just as Dennis was leaving my dressing room, he stopped at the door and looked at me and said, "You know, this is really working out well. You're a good actress, Yancey. I must admit, I was one of the ones not so high on the idea when Madison approached us about hiring you, but I think it's turning out well for everyone concerned," Dennis said.

I was surprised, and I gave Dennis a puzzled look, making sure I'd heard him correctly. "Madison came to you guys and asked you to hire me?"

It was his turn to be surprised. "Yeah, I thought you knew. She said you'd run into some hard times and that she and Derrick wanted to help you. She even offered to forfeit some of her salary if money became an issue."

I'd never heard such welcome news. "Are you sure about this?"

"I'm sure. I was in the meeting. Like I said, I'm glad it worked out."

"Yeah, me too," I said.

When Dennis left the room, I tried to get back to memorizing my script, but I couldn't get what he had said out of my mind. Why had Madison gone to bat for me to get this job? Here I was thinking I got it on giving a great audition when now I was finding out that I could have come in looking and sounding like a soap opera actress and still would have gotten the job. Maybe Derrick was the real reason I got the job and not Madison, as Dennis said.

I had opened the script to the first page that had my character's name when there was another knock at my door. I figured it was Dennis most likely recanting or telling me not to say anything about what he'd just told me.

"Come in," I said. A few moments later in walked Madison and Derrick.

"You got a minute, Yancey? I think Madison has something she wants to tell you."

"Sure," I said, so happy to see her now that I knew the truth.

"Okay, Madison, tell Yancey what happened."

Madison took a deep breath and rolled her eyes at Derrick and then at me.

"This girl came to see me at the studio yesterday. I don't know why me and if she's telling me the truth or not, but Daddy thinks you should know."

"Know what, Madison?"

"She said she had proof that you didn't

know anything about the drugs that were in the bag. She said your mother was the one who set you up."

All the happiness I'd felt a few moments before drained away. "Ava? Are you sure? Who was this girl?"

"She said her name was Lyrical or something like that."

"Lyrical? I know her. I wonder why she didn't just come to me."

"How do you know her?" Derrick asked.

"Ava introduced us. They met in prison. We didn't exactly get along, but she was going to be a part of my reality show as my assistant." When I thought about it, Lyrical had always been a straight shooter with me. She was just that kind of person, whether it made me mad or not. "Do you think she was telling the truth, or was she out for something?"

"Something like what?" Madison asked.

"She is under delusions that she might be a big recording star. Did she ask you to help her?"

Madison's young face became troubled. "Lyrical did mention to Thurston something about leaving a CD. Do you think she's making this up?"

"I don't know, but nothing about Ava would surprise me. I asked her if she knew the guy who I was taking the bag to, but she ignored the question." That made me think she didn't know him. But what connection did he have with my mother? "I never really thought about Ava and Marcus knowing each other," I said.

"Lyrical did mention some guy you were sleeping with who was involved in it with your mother," Madison said.

"Did she say it was Marcus?"

"I don't remember a name."

"Do you think maybe your lawyer can check it out?" Derrick asked.

"Yeah, you're right. I should tell Raymond. We've been concentrating on how to find Marcus and get him to admit to this." I shook my head, considering this latest betrayal. "Damn, Ava. Do you hate me this much?" I mumbled.

If I was going to get Ava to admit that she was in cahoots with Marcus against me, I had to beat her at own game. I couldn't let on that I knew that she was involved. But how was I going to get her in the same room with me and Jeff so he could tell me if she was the one who had an affair with Marcus's father?

I thought back on the afternoon at the studio with Madison, and a plan sprang to mind. I picked up my cell phone and dialed Ava's number. I blocked my phone number because I knew she might not answer if she knew it was me.

"Hello."

"Hello, Mother," I said in the fakest cheery voice I could muster.

If she was surprised, she sure put up a good front. "What do you want? Why is your number coming up private?"

"Oh, Mother, I have the most wonderful news."

"What, they've promised you a private cell when you go up to the joint?" she said snidely. "I guess they would want to keep a celebrity like you from the general population."

"I might not be going to jail, but that's not my great news."

"Oh, I think you're going to jail, Yancey. If I were you, I'd prepare for that."

I didn't let her get to me. "I've reconciled with Madison and I'm so happy. You know, that's how I got out of jail. She is more loaded than we ever expected."

Her tone changed from offensive to suspicious. "How did you manage that?"

"I'm doing her television show, playing her mother, no less, and we've just grown closer. And guess what? I told her about you and she wants to meet you. And, Ava, I think she wants to be in your life as well."

"You're kidding, right? Does she think I'm going to let her call me grandma? I don't think so." Yet she was confused, I could tell. She was taking the bait. "How much you think she's worth?"

"At least fifty million," I said.

"That little bitch worth that much? You're kidding, right?"

"No, I'm not. And I think once she meets you, she might be willing to write us both a check. Madison has told me how all her life she's longed to know her mother and grandmother. She's even buying me an apartment in the Four Seasons, where she and Derrick live. I bet she'll want to buy you one as well."

Typical of my mother, she found an objection even to an offered gift. "Well, if she's in a buying mood, then she needs to be looking in California because that's where Ava is heading."

"I'm sure that can be arranged, Ava."

She didn't reply right away. She was probably adding up all the demands she would make. "So when can I meet this spoiled brat? She doesn't act like a big star, does she, because I'm not putting up with that."

"The sweetest girl you'll ever meet, Ava,

and she belongs to us."

I must have been laying it on too thick, because she became leery again. "Why you being so nice to me, Yancey? Something ain't right about this. You were pretty upset when I took over your little house."

"I'm over that," I announced, peaceful as Buddha. "Becoming close to Madison has solved all my problems. All she wants is a family and that's all I want. Come on, Ava. Please, just meet her. If you don't like her, you can leave."

"Why can't she come to me?"

The woman really had a lot of gall. "We can do that, but I have to bring her bodyguard with her."

"Bodyguard?"

"Yes, her bodyguard. Madison is quite popular. She can't go anywhere without her fans rushing her."

"So what if I come to her?"

"Then I will have Derrick arrange a private suite at the Four Seasons where you can meet with her."

She was sorely tempted. Fifty million was dangling like a bunch of grapes. "I have to think about this. I'm doing okay, but I guess you can't ever get too comfortable. A little more money in my checking account might not be a bad thing."

"So you'll do it?"

Ava didn't say anything for a few moments, and just as I was going to call her name to make sure she was still there, Ava said, "Okay, I'll do it. I'll meet Miss Thing."

"Thanks, Ava. You won't regret this."

Ava didn't respond and simply clicked off the line.

I was struck by the strangeness of the moment as I stood at the door of my town house. I took a deep breath and rang the doorbell. A few moments later, nothing had happened and so I rang it again.

The door suddenly swung open and there was Ava, in one of my robes. Ava's eyes were groggy and confused as she rubbed them. When they appeared to be wide open, Ava looked behind me and asked, "Where is she?"

"Aren't you going to invite me in?"

"Not until you tell me where the little money maker is."

"She's not coming here, Ava. Remember, you are coming to us."

"Then what are you doing here?"

"I need to talk to you."

"About what?"

I could only put up with so much. "Let me in," I said as I pushed my way into the house. I was surprised that Ava didn't offer much resistance, but as I headed toward the sofa Ava called out, "What do you want?"

I turned around and started to take off my coat. "I told you, we need to talk."

"You and I don't have anything to talk about until I meet Madison and see how much money she's going to give me."

"You're not getting a dime of Madison's money," I said.

She could tell I was dead serious. "You're crazy. Then why did you call me and tell me that? What kind of crazy mind games are you playing, Yancey?"

I snapped a finger toward her. "I should be asking you the same thing."

"What in the hell are you talking about? Have you been taking those drugs you were selling?"

"You know damn well I wasn't selling any drugs. Now tell me what's really going on."

The first crack in her veneer peeked open. "How would I know?"

"That's not what Lyrical said."

The crack suddenly got a lot bigger. "What does that lying bitch know? You know she's an ex-con and once a con always a con, Yancey. Don't be so stupid, girl."

"Obviously Lyrical knows quite a bit. And if you don't go to the police to tell the truth, then Lyrical and I will."

"Get your crazy ass out of my house," Ava said weakly as she headed toward the door. I followed her and pulled her left arm. She looked startled by my aggressiveness.

"Bitch, let me go," she screamed.

"It was you, wasn't it?" I hissed, right in her face.

"What was me?"

"It was you who set me up. Does Marcus know you were the one who was really having an affair with his father? That you were the reason his daddy's marriage broke up and his mother killed herself?"

Her eyes danced around like a trapped animal's. "What he doesn't know won't hurt him."

"How did you do it, Ava? How did you convince Marcus that it was me who had the affair?"

She regained some of her bile. "That wasn't hard," she sniffed. "Your reputation has preceded you in certain circles, darling."

"What are you talking about? You're going back to jail."

Now she looked frightened. "You don't go to jail for a few fibs. It's no law against lying about love and a few pounds, the last time I checked."

I pushed her away, disgusted. "So Lyrical

was telling the truth. You used my name, didn't you? This is how it all came about. You've done it before, so I shouldn't be surprised." Still, I was hurt. She'd been totally callous toward her own daughter. "Why can't you leave me alone? Use your own name with your little games."

"Don't tell me what to do, bitch."

That was the last time she was going to call me that. I grabbed her arm so hard, she winced. "You're going to tell the authorities the truth."

"You're going to jail, bitch, for a long time. Now you will realize how I felt stuck in that hellhole that you sent me to."

I couldn't believe it. "Is that what this is all about, Ava? Because I told the truth about the shooting you want to get me back. How childish."

"Don't you call me childish."

"Do you hate me that much?"

She roughly pulled her arm free. "I don't even think about you, Yancey. Don't flatter yourself."

"Where is Marcus?"

"I don't know what you're talking about."

I caught a glimpse of the hate in her eyes when she looked at me. I don't know why, because I consider myself a tough cookie, but I suddenly felt a tremendous sadness that the woman who brought me in the world held me in such disdain. If she hated me that much, why hadn't she given me up? Or was giving up a child an act of love?

"Ava, you're my mother. You're supposed to love me," I said, almost pleading. I was trying to stop the flood of tears I felt coming.

"Who in the hell do you think I am? Jesus. I don't have to love you, bitch!"

After my big fight with Ava I retreated to the studio and my dressing room. I'd asked the director if I could run lines with Madison's stand-in and he'd agreed. Just as I put the finishing touches on my makeup I heard a familiar voice.

"Knock, knock. Can I come in?"

"Is that who I think it is?" I asked as I closed up my robe.

"It is," Dalton said as he walked in with his arms open. I didn't know he was coming back to New York so soon. I jumped up from the chair and raced to give him a hug. But just as I got close to him I stopped. My eyes moved from his face down toward the floor. The right side of his face was badly burned.

"I know it looks bad but it doesn't hurt as much, Yancey. I promise. The doctor gave me some cream and he said before long it will simply look like a birthmark."

"Why, Dalton? Why?" I screamed. I wanted to cup his face in my hands and try to make it better. But I knew I couldn't without facing my own demons.

The sight of Dalton's face and the force of a childhood memory brought on uncontrollable sobs. Dalton held me tightly to his chest as I screamed and cried. He began rocking me like I was a baby and before long I was sharing with him the horror I'd experienced at the hands of the woman who gave birth to me.

"Look at this, Dalton," I said as I slowly removed the robe and pointed to the discolored patch on my right arm.

"What's that, Yancey?"

"I call it my birthmark but in reality it's an iron burn. Is that what Anderson did to you?"

Dalton eyes went downward and he muttered, "Yes, Yancey. Anderson did this to me."

I began to share with Dalton what seemed like an ocean of time ago.

"I was getting ready for my first dance recital. I was in the fifth grade and I had the only solo. We were going to wear black leotards and white blouses. We had white ribbons for our hair. I wanted my ribbons ironed and so I asked my mother to show me how. I had never ironed before. I wanted my ribbons to be perfect and so I was doing it very slow. I guess I left the iron on the end of the ribbon too long and it turned a dirty brown. I was so upset that I started crying and this made my mother mad. Really mad."

I paused as my mind went back to the tiny house where Ava, my grandmother and I lived in Jackson, Tennessee. It wasn't really a house but more of a trailer on a foundation. I hated that house and I hated it even more when my friends wanted to visit me. Now I was going to show up at the recital wearing a dirty white ribbon.

"What happened, Yancey? What did your mother do to you?" Dalton asked as he took my hand and began to rub it in a soothing manner.

"She started yelling at me, calling me a dumb, stupid bitch and how I was going to make her look bad. I started to cry harder, demanding to know why she and my grandmother were always so mean to me. All I was trying to do was make them proud. Before I knew what was happening, Ava jerked the iron cord from the wall and pressed the still hot iron against my arm.

The pain was unbearable but what I remember most is the feeling I had. It was like something inside of me died that day and I felt no one would ever care or love me again. I was damaged goods and I would have this mark to remind me."

"You're not damaged goods, Yancey. You're a beautiful woman who has a lot to offer the world. Don't allow your past to haunt your future."

"It's too late. It already has. I took my mother's hate and made it my own. It forced me to give up one of God's most precious gifts."

"What do you mean?"

Just as I was getting ready to tell Dalton about my secret, my door flew open and there standing before us was my daughter, Madison.

CHAPTER 17

Madison had stood at the door of Yancey's dressing room in full eavesdrop mode. She had seen the strange man knock on her door and wondered who he might be. Was he a suitor who Yancey would choose over her father and crush his dreams of a reconciliation?

Instead Madison had become so engrossed with Yancey's sad and terrible childhood story that she lost her balance and suddenly was standing face-to-face with Yancey and her friend.

"Madison, how long have you been standing there?" Yancey asked. A panic-stricken look covered her face.

"I'm sorry about what happened to you, Yancey. I can't believe your own mother would do that to you," Madison said. She glanced at Yancey's arm and then Dalton's face and then lowered her head in shame.

"Dalton, this is Madison. This is my

daughter."

Dalton did a double take. He first looked at Yancey and then quickly at Madison and back at Yancey again.

"Nice meeting you, Madison. I'm Dalton, a friend of your mother's. I voted for you every week on *American Star*."

"Thank you, Dalton, and it's nice to meet you."

"Same here," Dalton said as he smiled at Madison and then at Yancey whose eyes glistened with tears. Her face had a stricken expression.

Madison suddenly felt a rush of tenderness for Yancey, her mother, but didn't really know what to say. Should she tell her that she now understood that her seemingly narcissistic personality was only an armor to protect all the hurt that she'd endured?

That she finally understood why she couldn't be a good mother since she had never known one. For the first time Madison understood why Yancey had given her up and why God saw fit for her aunt Jenny to raise her as a child and for her daddy to do double duty when Jenny died. Nicole had been right about how God always equals things out.

"Yancey, would you like to go with Daddy and me to eat some sushi? I want you to meet my best friend, Caressa."

"I just came up with a brilliant idea," Dalton said as he clapped his hands in glee.

"What?" Yancey asked.

"You two have to record 'Dearest One.' Your voices together would be perfect."

"I thought you said it needed a rap to go with it."

"What are you two talking about?" Madison asked.

"Dalton is a wonderful songwriter and I think he has some songs you could use for your debut release, Madison."

"Really?"

"I don't know if I'm all that but I do okay," Dalton said with a laugh. His personality was taking all of the doom and gloom from the dressing room and for the first time Madison and Yancey exchanged honest, sincere smiles with each other.

"Why don't we talk more about this over sushi?" Yancey suggested. She suddenly noticed the sunshine streaming through her dressing room window in a buttery yellow glow and for the first time in a long time felt a bone-deep sense of peace.

"Yancey," Madison called out.

"Yes, Madison."

"Don't worry about your mother. Daddy

and I will make sure she never hurts you again."

Yancey simply smiled.

CHAPTER 18

It was a cold New York afternoon when the doorbell rang. Ava was thumbing through a magazine, trying to get ideas for her new California home. She looked at the phone and started to call Steven to see if he had gotten the approval for her to make the move back west as he had promised. Just as she headed toward the phone, someone knocked on the door. Ava swung it open and was greeted by two men wearing trench coats. They looked like policemen and they were.

"Ava Middlebrooks?" the white officer asked.

"Yes, I'm Ava Middlebrooks," she said, tightening her robe. "How can I help you?"

"We're Officers Justice and Anderson from the New York State Parole board."

Ava immediately put on her outraged citizen act. "Oh, do you have some more questions about my daughter?"

"No, Ms. Middlebrooks, we're here to see you."

"About what, Officers?"

"You're under arrest for parole violations," Officer Justice said.

"What are you talking about?"

"You might want to put some suitable clothes on, Ms. Middlebrooks, you're under arrest," Officer Anderson said.

"There must be some mistake," Ava said as she pulled her robe tighter across her breasts. There was no way she was going back to prison willingly. The cold wind from the outside brushed her face.

"Here is the order right here, Ava. Read it and then we need you to come with us."

Ava snatched the paper from the officer's hands and started to read it. It looked like she was going back to prison. Had S. Marcus double-crossed her? Ava started shouting at the top of her lungs, "Oh hell, nah. This shit isn't happening. I'm not going back to that hellhole. You motherfuckers better pull out some guns or something if you think I'm leaving this house. Do you know who I am? Do you know that my granddaughter is one of the biggest names in show business?"

"Mrs. Middlebrooks, none of that matters. You just need to come with us and let's not make this more difficult than it has to be."

"I need to call my lawyer," Ava said.

"You will be able to do that after you've been processed," Officer Anderson said.

That's when Ava let out a deep gasp, put her hand across her forehead, and fell flat out on her back, totally blacked out.

EPILOGUE

I had a dream last night. A beautiful dream. In my dream, I live in a beautiful house surrounded by nothing but God's magic in colors of green, gold and blue. I have a wonderful husband whose love for me is real and true. When I see him or hear his voice, I glow from the inside.

In my dream, I have a precious daughter whom I watched grow from a girl into a young woman. The pride I feel as her mother makes me tingle with happiness down to my soul. I have never imagined a love so deep or so pure, until I felt — with every ounce of my skin and bones — a mother's love for the child who grew from her own flesh and blood.

I know she really doesn't need me now, but I love the fact that when she's around me, she brings a child's heart that puts everything in perspective. She has taught me what's important, what matters:

love. Period.

Because the unconditional love that sparkles at me from her eyes fills me with so much joy that tears glaze my eyes. Everything goes blurry, yet it becomes so crystal clear. She is my most precious gift from God, and I celebrate her, and what we share, every day, in the simplest yet happiest ways.

Sometimes we sit up in bed in matching pajamas, eating popcorn and watching old movies. Sometimes we gather around the piano and sing songs together, songs that become number one hits with our friend Lyrical rapping the intro. Sometimes we shop for hours, but don't buy a thing because we're just simply enjoying each other's company. She listens when I warn her of the danger of growing up too fast and how show business is simply that . . . business. Sometimes we eye each other when her father tells a joke and fails to deliver the punch line. I think he knows we're not laughing at him, but with him.

On days when I doubt myself and my ability to be a good mother, I depend on a good friend who knows what it's like to be a good mother. Nicole Springer-Stovall and I have developed a good friendship, a true friendship. She tells me that no mother is perfect but when you do things in love they have a way of turning out right. Even in my wildest dreams I never dreamed of trusting another female the way I do Nicole.

Sometimes in my dream, it seems as though the days are passing with dizzying speed. And there are times — the good times — that pass at a snail's pace. Other times, bad memories return. But I welcome them in like old friends, because the contrast of remembering how bad I once felt helps me appreciate how good I feel today.

Yes, it's good to remember that once, in my past, I was haunted by dreams about people in my life showing up to steal my moment of glory. In those dreams, as I stood in the world's spotlight, winning awards and being celebrated for my talent by the likes of Denzel Washington, that's when friends and family would bogart onto the stage to shove me back into darkness and misery.

Today, though, I actually have friends. Real friends. People who want me to feel happy and be successful.

As for Ava, well, deep down, I wish I could have enjoyed the comfort and security of feeling a mother's love the way I spoil my daughter with encouragement and love.

But the reality is, I've accepted the fact

that I'll never really have a relationship with my mother. And I'm finally at peace with that.

She never wanted to be a mother because her mother somehow lacked the maternal instinct to love and cherish one's babies.

So this problem has plagued my family for at least two generations.

Now, someone has to break the cycle. For Madison.

And I believe that someone is me.

Today, I have the power and strength to do that, because I'm blessed with the understanding that nothing is more important than love and family. And I realize that I can be happy with my life, even though I can't forget all of its sadness. I'm stronger. I really am confident. And I'm loved.

My dream showed me that every day is an opportunity to begin a new life, and I intend to take advantage of that promise.

So I've traded in my diva card for a mommy card. The card is green, but hopefully it will turn to platinum when the twin boys arrive.

Best of all, I'm facing a future full of sweet dreams.

ACKNOWLEDGMENTS

Sometimes change is necessary for growth.

But some things never change, like my belief and love for my Lord Jesus Christ, and my love and thanks to my family and friends who have supported me in good times and bad.

Another unchanging fact of my life is being grateful for a career as a novelist and the people who support me so fiercely.

I'm thankful for the people who encourage and enable me in this career. That includes agents, lawyers, accountants, editors and so many people who keep my life working.

I must offer special thanks to my writer-sister-friend Elizabeth Atkins, for being one of the best line editors I've had the opportunity to work with. I look forward to our future projects.

Special thanks to my niece Bria Barnes for helping me with the Madison character and Shunda Leigh for test reading my manuscript.

A major part of change for me has been selecting a new publisher. I can't close without mentioning my new publishing family and how grateful I am for them taking me in with open arms. Karen Hunter and Karen Hunter Publishing came into my life and made my choice an easy one. Carolyn Reidy and Louise Burke offered leadership and the promise of a lasting friendship. Jean Anne Rose and Kerrie Loyd came with fresh ideas and enthusiasm on making my fan base even bigger. Finally, Brigitte Smith made sure everything ran smoothly and gave me the security that things at my new home would be just fine. And they were.

I have to thank all of you who write me on the website and Facebook because you make me feel so special every day of my life. I know a lot of you are experiencing change in your lives as well, and I want to be the living proof that *change* is a good thing. Trust me.

E. LYNN HARRIS
June 2009
Atlanta, Georgia

ABOUT THE AUTHOR

E. Lynn Harris is the author of eleven previous novels and the memoir *What Becomes of the Brokenhearted.* His recent novels *Basketball Jones, Just Too Good to Be True, I Say a Little Prayer, A Love of My Own,* and *Any Way the Wind Blows* have hit bestseller list including the *New York Times,* the *Wall Street Journal,* the *Washington Post,* and other publications. Harris divides his time between Atlanta, Georgia and Fayetteville, Arkansas.

The employees of Thorndike Press hope you have enjoyed this Large Print book. All our Thorndike, Wheeler, and Kennebec Large Print titles are designed for easy reading, and all our books are made to last. Other Thorndike Press Large Print books are available at your library, through selected bookstores, or directly from us.

For information about titles, please call:
  (800) 223-1244

or visit our Web site at:
  http://gale.cengage.com/thorndike

To share your comments, please write:
  Publisher
  Thorndike Press
  295 Kennedy Memorial Drive
  Waterville, ME 04901